Maggie Fromm moved to LA to follow a dream: to become an actress and live happily ever after with her high school sweetheart. When her heart is broken after a year of eking out a living, Maggie finds herself fighting for her dream alone. Her luck may change when she meets Gwen Knowles, a talented and spirited director drawn to Maggie's energy on stage.

As they work to bring an independent play to life, Maggie and Gwen face shadows from their past—but this time, they have each other.

GETTING TO KNOW

YOU

Jennifer MD Cox

A NineStar Press Publication
www.ninestarpress.com

Getting to Know You

First Edition, May 2024

ISBN: 978-1-64890-764-7

Also available in eBook, ISBN: 978-1-64890-763-0

CONTENT WARNING:

This book contains discussion and depiction of being stalked by an ex; verbal, psychological, and physical abuse; violence with a knife; recovering from unhealthy relationships; discussion of family abandonment due to sexual orientation; cheating by an ex; and police involvement.

This book is dedicated to Benny, a dear friend who asked me in 2010 to write a same-sex love story "where no one dies at the end." Sorry it took me so long.

In a way, it is also dedicated to my past self and my child's future.

Author's Note

This book includes themes of surviving and overcoming domestic violence. If you or someone you know is unsafe, there is help. Please reach out to:

United States: The National Domestic Violence Hotline at 1-800-799-7233

England: Refuge's National Domestic Abuse Helpline at 0808-2000-247

Northern Ireland: Domestic and Sexual Abuse Helpline at 0808-802-1414

Scotland: Domestic Abuse and Forced Marriage Helpline at 0800-027-1234

Wales: Live Fear Free at 0808-80-10-800

The Men's Advice Line run by Respect is a confidential helpline specifically for male victims in the UK, at 0808-801-0327

You may also consider donating your time or money to organizations such as Peace Over Violence. An opportunity to support survivors in your community is no farther than a quick Google search away.

Chapter One

THE WORST PART about sitting in the waiting room was having to look at all the other girls.

Maggie tried to practice slow breathing, but she could feel her cheeks burning regardless. She couldn't help it. She was in a room filled with dozens of attractive women. And most of them were redheads–but why?

Maggie's own thick, curly, walnut-brown hair fell across her face as she jerked her head down to reread the posting clutched in her hands. Nothing in the casting call said anything about red hair; she was certain. Her headshot, paper-clipped to her short resumé, didn't conflict with any of the listed requirements. She was between five and five and a half feet, she was light skinned, and she could do a believable Irish accent. She'd even googled "Irish fashion" and assembled an outfit of warm jeans with a long, flowing sweater to better look the part of "Irish girl in St. Patrick's Day commercial." When she left the apartment that morning, she was at least half convinced she had a shot at being chosen to sell beer on national television. Several hours later, as redhead after redhead had passed her in line, she felt what little optimism she had deflating.

The girl next to Maggie, who'd clearly added freckles with makeup, had been chattering to her in an exaggerated Irish accent for hours. She also noticed the red hair trend. "T'at's silly o' t'em," she said. "Don't t'ey know t'at t'e most common 'air color in Éire is dark brown or black?"

Maggie only nodded with a small "Mmhmm" in return.

"T'ey're overdoing it," said the freckled girl. "Pro'lly new to t'e scene. Not like you, now, you didnae over t'ink. Have you been doing t'is long?"

Maggie thought about the hours she had spent trying to choose a sweater and practicing her accent in the bathroom mirror. "Not really," she said quietly. "Just about a year."

Freckles beamed encouragingly. "A year? Wow, good for ye! Are you new to t'e area t'en?"

"Um…my girlfriend and I moved here together not long ago."

"T'at's good you had a friend wit'ya. It's awful to move somewhere wit' no friends. I was here six months 'fore I had any friends t'ang out wit', and my first roommate was a nightmare. In fact, I'm looking fer a new roommate right now. She quit and moved back 'ome t'er folks in Mississippi. I better find someone soon, rent's due next T'ursday."

Maggie cringed and opened her mouth, debating whether it was worth correcting the stranger's use of the word "friend," but Freckles continued.

"If you're new to t'e area, ye should join m' group on Facebook. It's fer girls like us, trying t' make it. Never know when y' might need advice on an audition or where the safest sushi t'eat is."

Freckles scribbled the name of a group on the back of her copy of the audition advertisement, tore it off, and handed it to Maggie. "Thank you," she said, and she meant it.

Freckles might be a chatterbox, but she was right. It was difficult being new to the area with no friends, even though Maggie was lucky enough to not be alone.

The door at the far end of the room opened, and a voice called, "Margaret Fromm?"

Freckles gave her a big thumbs-up. "Luck of t'e Irish, girl!"

Maggie gave her a small wave and walked into the audition room, knowing she wouldn't get the part. She was fairly certain Freckles wouldn't either.

*

MAGGIE OPENED THE apartment door and half fell into the kitchenette. Waiting for the "Irish girl" audition had taken all morning, but the evening's "young adult for romantic winter fashion" audition wait had been even worse. Why was it you waited for what felt like days, only to walk in, say a few short lines, and hear "We'll call you"? All that stress for a handful of seconds. And the evening audition had been in groups. Why was the wait so long if they auditioned in groups?

She glanced at the digital clock on the stove: 12:00. It was at least fifty minutes off, meaning it was closer to 11:10. One of these days, she'd take the time to fix it. Tonight, her exhausted hands couldn't be bothered. But there was one more thing she wanted to get done.

With a heave, Maggie used the last of her strength to lift grocery bags onto the kitchen counter. The bags contained a combination of frozen meals and instant ramen. Maggie smiled as she put away the shrimp flavored ramen; Jess's favorite had been on sale, and Maggie had bought extra. When Jess came home in the early morning, Maggie could fry a few eggs and serve some quick brunch ramen as a hot meal. To satisfy her growling stomach until then, she threw popcorn in the microwave while she went to the bathroom to prepare for the night.

Makeup off, snack eaten, teeth brushed, and changed into her set of comfy sweatpants and hoodie, Maggie looked at the clock. Almost midnight. She grabbed a fuzzy blanket and curled up on the sagging loveseat against the wall, facing the door. She'd take a nap until Jess came home.

As Maggie pulled her phone out of her pocket, the thought crossed her mind to set an alarm for the morning before work. She furrowed her brows. No, Jess had promised—she'd definitely be home by 2:00 a.m. at the latest. Jess would definitely wake her up coming in. They'd eat, then go to bed, where Maggie's alarm clock would wake her. There was no need for an alarm on her phone. Not tonight.

Maggie forced herself to set the phone aside and burrowed under the blanket, but worry creeped up her back. Still, she was exhausted and quickly drifted off to sleep.

*

MAGGIE WOKE UP to sunshine in the apartment, golden beams spilling through the dusty blinds to highlight the crevices in the kitchenette tile. After a few hazy blinks and a slow realization of what had woken her—the gradual crescendo of her alarm from the bedroom—she launched to her feet. She stumbled through the door and slammed the alarm Off button before it could bother the neighbors.

Maggie stopped to get her bearings and turned to the clock first: 6:01. She then bolted back to the other room, grabbed her phone from the arm of the loveseat, and scanned her lock screen. There was a text from Jess. Maggie mistyped her password once before managing to open the message.

Staying out tonight with the band. I'll be home at noon. Have a good day at work.

Its timestamp was 3:34 a.m.

Maggie took a deep breath and let it out slowly. Jess was okay; nothing bad happened. She glanced at the ramen she had left on the counter in preparation. She slumped her shoulders.

Sorry I didn't respond. I was asleep. I hope your gig went well. I can't wait to hear about it! I'll see you tonight after work. Love you!

Maggie sent her reply, put the phone in her sweats pocket, and went to find her work uniform.

*

FOUR HOURS INTO pouring coffee and placing muffins in paper bags, Maggie still couldn't shake her feeling something was wrong. She desperately wanted someone to talk to about it, to see if she was crazy. She would have even given a free donut to the smelly manbun customer who wrote a different "Act One, Scene One" in the corner booth every day if he'd just lend her an ear.

The truth was, she had no one but Jess.

She'd known Jess since kindergarten, but they hadn't gotten close until high school. At that age, Jess had embraced the punk aesthetic, cutting her dark hair ragged and wearing asymmetrical clothes to school. She could play guitar, piano, clarinet, alto saxophone, bass, and a little bit on the drums. Even in their class of about 300 at Ashland High School, she stood out. She seemed to make friends without trying, was constantly asked to play for any musical events at school and in the community, and, most of all, was openly gay. Maggie was fascinated by her. She'd spend hours standing to one side of the orchestra pit and watching Jess play while pretending she was there to support a friend.

Then, one day, Jess walked over to her, clarinet case in hand, and said, "Hey you. Let's get a coffee."

Maggie drank hot chocolate rather than coffee, but when Jess offered her a taste, she couldn't turn down the chance for an indirect kiss. They talked for hours about the school musical, Jess's dream of being in a successful band, Maggie's dream of acting, school drama, and strict parents.

Finally, Jess put her hand on Maggie's hip in a side hug and asked, "So, boys or girls?"

Maggie had never told anyone. She felt her face, which was already pink from giddiness and nervousness, flush a hot red. "Girls," she said, almost in a whisper. "It's always been girls."

Jess grinned. "I knew it. Cute, but no boyfriend. Guess it's my lucky day." She turned to face Maggie directly. "How would you like to be my girlfriend?"

Maggie nearly fainted. She covered her burning face with her hands and squeaked, "Okay." Beaming, Jess put her hand back on Maggie's hip and squeezed her close against her side.

The years of high school after that were a roller coaster. Maggie was so proud to be Jess's girlfriend she nearly burst. All their friends said they were the cutest couple in Ashland High. There was only one problem: Maggie's parents.

Jess's parents were "cool with it," as Jess said. They spent a lot of time at Jess's house, playing video games during giggly sleepovers or eating family dinners. Jess's mom and dad welcomed Maggie like another daughter. Maggie's, on the other hand, were most certainly not "cool with it." Maggie was well aware of their opinions. She'd worked hard for years to be the good little girl they expected her to be and held her tongue whenever her mom talked about "one day when you find a good man." Maggie explained to everyone that her parents needed to think Jess was a "good friend," and everyone understood, but it still wore on her. Over time, she and Jess built a plan.

Jess and a group of guys—Steve, Jay, and Ethan—had formed an alternative rock band named "Chimera" during their sophomore year. By the beginning of their senior year, they were the toast of the town. Jess threw all her energy into making the band a success, everything from song-writing and rehearsals to booking and performing shows. With graduation looming, it seemed the band was ready to turn professional, and Jess had her sights set on Los Angeles.

"It's the perfect place for acting," she told Maggie in the computer lab. "Come with me. We'll split living costs. A little apartment together in the big city."

Maggie glanced back at the college admissions essay draft on her screen. "I…I dunno. Wouldn't a college degree help? We'll be so young."

"College just puts you in debt and makes it harder to get started," Jess said, rolling her eyes. "It's talent that gets you in the spotlight, not de-grees. College won't help you." She reached for Maggie's hand and squeezed it, stroking her knuckles with her fingertips. "I want a future with you, Mags. Let's do it."

Maggie said she'd think about it, but the truth was, she already knew what she would do. She couldn't hide from her parents anymore. The pain of unspoken rejection was too much. LA was her way out.

They, of course, did not take the news well.

Jess was all she had now. Maggie's friends from high school were in colleges across the country, and as they became busy with their own lives, communication tapered off. Jess's bandmates made her feel welcome, but they didn't have a lot of interests in common. Jess herself had wasted no time in establishing the band's credibility in the city. Their apartment in North Hollywood put them right in the middle of a busy entertainment community, and the band had performances scheduled almost immediately. Between rehearsals, networking, and performing, Jess was rarely home at the same time as Maggie, and even more rarely returned home from performances when she'd planned.

And that was the crux of the problem. Maggie knew how hard Jess worked for the band. In the past year, they'd kept their feet firmly on the ground by working multiple part-time jobs. Over time, Maggie transitioned to one full-time job at the coffee shop. Jess still worked at one part-time job as a bartender, but more and more often her money came from the band's performances, and it seemed inevitable they'd be recognized professionally soon. Maggie understood success meant dedication, long days, and even longer nights.

But Jess had stopped coming home at night altogether. After a performance, the band was often welcome to stay at the venue, usually a bar, to party with the customers. Jess was choosing more and more often, it seemed, to stay until the bars closed and sleep it off in the unit where Jay lived and the band stored their equipment.

Maggie was snapped back to the present moment as hot coffee

dripped onto her thumb. She quickly wiped it off and shook her head at herself. She didn't want to stifle Jess, but the lack of communication about where she was and what she was doing—especially with the crime rate in NoHo—worried Maggie. Something would need to change.

*

A COWORKER CALLING in sick and a ten-hour day at the shop gave Maggie overtime pay. The owner, Sofia Marquez, gave her a burned, edible-but-unsellable cookie as a thank-you. Maggie chomped on macadamia nut and vanilla dough as the metro took her within three blocks of her apartment complex. She stopped by the corner convenience store and picked up a mix for pink lemonade, Jess's favorite. Maybe a difficult conversation could be made sweeter.

Maggie's spirits lifted a little as she pulled her way up the stairs. Jess had responded to her text about working overtime, reassuring her she'd be waiting at home. This wouldn't be so bad. Maggie played it out in her head. She would tell Jess how much she missed seeing her and how she worried about her being out all night. She'd ask what she thought they could do to smooth out their communication. Jess would give her a hug with hands on her hips and rest her head on Maggie's shoulder saying, "I'm sorry, Mags. Hand me that lemonade, and let's talk." No blame, no hard feelings, just problem solving. That's what adults in relationships do.

She had just finished imagining Jess suggesting a date night, maybe a funny bad movie night, when she went to open the apartment door and was suddenly halted. The door was locked. Jess usually left it unlocked if she knew Maggie was coming.

Heart sinking, Maggie pulled out her keys, unlocked the door, and stepped into the apartment. No one was home.

She pulled out her phone to call Jess and realized she'd missed a few texts from her bandmate, Ethan. She opened them hurriedly.

Hey. I kno this isnt how u should find out but I thought u needed to see this. Im here if u need to talk.

There were three pictures attached. Two in a bar, one at Jay's place. Jess making out with three different women.

The pictures, while hidden by the dark sleeping screen, were still up on Maggie's phone when Jess came home twenty minutes later. Jess walked in quietly, a little cautiously. She made eye contact with Maggie, who had sat on the floor in front of the couch facing the door.

"Hey," Jess said, her voice low and serious, but not apologetic. "We need to talk."

Her cheeks streaked with dried tears and throat swelled up anew, Maggie choked back a sob as she nodded.

Chapter Two

FRECKLE'S REAL NAME was Coral, and she still needed a roommate before Thursday. Jess was planning on rooming with Jay when September was up, so they both packed the apartment and split items based on need. Maggie found she hadn't gathered very many things, even with Jess agreeing with her keeping household items like a broom and plates. Desperate to be out, Maggie moved to Eagle Rock, LA within three days. Coral accepted her with almost no questions asked.

Staring at the ceiling in her new room, Maggie tried to sort her feelings. She couldn't afford to stay in bed and sob, despite feeling incapable of doing anything else. She had bills to pay. She had work five days a week handling hot coffeepots and ovens. *You need to keep it together, girl.*

Maggie slid her hand across the mattress and pulled her phone toward her. She hovered her thumb over the phone icon, suddenly tempted to call Jess's parents. To do what? Beg for comfort? Rage about their daughter's rock star lifestyle? To ask them to mail Jess's mom's perfect chocolate and peanut butter cookies?

She quickly deprogrammed their number from her speed dial and erased them, Jess, and the band from her contacts. There. Temptations removed.

Maggie returned her attention to the reason she'd reached for the phone. She opened her internet browser and scrolled through a bookmarked page of local casting calls. Her tension eased just slightly, and her shoulders and jaw relaxed. It felt stupid, but reading casting calls and trying to imagine being the character described helped to remove her from her problems. She wasn't Jess's frumpy ex-girlfriend, she was…"teen buying first car, no braces." She could imagine the commercial now. She'd play it like a spoiled but good-hearted rich girl. While the voiceover described the various safety features, she'd borrow her daddy's car to drive to parties and school events, always sheepishly asking for the keys until her daddy finally handed her a new set of keys all her own, and she'd give him a squealing hug.

Or, "movie theater patron." She was a young woman with the money and confidence to go alone to a public movie theater just because she wanted to be amazed by the newest blockbuster. And when the movie burst through the screen, she'd join in, racing the heroes and smashing her way through an engaging action scene. Or…

Frowning, Maggie scrolled through the list a little quicker. So many commercials. In the past year, she'd seen the occasional short film, and she hadn't turned down the chance to be a background extra for a paycheck every so often. But mostly, commercials.

She put her phone back down and rolled onto her side. She supposed it wouldn't be so bad to be the recognizable face of a brand, appearing as the same character in multiple commercials. But she'd dreamed for so long about bringing stories to life, lighting the same fire in others that movies and theater lit in her. And being the next face of home and car insurance bundling just didn't feel the same.

Jess had made it seem so easy, getting gigs immediately…

Nope. Nope, nope, nope. Maggie couldn't let her brain go that direction, not right now. She stood up and went to the living room for no other reason than to distract herself.

Coral's apartment had about the same square footage as Maggie's last one. This was remarkable since Coral's place managed to squeeze in an additional bedroom. To make up for it, the "kitchen" was hilariously tiny. At least Maggie's old kitchenette had a counter; this one just had a sink between an oven and a compact refrigerator. Against the other wall, Coral had a sectional, the kind that curved around the corner. An old wooden table sat in the middle of the floor. Its hinged leaves folded down, making the table bigger or smaller at whim. "My mom found it at a garage sale for ten bucks," Coral bragged when she first showed Maggie the place four days ago. Some folding chairs stacked in the corner completed the dining set.

Coral sat in the sectional now, a library book on magic tricks in her hands. Coral apparently hoped this would give her an edge in a future audition. Like Maggie, she regularly scanned the casting calls. Unlike Maggie, she seemed to find a way to go to all of them and still keep a part-time job as a hostess for a small art gallery in town.

Coral looked up and smiled as Maggie entered. "Hey, what's up?"

Her voice was rather pleasant when she wasn't forcefully practicing an accent for an audition. She had an uplifting tone, but Maggie shrugged dejectedly in response.

"Was just looking at some casting calls. I'm sick of seeing the same commercial ads."

Coral nodded sympathetically. "Not interested in being the queen of toothpaste or another clothing model?"

Maggie nodded. "It's all posing for products. I miss having a story, you know?"

Coral stood up, stretched, and set the magic book on the table. "I get it. You're in a creative rut. When was the last time you really got to perform for someone?"

Maggie watched as Coral walked to the pantry—really, shelves nailed above the sink—and reached for a box of graham crackers. "Honestly? Not since high school." She felt a twinge of…loss? Nostalgia? Right now, she'd give anything to be in Dorothy's classic blue gingham, dancing down a yellow brick road, with Jess's parents clapping in the audience.

Coral tore open the plastic wrap around the crackers. "Like a year ago, right? No wonder you feel stuck. You can't let your acting chops get rusty." She pulled out three crackers, set them on a plate, and reached for the peanut butter. "You need a creativity warm-up. Tell you what, are you free Saturday evening?"

"Yeah, I have the day off on Saturdays."

"Great." Coral grinned as she spread peanut butter on the crackers. "Every Saturday, I hang out at an improv club. It's free attendance every other meeting, and it's only a couple bucks each time you pay. The group's run by a drama professor from AMDA. Why don't you come with me this week?"

"Would that really be all right, if I just show up at random?" Maggie asked, surprised.

"Of course. It's very informal." Coral set her knife down. "People come and go in the group all the time. But it's a great way to stretch your creative muscles, not to mention make some friends." Coral handed the plate to Maggie, who took it with a questioning look. "Now eat. You've barely touched any food since you moved in, and hunger does not help your mood."

Maggie watched in surprise as Coral proceeded to make a new plate of peanut butter crackers for herself. "Oh…you didn't have to—"

"I know I didn't." Coral smiled kindly at her. "I like you. And I can tell you're going through a hard time. You did me a huge favor helping me pay the rent right when I needed it; the least I can do is give you some crackers. Now, don't waste them; eat up."

Maggie's first bite made her realize just how hungry she was. The crackers disappeared in seconds. She closed her eyes and took a deep breath, resolved to focus on getting through the next few days of work and building the courage to go to this improv group. Who could say? Perhaps it would be just the change she needed.

*

MAGGIE'S MORNING ROUTINE consisted of fighting to get a brush through her thick curls and forcing them into a ponytail, with an extra elastic around her wrist for the inevitable moment when the one in her hair snapped. On Saturday, she'd pulled the brush through her locks only for a whole section of bristles to snap off. Maggie sighed deeply, staring at the broken brush and deciding today was a comb-with-fingers-and-wear-a-hat day. She spent the whole day wondering if getting a pixie cut right after a breakup was too cliché. This pondering kept her so distracted, she forgot to be nervous about the improv group until Coral got home from work. An hour after that, Coral knocked on her bedroom door, purse and metro pass in hand and a huge grin on her face.

Maggie grew increasingly nervous during the trip over. They eventually made it to a small community theater, squeezed between an art gallery and a bar. Maggie would have passed over it completely if Coral hadn't been there to point it out. Despite the unassuming exterior, Maggie's spirits lifted as soon as she entered. There was a small front lobby, a ticket booth, a concessions stand, stairs leading up to balcony seats, all in the iconic aesthetic of a proud theater constantly going through some small repairs.

She felt truly at home once they walked into the auditorium. The faded velvet curtain was raised to show a well-loved wooden stage, littered with the remnants of marking tape, scratches from sets, and scuffs from dancing shoes. There was no set backdrop lowered, revealing a rough brick wall and various large sets and props: windows, doors, the kinds of necessities that would be repainted and reused.

Coral beamed at her, perhaps able to see how much lighter Maggie's heart was in the way she held her head just a little higher. "Isn't it great? Twilight Tales Theater has been open since the fifties. It's been through a lot, but it's my favorite stage in the city."

Maggie turned in every direction to take in the size. "This can't seat more than a couple hundred. What kind of performances are usually done here?"

"Just the small, classic community theater that really keeps stage performing alive," Coral said, walking toward the stage. "Plus, field trips for school kids, that sort of thing. What I love most is their collaboration with independent directors and playwrights. A lot of original work gets its time in the spotlight here."

Following Coral to the stage, Maggie realized a few front seats were occupied. Coral tapped the shoulder of a tall gentleman with umber skin in a suit jacket and jeans, cutting into his conversation. When he turned to her, Maggie was struck by his bright eyes and wide grin.

"Professor, I want you to meet someone." Coral gestured to Maggie as the man rose to his feet. "This is Margaret Fromm, my new roommate. Maggie, this is Professor Bascomb. He leads the group. Oh, and he's the one you give the money to."

Maggie started to rummage for her wallet, but the professor gently stopped her and shook her hand firmly.

"You may wait until after the session, Miss Maggie. Welcome to our little troupe. And please call me Max." His eyes twinkled welcomingly. "Are you here by choice? Or did my most enthusiastic participant coerce you?"

"Whaaaat? Professor Max, I'd *never*," Coral protested, a hand resting above her heart.

"I'm grateful to be here, sir," Maggie assured him.

"Maggie's an actress," Coral explained. "Not like that blogger I brought last time."

"Really?" Max asked, glancing at Maggie for verification.

Maggie shrugged. "Well, I'm afraid I haven't had much luck. Just some background roles recently."

Max smiled. There was something in the smile that was kindness but also a reminder of higher expectations. "Ah, yes, I understand. But don't forget, even the smallest background roles require our fullest efforts."

As he turned away, Maggie clutched her wallet in her pocket and whispered to Coral, "Does he always talk like he's giving a class lecture?"

"Yeah, everything's an important life lesson with this guy," Coral said cheerfully.

They set their things down in a couple seats as the last minutes before starting ticked by. A few more people filed in until the clock hit six.

Professor Max stepped onto a set of stairs that led from the auditorium floor to the stage, calling, "Ladies and gentlemen, let's begin. Please form a circle with me."

Maggie stood between Professor Max and Coral. The circle consisted of eleven people total. Maggie started to deep breathe again, fighting growing tension in her shoulders. She did better with large audiences than small groups. It was easier to perform when she couldn't see individual reactions.

"All right, everyone," said the professor. "We're going to start with some stretches. I'll lead by example. As we stretch, we'll go around the circle and introduce ourselves. Please give your name and a fun fact about you. And make sure you give your neighbors enough space."

He started rolling his head in a circle, letting it fall around his shoulders in a deep neck stretch. "My name's Maxwell Bascomb, and my fun fact is I've been in a prank war with my sister since we were children. It's her turn to prank me." Giggles rippled around the circle. Professor Max nodded to the neighbor to his right, who started speaking as he changed the stretch to an exaggerated shoulder shrug.

Maggie tried to pay attention to everyone's introductions but, in the back of her mind, furiously scrambled for a fun fact. What was "fun" about her? She'd won academic scholarships and rewards all through high school. Did that count? Maggie cast it aside as pointless bragging. She considered sharing her favorite role, the time she was cast as JoJo in *Seussical the Musical* her sophomore year. But when a brunette across the circle shared her fun fact—"I'm starting rehearsals as a dancer in *Cats* next week!"—Maggie suddenly felt that high school performances didn't make the mark.

There were only two people left before her. Maggie tried desperately to think of something unique about herself, frustrated by her blank mind, until—

A door at the back of the auditorium swung open, and a strong voice called out to the stage. "Sorry I'm late, Max. Bad news, no donuts this week. Good news, I have a great idea for an improv scene."

Maggie whirled around to see a tall woman striding toward them. She wore jeans, sneakers, and an unconventional robin's-egg blue, sleeveless, vestlike top with a drawstring hood. Her exposed arms were lean and muscular, and the hug of the top and her jeans highlighted a fit frame. Her shoulder-length, straight blonde hair flowed as she walked. Head high, arms swinging, stride long, she had an air of easy confidence in every movement.

Her cheeks flooding hot, Maggie quickly turned away, returning her eyes to the center of the circle. *Checking girls out only days after a breakup?*

Professor Max waved in a careless manner. "By all means, just waltz on in at your convenience. It's not like we're in the middle of anything."

The group laughed, including the new woman, who walked up on stage and joined the circle at the point directly across from the professor.

"As punishment for your tardiness, you will go last in our introductions," Max stated as he demonstrated a leg stretch. The woman, stretching a pair of strikingly long legs, grinned sheepishly at him.

Professor Max nodded to Coral, who followed her cue to introduce herself.

"My name's Coral Fletcher, and my fun fact is I'm about to be an aunt. My older sister is having her first baby in a few weeks."

As members of the circle echoed their congratulations, Maggie's eyes lit up. Babies—that was it.

As Professor Max changed the stretch to arms across the chest, Maggie caught his nod and took a deep breath.

"My name's Maggie Fromm, and my fun fact is my first theatrical performance was as baby Jesus—even though my family's Jewish."

Surprised laughter erupted around the circle, and the blonde spoke with a huge grin. "I *have* to know the story behind that one."

Even with her pink cheeks, Maggie encouraged herself to keep eye contact as she answered. "Well, a local church wanted a real couple and their baby for a Christmas pageant, but the first couple got sick and couldn't do it. My mom was coworkers with someone from the church, and I was, like, four months old at the time, so they asked my parents to do it. They thought it was funny."

"It's accurate," said a gentleman to the left in the circle. "Jesus, Mary, and Joseph were all Jewish."

The group laughed again, and Maggie grinned with relief.

"All right," the professor declared, "as my tardy assistant introduces herself, let's shake out those limbs and loosen up." He proceeded to lightly shake his limbs one by one.

Across the circle, the blonde woman did the same. "Hi, everyone. My name's Gwen Knowles. I help out with the group, usually by bringing snacks." She smirked. "I wasn't successful today. Sorry. My fun fact is…hmmm, how to follow up being baby Jesus?" She paused until the group's giggling subsided. "Well, how about: I'll be directing a play at this theater soon, and I'm really excited about it." Gwen finished shaking her limbs and gave the group a sweeping bow. "And welcome, everyone, to our little improv group."

*

AFTER A BRIEF vocal warm-up of tongue twisters, which threw Maggie and Coral into fits of giggles, Professor Max turned to Gwen. "All right, what is this improv exercise idea you're so excited about?"

Gwen beamed and stepped forward. "As some of you know, I usually bring a snack to contribute to the table. You may have noticed I came late and without a box of donuts. Are any of you familiar with how a line at a coffee shop works?"

The group members looked at her, puzzled. A few responded with a confused, "Yeah…?"

"Good," Gwen replied. "Because today I had the misfortune of encountering a woman who seemed unfamiliar with the concept, facing an employee who seemed too inexperienced to defeat her stupidity." Gwen spread her arms, palms up. "Imagine, if you will. It's five fifteen. Your neighborhood coffee-and-donut franchise is packed with customers in the evening rush. There's a line reaching nearly out the door. In the middle of the line is yours truly. At the head of the line, a woman demanding her order. She has requested a box of their promotional donuts. It appears the store has sold out of these specific donuts for the day and is awaiting the morning delivery. Does this answer quiet her? Not at all. For she is convinced the workers are hiding their donuts 'back there.' Now, anyone with eyes can tell there is no 'back there.' This is a tiny establishment that has the square footage of a broom closet. Yet such is the argument between customer and employee. For ten. Long. Minutes." Gwen sighed. "At which point I left, donut-less, to come here and bear sad tidings."

The group murmured incredulously. "Where the hell was the manager?" spoke up one gentleman.

"I bet I know which place you were at," said a lady. "It's always packed, and the evening manager never leaves her office, just sits at a desk and watches movies. The staff are on their own running the place, poor things."

Gwen nodded. "Well, to honor the donut shop horror customer, I have an idea for an improv scene. Could everyone do me a favor and stand in a single line?"

Gwen, placing herself second in line, gave directions as the group members assembled themselves. "You're all going to be customers standing in line, but for this exercise I'm going to ask that you all be coldhearted bystanders—like, I suppose, myself—who don't intervene to save the poor employee. The first person in line faces the second person in line. The first person is the employee at the register, the second person is the horrible customer. The customer wants a specific order the employee is unable to provide. The 'whats' and 'whys' are up to you. Max, could you keep time for us? The goal is to keep the scene running for… How long do you think would be appropriate?"

"If you're including the innocent beginnings of the transaction? Two minutes, I should think."

"Sounds good." Gwen turned to the first person in line. "Ready, Debra?"

"Ready."

Maggie was about three-fourths of the way down the line, which meant she didn't have a very clear view of what was happening. She watched and listened, peering around the backs of people's heads, as Gwen and Debra, with a nod from Professor Max, began the scene.

"Hi, what can I help you with?" Debra started with the familiar tone of a customer service employee.

"I want a box of your Summer Soothing donuts," Gwen replied. It seemed like her arms were crossed over her chest. "And hurry, I have a meeting."

"I'm so sorry, ma'am, but we are sold out of Summer Soothing donuts," Debra replied, sounding apologetic. "Can I offer you—"

Gwen's voice immediately became a screech. "What do you *mean* you're sold out? I can see the donuts right behind you."

Maggie listened attentively, craning her neck around the line to watch as Debra and Gwen continued in a back-and-forth manner until Professor Max called, "Time."

The group clapped politely, and Debra announced, "Phew, that was difficult! Who knew two minutes could feel so long?"

Gwen laughed, stepping out of line to face the group. "No kidding. There are only so many ways you can demand donuts, and only so many ways you can say you don't have them. Thank you so much Debra. Could you move to the back of the line? You'll be our last customer of the day. I'll be the cashier next, the next person in line plays the customer, and that's how we'll take turns moving forward."

As Debra walked around the line and Gwen stepped back in, Professor Max spoke up.

"Before we move forward, I'd like to ask the group— What kinds of lessons do you think we can learn from this activity Gwen has created?"

There was a pause, and then a group member said, "Well, we have to be creative and try to state our character's goals in multiple ways."

People nodded. "And we're demonstrating a relatable real-life scenario," said another individual.

Maggie, her brows furrowed thoughtfully, spoke up. "I actually learned a lot about blocking, body language, and tone."

Professor Max looked at her with interest. "Indeed? Let's hear more about that." He turned to the group. "For those of you who don't know, 'blocking' is the way actors are positioned and move on stage. Maggie, could you elaborate?"

Maggie felt the initial heat slowly leave her cheeks as she spoke. Professor's interest inspired a little confidence in her answer. "Well, as the audience, we're in a very unusual position. The farther down the line you are, the less you can actually see. I really only had the actors' voices to go off of. In a stage performance, it's important to remember things like limited perspective when you plan your blocking, because people sitting to the far left or right in the audience won't have as clear of a view as people sitting in the center." Maggie tilted her head thoughtfully. "But body language will always matter in improv because the actors read one another for clues about how to move forward and express themselves."

The group murmured in agreement, and Gwen stepped out of line with a smile.

"That's exactly why I like to make you guys break out of the beloved circle formation sometimes. When you're acting, you need to remember both the audience's perspective and your costars'. Very nicely said."

The blush Maggie had fought so hard to keep down flooded her face as her eyes met Gwen's. She nodded and quickly looked to the side.

Gwen stepped back in line, and the exercise continued. Maggie giggled, gasped, and clapped her way through multiple performances of customers demanding donuts or coffee. Some individuals had a natural flow, some kept halting to titter nervously, but everyone seemed to enjoy themselves.

Eventually, it was Maggie's turn to play the horrible customer. She looked up at the face of a tall, skinny man about her age with a massive halo of fluffy black hair. She looked over at Professor Max. "The customer can ask for anything, right? The employee just can't provide it for some reason?"

He blinked. "Yes, that's what Gwen said. The 'whats' are up to you."

"Great. I'm ready."

"Go ahead."

Kevin, her acting partner, smiled down at her. "Hi, thank you for coming today. What can I get you?"

Maggie put a finger to her lips. "Let's see…I'd like a medium coffee with sugar, a blueberry muffin…and your number."

Kevin, mouth opening to reply, froze. Someone back in line (sounding a lot like Coral) guffawed. Regaining his composure, Kevin smiled. "You're very sweet, but I'm afraid we're all out of muffins."

"That's all right," Maggie purred, leaning closer. "I'm not really hungry for food. But I'd love to take you for dinner."

Kevin's eyes widened as he realized, oh yes, she was doing this. "That's very kind of you, but I, um, I have a girlfriend."

"Oh, is she pretty?"

"Very. She's the most beautiful girl I've ever seen."

"Then I bet she gets a lot of guys hitting on her."

"Um…I guess so?"

"You poor thing," Maggie exclaimed. "No girl should parade her looks around to get hit on when she already has a man. You deserve better."

Kevin looked appalled. "No, I'm lucky to have her, actually. I don't—"

"C'mon, let's have some fun together. I promise I'd pay attention to you and show you a good time."

Kevin pretended to type in a cash register. "Let me get that medium coffee going for you. Your total is three dollars and fifty cents. Is there anything else I can get for you today?"

"Still waiting on that phone number, hot stuff."

Kevin choked, but pressed on. "One coffee with sugar. How many scoops?"

"Two. One for each of your perfect biceps."

Coral was definitely laughing back in line, along with a few others.

Kevin seemed to swallow a chuckle himself. "Cash or credit?" As Maggie pretended to hand him her card, she brushed her hand along his. Kevin quickly mimed through pouring a coffee and adding sugar, handing it to Maggie as fast as possible. "Here's your coffee, have a great day!"

"Hey now, I ordered coffee with sugar." Maggie raised her pretend cup. "Here's my coffee. Now give me some sugar, handsome."

Kevin looked at Professor Max, aghast.

The professor waved him on. "Keep going; you have thirty more seconds."

Kevin took a deep breath and turned back to Maggie. "Thank you for getting your coffee with us today. I'm afraid I won't be giving you my phone number because that…that would be inappropriate to do at work."

"Don't be so frigid, sweet cakes," Maggie responded.

"Really, lady, I'm clearly at work."

"Fine, then, when do you get off work?"

"I don't. Want to give you. My number," Kevin said very slowly.

"Typical," Maggie spat. "Thanks for being a real dick and leading me on. I guess that's what I get for being a homely nice girl. I hope your hot bitch girlfriend cheats on you." She mimed throwing her coffee on him, and he jumped back with a yelp.

"And time!" Professor Max called.

Maggie beamed as the group clapped. She and Kevin high-fived.

"You were great," he said, grinning ear to ear. "I have never felt so uncomfortable and cornered in my life."

"You were great too. I like how you tried all the polite responses first and gradually increased your assertiveness. Nice touch."

"That wasn't intentional. Your persistence made me increasingly desperate to get you to stop. It was like you had an answer for everything I said."

Maggie felt a warm glow in her chest as Kevin walked away and she turned to face the next person in line. It felt so good to be immersed in a character. A nod from Professor Max, and she was ready to do it again. She plastered her face with a customer service smile, familiar and yet somehow fresh.

"Welcome. Can I help you with anything today?"

*

AT THE END of the group, a few members hung back to chat a little. As Maggie listened to Coral complimenting Kevin on his tongue twisters from the vocal warm-up, she noticed Gwen approaching and was surprised when the tall blonde tapped her shoulder.

"Hi, Maggie, right?"

"Y-yes, hi," Maggie said, shaking Gwen's outstretched hand.

"You did a fantastic job today," Gwen said warmly, her green eyes glinting. "Something about your performance in the improv scene leads me to believe you have lots of experience with being harassed at work."

"Oh, not so much." Maggie shrugged. "I just wanted to do something a little different."

"I'm glad you did." Gwen pulled her hand away and turned to Coral, who had ended her conversation. "Where did you find this one? She's very creative; I like her."

Coral beamed. "This is my new roommate. She's an actress and just needed a place to stretch the performing muscles."

"An actress?" Gwen smiled at Maggie. "If you don't mind me asking, what kind of experience?"

"Recently, mostly background extras," Maggie admitted sheepishly. "I haven't had a starring role since I graduated high school a year ago."

"Well, your school must've had a strong performing arts program. You have a great skill for thinking quickly on your feet. I hope we'll see you again?"

"Absolutely," Maggie replied quickly. "I wouldn't miss it for anything."

Gwen placed a hand lightly on Maggie's shoulder. "Wonderful. I look forward to seeing you then."

Maggie watched Gwen walking away, blonde hair flashing in the light, and felt a strange lingering on her shoulder.

Chapter Three

CORAL WAS THRILLED when Maggie expressed an enthusiastic desire to return to improv group. She filled Maggie's week with gossip about different members who fluttered in and out of participation, outlining their interests and experiences. There didn't seem to be a participant Coral didn't know in some detail.

Maggie spent a few days working up the courage to ask more about the confident, athletic blonde who had captured her attention, but thankfully, she didn't need to. They were working together, cooking boxed mac and cheese when Coral mentioned her organically.

"Oh, when it's our turn to bring snacks, we have to bring mac and cheese bites. Those are Gwen's favorites. She says she can't resist cheddar."

Maggie acted nonchalant as she stirred the pot. "How'd you find that out?"

"Because when I brought them to the group she ate, like, half of them before group was over." Coral laughed at the memory. "She bought me a box of Kraft mac to make up for it. Sometimes, she acts like a college student with no dining plan!"

"How old is she?"

Coral reached into the freezer for a package of frozen peas. "She's about…twenty-five? Definitely young for someone in her position. Rumor is, she took a two-year theater program and then launched straight into working. I think she helped found the improv group with Professor about four years ago."

"Was he her teacher?"

"Nah, I don't think so. I think they met working on a stage production of *The King and I*. He was the director; she was…I think the assistant stage manager?"

Maggie laughed. "Next you'll tell me you might know her blood type and what she ate for dinner last night."

Coral waggled a spoon at her. "Don't judge my powers of observation and memorization, thank you. We all have our gifts."

"Well, some of us have gifts."

A frozen pea hit the side of Maggie's head. "What's with that self-deprecation?" Coral demanded good-humoredly. "I seem to recall you being quite quick-witted during group. Even Gwen said so."

Maggie shrugged, turned the heat off under the pot, and redirected Coral's attention with her next question. "So, is she a full-time director?"

"Mmmm, that would be an optimistic way of putting it," Coral said, tapping microwave buttons. "She's a part-time everything. She's freelance, but she has a great resumé. From what I can tell, she's not hurting for work. She has a solid repertoire of passion projects and paid labor under her belt.

Mostly works in directing, stage managing, those aspects, but I've heard she kicked ass as Emily Webb when the Twilight crew did *Our Town* a couple years ago."

Maggie moved the pot onto a hot pad on the table and added the secret ingredient: parmesan cheese. "Do you know anything about the play she said she's directing at the Twilight?"

Coral pulled down two plates. "Only that it's a small production. Hey, hand me a fork?"

For the next several minutes Coral and Maggie ate in silence. Unsurprisingly, it was Coral who spoke first.

"Can I ask you a question?"

Maggie looked up from her plate and nodded, cheeks stuffed with peas.

"What went wrong with your last roommate?"

Maggie tried to swallow, choked, and gulped down a mouthful of water before she could reply. "Um…honestly, it'll probably sound silly."

"I'm not asking to be judgy," Coral emphasized. "I didn't get along with my first roommate, and I tend to rush things. So far, I like living with you, and you really saved my butt with the rent when you moved in. But I know almost nothing about you." She resumed eating as she continued. "I'm not kicking you out or anything. I only wanted to know if what happened was something we should be working on together as roommates."

Maggie laughed before she could stop herself. "Trust me, we're not going to have the same problem."

Coral raised an eyebrow. "You don't know. I could be another psycho."

Maggie shook her head. "Jess wasn't a psycho. She just… We decided on different paths, and I wasn't going to have a place to stay."

Coral chewed slowly. Maggie took another nervous sip of water, then pressed on.

"Really, that's all it was. She decided to move in with her bandmates, and I couldn't keep the apartment by myself."

"Mmmhmm." Coral swallowed but didn't speak. After a moment, she sat forward on her seat, resting her chin on her hands. "I'm not trying to be pushy, but, again, I feel like I know nothing about you. I know you're Jewish, an actress, and going through something hard right now. You never talk about yourself." Coral wagged a finger at her. "And you haven't liked any of my memes on the Facebook group, which is just rude."

Maggie rolled her eyes at her and quirked her mouth to one side. "Post better memes, maybe?"

Coral smirked but kept eye contact. "Look, if you don't wanna talk with me about family and schooling and best friends, I'll let you on your own time. But I think, as your roommate and as someone splitting the bills with you, I have the right to ask a couple questions about your immediate plans. We haven't really talked about apartment rules either. Is it okay if we have that conversation now?"

Maggie nodded. Anything to keep the conversation off the past.

"Let's start with jobs. We're both looking for roles. But how secure are you with your job at the bakery right now?"

"Pretty secure. The boss likes me, and I have regular hours. I might become a full-time brew maid at this rate." Maggie sighed, resting her cheek on one hand.

"Nuh-uh, keep that chin up, missy." Coral reached across the table to poke her wrist. "You're hoping for a big story role, right? Movies, television?"

"Whatever I can get. I'd love to do stage, but…everyone around here seems so…"

"Networked." Coral scrunched up her nose. "If you didn't go to school for acting around here, or anywhere good, it's hard to elbow your way in and know where to go to insert yourself. But! Not impossible."

Coral sat back. "Well, for myself, the art gallery's a solid position, but at some point, if I'm there too long, they'll either try to make me switch into a full-time position or they'll trade me out for a local art school grad getting school credit."

"That must be stressful for you."

"Eh, I just need to get myself a rolling repertoire of work like Gwen has. Then I won't need it to keep the bills paid." Coral grinned. "I've got a good feeling about this next audition. Seems like a chance for a recurring job too." She scooped more mac and cheese onto her plate. "So it seems like neither of us will be hurting for money in the near future. Next, house rules. Anything you're strict on?"

"Not really. I keep my food kosher, but that's just me. I don't really expect much."

"Well, that's not good. This is your living space; you should have some boundaries around it. Obviously, your room is your space, for example. All I ask is you don't turn it into a mildew and fungi garden." Coral's nose scrunched again. "The smell…you never forget it."

"Is that what your first roommate—?"

"Oh, no, that was a cousin of mine. Teenage boys, you know." Coral shuddered. "So gross. Anyway, here's some things I'm a stickler for." Coral started counting points off on her fingers. "Firstly, if you cook or eat with it, please wash it. It doesn't have to be right away, but longer than forty-eight hours is a problem."

"That's fine by me."

"Secondly, if it's trash, it goes in the can. I don't mind being the one who takes the trash out to the bin, but I hate having to pick it up along all the floors and furniture."

"Also fair."

"Thirdly, any lovers stay in your room, and wear pants in the living room." Coral looked up. "Did you say something?"

Maggie, choking on her words, coughed and took a sip of water.

"Okay. Fourthly, most of my food is up for grabs, but if I write something on it, it's mine. And that's about it. Cool with you?" Coral extended a hand.

Maggie reached out to shake Coral's hand. "You got a deal. And don't worry about lovers, I'm not really looking to date right now."

*

MAGGIE BREATHED IN deeply and let her shoulders relax as she stepped into the theater. Twilight Tales Theater greeted her with warm lights and echoing voices from the stage, a cleaner brushing away popcorn and humming "Hello Dolly," and a flood of welcome memories. She couldn't stop a smile from spreading across her cheeks as she walked with Coral toward the improv group.

It felt more natural than the time before. Kevin gave her a high-five, and other familiar faces smiled and waved at her. Even Gwen grinned at her as they formed a circle. Warm-ups included another icebreaker activity, this time asking everyone to give their favorite jokes as Professor Max guided their stretches.

As the group members finished shaking out their joints, Professor Max called out, "For today's activity, we're going to split you into pairs randomly. So, make two lines, please, facing one another."

There were nineteen people present. Professor Max joined the short line to even the group.

"All right," he said. "Everyone, hold hands. People on the ends of the lines, hold hands with the person in front of you. We're all going to step one spot to the right. If you're on the end and there's no one to your right, that means you switch to the end of the other line. Make sense?" The group murmured understanding. "All right, go."

There was some stumbling and some chuckling, and everyone moved one person to the right. "Okay, not bad, no one fell down," Professor Max declared with what seemed to be pride. "Let's do that two more times." The group did so. "Okay, everyone look at the person across from you, that's your partner."

Maggie looked up, heat rising to her ears as she took in Gwen wearing a green short-sleeved hoodie with a zipper cutting across the chest diagonally, jeans cut off above the ankle, and a charming grin.

"This'll be fun," Gwen said in a low, friendly voice. Maggie nodded, sucking her lips in between her teeth and turning to listen to Professor Max.

He'd stepped away from his partner to retrieve a small plastic bucket. "Send up one person to pull a piece of paper from this bucket. Each has a type of location on it. Keep it secret. When you return to your teammate, separate from the group and talk–*talk!*–about how you two can act like two people who are in this location. Don't practice acting it out. After about three minutes, each pair will take turns acting out their location in front of the group for two minutes. The goal is for the group to guess your characters' location without your characters saying it!"

"I'll grab it," Maggie offered and moved into line. She was joined by Coral and eight others, who quickly fished for a slip and hurried back to their partners. Maggie took one of the folded pieces and hastened back to Gwen, who had stepped away from the group to stand backstage.

"What'd we get?" she asked as Maggie unfolded the paper. She read it over Maggie's shoulder. "Oooh…Ferris wheel. Tricky."

Maggie folded and unfolded the corners of the paper, thinking. "What kinds of things do people usually do on a Ferris wheel?"

"Depends on who they're on it with." Gwen shifted her weight to her other foot. "If they're parents and children, they'll be busy looking at all the sites. If it's lovers on a date…" Gwen smirked knowingly. "You hope to get stuck on top for a little bit."

Maggie laughed a little too loudly. "Last week, I hit on a coffee shop cashier. Acting like lovers on a Ferris wheel? I'm afraid I'll get typecast."

Gwen shrugged comically. "Well, those are the two options I can think of."

Maggie tapped the paper a couple times, then grinned. "I have an idea."

After some fervent whispering, Gwen's grin quickly matched Maggie's.

Minutes later, Professor Max announced, "All right, folks, we're going to get started. Check the pieces of paper with your location on it for a number. That's the order you're going to be performing in."

Maggie checked the paper and found "3" in the corner. She and Gwen joined the rest of the group seated in the front seats, leaving Kevin and Coral onstage to perform.

"And, begin," signaled the professor.

Coral and Kevin immediately stooped their backs and started walking in a line, cautiously, with their hands out in front of them. "Can you see anything?" Coral asked.

"Nothing," Kevin answered. "It's pitch-black down here."

"Keep going. There has to be a way out."

Kevin started to straighten up, then cried out in pain and clutched his head. "It's so cramped down here."

"And it smells."

"What are we even doing down here?"

"Trying to find…my lost puppy."

Kevin and Coral continued to feel their way in a twisting, winding path, until eventually, Professor Max yelled, "Time!"

Kevin and Coral straightened up, hands at the base of their spines and relief on their faces. The group clapped for them.

Professor Max asked, "Who can guess where this scene took place?"

Hands flew up, and voices rang out.

"The sewer?"

"A train tunnel."

"Catacombs!"

Professor Max turned to the stage, and Kevin grinned.

"We got 'underground.'"

Group members muttered and gave another small round of applause.

The professor stood as Kevin and Coral exchanged places on stage with the next couple. "What does this exercise teach us about acting?"

"The importance of a good set," cried out one voice. Professor Max grinned, but his eyes were serious.

Maggie raised her hand. "Actually, one of the most popular musicals right now has almost no set pieces at all. *Hamilton* has one set of barely changing scenery that represents many settings."

"That's true," Professor Max said, pointing to Maggie. "So, what's the key? What do the actors do to make the setting come to life?"

Maggie was at a loss for words, but an older lady with straightened gray hair spoke up.

"Familiarity."

"Say more."

"Actors on a sparse stage use their dialogue or actions to guide the audience to imagine something they're familiar with." The lady cocked her head to one side. "So all the places we got on our papers should be something we're basically familiar with and only need reminders to imagine."

"Exactly." Professor Max folded his hands behind his back and swept his gaze across the group. "When you're presenting a familiar setting, the audience already has an expectation for how people in that setting are going to act." He gestured toward Coral and Kevin. "People underground, for example, often feel cramped and constrained in their movements. Well done."

Maggie sat back and digested Professor Max's words, even as she laughed and clapped along with the group as the next pair acted out visiting the zoo. The next minutes went by swiftly, and then it was their turn. Maggie and Gwen climbed up the stairs to the stage, grabbed a couple chairs from backstage, and brought them to center stage.

Professor Max looked at his watch as they sat down. "Okay, go ahead."

Gwen immediately grasped the edge of her chair and looked to the one side. "Maggie, I don't think I can do this."

"Of course you can do this," Maggie said calmly. "It's perfectly safe, and I'll be with you the whole time."

Gwen leaned forward hesitantly, peering down. "Has anyone ever died in one of these things?"

"Don't worry about it. Look, here we go."

Gwen and Maggie straightened their backs and rocked slightly side to side. Gwen started whimpering, "Oh, oh no, oh no!"

Maggie patted her arm reassuringly. "See, it's not so bad… Look, isn't it a nice view?"

"I don't want to look!" Gwen covered her eyes and put her head down in her lap.

"C'mon, Gwen. You can do this. I believe in you. We're getting close to the top, ready?"

"No!"

"C'mon, Gwen. You promised yourself one look. I'm right here, okay?"

Gwen slowly, cautiously raised her head and peered over the edge of her chair. Then she shrieked and practically leaped into Maggie's lap. "Oh my God, it's so high! Get me down get me down get me down!"

Maggie almost froze. Blushing, she shook off her surprise and started rubbing Gwen's back. "Look, we're going down right now. Focus on the horizon, not the ground. Do you see that sunset? Isn't it beautiful?"

Gwen, settled into her seat, then reached and clutched Maggie's hand. "Okay…okay, the horizon, not the ground…" She took several deep breaths as she and Maggie slowly slumped in their seats, and then at Gwen's subtle signal of a hand squeeze, they both gave a soft jerk.

"And we're stopped. You survived, Gwen," Maggie said proudly. "You did so good."

Gwen laughed and sank her head into her hands. "Never make me do that again."

"This was your idea!"

Maggie and Gwen stood and mimed opening a small gate to the side and stepping down onto a platform, continuing to talk and laugh.

Professor Max said, "You're a little short on time, but I'll allow it. Good job, guys."

Gwen and Maggie gave short bows as the group clapped. The professor called for guesses, and the voices were unanimous. "Ferris wheel!" Maggie smiled brighter as Gwen gave her a high-five.

The other groups moved through their skits in what seemed to be no time at all. Maggie sat near Gwen and Coral and thoroughly enjoyed herself, right up to when Professor Max thanked everyone for their participation and invited them to share in snacks. Before Maggie could get up to retrieve a cookie from the table on the stage, she felt a hand on her shoulder.

"Hey, Maggie, can I speak with you for a second?" Gwen asked.

"Sure."

Gwen stepped backstage into the harsh light of a single large bulb illuminating the prop table and mic charging stations. Maggie followed hesitantly, leaving Coral and the other group members chatting in the floodlights. When they were alone, Gwen leaned against the table, hands curled over the edges at her sides, feet crossed on the floor.

"I'm directing a play here with a local playwright," Gwen said, "and I want you to audition this week."

Maggie's face flushed so fast she felt lightheaded. She swallowed and tried to act calm. "What's the play?"

"It's an original, so it's not going to draw great crowds or anything." Gwen looked to the side and shrugged. Her blonde locks flowed across her neck as she moved, and she pushed them back again impatiently. "But it's a story I'm passionate about. It's about the women's liberation movement in the seventies, all female characters. And I think you should try out." She looked back at Maggie, straight into her eyes. "You have exactly the energy I want onstage. You're creative and quick on your feet. I want your talent. I know you're looking for work, and it's a paid role. What do you say?"

Maggie's chest filled with a sensation she'd been missing all year. "When's the audition?"

"Tuesday, six p.m. to ten. Will you be there?"

"Absolutely." It was short notice, but her boss would understand. She'd have to. "I wouldn't want to be anywhere else."

Gwen beamed, shining a new light across backstage. "Fantastic. I'll be there, with the playwright and a producer. Don't worry about trying to prepare. We're just going to test out a few lines, nothing to memorize. And for the love of God," she added, her voice dropping to a whisper, "don't let Coral try to teach you a Valley girl accent."

Maggie giggled. "Got it. I'll be there."

Gwen reached to shake her hand firmly, then strode back onto the stage and effortlessly rejoined the group conversation. Maggie lingered behind for a moment, breathing deeply, before walking as quickly as she dared to find Coral. *Forget how pretty Gwen is—she might be offering me a job!*

Chapter Four

MAGGIE'S BOSS, SOFIA, was very understanding. A young business owner, she had many dreamers in her employ and was determined to support their efforts. Although she originally had Maggie scheduled to close on Tuesday, she gave her permission to leave at five thirty in exchange for covering a coworker's half shift the following Thursday. Elated, Maggie had thrown herself into the day's shift with a renewed vigor. She couldn't stop herself from smiling.

Well, at first. Give the Sunday after-church rush enough time, and it would wear down the cheer of even the most hopeful customer service worker. Maggie's spirits deflated slightly after one too many harried people in suits and dresses complained about wait times.

"Please," Maggie muttered to a coworker as she took a coffeepot to the back for cleaning, "forgive me for the two-minute wait it takes to make your frappe mocha dairy-free venti sugar crash." They laughed and moved on with the morning.

Thankfully, the rush of customers eventually trickled down to a manageable line of patient people. "I can help who's next," Maggie called.

A young woman stepped up. Tall, black hair, workout clothes, and a hoodie. She placed a five on the counter. "Medium coffee, black."

Maggie rang up her order. "Medium black, okay. Anything else?"

"No."

"That'll be four-thirty."

Maggie opened the register and counted out the customer's change. When she raised her eyes, the woman was gone. She leaned across the counter, searching, and shot an incredulous look at the next customer in line.

The customer smiled and shrugged. "I think she got an important phone call or something. She picked up her phone and just ran out."

Blinking, Maggie placed the change in the tip jar. "Well, that was weird. How can I help you?"

*

PIZZA, MAGGIE THOUGHT as she tugged on the door to check the locks of the shop one last time. Tonight, she deserved pizza. She could share half with Coral. She waved good night to her boss through the window, who waved back cheerily before walking to the back exit to lock up there.

Stepping onto the sidewalk, Maggie turned in the direction of home when movement caught her eye. A tall woman with black hair, wearing workout pants and a hoodie, swept up to her from a side street. Maggie had enough time to recognize the runaway customer before she was in her face, blue eyes bearing down on hers.

"I don't know what she sees in you, Maggie," the woman said, her voice cold and clipped.

Maggie took a step back. "I'm sorry, do I know—"

"I'm going to say this once." The woman jabbed a finger into Maggie's chest. "Stay away from Gwen Knowles." She turned on her heel and marched away, leaving Maggie breathless and shaking. After several deep breaths, Maggie resumed walking home with her hand wrapped around her phone in her pocket.

*

"CORAL?" MAGGIE CALLED out the moment she opened the apartment door.

"Yeah?" she yelled back from her bedroom.

"Is Gwen's last name Knowles?"

Coral stepped out with her hair up in a towel as Maggie set the plastic bags full of convenience food on the counter. "That's how she introduces herself. Why?"

Maggie pulled out the frozen pizza and set the oven to preheat. "Do you know anyone with long black hair and blue eyes who has some connection to her?"

"No idea. What happened?"

After Maggie described the two incidents with the customer, she explained, "I wasn't sure if maybe she was someone from improv group I hadn't met yet. She seemed to know me, and definitely knows Gwen."

"Geez," Coral said, bewildered. "That's mildly terrifying. Are you okay?"

Maggie stuck the pizza in the oven. "I'm fine. She just…startled me."

"What do you think she wanted?"

Maggie laughed wryly. "I think she made that very clear. She wanted me to stay away from Gwen." Maggie started putting the rest of the food away. "She's probably interested in trying out for the play and is scaring away competition. I had a classmate like that in high school. Used to threaten people not to try out for the parts she wanted. No one took her seriously."

Coral didn't seem to share Maggie's casual attitude. "Maggie, this person called you by name."

"She saw me at work earlier. I had my name tag on."

Coral shook her head. "But what was she doing at your work? If she wanted to scare you away from auditioning, couldn't she do it at the audition itself? From the sound of it, she spent a large part of her day watching you. There's a six-hour gap between when you met and when she threatened you."

Maggie paused, leaning against the counter. "That's…definitely weird, I agree."

Coral reached for her phone. "I think you should report it. We can call the nonemergency line and make a statement."

"The police?" Maggie furrowed her brows. "What would I tell them? I have no idea who this chick is."

"I know. But it's important to leave a paper trail. Best-case scenario, you're just being cautious. But worst-case scenario… If this woman comes back, you're going to want your encounters with her documented."

Maggie examined the phone with skepticism. "She didn't exactly threaten my life or anything. I don't think they're going to take it seriously."

Coral looked at Maggie, sighed, and put her phone back in her pocket. "If you change your mind, let me know. And I'd feel safer if you text me after you leave the audition tomorrow."

"You're going to be at *your* audition," Maggie reminded her.

"Don't care. If I get home and you're not there, I want to know what time you headed out. Fair?"

Maggie rolled her eyes at her and went to retrieve plates. "I never thought you'd be a worrywart."

"And honestly, Maggie, the way you act?" Coral retorted, retreating back to her room. "I never thought you'd be so carefree about your own safety."

Maggie opened her mouth, but closed it, surprised by her own thoughts. There simply wasn't any reason to be afraid. Personal threats happened to interesting people who had something others wanted. *This was just an insecure actress,* Maggie told herself. When she saw her at the audition the next day, she'd show her measly threats couldn't hide talent and hard work.

*

BUT SHE WASN'T at the audition. Maggie saw a number of people she recognized, even a couple ladies from the improv group, but no black-haired stranger. Perhaps, she had simply buckled under pressure.

Maggie had arrived at the Twilight just before six. She found the others congregated in the main lobby. A table held two stacks of paper packets. After checking with the others, Maggie retrieved a packet from one pile and left her resumé in the other. Her chosen packet, titled *Scene Three,* had the number thirty-eight in the top corner.

Maggie sat on the stairs leading to the balcony seats, set her belongings next to her, and started reading the script. She had no context for the characters, no descriptions or explanation for the scenes preceding this one.

Yet, in only a page or two, the characters burst into life in her imagination. In the scene, two women debated about organizing a protest. One of them, Ruth, wanted to march through the streets and swarm the city hall; the other, Mary, wanted to pass out flyers on the street in front of the local library.

Maggie didn't have time to finish reading before the door to the auditorium opened. Gwen stepped through first. Maggie blinked in surprise. Unlike the casual but edgy outfits she'd worn to the improv group so far, Gwen was dressed in a pantsuit. Her pressed black trousers, white blouse, and black blazer somehow refined her frame, giving her an air of prestige. She looked like a boss, yet her smile had the same energy that lit up the stage the previous Saturday.

Behind Gwen, two more figures stepped out. To her right stood a woman with deep hickory skin and an even deeper kindness in her eyes. Her black hair, braided tight against her head, made her eyes and smile stand out. She wore a flowing green dress that shimmered as she turned to laugh at something her companions had said. To Gwen's left stood a short, lean man of fawn complexion who could have fit in the woman's dress twice. He wore dark jeans and a navy blazer over a plain gray tee. If his clothes were more interesting, Maggie couldn't tell, too distracted by his bright blue hair. He also wore a serious expression on his face—a complete contrast with his hair color.

Gwen clapped her hands several times, and the room quieted. "Thank you all for coming. We're about to get started. I'd like to introduce us first. This lovely lady is Haleigh Johnson, the author of this remarkable play."

Haleigh Johnson waved jovially. "I've studied the women's liberation movement for longer than I care to say. This is finally our chance to give its message a true spotlight."

"And here, I want to introduce the fantastic Caleb Hughes." Gwen gestured to the gentleman with blue hair. "Caleb is a member of the board for Peace Over Violence, which is helping produce the play."

Caleb Hughes stepped forward and cleared his throat. "Peace Over Violence is an organization dedicated to healing communities and families suffering from violence, with a particular focus on the pervasive harm done against women. We are rooted in feminism and multiculturalism. We're honored to be partnering in the production of this play with Gwen and Haleigh, to raise awareness for our services to the community."

"Part of the proceeds of this play will be donated to Peace Over Violence," Gwen added. "We ask that you take this production seriously. We are grateful for all of you who are here to lend your voice to this message." She made a small mock bow. "And I'm Gwen Knowles, your humble director."

Gwen straightened, clasped her hands, and spoke with a businesslike tone. "Please look at your packet for your number. We will call you in one at a time. Please wait out here and respect the privacy of the individual on stage with us."

"Could number one join us?" Haleigh said, gesturing with open and welcoming hands. "Oh, and please bring the pile of resumés."

Rustling filled the lobby as number one emerged from the crowd and stepped forward, the other actresses moved back, and the three leading figures returned to the dark auditorium. Maggie looked at the thirty-eight scrawled on her script and sat against the steps. She had a long wait ahead of her.

Chapter Five

MAGGIE HAD STARTED to grow stiff from sitting on the steps before the doors opened and Gwen's voice called out, "Thirty-seven, please!"

Finally, Maggie thought, straightening up. She started her stretches and opened the script one more time to study it. As she imagined the tone and posturing of each character, curiosity about what she'd be asked to do crept in. Some of the actors had returned to the lobby after their turns and taken another seat. Others had simply left right after. She sensed the ones who left were not the lucky ones.

Maggie anticipated they'd ask her which character she was interested in auditioning for. That was how her high school had always done it. There were only two characters to choose from in this scene, but she was leaning toward Mary. Mary seemed to be a soft-spoken but determined woman who was kind, understanding, and sweet. Her argument for handing out flyers definitely resonated with how Maggie would feel in her situation. She imagined herself handing a cup of tea to Ruth and pausing to rest her hand on hers, saying, "You accomplish nothing by being brash. If you want to be heard, be polite, or they'll cast you and your message aside."

When Gwen called, "Thirty-eight?" Maggie strode forward with confidence, Mary's steady but comforting demeanor firmly in mind. She passed the last three auditioning actresses and approached Gwen with a smile. Gwen smiled back at her, which did nothing to settle the fluttering in her stomach. "How are you?"

"I'm ready," Maggie said, giving a thumbs-up.

"Perfect." Gwen let the door close as Maggie entered the darkness. "I'm excited to see how you do. Come join us on stage."

Haleigh and Caleb sat in the front row. Gwen joined them as Maggie stepped onto the stage. Maggie had to squint for a moment, but her eyes quickly adjusted to the stage lights.

She smiled broadly. "Thank you so much for having me."

"Thank you for coming," Haleigh said brightly. "I assume you've taken a look at the script?"

"I have. I love it already. The dialogue paints such a clear picture of these characters. I can't wait to see them come to life."

Haleigh laughed merrily.

Caleb stated, "Well, we're about to see one come to life now."

"We'd like you to turn to page five," Gwen said. "Haleigh will read the lines for Mary. We'd like to see you act out Ruth."

For the barest split second, Maggie felt whiplash. But her stage presence was foremost in her mind, and she shook it off as quickly as it had come.

"Sounds great." She started turning pages, with the back of her mind frantically working to change her character style. Where Mary was soft-spoken and polite, Ruth was brazen, blunt, quick to speak, and at times angry, but she had a kinship with Mary all the same. By the time Maggie reached page five, she had an image slowly coming together piece by piece. "Ready."

"Let's go right from the top of the page," Gwen said. "Mary starts."

"I can't speak to you when you're like this," Haleigh read, her voice sad and frustrated. "Mom always said there was never any changing your mind."

"Don't talk about Mom." Maggie stood stiff, one hand curled into a fist. "She didn't know me."

"It's true. Once you're set in your mind, you're set like concrete. You won't move to save yourself any kind of trouble."

"Trouble?" Maggie pointed accusingly at Haleigh. "If I'm concrete, you're powdered sugar. So sweet you attract flies, so weak you can be blown away. You're so scared of *trouble* you'd rather things just stay the same!"

"You know that's not true. I'm here, and I'm participating. I'm doing my part."

Maggie laughed, bitter and harsh. "Your part? The part where you sit demurely on the library steps and pass out flyers to people who take pity on you?"

Haleigh began to speak, but Maggie, as the script queued, cut her off.

"No, listen. We're not here to be polite. We're not here to just shut up and take it anymore. I'm sure you're going to be the town darling—oh, that sweet Mary, she certainly means well. But they know if they ignore you, you'll accept it. You'll be sitting with your flyers until nightfall, and no one will have taken you seriously. Now me?"

Maggie's voice choked a little, as though tears long submerged were bubbling to the surface. "I'm no one's darling. I have nothing to lose but my self-respect. People already see me as the loudmouth. But if I have a loud mouth, by God, I'm going to use it, and I'm going to *make* them hear me!"

Maggie stepped downstage, a finger pointed at Haleigh, eye contact steady and script forgotten in her other hand. "If you want to be just like Mom, that's your choice, and you can watch the world move on without you. I'm not going to be the submissive child the world wants me to be, because something, *someone* has to change."

Maggie expected Haleigh to respond with Mary's lines of comfort and warning, but instead, the playwright stood and clapped.

"Brava!" she called. "I don't need to hear the rest of the scene. Gwen, I see exactly what you mean."

Caleb nodded curtly. "She has the energy."

Maggie's cheeks flushed hot, and she chuckled. "I was just getting started. That was barely a minute."

"Oh, you're not done," Gwen said, smiling. "This is just part one. Haleigh, feedback?"

"I wanted to see how quickly you could step out of yourself and into a character with little preparation," Haleigh stated. "This is a highly emo-tional moment for Ruth, and it's hard to lean into that moment without getting to know the character deeply. I felt…sincerity and passion in your performance." She sat back down. "And quite quickly too."

Gwen nodded. "I wanted to see confidence in the face of uncertainty. This is a very short excerpt of the scene, but it includes a lot of lines with little interruption or movement. With no memorization or real practice, you were articulate, emotive, and confident."

Gwen and Haleigh turned expectantly at Caleb. He leaned forward in his seat. From the floor, he pulled up the pile of resumés and picked Maggie's from the top.

"Margaret Fromm?"

"That's me." Maggie realized he was seeing her resumé for the first time.

Caleb, Gwen, and Haleigh studied it briefly.

"You'll forgive my asking," Caleb said, "but I'm seeing no named roles past about a year, two years ago."

"And those roles are high school roles," Haleigh added.

"Can you tell us about your acting experiences?" Gwen said kindly.

Maggie's ears turned hot, but she forced herself to sound calm. "I moved here right after high school graduation. As you can see, I was cast in multiple school and community performances during that time. Since moving here, I've auditioned repeatedly, but it's...very competitive."

"It certainly is," Haleigh muttered.

"You didn't go to school for acting?" Caleb asked.

Maggie shook her head. "I work at a coffee shop full-time, but audition almost every day off. Sometimes twice a day."

"That's certainly hard work all on its own," Caleb acknowledged.

"What would having a role in this play mean to you?" Gwen asked.

"Everything," Maggie said earnestly. "Telling stories by becoming those stories—it means everything to me. And I want to tell this story. I don't know much about it, but I feel as though I know Mary and Ruth so well already."

Haleigh sat back in her seat. "Tell me what story you see in this scene that you want to tell."

Maggie took a moment's pause to collect her thoughts. "These are two sisters who have similar beliefs, but their ideas about how to promote change are radically different. There's an unspoken history there, too, like they had very different relationships with Mom, and that changes their relationship with each other. But at the end of the scene, it's clear they still love each other, even if they're taking different paths."

Caleb lifted an eyebrow. "They're screaming at each other at the end of this scene."

"They could only scream with that much emotion if they truly cared," Maggie replied.

Gwen nodded. "Thank you, Maggie. Haleigh, Caleb, your thoughts?"

"I want her for round two," Haleigh said firmly.

"I agree," said Caleb.

"Maggie, could you return to the lobby and wait?" Gwen asked. "I believe we have three more individual auditions. Then we'll ask those remaining to return as a group. Can you stick around a bit longer?"

"I can wait all night," Maggie said eagerly.

*

ALTHOUGH THE SECOND wait was shorter, Maggie found herself more anxious than the first time. At least then, she had a script to read and study. Now, as she waited through three auditions that seemed much longer than hers, she had nothing but her phone to keep her mind occupied. And there simply wasn't anything on social media that could overpower her racing thoughts.

When the second round finally began, Caleb came to the door to call the remaining actors into the theater. It was a much smaller crowd that walked onto the stage.

Haleigh called out merrily, "If everyone could arrange yourselves to stand in a line, we'll get started."

Maggie did a headcount quickly as they moved into their places. With shock, she realized the circle only contained twenty-three individuals. She glanced around and tried to read the faces of the room. The group seemed to be entirely young ladies or middle-aged women. Faces were a blend of excited, calm, and stern.

Haleigh went stage left, and Caleb stage right. Gwen, standing at center stage, spoke with high spirits.

"Congratulations, everyone, on being asked to participate in round two of our audition. We want to thank everyone who came today with determination and dedication to the craft. We have one more exercise, and then the audition will be completed."

Haleigh handed a stack of paper to the lady at the end of the line. "Please take a packet, then pass the rest on. Take a couple moments to get familiar with this scene. You'll be taking turns acting out the scene in groups. We'll call you up by name."

Maggie read through her packet as quickly as she could, flipping through what appeared to be a scene in a grocery store. At least four more characters were in this scene in addition to Ruth and Mary. Very quickly, she heard names being called. She wasn't called in the first group, so she read along as the first six acted out the scene.

After a few minutes, Gwen and Haleigh asked some of the women to return to the line, some to come forward, some to change roles with one another. When Maggie was called up, she was given Mary's role to read first, then Ruth's, then a character named Susan, and then Ruth again. She was asked to move back in line, and then was called up ten minutes later. With each change, she watched anxiously as Gwen and Haleigh murmured together, writing notes. The people in the group cycled in and out fluidly, but Maggie started to notice a pattern. She was frequently matched with a young lady with wavy brown hair, a dirty-blond-haired woman with broad shoulders, and an actor with startling bleached hair. Maggie fought the urge to cross her fingers. *Maybe frequent matching means they think we work well together?*

After what felt simultaneously like hours and seconds, Haleigh and Gwen stopped calling names and jotting down their thoughts.

"All right, everyone, that concludes our audition tonight," Gwen announced. "Thank you so much for your patience. We will contact you by Friday evening with our decision. Be safe going home tonight."

Maggie and the rest of the actors walked to the edge of the stage, preparing to exit. As she did, she felt Gwen approach beside her.

"May I chat with you for a moment?" Gwen asked.

"Sure." Maggie once again followed Gwen backstage. Still within the glow of the lights, Gwen offered a handshake. "I just wanted to thank you so much for coming. You did exactly as well as I knew you would. Haleigh was delighted to meet you."

Maggie blushed but smiled as she shook Gwen's hand firmly. "I'm the one who should be saying thank you. This is the first opportunity I've had in a long time to be a real storyteller again. I'm not sure why you asked me to audition, but I'm so grateful you did."

To Maggie's surprise, Gwen didn't let go of her hand.

"I'll be honest," she said. "I asked a lot of the people here to audition. A couple people responded to casting calls, but most were invited here by myself or my colleagues." Gwen's eyes locked with Maggie's. "But I was most excited to see you here. I have a strong feeling about you… I think I would very much like to work with you." She let go of Maggie's hand and smiled again. "I'm sure we'll be calling you soon. Go get some well-earned rest."

Maggie stammered her thanks as she and Gwen parted. As she hurriedly left the theater, texting Coral to let her know she was on her way home, the image of Gwen's brilliant eyes and smile filled her mind. She floated to the bus stop with a giddy grin, pausing only once when she thought she saw a flash of black hair across the street.

Chapter Six

IN THE PAINSTAKINGLY slow days leading up to Friday, Maggie had trouble finding ways to keep her mind busy during her rare downtime. Thankfully, she had the opportunity to pick up additional hours at work, but more than once, Coral found her in her room alternating between restless pacing and frantically scrolling through casting call advertisements.

"Will you calm down?" Coral said Thursday evening. "You said Gwen and Haleigh seemed impressed, right? I'm sure you've got this, and stressing out is doing you no good."

Maggie buried her face between her knees, hands still clinging to her phone where an ad for "'brunette for shampoo commercial" was displayed. "Lots of talented people don't get auditions just because there are only so many roles. They cut down on half of the actresses between rounds of the audition, and I bet they have to cut down at least by half again. Even if I did impress them, someone else might be completely perfect for the role and—and—I gotta find another audition to go to so I have something to focus on in case I don't—"

"Oh my God, you're going to give me an ulcer." Coral headed to her room, calling over her shoulder, "Tell me when you finally get the news, and I'll buy ice cream."

Maggie woke up Friday morning, nauseous with anticipation. She stared at herself in the mirror, working up the courage to go to work. She'd never felt this nervous before. She'd passed every audition she'd ever attended—well, every audition until graduation. A year of few callbacks seemed to have hit her harder than she imagined. Straightening her back, Maggie clapped her hands against her cheeks and forced herself to smile at her reflection.

Maggie asked Sofia for permission to keep her phone on while she worked, explaining she was waiting for an important call. She was in the middle of pouring a particularly hot brew from the pot when her phone buzzed in her pocket. She jumped like a startled cat and hastily set the pot down before rushing to the back. Her shaking fingers almost hung up the call before she managed to answer and hold the phone to her ear. "H-hello, Maggie Fromm."

"Hey, Maggie, it's Gwen."

Even separated by the phone, Gwen's voice had a warmth to it that brought a smile to Maggie's face.

"I have exciting news for you. You're in!"

"Really?" Maggie breathed, clutching the phone with both hands. "I passed the audition?"

"With flying colors." Gwen laughed. "Haleigh said she just *had* to have you for the role of Ruth. Congratulations."

Maggie slumped against the wall, a wave of relief flooding her. "Oh my gosh…I'm so excited! Thank you!"

"We'd like everyone to meet at the Twilight Tuesday evening," Gwen said, papers shuffling in the background. "If you want to be paid by direct deposit, bring your bank routing number because we're going to be discussing contracts and pay. We're also going to set up rehearsal schedules."

"When's the show?"

"In about four months, late February. So we're looking, at minimum, at a weekly commitment, with daily rehearsals in the last couple weeks. Can we count on you?"

"Absolutely!" Maggie would talk to Sofia, but at this point, she'd quit her job if it meant staying in this production. As nice as the boss was, other coffee shops existed and were constantly hiring. But this play? "I won't let you down. I'm completely dedicated."

"I knew you would be," Gwen said as a blush spread across Maggie's face. "I'm so excited to work with you. I'll see you Tuesday at six p.m. at the Twilight. Oh, and bring something to share, we're having a potluck to celebrate. Nothing messy though."

"Tuesday at six, with food. Got it."

"I'll let you go. Congrats again, Maggie."

"Thank you." Maggie hung up the phone, cradled it to her chest, and let herself squee in excitement.

Sofia poked her head in the doorway. "Did you get the part?"

"I got the part." Maggie wiped tears from the corners of her eyes and ran to her boss. "I got the part!"

Sofia clasped Maggie's hand in an enthusiastic high-five. "*¡Felicidades!* Hey, get me a poster or something for the play, and we'll put it with the rest in the window, okay?"

"Yes." Maggie clapped her hands to her cheeks. "I can't believe this is happening."

Sofia laughed and patted Maggie on the head. "All right, starlet. Give yourself a minute so you can focus when you get back on the floor."

Maggie, of course, texted Coral before putting her phone back on silent. At the end of her shift, she turned her phone on to find a string of texts from Coral congratulating her and debating on which ice cream flavors were appropriate enough to celebrate. *Thank goodness for Coral,* Maggie thought to herself as she headed home. This exciting news brought a new waiting period—waiting for Tuesday—and she didn't know how she would have stayed sane if she'd been alone in her apartment like she used to be.

She wondered what Jess's parents would say if they heard about her audition. What would *her* parents say?

Maggie shook her head, quickly shooing such thoughts from her mind. That was the past. This was now. She was going to be on stage again, with a named role, and that was all that mattered. She ran toward the bus stop with a new spring in her step.

*

TUESDAY EVENING, MAGGIE practically bolted through the doors of the Twilight, partially from excitement, partially to get out of the rain. Shaking off her umbrella in the lobby, Maggie took a few deep breaths, then stepped through the doors to the auditorium, casserole dish filled with latkes in hand.

She was surprised at how small the group was. In addition to Haleigh and Gwen, there were only five others present. Gwen, dressed in jeans and an asymmetrical hoodie, waved her over.

"Perfect timing, Maggie! That's everyone. I'd like everyone to grab a plate of food and take a seat so we can get to know one another and discuss roles. Oh, and grab a packet. That has your script and contracts."

Three long tables, set up in a triangle, allowed the eight participants to sit, eat, and read the script with relative ease. Maggie filled her plate and sat at the end of one table. Haleigh, from where she was sitting, rattled a mug.

"Does anyone want a highlighter?" she asked. "We're going to start a group readthrough today, assuming we have time. Or a pen for your signature?"

The mug was passed around, and Maggie grabbed a highlighter and a pen. She took a bite of bagel as she flipped through the packet, listening to Gwen's instructions. Gwen navigated them through the contract and its expectations. Maggie was surprised to see the employer was listed as the University of Southern California.

"This play production is possible through a grant Haleigh and I applied for," Gwen explained. "That grant money is what will allow us to pay you but still give proceeds to Peace Over Violence. As I'm sure you can imagine, that also puts some unique pressure on us to do well. If this production is successful, we pave the way for future independent productions like this one."

As Maggie signed the documents, she felt the weight of Gwen and Haleigh's earnest efforts settling on her shoulders.

Eventually, the logistics of payment, schedules, and cast expectations were ironed out to everyone's satisfaction. Gwen went around the tables collecting signed and completed papers and went to make copies for the actors to take home as Haleigh moved forward with the evening's activities.

"I'd like us to go around and introduce ourselves. As you do, I'll inform you of your assigned role. Please give your name, your preferred pronouns, and a brief description of your acting experience. Could we start on my left?"

Maggie was delighted to see the dirty-blond-haired woman with broad shoulders from the audition. She smiled with a good-natured wave.

"Hi, I'm Georgia. My pronouns are she-her, and I'm an off-again-on-again instructor with 3-2-1 Acting Studios. I've been doing this for about…twenty-five years, I would say."

"Thank you, Georgia. I'm so happy to have your experience with us!" Haleigh beamed at her. "You'll be playing the role of Mary."

The woman to Georgia's left had dark-brown hair tied in a tight ballerina bun. She gave a casual wave. "I'm Alyssa. My pronouns are she-her. I just graduated from the University of Southern California last semester. I've mostly been doing roles as extras and understudies since then." Haleigh announced Alyssa would play the role of Joanne, a traditionalist who opposed the liberation movement.

To Alyssa's left, Maggie recognized the young lady from the audition with a tiny frame and wavy brown hair. "I'm Isabella, but please call me Bel! My pronouns are she-her. I'm a student with AMDA College of the Performing Arts, just starting this semester!" Bel was cast as Nancy, a young and enthusiastic new member of the liberation movement.

Maggie followed Bel. When she turned to her left, another familiar individual, the actor with bleached hair cropped short against their face, gave a stiff wave. "I'm Skylar. My pronouns are they-them. I'm an associate professor with CalArts. I've been in productions for the past fifteen years, first in New York, now here." Skylar was cast as Bonnie, another traditionalist in opposition to the movement. Based on their laugh, Skylar seemed to find this ironic.

Lastly, a woman with straight dark hair spoke. "I'm Donna, and my pronouns are she-her. I, oh gosh, I haven't been in an actual play for a while. I'm a professor with LMU for acting but went part-time to raise my kids for a while. I guess you could say I've been in this business for…thirty years? It's so exciting to be back." Donna would play Susan, the mayor's wife, whom Haleigh described as a neutral party representing "national public opinion."

Just as Donna was finishing, Gwen arrived and handed out copies of their signed contracts to keep. As she did so, Haleigh spoke.

"Well, as you'll remember from the audition, I'm Haleigh Johnson, the playwright. This script"—she lifted the packet—"is *Petty Oppression*, my baby of five years. I'm a professor with the USC School of Dramatic Arts."

"And I'm Gwen Knowles," Gwen said, returning to her seat. "I'm in freelance theater. I've had my finger in about every pot for nearly six years now."

With all participants introduced, Haleigh opened the script and invited the cast to start an initial readthrough. "This is just act one," she explained, "because I'm in the middle of a massive edit of act two."

Maggie's excitement grew as she highlighted her lines and listened closely to the others. Between scenes, Georgia decided to switch seats with Skylar so she could sit next to Maggie.

"If we're going to be sisters on stage," Georgia said, "we best get used to working closely."

As they read together, it was as if their real identities melted away.

Around the table, Maggie saw the actors trying on new characters like costumes, a new light growing in their eyes that set a spark burning in her own heart.

Haleigh was just about to guide them through a reading of scene three when the sound of a heavy door opening came from somewhere backstage. A young man stomped onstage, tying his long brown hair back into a ponytail.

"Gwen, for God's sake, I have set pieces to paint. Get out!"

"Roy!" Gwen stood with a sheepish grin. "Everyone, I'm afraid we have to end here for the night, but before you go, please meet Roy Sharpe. He's the stage manager for the Twilight. He's—"

"Going to kick your ass if you don't stick to schedule," Roy said, throwing a paint-stained rag toward Gwen. "You know we're doing freaking *A Midsummer Night's Dream* in less than two weeks. I need to work."

Haleigh, who was helping gather highlighters and pens, informed the group, "Starting Thursday, we'll be able to rehearse in The Sanford Meisner Center. Talk to me if you need directions to it. And as you leave, Gwen will let you know if there are any issues with your signed contracts. Thank you all for coming. Can you help move these chairs for Roy?"

Maggie helped carry her chair off the stage, then went to grab her umbrella. As she reached for it, Gwen called her name.

"Was there an issue with my deposit slip?" Maggie asked as she walked over to her. "I'm pretty sure I did the contract right, but I never seem to get account numbers and routing numbers straight."

Gwen placed a hand lightly on Maggie's shoulder and guided her to one side of the auditorium, out of the way of both the exiting actors and Roy's incoming crew. "No, your paperwork was fine. I actually have something else I want to talk to you about."

Maggie blinked. "Oh. Well…what's up?"

Gwen stood close to her and lowered her voice, not a whisper but low enough so the words wouldn't carry throughout the theater for others to hear. "I want you to know that, as your director, I'm always going to be honest with you. It's my job to see your potential, catch your shortcomings, and guide you to success. Do you trust that what I'm about to say is because I respect you as an actress?"

Self-doubt tugged at Maggie's thoughts, but she was reassured by Gwen's earnest gaze. "Yes, ma'am. I do."

Gwen nodded, then continued. "Like I told you last week, almost everyone who auditioned was invited by Haleigh and myself. Consequently, everyone else in this cast is either receiving training in acting or is already educated and experienced. If you'll forgive my saying so, your lack of higher education could hold you back."

Maggie felt a bitter sting in the back of her throat. She swallowed it down. "It certainly is…intimidating."

Gwen's eyes softened. "Hey, don't let that get you down. Bel only just started her education a couple months ago. You're not on as uneven footing as it seems at first." She turned to the stage, where Roy was yelling out directions and distributing tape rolls. "I asked to talk to you because I want to help you. You got this far on raw talent and dedication. I want to help you go even further." She glanced back at Maggie. "I'd like to teach you acting. I'm not an official professor like Max, but between the two of us, I think you could get a well-rounded boost. What do you say?"

Maggie, stunned, stammered out the first questions that came to her head. "W-what would it cost? What would I have to do?"

"Oh, no no no no, it wouldn't cost anything. Consider this part of me working with you as the director of this play. We'll meet at, say, the library to study once a week and, of course, keep coming to improv group. At improv, you'll get lessons from Professor Max on the basics. At the library, we'll dive into acting theory and fine-tune your talents." Gwen held out her hand. "What do you say?"

Maggie didn't have to think twice. Grabbing Gwen's hand tightly, she shook, fighting not to blush. "I would be honored. I'm so grateful for the opportunity."

Gwen smiled. "It's my pleasure."

*

MAGGIE WAS PRACTICALLY floating on air as she walked to the bus stop from the theater. Her umbrella swung jauntily at her side now that the rain had ceased, and the streets shone silver in the lamplight. As she came to stand at the stop and checked her phone for the time, she decided to take a moment to type up an email to Sofia with her new schedule. Rehearsals Tuesday and Thursday evenings, improv group on Saturdays, and study sessions with Gwen on her days off on Wednesdays starting next week. Suddenly she had gone from long fruitless weeks to a packed schedule.

She clicked Send and set her phone in her pocket, glancing down the street for her bus. But it wasn't a bus that caught her eye. A figure with long black hair tied in a high ponytail walked straight toward her.

"You!" Maggie said in surprise. She clutched her phone. Where was that stupid bus?

The woman didn't stop until she was uncomfortably close to Maggie, toe-to-toe. When Maggie stepped back, she stepped forward. "What kind of gunk do you keep in your ears?" she snarled. Icy blue eyes flashed in the light of passing cars. "I told you to stay away from Gwen Knowles. That not clear enough for you?"

"What is your problem?" Maggie demanded. "Who the hell—"

Maggie's head snapped to one side, and a stinging pain seared across her face. Vision reeling, she raised a hand to her cheek. When the stranger lifted her hand again, Maggie realized she had just been slapped. She gasped as the figure grabbed her shirtfront and pulled her close. As she spoke, spittle sprayed Maggie's face.

"I don't need a little *child* like you to be acting so *clueless*. I don't know what you did to get her attention, but you don't deserve it."

As Maggie struggled against her grip, a gentleman walking by paused and interjected.

"Hey, there, let go. Is there a problem here?"

The black-haired stranger glanced at the man, then shoved Maggie backward. Maggie tumbled to the ground as the woman brushed off her hands. "If all you want is the play, fine," she spat. "But I'm watching you. You get any closer to Gwen, there will be consequences." She turned and ran the way she'd come.

"Get back here!" yelled the gentleman as he helped Maggie to her feet. "Who was that?" he asked her. "Should I call the cops?"

Maggie shook her head dazedly. "N-no…no, it's fine. I just want to get home."

Chapter Seven

"WE'RE CALLING THE cops."

"Coral, please, it's fine—"

"Like hell it's fine!"

Maggie certainly hadn't known Coral for a long time, but she found it hard to believe anyone had ever seen Coral this angry. She'd dropped her practice juggling balls and was searching for the nonemergency police number on her phone. Her lips were set in a tight line, her shoulders tense, and her eyes had a hardness Maggie had never seen.

"This person just physically assaulted you, Maggie, in the middle of the street. She's made it very clear it's not about the play. You really think it's safe to let someone like that roam around unchecked?"

Maggie sat on the sectional, a feeling of unreality clouding her mind. "Coral, listen, they won't take me seriously. I have no idea who she is and—"

"And she sure knows who you are, and who Gwen is. Maggie, snap out of it. I know it can be scary to tell strangers about something that happened, especially when you don't understand it yourself. But your safety is too important to just ignore this!"

"I…I know that, but…what do I even say?"

Coral seemed to calm down a little. She reached for a blanket draped across the back of the sectional and placed it on Maggie's shoulders. Sitting next to Maggie, she wrapped an arm around her and pulled her tight. "Maggie, be honest. Why don't you want to call the cops?"

Maggie curled her legs up against her chest and hugged her knees, allowing herself to be enveloped. "I…I do want to call. It just… I know it's silly."

"Calling the cops can be nerve-wracking for anyone," Coral said soothingly. "It just seems like you might have something specific in mind."

"Mmm." Maggie chewed on her bottom lip, then sighed. "It might be because my dad is a cop. I know he doesn't have anything to do with LAPD, but it still kinda feels like telling my dad."

After a moment's pause, Coral gave Maggie's shoulder a squeeze. "You don't talk about your parents."

"We don't talk."

Coral nodded in understanding. "This will be nothing like talking to your dad. I promise. We'll put the phone on speaker, and I'll be with you the whole time. Okay?"

Maggie took a deep breath and let it out slowly between her teeth. "Okay."

"Atta girl." Coral hit Dial on her phone. As it rang, she pointed out, "This will keep Gwen safe too."

"I know." That thought gave Maggie comfort. "I'll do my best."

*

GWEN WAS WAITING for Maggie at the door to the rehearsal room on Thursday evening. She took Maggie to one side in the hallway, brows furrowed. "I got a visit from LAPD yesterday," she said. "Are you okay?"

"Oh! Oh, yeah, I'm fine." Maggie worked to keep her voice casual.

Gwen put up her hand. "No, really, I'm asking sincerely. They said you were assaulted, and I've been worried sick about you."

Maggie's heart leapt to her throat. "Well…it was a bit of a shock."

"I'm sure," Gwen murmured. "I don't want to pressure you, but can you tell me your side of the story?"

"Rehearsal is starting soon. I don't want to make you late."

Gwen made direct eye contact with her, green eyes boring into hers. "Haleigh will lead warm-ups. What happened to you matters to me. Please."

Maggie told Gwen everything, starting with the stranger standing in line at the cafe, acknowledging that Coral had urged her to call police the first time, but she had chosen not to. When she told Gwen about getting slapped the second time, Gwen's hands twitched as if to reach out and hold her, but she restrained herself. There was a pained look in her eyes when Maggie finished.

Gwen asked slowly, "Can you describe the person? As best as you can?"

"Long, black hair. Like, at least down to her waist. Really blue eyes. Pale skin." She thought hard. "I'd say she had a…pointy chin. And she's a little taller than me, but not as tall as you."

"And she hit you?"

Maggie laughed nervously. "It was quite the wallop, actually."

Gwen stepped back and leaned against the wall, breathing deeply. She folded her arms against her chest, fingers fidgeting. "And you still want to be in this play? Have study sessions with me? Honestly, if you back out of the study sessions and improv group, I won't blame you, but if you can at least stay in the play—"

"No, no, I absolutely don't want to give up on study sessions!" Maggie replied. "I don't know who she is or what her problem is, but it's not going to stop me from doing my best for this play."

Gwen's lips twitched, as if she couldn't help smiling. "As always, your energy lights up the room, Miss Fromm." Maggie's cheeks grew rosy, but Gwen's eyes were serious. "If I'm right about who the person is, it's Valerie Harker. Maybe it's not, but…she's the only person I know who fits that description and would do something close to that crazy."

Gwen stroked her chin with one hand, eyes focused on the floor. "She's…someone I used to know really well. We were very close for a long time. But…she isn't the healthiest person, you know?"

"Uh-huh."

"Still," Gwen continued, "I had no idea she would still have such, let's say, hard feelings. And last I knew, she wasn't even still in the city. If she's back, and if she's telling people to stay away from me…"

She straightened up and put her hands in her pockets. "I think I'm going to have to talk to the group today. I'll have to warn everyone working on this production to be safe. She picked you out first, but there's no guarantee she won't target the others too." Gwen turned to face Maggie. "I won't say anything about what happened to you specifically. But I think the others should know."

Maggie nodded. "Of course. And Gwen…I'm sorry I didn't take this seriously the first time."

Gwen reached into her back pocket and pulled out her phone. "Here, I'm texting you so you can save my number in your phone. If anything else happens, after you tell the police, tell me, okay?" She finished typing and slid her phone back into her pocket. "Don't play reckless with your safety, Maggie. We're counting on you."

Maggie gave a salute. "Aye aye, captain!"

Haleigh paused warm-ups as Gwen and Maggie entered.

"I'm sorry to interrupt," Gwen said as she walked to the front of the room, "but I need to borrow everyone's attention for a moment before we get started today." She looked around at the faces in the room and, bouncing a little on her heels, dove right in. "It's come to my attention that a past acquaintance of mine may attempt to target members of this play, mostly with verbal threats but possibly with physical violence."

There was a collective look of shock from the group, but everyone kept quiet, listening closely.

"I don't wish to alarm you," Gwen continued. "If any of you have been troubled by someone for your participation in this play, I invite you to come speak with me in private so we can discuss any concerns you have."

Georgia half raised a hand to quietly interrupt. Gwen nodded to her. "Dear, are you okay?" she asked, concerned. "This sounds unsafe for you."

Gwen shook her head. "I'm perfectly safe, I promise you. I don't understand her motives, but she's made no attempt to contact me so far."

Skylar, with crossed arms, tapped a finger against their elbow and raised an eyebrow. "Well, we'll keep an eye out for such a person. It sounds like jealousy to me."

Alyssa nodded. "I wouldn't be surprised. Gwen, you remember when you and I were in the same production of *Take Me Out*, what, a year ago? Year and a half? And there was that guy who stood outside of the theater burning playbills and telling people not to see it because he didn't get a part?"

Gwen groaned and rolled her eyes. "Oh, lord, that guy. Left ashes all over the sidewalk; it was awful."

Bel clapped a hand to her mouth, stifling an incredulous giggle. "People don't do stuff like that often, do they?"

"Honey, the things I've seen," Donna said, spreading her hands. "Theater tends to attract...well, the dramatic!"

The group laughed, falling into chatter of their own examples of jealous and petty coworkers until Gwen quickly called for their attention again.

"Again, it's not my intention to alarm you," she said. "I just want you to be informed about your participation in this play."

The actors looked around at one another. Maggie saw mostly grinning faces.

Alyssa spoke first. "Gwen, relax. We'll stay cautious, but it's going to take more than one person with some scary words to make us stop."

"Yeah. They're just jealous they couldn't be a part of this," Bel said passionately, eyes alight.

Gwen seemed to relax, shoulders falling into a more natural position. She looked over to Haleigh. "Well, I guess that settles it. Time to get to work."

Rehearsal started with Haleigh and Gwen breaking the actors into two groups to learn lines. Maggie, Georgia, and Bel ended up together since they shared the most scenes with one another. Haleigh sat with them as they picked through the script, sometimes filling in for absent characters. Although they started out sitting on chairs, Maggie noticed, across the room, Skylar on their feet, seemingly with Gwen's encouragement.

"They seem pretty into it over there," she commented.

Georgia glanced over and grinned. "Ooh, I like the enthusiasm. Come on, let's get up!" She stood, stretching. "It's not like Mary and Ruth talk through everything sitting down."

Maggie rose to her feet. "I guess that's true."

Haleigh stayed seated, but Bel rose too. "Okay, great. Georgia, it's your line."

Georgia cleared her throat, then changed the way she was holding the script, making it seem like a bundle of pamphlets she was handing out. "Nancy, dear, do your parents know you're with us today?" she asked with a motherly tone.

Bel mimed handing a pamphlet to an invisible passerby. "Oh, they don't mind. I just told them I was studying."

Maggie joined them, pretending her passerby had refused a flier. "You haven't been honest with them?"

"It's not lying," Bel protested, crossing her arms and huffing. "I'm studying feminism. Right?"

Georgia wrapped an arm around Bel and hugged her close. "That's exactly right, dear. I—" She paused, then flipped back and forth a few pages. "Haleigh, I have a question. There aren't actually going to be people walking across the stage as we do this, right?"

"This is more like the three of you are setting up and preparing, not actively talking to the public yet," Haleigh agreed.

"Ah. Well then." Georgia set her script down on the floor and hoisted a folding chair, pretending to fuss about its placement. "Maggie, how do you think Ruth would be feeling in this scene?"

"Frustrated," Maggie replied quickly.

"Well, let's see you lift *two* chairs, and give a good scowl." Georgia rubbed her hands together. "Bel, let's go back a couple lines. I want to try sounding a little more confident and less patronizing."

"Are you being bossy over there?" Alyssa's voice called from across the room. "We can hear you giving orders!"

Georgia looked at Bel and Maggie with a slightly worried face. "Am I being bossy, ladies? I tend to have a bit of a large presence in small groups."

Maggie shook her head.

"I'm enjoying this," Bel said cheerfully. "Reciting lines in different ways is helping me with my memorization."

"You hear that, nosy?" Georgia called over to Alyssa. "She says I'm helpful!"

"You mean like that time in *The Crucible* when you made me rehearse the same line for half an hour because you couldn't decide on how to say yours?" Alyssa responded, with Donna chuckling behind her.

"You stay in your group, young lady!" Georgia said with mock sternness, waving a finger.

Gwen waved her hands in the air. "Ladies, ladies, we're losing focus! What's going on here?"

Alyssa and Georgia broke into sheepish laughter.

"I'm always giving her a hard time," Alyssa said. "We've been in a couple things together, and she can get—"

"Bossy!" Georgia cut in. "But it's not my fault this time. We were watching your group moving around and thought it would be great to try."

Gwen nodded, setting her hands on her hips. "When I'm working with you, I encourage you to move around and try to act like your character would in the setting. It's going to help inform you of how you want to say your lines. Here, let's use an example. Sky, Alyssa, go to page twenty please."

Donna stepped back, and Alyssa and Sky flipped through their scripts. Alyssa started, miming as if she were setting a table while still holding her script within her line of sight.

"I wouldn't expect such people to know how to behave themselves at a proper church dinner," she said, her tone aloof.

Skylar *tsked* between their teeth, putting chairs into place around an invisible table. "The least they could do is contribute some food. I've nearly burned my hand on that horrid stove every year. But these young people don't know how to cook properly anymore, do they?"

"I suppose they haven't the time," Alyssa responded. "All this running around, marching, demonstrating."

Skylar paused, finding their place on the page. "Seeing such a public display of degeneracy… It sickens me."

"Well, they're foolish," Alyssa said demurely, continuing to set the table, "but I'm sure they'll come 'round. When they grow, they'll find there just isn't enough time or energy in life for all these…these high-flying ideas. They'll settle down just as we all did."

"You think these ideas are harmless? They eat away at everything that keeps us whole. They're rotten." Skylar slammed the feet of a chair against the floor in anger.

Gwen cut in. "Yes! A bit forceful for what's supposed to be a middle-aged woman in the 1960s, but that's the right energy. Now imagine that energy restrained. Hold it inside yourself like it's bursting through your seams."

Skylar nodded. "You think these ideas are harmless?" they repeated, tightly gripping the chair, eyes blazing, fingers white at the knuckles—the image of a well-mannered individual attempting to contain their rage. "They eat away at everything that keeps us whole. They're *rotten.*"

Georgia, Maggie, and Bel gave a brief round of applause, which Skylar and Alyssa returned with mocking bows. They returned to their separate groups, encouraged to act bolder and larger, to feel their characters in both motions and words. Near the end of rehearsal, Gwen instructed the group to recite scene one without stopping. In this scene, every character made at least a brief appearance, walking through a neighborhood corner store and discussing the national news about women's marches in major cities. Maggie proudly recited her lines from memory and pretended to pick up and return items on shelves as she and her character's sister did their shopping.

At the end of rehearsal, the actors drank water and heard feedback from Gwen.

"I'm impressed to see how well everyone is doing getting off book," Gwen said, "but I don't want you worrying about memorization yet. You have plenty of time. What I want you to focus on is getting familiar with the setting of the play. The 1960s might not seem that long ago, but they had their own unique culture and political climate. I'm more focused on you inserting yourself into the setting and having it feel as natural to you as our modern world."

She waved her copy of the script. "Your homework is in two parts. Firstly, I want you to tell the story of the play out loud to someone. That will help you connect to the story. Secondly, I want you to think about how you would experience the sixties from your own cultural lens. Not your character's—I know some of you are playing women who don't quite have identical experiences."

"No kidding," snarked Skylar.

Gwen nodded. "The play itself focuses on gender, but the liberation movement would have different impacts based on race, creed, etcetera. I want you to insert yourself into this movement and reflect on how you would be impacted, culturally and politically. It will help make the setting more grounded for you. I don't need a typed report or anything, but I'd like you to talk about it a little to the group on Tuesday."

*

THE NEXT EVENING Coral picked up the dinner plates. "All right, I'll wash up, and you tell me this story. Then I can tell Gwen at improv group tomorrow that you did your homework."

Maggie sat backward in her chair, watching Coral work as she spoke. "So the whole thing is about the women's liberation movement in the sixties, which Wikipedia tells me was a global social movement to draw attention to sexism, gender inequality, and general mistreatment of women."

"Huh," Coral muttered. "Good thing we live in a time after they solved all that."

Maggie laughed but continued. "There's no real main character, but it's largely through the eyes of Mary, Joanne, and Susan. Mary is my character's older sister. We both want to bring the movement to our small town, but I want to be loud about it and march in the streets. The audience eventually learns I got pregnant out of wedlock and had a miscarriage, but the town thinks I got an abortion. I want to fight for women having more say in their reproductive health. Mary is a widow whose husband died in Vietnam. The town loves her. She's trying to reach the people in a more friendly, personal way, trying to have personal discussions with the people who respect her. She wants to focus on women having more recognition and equality in the workforce since she has to work to provide for her family now."

"So you work together on organizing stuff?" Coral guessed.

"We try to, but my character keeps butting heads with Mary, telling her she's being too soft, while Mary keeps telling me I'm being too abrasive. By the end of act one, we're practically not speaking to each other. We have some kind of difference of opinion about our mom. I think Mary was the favorite child. I'm hoping that gets explained more in act two."

"You don't have act two yet?"

"Not just yet. Haleigh said she's going through an overhaul of some scenes."

Coral glanced over her shoulder. "She's rewriting a script that she got grant money for?"

"It's not that unusual. Some shows go through rewrites right up through dress rehearsal."

"Ah." Coral returned her attention to the dishes. "So what about the other characters?"

"Well, in opposition to Mary and Ruth, there's Joanne and Bonnie. They're traditional housewives and close church friends. They seem to see the movement as an attack on the sanctity of marriage and family dynamics. They start out really close, but their friendship gets strained as Joanne realizes Bonnie is, well, fanatical. Joanne believes the movement is bad because it will encourage promiscuity, abortion, divorce, or women choosing work over caring for their children."

"Apple pie and motherhood," Coral commented.

"Right. But Bonnie straight up believes God made women to be subservient to men, and rejecting that role or doing anything other than serving a husband or being a nun means rejecting God. Joanne doesn't actually believe women are less valuable or capable than men, and she's not sure how to confront this difference with her friend."

"So both sides have their disagreements and conflicts."

"Yeah, it's pretty balanced."

"What's it like being a loud, abrasive revolutionary?" Coral asked with a smirk. "That doesn't seem quite your speed."

"I know! I was so surprised they wanted me as Ruth and not Mary. But honestly, I get so riled up reading her lines. This play might make a revolutionary out of me." Maggie giggled as a thought crossed her mind. "The actor playing Bonnie is her exact opposite. It's actually really funny to watch."

"Who's playing Bonnie? Maybe I know her," Coral asked.

Maggie hesitated, then chose her words carefully. "Skylar? Um…super short silver hair. I think about twenty-five, thirty years old?"

"I know them," Coral said excitedly. "Skylar is playing a conservative church wife? That's hilarious. Wonder why they didn't post anything in the Facebook group about it?"

Maggie felt a small wave of relief. Coral knew Skylar, and their preferred pronouns. This was followed by a sudden thought: *If she's okay with Skylar, maybe she'd be okay with me?*

Filing the thought away for later, Maggie continued telling her story.

"There are two other characters who don't have as much happen in the first act. Nancy is a young movement member. She's filled with enthusiasm and energy, but she doesn't seem to fully grasp the importance. She follows Ruth–me–around because she finds my ideas of marches and protests exciting. She seems to be in it for the fun. She agrees with the message but doesn't seem to have a personal stake in the message like others do."

"How young is she?"

"She's graduating from high school."

"Well, that's why," Coral said confidently. "If she has a decent family life, she maybe hasn't experienced anything that would motivate a more serious participation."

"Maybe," Maggie mused, "but there's a whole second act I haven't read yet. And the last character is Susan. She's the wife of the town mayor, a stand-in for the public opinion and leadership response. She mostly interacts with the other women as they try to set up their protests and counter-protests. Talks a lot about her husband and tries to be friendly with everyone involved."

"That makes sense. Her family benefits from society being the way it is. If a bunch of women successfully overthrow the patriarchy and her husband isn't mayor anymore, the family needs a new form of income and support and loses their socioeconomic status."

"Huh, I hadn't considered that," Maggie muttered. "Scene four makes a lot more sense now. She's in a sewing circle with Joanne and Bonnie and makes a lot of comments about how women are doing just fine in the home."

Coral nodded and reached for a towel to dry the dishes. "So, is the mayor's wife what ties everything together?"

"Not quite. There's also a march at the end of act one. The goal is to gather the women in the park to talk about their individual experiences and raise awareness of the sexism the town experiences and perpetuates. Ruth and Nancy spend most of the act helping organize it, with Mary on the sidelines supporting in a quieter way. Joanne and Bonnie plan a counterprotest. Susan's trying to keep the peace. At the end of the scene, Nancy gets sick and reveals she's pregnant."

"Ooh, I love a dramatic cliffhanger right before intermission." Coral stacked the plates to put away. "So now that you've recited the story to me, what are your thoughts?"

Maggie tapped her foot thoughtfully. "I can see the parallels between Ruth and Nancy. But I feel like I'm missing an important piece of information about each of the characters. I'm not sure what to think, to be honest."

"Well, I can't wait to watch it." Coral grabbed a box of Oreos and went to sit on the sectional. "You'll get me tickets, won't you?"

"I don't know if—"

"I'm kidding! Of course I'm going to pay for my ticket." Coral tore open the box and selected her first cookie. "Any cause Gwen thinks is worth contributing to, I'm gonna pay my dues."

Maggie smiled in gratitude. "You're a true pal, Coral."

Coral held out the Oreos invitingly. "How's Gwen doing? I know the cops mentioned talking to her."

Maggie joined her on the sectional and accepted a cookie. "I forgot to tell you—she talked to me about it yesterday. Asked me to tell her what happened."

"What'd she say?"

"She said she'd understand if I stopped going to improv or didn't study with her," Maggie said, breaking her cookie open. "But she hoped I'd stay in the play. And she decided to tell the cast in case they get targeted next."

"Did she have any idea who it could be?"

Maggie licked the cream off one cookie half. "Someone named Valerie. Said they used to be close. Apparently, it was a surprise to find out she might be back in the city."

Coral's face went suddenly solemn, and she set the cookies down. "I've heard that name before. Maggie, please be careful."

Maggie reached for another cookie. "I'm going to be careful; I promise. But Gwen seems to think it's not about me."

"Gwen's being cautious, as she should be," Coral said, "but…well. Just promise you'll be careful."

Chapter Eight

THE WEEKEND PASSED uneventfully. Coral was particularly vigilant on their journey to and from improv group, but they caught no glimpse of Valerie. This left Maggie free to focus on the acting exercise Professor Max had designed—creating a story with a partner, without speaking, using only facial expressions and body language. She partnered with a jolly gentleman, and together, they created a story of dear friends comforting each other after some kind of loss. Coral and Gwen's story was more humorous and appeared to feature a woman standing up to her bully.

Maggie spent the remainder of her free time before Tuesday's rehearsal working on the second part of her homework. Maggie had tried to go "off the cuff" initially but realized she didn't know a lot about the liberation movement as a whole, let alone how it would impact her unique cultural lens. Determined to have something meaningful to discuss on Tuesday, she rolled up her sleeves and started researching. Coral let her borrow her laptop to make things go more smoothly. Maggie was bent over the keyboard, alternating between furious typing and clicking between tabs, when Coral poked her head in.

"You look like a college student," Coral said with a chuckle.

Maggie grinned wryly. "Well, I was a good student. I'm almost done. I'm going to email this to myself in a few minutes, and you can have your laptop back."

"Keep it as long as you need," Coral called nonchalantly as she retreated to the kitchen. "I haven't needed it in ages."

With her talking points saved in an email on her phone, Maggie walked into the rehearsal room Tuesday evening with a mixture of anticipation and anxiety. She felt certain she had addressed the homework, perhaps even in more detail than Gwen anticipated. But she wondered what form the discussion would take and if she'd be expected to answer any questions. A lingering memory of her AP English teacher rose to the surface and suggested perhaps she should have cited her sources.

The cast, Gwen, and Haleigh sat in a circle on the floor. Gwen gestured to the printed script.

"How did it go with your homework? Did everyone find someone to tell the story to?"

The group responded in assent.

"Great. Then let's focus on the second part. I want to hear the personal and cultural connections you were able to make to the liberation movement. It will help me know how best to help you connect to the story. For example," she said, pointing to herself, "I am very, very gay."

Maggie's head snapped up, heart jumping to her throat as Gwen continued.

"Like, I've known I was a lesbian since I was a young child. Thank goodness my mom accepted me, but historically, you could call us an invisible minority at best. That's a huge part of the liberation movement I connect to. I love the fact that a movement that emphasized sisterhood was the place where the lesbian liberation movement found acceptance. I'm grateful to live in a time when I can be open about who I am, and I give the women's liberation movement a massive amount of credit for that."

Time seemed to grind to a halt for Maggie. Thoughts flooded her brain, all of which got lost somewhere in her throat. *She's…she's gay? Me too! I'm not the only one. Wait, no, don't stare at her, don't stare. Who's talking? Look at who's talking.*

Maggie turned her attention to Skylar, who was gesturing at themself.

"The women's liberation movement didn't really have me in mind. When sexism gets discussed, it's always in this two-box system, and I don't fit in either box."

How do you know what your sexual orientation is when you're agender? Maggie's thoughts kept racing. *Wait, crap, don't think about that, just listen. Focus.*

Haleigh reached across the circle to shake Skylar's hand. "Thank you so, so much for sharing your insight," she said, her voice low and earnest. "I recognize my script divides the issues of the liberation movement along a gender binary, when we know that's not an accurate understanding of sex and gender anymore. You definitely shed light on part of the story that needs to be told."

"No more script rewrites," Gwen interjected, nudging Haleigh in the ribs with her elbow.

The interaction brought a flash of memory to Maggie. *Oh my God, she's gay, and she cuddled me on our pretend Ferris wheel; how did I not notice that? She was totally acting like we were dating, not just friends! I should have—should have what? Focus, Maggie, look for who's talking and pay attention.*

"I had no idea the movement took place in so many countries," Bel was commenting as Maggie brought her attention back to the group. "I actually read all about a march to Monumento a la Madre in Mexico City, protesting the belief that women are all destined to be mothers, on *Mother's Day*. I know if I did that, Abuela Adelina would be so mad." She changed her voice to imitate an aging woman. *"Mi nieta* would rather spend Mother's Day marching the streets than spend it with me, *¡qué lástima!"*

"I know exactly what you mean," Alyssa replied. "I think my traditional Indian mother would be the same way. She'd be all like, 'So motherhood is too good for my daughter now, huh? After I dedicate my life to raising you?'"

Maggie couldn't focus on the presentations. *Does Gwen want to be a mom? I never thought about kids after figuring out I was— Dammit, Maggie, this isn't about Gwen. This is about the group. How long have you been thinking about this? What did I miss?*

"Nearly half a century since this movement," Georgia was commenting, "and women are *still* second-class citizens in the church. Third class, even, if we consider gay men to be second class. At least gay men can become priests to 'hide their shame' and still gain power over the congregation, as problematic as those implications are." Georgia sighed deeply. "Sometimes, I'm ashamed to admit I'm still Catholic. We're not anti-science, but we're anti-progress with everything else."

Gwen just told everyone that she's gay, in front of a freaking Catholic, Maggie thought, bewildered. *She didn't even stop to think what the group might think about her. How does she do it? She doesn't even look scared; she looks completely— Shit, I'm staring at her! Look away, look away; look at whoever's talking.*

"There's this huge stereotype that Asian women are docile and submissive and make good wives," Donna was commenting. "Before I met my husband, I was so nervous when I was dating because there were all these expectations. White guys wanted me to act a certain way, my parents wanted a quality husband to help make future grandkids, and I just wanted to go to college and have some fun, you know? But I think the worst part was when I had friends who would be like, 'You're Asian? I had no idea; you look and act so white!' And my parents were proud of how well I passed as a white woman."

Gwen could have passed, Maggie told herself. *She didn't have to tell anyone. She could have gone this whole time, and no one would have guessed otherwise. Why would she—*

"Hey, Maggie." Gwen's voice cut into her thoughts. "You've been pretty quiet over there. Could you share your thoughts with us?"

"Um, yes!" Maggie blushed from ear to ear. Her head, filled to the brim with thoughts a moment before, was suddenly empty. She fumbled with her pocket for a moment, about to pull out her phone and read off her notes, when she realized no one else was holding any papers or references. She took a deep breath, let go of her phone, and sat up a little taller.

"I honestly had to do a lot of digging to find anything, but... I found out there was a prominent Jewish movement within the liberation movement. Like what Donna was saying, there was this push for Jewish women to embrace their heritage and not try so hard to 'pass.' And like what Georgia was saying, in the religion itself, women and men are treated very differently. We're still seeing impacts today; different sects of Judaism have different stances on gender roles and modesty, and some sects are very progressive. So even though there isn't a lot of historical recognition, it's safe to say Jewish women were heavily involved in the movement, and I think that's exciting."

There was a murmur of agreement from the cast, and Maggie sat back, breathing deeply. *I can't let her find out I'm gay, she'll know I think she's—*

Wait, what do I think she is?

Maggie forced herself to return her attention to the group one last time, just as Gwen was wrapping up the discussion. Everyone stood and stretched as Gwen and Haleigh started giving instructions. Maggie went to stand by Georgia, who gave her a smile.

"Ready, sister?"

Maggie smiled back. "Always. While they're working on the church scene, can we practice our lines for scene five?"

As Georgia flipped through her script, Maggie glanced at Gwen once more over her shoulder. There she was, just having revealed her sexual orientation to the whole room and somehow standing as confident and self-assured as ever. She made a low comment to Bel, and the two of them laughed together. Shining eyes filled with focus, hands on her hips, an assertive but supportive authority in her voice. There was something…*amazing* about her.

A tiny flutter nestled in Maggie's chest, fragile but lovely as a butterfly, and she hastily turned away.

*

MAGGIE'S THOUGHTS WERE still flustered as she made her way back to her apartment that night. She tried to distract herself with planning a grocery shopping list, rereading her script, and memorizing her lines as she scrolled through social media. She would be successful for a little bit, then find her mind wandering back to: *Gwen Knowles likes girls.* By the time she stood by her front door, Maggie was exasperated. She shook her head sharply at herself. *It's not that big a deal. Stop it. Go inside, get yourself a cup of water, and don't think about the fact that tomorrow you and Gwen will be alone together in a library studying acting. It's not. A. Big. Deal.*

Entering the apartment, Maggie was surprised to find small cardboard boxes and plastic bags scattered across the floor. "Coral?" she called out.

"Oh, hey!" Coral came out of her bedroom. In one hand, she held a rainbow flag in the air. In the other, she lifted a pink, purple, and blue flag. "Look what finally came in. I ordered my pride flags, like, three months ago. Totally worth the wait though. Feel the fabric."

Maggie snapped. Slumping onto the floor, she giggled first, then slowly escalated into hilarity. Coral watched in confusion as Maggie devolved, tears leaking through tightly squeezed eyes.

After a few moments, Coral asked cautiously, "Maggie, why are you crying and laughing at the same time?"

After Maggie finally composed herself, she told Coral everything. Everything about Jess, high school, coming out to her parents, moving to LA, the breakup, and finally, Gwen coming out to the cast. She talked as though she couldn't stop herself, words spilling from her mouth as though she'd broken a dam. When she finally finished, she poured herself a glass of water and gulped it down, a strange sense of calm washing over her.

Coral sat at the dining table, flags draped over her chair behind her. "Wow," she murmured as Maggie refilled her water glass. "I had no idea you were holding all this in."

Maggie half-chuckled as she continued drinking, more slowly this time.

"Firstly," Coral said, "I am so, so sorry you didn't feel comfortable being honest with me about your situation before now. I like to think I'm this big LGBT-plus advocate, but—"

Maggie cut her off. "Please, don't apologize. You never did anything to make me feel unsafe. I didn't know that you…y'know."

"That I'm bi?" Coral laughed. "I don't hide it, but I guess it never came up in conversation. But now you know, so…" Coral lifted her bi pride flag off the chair and gave it a wave. "Woo!"

Maggie laughed and leaned against the stove. "You have no idea what a relief it is. Jess was the only one I ever knew who, y'know, wasn't straight. I mean, I knew there were other gay people in our high school, I just wasn't friends with them. And now that we're not…" Her voice trailed off.

Coral tapped her foot on the floor thoughtfully. "Well, a lot of stuff makes sense now. I can't believe you've gone this long with no gay friends. You didn't reach out to people online?"

Maggie shook her head. "I never felt comfortable trying to talk to people I don't know online. Plus, I was scared my parents would see what I was doing on the family computer."

"Yeesh. I can't imagine having parents constantly watching my business."

"You call your mom every week," Maggie replied.

"Yeah, but I *choose* to tell her my business," Coral retorted. "There's a difference. Maggie, it feels like you need more gay in your life."

Maggie blushed. "I don't think I'm ready to date again just yet."

Coral blew a raspberry. "Who said anything about dating? I have zero interest in a relationship right now. Haven't you ever seen, like, a pride parade?"

"I've seen pictures in the paper, yeah. Mom and Dad didn't like that; they said it shouldn't be out in public."

Coral waved a hand dismissively. "With all due respect, your parents can f—mind their own business. Look, the point of pride is to build community. It's important to have friends with shared experiences and who understand you. The fact that you're acting like your sexual orientation is this big, heavy secret… That's not great for your mental health, you know."

"I guess…"

"Listen," Coral said, standing up with a grin on her face. "I have another Facebook group you should join. Can I take your phone?"

Maggie handed it over, and Coral opened the app, searching for the group.

"This is just some friends in the area. It's all LGBT-plus or allies. Sometimes we hang out; sometimes we host fundraisers for different events and charities. But honestly, the biggest thing we use the group for is sharing memes." She handed the phone back to Maggie. "Let yourself see what the community is like outside of dating. And you should totally come to our next party."

"Party?"

"It's a fundraiser for the Los Angeles LGBT Center, but it's also a casual mingle party. It's open to the public, but, like, *all* my friends are going to be there. You can hang out and talk with people. Get a little platonic gay in your life." Coral lifted her flag. "The last party was where I ordered this."

"When is it?"

"Next Saturday. And there's no improv group next week. They're going to be running *A Midsummer Night's Dream* for about a month, so improv group is on hold. C'mon, what do you say?"

Hesitantly, Maggie nodded. "Yeah…I want to go. I'm tired of still being in the closet like this. The way Gwen could just tell everyone she's a lesbian without thinking twice about it… I want that."

"Now, I'm not saying you have to be exactly like Gwen. She's always said she'd rather go without a job than work for someone who couldn't fully accept her."

"That's…incredible," Maggie said wistfully. "She's so confident about it."

Coral glanced at her thoughtfully, then picked up her flags and walked back to her room with a cheeky grin. "Careful, Maggie. Keep talking like that and you might fall for her."

"Coral!" Maggie shrieked, clasping her hands to her cheeks.

"Aren't the two of you meeting to study in the library tomorrow? Just the two of you, all alone, surrounded by high bookshelves…"

Maggie ran to Coral's room. "Shut up!"

Coral, who was in the process of hanging her bi pride flag, stuck her tongue out at her. "Don't be mad at me for speaking the truth. She's pretty, she's smart, she's charming, and you found a way to get her aaaaaallllllll to yourself for almost a whole day a week—"

Maggie grabbed Coral's fuzzy throw pillow and threw it at her before rushing back to her room. "I'm not listening to you!"

Maggie closed her door, Coral still laughing. As she changed into her pajamas, Maggie tried to put her busy thoughts to rest. She mulled over how things had changed for her so rapidly in one day. Yesterday, she'd felt like the only lesbian in LA—at least, the only one who wasn't following Jess and her band around. Today, she felt surrounded. When she opened her door to go brush her teeth for bed, she saw Coral's two pride flags hanging on the opposite wall, and she smiled. For the first time in a long time, she felt at home.

Chapter Nine

MAGGIE WOKE UP Wednesday morning and, for a second, thought she'd set her alarm to make sure she made it to another audition on time. It was only when she was brushing her teeth and realized she couldn't remember what audition she was supposed to be going to that she finally remembered: today was her first study session with Gwen.

Gwen had suggested they get together at the Doheny Memorial Library, explaining she had an eight a.m. class at USC Wednesday mornings and could meet Maggie there immediately after for a full-day study session. Anticipating sitting for an extended period of time, Maggie dressed in leggings and a light dress. She searched for the best bus route while eating breakfast. This was something she'd gotten fairly skilled at; between auditions and filming sites, she'd been all over LA in the last year. She had a pang of nostalgia as she realized she hadn't entered a library of any kind since high school. She grabbed a packed lunch, took a deep breath, and headed out into the autumn morning.

The bus ride was long enough that Maggie arrived at the library's signature fountain just as Gwen did. Gwen wore jean capris and a sleeveless green shirt with a turtleneck, a messenger bag slung over one shoulder. Maggie was starting to wonder if Gwen had something against sleeves. She didn't linger on the thought for long as she and Gwen closed the space between them.

"We're just in time to get my favorite study space," Gwen said brightly. "C'mon."

"This place is huge," Maggie commented, gazing around her in fascination as they walked up the stairs together.

"And it's not the only library on campus. But I like it for its spaces. Anytime I try to study at the other libraries, either there's nothing free, or I get kicked out because 'this is for *our* program, not *theater*.'"

Maggie fell in love with the library the moment she stepped inside. It was monstrous compared to the library in her hometown. Gwen seemed amused to watch her stare at each passing attraction—stained glass windows, winding bookshelves, library card catalogs that covered whole walls. Finally, they found themselves in a large but quiet room with mostly empty long tables. Maggie noticed a few students with laptops out or piles of books, none of whom paid her or Gwen any mind as they chose a table near the back.

Gwen set her bag down on the table with a muffled thud. "I brought some reading material, more as a guide than anything else," she explained, unlatching the bag and digging books out to set out. "But the biggest thing I want to talk with you about today is personal theory. Did you bring anything to write with?"

Maggie shook her head. "I didn't think to, sorry."

Gwen handed her a spiral notebook and a pen. "I got extra. Take a seat. I want you to start by talking with me about why you decided you want to be an actress."

With a bittersweet taste at the back of her throat, Maggie felt the same pang of nostalgia. "I just always have. I've never wanted anything else. When I was a kid, I used to play pretend theater with the other kids in the neighborhood. You know, act out movies we liked or write our own plays based on fairy tales. I started trying out for school plays as soon as I was allowed, in fourth grade. But even that wasn't enough, and I would beg to audition for community plays. I was in two or three performances a year. The older I got, the more roles I was cast in, and the more fun it became. I love bringing stories to life, making them more alive than they could be in your imagination. I like reading just fine," she clarified, "but there's something different about being able to watch a story, as if it's real. And that's all I've ever wanted to do—make characters and stories *real*."

Gwen listened patiently, hands folded under her chin. When Maggie was done speaking, she replied, "That certainly shows me your dedication and hard work, as well as what you find enjoyable about storytelling on stage. But I want to know why you chose to pursue acting professionally. Right out of high school, to boot. Were you, as we say, dream chasing?"

Maggie shrugged. "Maybe a little, but…I wasn't silly enough to think I was going to show up in LA, get cast in a big-budget movie, and live pretty for the rest of my life. I'm not interested in celebrity status. I came here knowing I would have to work hard to get any roles. But I didn't care what I got, I've been an extra in so many things, no credit or anything, but I love helping bring the scene to life. All those people in the background of scenes are crucial to making it feel realistic." She sat back, paused, and added, "I sound desperate, don't I?"

"I don't think so. I think you sound passionate. So your priority is storytelling. Bringing stories to life. You're not interested in fame and fortune?"

Maggie shook her head. "I don't need the whole world to love me. I just want to do my best and…ah…" She blushed, biting back words that felt presumptuous. But Gwen sat across from her, the embodiment of confidence, attentively listening to her. Maggie took a breath and plunged forward.

"I want to be so good at it that whoever sees me can't possibly imagine anyone else as that character. The way Emma Watson is the face of Hermione Granger, or Vivien Leigh is Scarlett O'Hara. I want to make a character so real to the audience that my body is the character's body, my voice is her voice. But I don't have to be a celebrity," she repeated hastily, voice trailing.

Gwen's face broke into a wide smile, and she put Maggie's nerves at ease. "That's what I wanted to hear. It's one thing to say you like acting because you like storytelling, and that's important, definitely. More important than trying to make yourself a celebrity. But if you're going to make a career out of it, you have to have a personal stake in it. And that personal stake will strengthen your acting process, the way your inspiration—which, for you, is storytelling—informs your technique." Gwen reached into the pile of books and pulled out one with the face of an elderly gentleman wearing a bow tie on the cover. "Let's start with Stanislavski."

Maggie became swept away. Gwen's books were heavily highlighted, tabs lining the pages, making it easy for her to locate the parts she wanted

Maggie to read from as she explained the day's lesson. Maggie, who had never heard of Konstantin Stanislavski before that morning, found herself enamored with his story of amateur acting and directing before finally founding the Moscow Art Theatre. When Gwen flipped the book open to the Stanislavski system, a giant diagram demonstrating everything he believed contributed to the perfect performance, her brain ground to a halt in a joyful blend of fascination and perplexity. She wrote notes in the notebook Gwen had given her as though her life depended on it.

It wasn't until Gwen closed the book and suggested they go find a place on campus to take a break and eat that Maggie paused long enough to feel the clawing pain of hunger in her stomach.

She groaned as Gwen started rummaging in her bag. "I didn't know how much there was to learn. We've spent the whole morning on just one person?"

Gwen pulled out a piece of cardboard that read, Out for Lunch—Coming Back—Please don't move my books. She placed it against her pile of books so it could be read by passersby. "Yep. To be fair, I chose to start with Stanislavski because he's a great middle ground between what you seem to enjoy about acting and my own beliefs about it."

Maggie and Gwen stood, grabbed their packed lunches, and walked out of the library.

"But there's a whole book about one man," Maggie reiterated. "I'm realizing this is how people can actually study acting for four years. I guess I thought when people went to college for acting it would be more…y'know, hands-on. Now that I know how much there is…" She sighed. "I'm never going to catch up."

Gwen glanced at her sideways as they made their way to the door.

"Are you always so quick to give up on yourself?"

Maggie blushed. "Well…no. I get frustrated; then I buckle down and work."

"Good. I don't want you to give up on me just because of Stanislav-ski."

"Oh no. I want to learn more," Maggie cried. "I…I feel a little in awe. Like I'm staring at a whole world I didn't realize existed. And I'm a little jealous of the others because they already know."

Gwen shrugged nonchalantly. "Bel doesn't know much more than you do, and the rest can tell you that after you choose the parts of acting theory you care most about, you tend to forget the rest. But that's why it's important to work in groups, keep your mind open." She grinned. "And you have an advantage—your mind is completely open to new ideas. You're not set in your ways from decades of practice."

Gwen led Maggie to a common space on the campus and found a bench for them to sit on. "I don't have a dining plan," she explained, opening a bologna sandwich. "So I end up squatting somewhere to eat and hope I don't choose a spot that pisses off campus security."

Maggie bit into her peanut butter sandwich, too famished to respond. For a moment, the two of them were content to eat. After finishing her sandwich, Maggie reached for an apple, saying, "I told you what I like about acting. I think it's fair if I ask you something."

Gwen swallowed, nodding. "Sure, what do you want to know?"

"How'd you get into professional theater? You seem young to be a director. You're a college student, but you get paid jobs. How'd you do it?"

"That's a lot of questions." Gwen laughed. "Let me start with what you care about—passion." She peeled an orange as she spoke. "I like what you said about making stories real for the audience, but that's not quite how I approach theater. I'm more interested in making a living, breathing piece of art, and I'm not too concerned about making it 'real.' But it's art with a unique challenge to it. Like, a painter has complete control over their canvas. They can still mess up if they don't know the proper technique, obviously, but the canvas isn't going to quit on them or insist on being given star treatment."

Maggie giggled as Gwen continued.

"Versus, in theater, in order to make the finished product, you *need* multiple people, and each of them has their own idea of what the product should look like. The actors, writer, prop director, costume designer, stage manager, lighting, sometimes music… What I love is that all those people come together to create one cohesive piece of art. And every time it's performed, it's fresh and new all over again; it's never quite the same as the night before. That's why my favorite jobs are stage manager and director. I like getting all those parts to work together in harmony, collaborating until it all works like it should."

"Sounds like a job for a…a control freak."

Gwen half smiled. "Actually, I think being a control freak is bad for being a director. You can't possibly hope to perfectly control every aspect of theater. You need to be a good organizer, negotiator, problem solver— but you can't control everything that happens after the curtain lifts. My favorite parts of a performance are fixing those mistakes and arguments in the dark of backstage. If we do our job right? The audience never finds out. But *we* know that we kept the show going."

Maggie nodded with understanding. "I've heard you've done acting roles too?"

Gwen laughed. "Mostly when someone was sick or quit and we couldn't get a good replacement. I suppose you heard about the *Our Town* performance? That was a nightmare. I was the stage manager's assistant. Our Emily Webb quit during dress rehearsal week. I was the only one who knew all the lines."

"Oh my gosh, what did you do?"

"What do you think I did?" Gwen raised her orange dramatically. "The show must go on! I put on the freaking dress that was not made for me, I went out on stage, and I did what I imagine you would have done. I became Emily Webb."

"That sounds terrifying," Maggie murmured. "I can't imagine doing a role with only a week's notice."

"Four days," Gwen corrected. "Oh, it was awful, don't get me wrong. But that's what I love about theater. It's a wild, unpredictable world that creates amazing art that people will remember and talk about for years—an experience you live and breathe and admire. And somewhere in the background, there's a stressed stage manager with pins in her mouth helping the costume department fix a skirt that ripped on the scenery."

"I remember a time when my high school was doing *White Christmas*, and the machine for the snow fell on stage during the 'Love and the Weather' song. I was backstage watching. It almost hit Kyle on the head!"

Gwen laughed. "Oh no. How did they manage that?"

"They finished the song, and we closed the curtain to sweep up the stage for a few minutes. Kyle was telling people about it for weeks."

"I would have too. He almost paid the ultimate sacrifice for art." Gwen threw her orange peel in a garbage can beside the bench. "I wasn't as involved as you were; I didn't get to perform in school musicals or community plays. But my mom used to work in a theater, and I'd get to watch. I guess you could say I grew up backstage."

"What did your mom do?"

"She was a janitor." Gwen leaned back and smiled wistfully. "Sometimes, the crew would let me try out different things while she was cleaning the seats and halls. I learned how to aim a spotlight, sew a hem, and do a mic check thanks to those guys. They wrote letters to help me get into college. I send them Christmas cards every year."

"That sounds almost magical." Maggie could imagine a teenage Gwen, intent on her task, being guided by wiser and more experienced hands. "I wish I had something like that."

"A theater family?" Gwen nudged Maggie gently with her elbow. "You're making one right now. And on that note, are you ready to get back to work?"

Maggie swallowed the last of her apple. "Absolutely!"

*

GWEN AND MAGGIE studied Stanislavski, his history, and his system for the rest of the day. As the sun started dipping under the horizon, Gwen handed Maggie a couple books.

"Here, borrow these for next week. I'm not sure what type of reader you are, but if it's helpful to reread some concepts, these are the books I find are the clearest."

"Are these library books?"

"Nah, they're my textbooks; that's why they're all marked up. Do me a favor and come up with some ways you plan on connecting what Stanislavski's taught you to your role as Ruth. We'll review them next week before we move on to the next topic."

Maggie saluted as she tucked the books under her arm. "You got it."

Gwen insisted on walking Maggie to her bus stop. "What's your plan for the rest of the night?"

"Sleep. I have work before rehearsal tomorrow."

"At the bakery, right? Where the cashiers always get hit on?"

Maggie giggled. "It's a coffee shop, but yeah."

"Do you like it?"

"Yeah, it's nice. The boss hires a lot of creative types, college students, that type of thing, so she's great at managing changing schedules. I get Wednesdays and Saturdays off. I've been there for about a year now."

"That's good. I've never worked customer service. I knew I would punch someone eventually if I did. I did telemarketing for five years, and that was bad enough."

"What do you do when it's not time for rehearsal or improv group?"

"Right now, my biggest job is actually on campus. I'm assistant stage manager for USC. Eventually, I'll get ahold of some other jobs. I bounce around."

"Is that how you like it?"

Gwen paused before answering. "No. I want a permanent position. I'd love to be at a theater like the Twilight full-time, maybe with freelance directing on the side. But I need to finish all my classes before I qualify for competitive pay. So I'm making up for it by building my resumé."

Maggie smiled reassuringly. "I'm sure you'll get that opportunity soon. It seems like you're really well-known around here."

Gwen chuckled wryly as Maggie's bus came around the corner. "Well…I feel better knowing you're cheering me on. Have a nice night,

Maggie. I'll see you tomorrow."

After she waved goodbye and took her seat on the bus, Maggie glanced back through the window, straining to see Gwen walk away from the stop. Gwen seemed a little more slumped than she had a moment before. As the bus closed its doors and started to pull away, Maggie thought she saw Gwen's shoulders lift, as though taking a deep breath, stretching and bringing energy back into her. Then she was around the corner and out of sight.

Chapter Ten

MAGGIE WALKED INTO rehearsal the following night and, for a moment, thought she had walked into the wrong room. It took a second for her brain to register that she was staring at Skylar in a wig, which Donna was wrestling with a brush.

Bel, Alyssa, and Georgia were right behind Maggie.

Georgia, her voice straining politeness, asked, "Sky, dear, what are you wearing?"

Skylar pointed at the white, bushy mop balanced on their head. "Oh, this? This is Bonnie the Bonnet."

"You look horrible," Bel said.

Georgia looked alarmed, but Skylar just laughed.

"It's the best we could find on short notice. It was Donna's idea."

"I thought it would help Sky embrace the feminine side of their character," Donna said from between gritted teeth, giving a can of detangling spray a preparatory shake. "It's an old wig from Halloween ages ago. I'm trying to make it resemble a seventies hairstyle. But I didn't store it very well in my closet, did I?"

Maggie stepped forward and lifted her hands in invitation. Skylar bent their head so she could remove the wig.

"Let's find something else to mount this on," Maggie suggested. "I think I saw a few headdress busts in the hallway."

As Maggie and Bel retrieved an empty bust, Georgia fished out some hairpins from her purse.

Alyssa spoke up as Maggie pinned the wig in place. "Sky, when you auditioned for the play, I assume you knew all the characters are women. Are you afraid people might…I dunno…are you afraid of how people will react or label you for being in this?"

"You mean, will people make assumptions about my assigned sex and then treat me as that gender? That happens every time. There aren't exactly a lot of agender characters." They smirked. "I play a male character, and people start using he-him pronouns and treating me like a dude. I play a female character, and people start using she-her and ask way too many questions about my personal anatomy. But I talked with Haleigh about it, and I actually have some personal family history with the liberation movement. I have photos of my mom and grandma marching and everything. And now playing as Bonnie? Well"—their eyes twinkled—"everyone wants to play the villain at some point."

"Is it accurate to call Bonnie the villain?" Georgia wondered. "I mean, she's on the wrong side of history, that's for sure. But I don't know if we've seen anything that makes her a true villain. I see her as a victim of the times."

"A victim?" Sky repeated, raising their brows.

"Not a completely helpless one," Georgia said quickly, "but no one becomes that radical if they have a normal and loving upbringing, do they?"

"I don't know," Maggie muttered. "I've known some people who were loving and neighborly on the outside, but hateful and strict on the inside." She started pulling the fibers apart into different sections. "I agree with Sky, I think it's a choice."

"At the very least," Donna cut in, handing Maggie the brush, "I think it's safe to say it's her choice to continue in her line of hateful thinking. But I agree with Georgia that she must have learned it somewhere. I guess she's a cautionary tale. When I see Sky acting out Bonnie's lines, I think, 'There but for the grace of God go I.'"

Sky shrugged. "Choice or no choice, I say Bonnie is the closest this play has to a clear antagonist. I can't wait to see what she does in the second act."

"Did someone say, second act?" Haleigh said as she and Gwen walked down the hallway, and Haleigh gleefully held up a stack of paper.

Everyone jumped up and ran to retrieve their copies of the scripts, except Maggie. Georgia grabbed her a copy so she could continue detangling the wig.

"I am so, so sorry for the wait," Haleigh said as the group began flipping pages curiously. "Maggie, can you carry that with you so we can do a read through? And…what are you doing?"

"Sky, is this you?" Gwen asked, gesturing toward the snarled mess in Maggie's hands.

"Blame Donna!"

The cast members settled into a circle, Maggie still brushing the horrendous wig. Georgia sat next to her to help turn her pages.

"Second act starts right after the gathering in the town square," Haleigh said. "Scene one, Ruth and Joanne start. Ladies?"

Maggie dove into the script. There were moments when she almost forgot to keep brushing Sky's wig. Nancy had been sent to the hospital for early pregnancy complications. The small town was in an uproar. They blamed Ruth for corrupting Nancy, but Ruth revealed she didn't know Nancy was sexually active. Nancy wrote to Ruth asking for advice. Should she fight for her baby's life? Should she abort? She didn't know who the father was.

Mary was distraught, but she continued the fight for the movement while encouraging Ruth to lay low. She confronted Bonnie for spreading rumors about Ruth and Nancy, but Bonnie told her she was dishonoring her veteran husband's memory, and she should remarry because the baby needed a man of the household. Bonnie decided to focus her energy on attacking the reputations of the movement participants, and the consequences were dire. The police were called to investigate Mary's parenting, and Nancy and Ruth were both harassed at home. Eventually, Joanne swore off Bonnie's tactics, and Bonnie turned on her, having her shunned at church.

In an explosive scene, Ruth and Mary had one final fight. Maggie clutched her brush tightly. "You know the truth," she spat accusingly. "But you never stood up for me. Not once. Not a single word in my defense."

"That's not true," Georgia said soothingly.

"Don't lie to me. You could have stopped all of this if you'd been honest. Why do you lie to everyone?"

"It's...it's not my business."

"I'm not your business? I'm your sister!"

"But it's your personal—"

"I don't have personal business anymore," Maggie said, her voice catching in her throat as she read ahead. "Not…not since the doctor told the church board about my baby. But didn't tell the whole story. No. No one cares about the whole story. I'm just Ruth, the slut who got herself knocked up, then killed her baby—"

"Don't say those things—"

"But you could have told them." Maggie's knuckles were white on the brush. "You could have told the church board. Told them that it was Jared—what his treatment did to our baby."

"You shouldn't care what they think. Let people think what they want—"

"Do you realize ," Maggie said, cutting her off, "you're the only reason I'm still in this godforsaken town? You're the only family I have, Mary."

"I know that…and I love you, Ruth."

"Then why… Why won't you say anything?"

"When Mom died—"

"No, don't say it like that." Maggie turned the page so quickly she ripped the edge. "Say the truth. Say what happened. When—"

"When Dad killed Mom," Georgia read, and the group gasped collectively as she continued, "you and I told the police what he was like. How he used to treat her. And what did they do?"

"They arrested him."

"But, Ruth…" Georgia took a breath. "Ruth, I told them about him the first time he threw a plate at her. I went to the police all by myself to tell them. At first, I thought they did nothing. But years later, I found out that's why Mom lost her job at the library."

Maggie gripped the edge of her page so hard it creased. "I…I never knew. I thought you—"

"I tried," Georgia read, putting a sob in her voice. "I tried to save Mom, and I couldn't. So I thought…I thought I would try to play by their rules. I told people you had been misled, but I was taking care of you, and you wouldn't make any more mistakes. And they…they talked about you, but they left you alone."

The group kept reading to the climax, when all the characters came to a final confrontation in the town hall, speaking in favor of or against the town legislature passing a law that would make any actions done after the withdrawal of consent considered rape. They learned Nancy died from pregnancy complications. In the wake of her death, Bonnie was charged with slander. The play ended with Susan approaching Ruth and Mary, asking them to continue the fight but to please do so in a way that caused less division in the town. Ruth and Mary each refused.

After finishing the readthrough, all the actors were spent.

"You're one of those people who doesn't believe in happy endings," Skylar said to Haleigh accusingly.

Haleigh shrugged. "I wouldn't say that. But I thought it would be disingenuous to write this as though the liberation movement ended successfully in the seventies."

"I don't want to die," Bel whined. "I like Nancy."

"And all those fights about Mom," Maggie breathed. "I thought it was about who was treated better, but to know it was about who was doing more to protect the family…"

"Actually, with all the comments Bonnie has about marriages, the history of Ruth and Mary's mom, Nancy's harassment, Ruth's ex-boyfriend," Georgia said, flipping through the script, "there's a huge theme about domestic violence in this play."

"Now we know why Peace Over Violence is involved," Alyssa muttered.

"I hope reading this act has given you a new lens with which to look through the whole play," Gwen said. "Believe it or not, it's still a little rough, but we're confident the flesh of the story is complete."

"No more full rewrites," Haleigh promised.

Maggie handed Skylar their wig. "Well, I know one thing. I'm more determined than ever to give this role my all."

Skylar placed the wig on their head and gave a confident hair flip over their shoulder. "Let's bring down the house!"

*

THE DAYS SEEMED to fly by Maggie. When she wasn't at work, she was burying herself in the books Gwen had lent her. When Coral dragged her out of her room to eat, she'd subject her poor roommate to a verbal presentation of everything she had just read. After she ranted to Coral for a straight hour about Stanislavski's concept of the "Magic If," Coral reached across the table and grasped Maggie's hands.

"Maggie, I consider you a friend. If you don't stop reciting your homework at me, I'm going to scream. Please go nerd out in your room."

Overwhelmed with thoughts and ideas, Maggie found herself typing furiously on Coral's laptop. On Tuesday, when she got off work at midday, she made her way to the public library to find a book by Benedetti, finish typing her ideas, and print out everything she had written. It wasn't until she held the finished paper in her hands, citations and cover page included, that she realized she'd typed a full twelve pages. And that was after editing. She couldn't stop herself from flipping through the pages and rereading parts of it on the bus home. She'd drawn direct parallels between the Stanislavski system and her own attempts at method acting in past roles, written extensively on how she intended to strengthen her method of physical action, and even written out how she would use the system in her role as Ruth.

Maggie was flush with excitement Wednesday morning when she stuffed Gwen's books and her printed report into her old high school backpack. She wore a light hoodie to get her through the morning and another dress and leggings set. Golden sunlight illuminated the Metro bus windows and seemed to follow just ahead of her as she walked to the library.

Gwen was a couple minutes later meeting her that day but greeted her as brightly as the sun had. "I see you're prepared!"

Maggie hoisted the backpack on her shoulders. "Well, I'm a student now. Thought I'd lean back into some old habits."

"Like backpacks?" Gwen asked as they entered the library.

"Backpacks, studying, writing down my thoughts… I actually went to the library to get more books."

"Wow, I'm impressed. About what?"

"Stanislavski, but in more contexts. I wanted to read what other people thought of him and how his system has been used in modern works. I even tried watching a bit of opera on the library computer, but…well, I only speak English."

"I imagine that would make it difficult."

"I can't get over how thorough he was. He saw performance as so much more than memorizing lines and adding emotion and blocking. He saw it as a whole becoming, inside and out. I was thinking about Skylar and Alyssa a lot as I read, wondering what Stanislavski would tell them to do when acting a role that they fundamentally disagree with."

"I imagine he would have an interesting discourse with Haleigh about the whole thing," Gwen commented as they entered the study room. "Her writing largely uses the characters as symbolic representations of key social issues. He might encourage her to make them more fleshed-out individuals."

Maggie hastily put her backpack down on their chosen table and pulled out the books and paper. She handed the paper to Gwen, cheeks pink with excitement. "I know you said you wanted to start with connecting Stanislavski's teachings with being Ruth, but I had so many ideas that I…I went a little overboard. But I couldn't keep it all in!"

Gwen hesitated. After a pause, she slowly turned the pages, scanning them. When she looked back up, she wasn't smiling. "You wrote a twelve-page paper in a week?"

Maggie nodded. "I imagine you've written lots of these, so it's okay if you don't want to read it…"

Gwen set the paper down on the table and stared at it, hands clasped in front of her face. She spoke without looking at Maggie. "I'm…confused. Why didn't you go to college?"

Maggie blinked in surprise. "I, um."

After another pause, Gwen gestured at the paper. "Citations. Cover page. Freaking MLA format. Twelve pages. In a week. With a full-time job."

Maggie felt her spirits sinking. "Gwen, now I'm confused. I know it's not what you asked for, but you seem—"

"I'm annoyed." Gwen ran her hands over her eyes, then finally looked at her across the table. "I'm very annoyed with you, Maggie Fromm. This kind of writing shows you were a fantastic student in high school, probably above grade level. You could have gotten an academic scholarship. The work would have been a breeze. And you…chose not to?"

"It…it didn't seem like the right choice at the time."

"But for what reason?" Gwen's voice was hard. "People who can't go to college because of money don't move to LA to be brewmaids and actresses. People who don't go to college because they struggle at school don't write like this. So why?"

"Respectfully," Maggie said, face flushed red, "I don't see what business it is of yours. You don't have to read the paper if it offends you so much."

"Maggie, I can't read this."

"Well then, like I said—"

"I have a learning disorder." Gwen's eyes bored into Maggie's soul. "Something like dyslexia, my pediatrician called it a processing disorder. Reading takes all of my willpower and concentration, and I have to… I mean, you saw my books. All those highlights and tabs and underlines weren't only to help me remember important information. They were to force my brain to interact with the pages, to help me actually read, and I have to read everything out loud. Otherwise, I stare at the words, and nothing happens."

Gwen gripped the paper and waved it in the air between them. "This kind of paper would have taken me months to do. That's why I'm still trying to finish a four-year degree six years later. That's why I can't get the job I want yet. But you?" Gwen tossed the paper onto the table. "College would be so easy for you. You have the talent for acting and academic work. And you…threw that away?"

Maggie's blood pumped with indignation. She was about to snap back, throw the papers in Gwen's face, maybe even leave the library, and then she looked at the paper, where two little wet spots were bleeding the ink. Her heart squeezed in her chest, and she searched Gwen's eyes. Whatever tears had leaked through were now well contained, but those green eyes still glistened.

Gwen wiped her eyes impatiently. "Don't mind me… I cry when I get frustrated."

Maggie started to move, hesitated, then reached across the table to rest her hand on Gwen's. "I really admire you, Gwen. You've built a whole professional resumé, all on your own efforts. I don't think academics should matter, and you prove that. You've gotten so far without a degree."

Gwen snorted. "Sweet of you, but that's not how this works. I pushed myself through two years as a full-time student. Failed a couple classes and had to retake them. Focused so much on my classwork I barely had time for sleep. The Academic Resources Department was a huge help, and I was doing okay. But after two years, I…I couldn't keep doing it like that anymore. So I'm a part-time student now. And all the jobs I get? I get them through the connections I made here. I met Professor Max because he was a guest speaker in one of my classes, and a lot of my other connections have done projects with the USC drama students."

She looked at Maggie with softer eyes this time. "That's why deciding to act straight out of high school, no further training, is so risky. In addition to what you said last week—that there's so much theory to learn—you start out without having a professional network."

Maggie slumped over the table. "I guess I knew that was going to be a barrier."

Gwen took a deep breath and turned her hand over to hold Maggie's. "I'm sorry for snapping at you. But I really would like to know. Why didn't you go to college?"

Maggie told her about Jess's plan to move to LA with the band. She couldn't bring herself to call Jess her girlfriend. Something about coming out to Gwen was intimidating, but she explained everything else. The persuasion to avoid student loans, the promises of success based on luck and talent, and the eventual split as Jess's band moved on successfully.

Gwen's brows furrowed as she listened. When Maggie was done, she asked, "Did Jess ever tell you why she wanted to come to LA specifically?"

Maggie shook her head.

"If I had to guess," Gwen continued, "Jess and her band probably already had a contact in LA. Maybe one of them had a relative in the industry."

"I think a lot of their first performances were at a bar Steve's uncle owned," Maggie said quietly.

"Well, that'll do it. I'm not trying to criticize your friend, but I think Jess was ignoring the fact that she had an advantage that you didn't. I'm not doubting their talent, but if they started with a foot in the door…"

Maggie sat back in her chair, returning to that day in the high school computer lab. Jess's sheer confidence and reckless persuasion suddenly made more sense. "You must think I'm an idiot."

"Of course not." Gwen picked up the paper, more gently this time. "An idiot doesn't write twelve pages on personal use of the Stanislavski system in a week, with citations. And Maggie, you have talent. And now? Now you have a foot in the door." She gave Maggie's hand a slight squeeze before letting go. "I guess all I'm saying is, if you consider college, I think you'd do very well, and I'm jealous."

Maggie smiled dryly. "And I'm jealous of your resumé."

Gwen reached for her bag and pulled out a new set of heavily highlighted books. "Don't be. You're going to build your own resumé, easily. If you can forgive me for being a bit of a jackass for the start of this study session—"

"Already forgiven."

Gwen gave a small smile. "Well. Could you summarize your paper for me? I'm eager to hear your thoughts."

Chapter Eleven

THAT SATURDAY WAS the promised fundraiser party for the Los Angeles LGBT Center. Maggie, who hadn't attended a party since her and Jess's joint graduation party over a year ago, stared aghast at her closet.

Coral, mascara wand in hand, poked her head in the door. "Not to rush you, but you really don't have to think too hard about this. It's literally a hangout, nothing special."

"I know," Maggie groaned. "But I've never been to an event where I'm not straight, you know? How do you dress for that?" She started pushing clothes around on their hangers. "I've seen jokes about lesbians wearing plaid. Do I have to wear plaid?"

"Oh, you poor baby gay. You don't have to dress like anyone but yourself, silly goose. It's not your clothes that make you a lesbian."

"I just don't want to stand out." Maggie pulled out a sweater, glanced at it, and put it back.

"Look, would it make you feel better if I show you what I'm wearing?" Coral led Maggie to her bedroom and laid some clothes on her bed. "It's supposed to be a fun time, so I'm wearing my favorite tank top and skort."

"You have skorts?"

"I personally feel they are an underrated piece of clothing. And then, I'm accessorizing with my favorite hat." She tossed a fedora with a rainbow band on top of the outfit. "It's not a bad idea to have a little indication of pride."

Maggie shook her head. "I don't have anything like that."

"Then, bring cash or a check because that's what the fundraiser includes." Coral returned to the bathroom to finish her makeup. "Just stop stressing, please. I've never seen someone worry over small things as much as you do."

Encouraged by the simplicity of Coral's outfit, Maggie decided she would also aim for comfort. She had a three-quarter-sleeve top and jean capri combo she adored but didn't often have the chance to wear. The turquoise top had a sweetheart neckline, and the capris had butterflies embroidered along one leg. She remembered the birthday when her parents had given both to her; the memory left a bitter taste in the back of her throat. She shook it off and turned her attention to attempting to tame her curls. If the humidity was cooperative enough, she could get them pulled into a high ponytail.

After breaking a few bristles off her new cheap brush and touching up her makeup, she'd finally moved past her anxiety about her appearance for the party. Instead, she was headlong falling into anxiety about how to act once she got there. Patiently, Coral kept reassuring her each step of the way that she was only expected to be herself, and Coral would stay by her side the entire time.

"Unless you meet someone you want to be alone with," she said with a nudge and a wink.

The party took place in the courtyard of an apartment complex—a much nicer one than Coral and Maggie's. The yard had trees and wooden terraces draped with fairy lights and paper lanterns, giving it a gorgeous but casual party atmosphere. There were already about twenty people present, spread out across the yard in chatting groups. Maggie spied a table of food toward the back of the yard, numerous places to sit, and a small speaker system set up to play music.

Coral took Maggie by the elbow and guided her to one side as soon as they arrived. "C'mon, let's look at what they have to sell before all the good stuff gets taken. Then I can introduce you to people."

Coral steered them toward a table laden with various pins, flags, shirts, bags, and other pride merchandise. "Bobby!" she chirped to the brunette who appeared to be working the table. "What's new?"

"Honestly, not much, but I'm pretty excited with these fabric pride flower pins we got," Bobby responded, showing one with bi pride colors for Coral to examine. "Who's your friend?"

"This is Maggie," Coral said, placing a hand on her shoulder. "Maggie, this is Bobby. She's one of the masterminds of the group, constantly arranging events like this. She might be the most important voice for LGBT rights in the city ever."

"You exaggerate," Bobby said lightly, reaching across the table to shake Maggie's hand. "It's nice to meet you. Did Coral drag you here, or are you here by choice?"

"Why does everyone keep asking that?" Coral complained.

"I'm here by choice," Maggie reassured them. "It's nice to meet you too. I've never been to anything like this."

"Well, relax and have fun," Bobby urged her. "And if you want to help support the cause, you can buy anything on this table, or you can order from my book over here."

Coral and Maggie searched through the merchandise. Coral seemed quite interested in trying to buy the whole table. After a moment, a set of enamel pins caught Maggie's eye. She was about to pick up the rainbow pin but paused, fingers hovering.

"Coral? What are all of these?"

"The pride flags?" Coral joined her. "Oh, wow, Bobby, you have almost everything here. Has the bear pride flag been popular?"

"Nah, but Gene isn't here yet."

Coral laughed, then returned to Maggie's question. "So, you recognize the gay and bi pride flags, obviously, but some of these are more obscure. Like, here's the straight ally flag, that's the ace-aro flag… This one's interesting." She picked up a pin with five stripes on it: dark orange, orange, white, pink, to dark pink. "The lesbian pride flag, or at least the newest version."

"How many versions are there?"

"Oh lord, I have no idea. I don't know what it is with the lesbian flag, but the community just can't seem to settle on one. There's an extensive history of fighting over trans inclusion and femme versus butch representation. But if you wear this, most people who are familiar with the concept of pride flags will probably recognize it as a lesbian pride flag."

Maggie picked it up. Something about it resonated with her in a way that felt more personal than the rainbow flag. She checked the price tag on the table, then reached for her wallet. She handed fifteen dollars over to Bobby, who smiled.

"Great choice. The couple who makes these pins take a lot of pride in their work. Thank you for your support for the Los Angeles LGBT Center!"

Maggie stuck the pin on her shirt, over her heart. As she turned to face the growing party crowd, she felt different. Less like an outsider.

"It helps, doesn't it?" Coral said as she debated between a bi pride frog patch and a trans ally drawstring bag. "Obviously, everyone is welcome here, but it's nice to be able to show a little of what's inside on the outside."

Maggie nodded enthusiastically. She opened her mouth, about to ask Coral to hurry up so they could join the group, suddenly excited to participate. Her voice choked in her throat as her eyes fell on the entrance to the courtyard—where Gwen Knowles was walking in, wearing a stunning navy-blue sundress with a halter top and her hair tied back in a partial ponytail. Before Maggie could decide how to react, Gwen's eyes were on her, and she was headed straight toward the table.

"Oh, hey, Gwen," Coral said cheerily as she set both the frog and bag down, her attention now on a rainbow plushie bear. "Fancy seeing you here."

Gwen stopped, standing directly in front of Maggie. Her eyes settled briefly on the pin on Maggie's chest, and a strange smile graced her lips. "What a nice surprise to see you here, Maggie."

"Coral brought me," Maggie said, clearing her throat.

Gwen turned to her roommate, who had set the bear down and was closely examining a rainbow fleece blanket. "Coral, what do I owe you for continuously bringing the lovely Miss Fromm into my life?"

Maggie's cheeks and ears flushed hot as Coral responded.

"Hey, it's just luck that you and I have the same interests," she said. "I suppose Maggie is one of those interests." Coral held up rainbow earrings to her ears. "What do you think?"

"Smashing," Gwen said, "and they match your hat."

Coral laughed and put the earrings down. Bobby, who had just completed another transaction down the table, approached with a grin.

"Gwen, good to see you," she said. "How's your evening?"

"It's going very well. Did you sell Maggie this pin?"

"I did, would you like to see?"

Maggie bounced on her heels in confusion as Coral continued her indecisive shopping, eyes darting back and forth between Coral and Gwen. Gwen selected a lesbian pride flag pin, paid Bobby, and pinned the flag to the neckline of her dress. She glanced over at Coral.

"How long have you been here?"

"Shhhh," Coral said, waving her away. "I'm just going to take a look at the book real quick."

"Do you mind if I steal Maggie from you, then?"

"No, I don't mind. I'll catch up with you!"

Gwen turned to her, that strange smile dancing again. She gestured over to an open bench several feet away. "Shall we chat?"

Mouth dry and head dizzy, Maggie nodded and stiffly moved to sit. Gwen sat close to her so they could hear each other over the music.

"I hope you won't think me too forward," Gwen said, "but I'm happy to see you here."

Maggie laughed nervously. "I'm surprised to be here. Coral was very persuasive."

"Why's that?"

"Coral said it would be good for me to have a friend group that's, well, not straight."

"Mmmm…you're not openly out, are you?"

"I wasn't. I guess I am now?"

"I suppose so. Congratulations." She shook Maggie's hand. "And I'm happy for you. Is this your first time coming out to anyone?"

"Well, no, I told Coral a couple weeks ago. And lots of my high school friends know. The first person I ever came out to was Jess."

Gwen paused, then asked, "Your girlfriend?"

"How'd you guess?"

"Honestly, a young lesbian couple moving to LA straight out of high school is pretty on-brand for the LGBT community." They giggled, and she continued. "Well, I'm glad you're here. Coral's right; it makes a difference being able to hear from people who share your experience."

Maggie snorted. "I hope not a lot of them have my experience."

Gwen glanced at Maggie's hands, which were tightly gripped together in her lap. "You seem pretty tense. And frankly, since you didn't confide in me after I came out to the cast a few weeks ago—"

"I hope you don't think I lied to you. I'm new to this."

Gwen reached over and placed a hand on top of hers. "I understand. I only want to make sure you're comfortable being here. I know how en-thusiastic Coral can be, but participating in events like this is a personal choice."

"I know that. And I think I'm ready for this." Maggie took a deep breath. "In high school, my friends knew, but not their parents, and certainly not mine. It was always this secret. Jess and I were this sneaky couple none of the adults knew about except her parents."

"Her parents were accepting?"

"Oh, they were great." She sighed wistfully. "The best parents ever. It was like having another mom and dad."

"And…your relationship with your parents?" Gwen asked gently.

Maggie paused, gathering her thoughts. "What I told you about Jess talking me into not going to college was only part of the story. It was her idea, but I went along with it because…I just couldn't handle being closeted at home anymore, and I knew how my parents would react."

Gwen's hand squeezed hers as she continued. Words were falling from her mouth as though she was afraid she would stop talking, and Maggie suddenly needed to tell this story.

"My whole life, it was so hard, you know, pretending to be what they wanted, pretending I was going to marry some nice Jewish boy, all while they were saying these…awful, hateful things about people like me. We'd eat dinner, and I'd have to force myself to swallow my food while my dad and mom talked about how gay people are unnatural and indoctrinating children. So when I finally told them, I did it knowing they were going to kick me out, and my suitcase was already packed."

"Oh my God," Gwen said softly.

The words kept coming. "It was literally like, 'Hey Mom, Dad, I'm lesbian. Jess is my girlfriend. I'm leaving.' Mom screamed at me, and Dad was trying to lecture me about how I wasn't welcome anymore, and I was like, 'I said I'm leaving, didn't I?' And it was still just…yelling as I left. I'd never heard them yell so much. They didn't even stop when I got in the car."

Just as suddenly as the words had come, they stopped, and Maggie started to feel ashamed. Here she was at a party, and the first thing she did—to Gwen Knowles of all people—was spill her downer coming-out story. Before she could apologize, Gwen spoke.

"Maggie, I am so, so sorry for how I acted this week." She rubbed her forehead with the ball of her hand. "I'm an idiot. I got so focused on how jealous I was of your academic skills and got caught up in my own ideas about what you should do. I never stopped to think."

"It's okay—"

"No," Gwen said firmly. "It's not. I made an assumption I never should have, and I lashed out against you because of it. I know you said you forgive me, but I want you to know I'm going to do better. That was completely unfair of me."

Maggie nodded slowly. "It was a little hurtful. But understandable. I can't imagine what it's like to be so smart but struggle with reading."

"And I can't imagine what kind of person I'd be if I thought my mom hated the real me growing up." Gwen stood. "Come get a drink with me. I want to start over. No lectures or confrontations today."

Maggie rose to her feet with a smile. "Yes, please. I don't want to be a party pooper."

"Oh, don't stress about that," Gwen reassured her as they made their way to the rear. "First time in a LGBT safe space? This is when most people process things like that. But it's also a time to just enjoy ourselves."

Maggie tried to take her words to heart and urged herself to calm down. After she and Gwen had procured their fruit punch and cupcakes, Maggie heard Coral calling for her.

"There you are," Coral said, weaving through the party. "Gwen, I'm taking Maggie back. There are people I want her to meet."

"Can I follow?"

"Of course." Coral took Maggie's hand and brought her to a circle of lawn chairs, two of which were occupied. A tall, broad-shouldered gentleman with black hair and hazel eyes was laughing with a slim man in rainbow suspenders. "Maggie," Coral said as they approached, "this is Gene and Darren. Gene, Darren, this is Maggie. She's new around here and doesn't have a lot of friends."

"Oh my gosh, hi!" said Gene, standing to his full six and a half feet and extending a hand. "Welcome to our little gathering. How are you?"

Maggie, completely dwarfed by this man, shook his hand a bit hesitantly. "I'm doing well. How do you know Coral?"

"Mostly events like this," he replied, sitting down and gesturing for the ladies to do the same. "She seemed quite intent on introducing us though. How do you know her?"

"We met at an audition, and now we're roommates."

"Oh, you're an actress like she is?" asked Darren.

"Yeah. Do you work in acting?"

"No, I work in IT," Gene replied.

Darren poked Coral with a campfire stick. "Spit it out. Why'd you want us to meet her so bad? She's cute, but she's not exactly our type, y'know."

Coral batted the stick away. "Can't a girl just introduce her roommate to some new friends? Who might, I dunno, also practice the same religion and might be able to help her feel a little bit more welcome in that regard?"

"Oooooohhhh," Maggie and Gene exclaimed. Looking closer, Maggie saw Gene's kippah.

"Coral, you're such a busybody," Gene chided.

Coral threw up her hands. "Fine, but is there another loving gay Jewish couple you recommend I introduce a baby gay to for spiritual support?"

Darren rolled his eyes. "Not everyone needs or wants spiritual guidance. Maggie, are you here by choice, or did Coral drag you—"

"I swear if one more person asks that question—" Coral started as Gwen, laughing, pulled her back into her seat.

Gene turned to Maggie. "Have you found your place in the local Jewish community? Or do you prefer to worship at home than in a synagogue?"

Maggie tried to hide a blush. "I haven't really been practicing. It feels like a different part of my life."

Gene and Darren looked at each other and then at her, responding simultaneously. "Conservative parents?"

"Y-yeah, how did you know?"

"Tale as old as time, honey," Gene said with a laugh. "And what about you?" he asked Gwen as she unwrapped her cupcake.

"I'm just following Maggie around," Gwen replied. "I wasn't raised religious."

"Fair enough." Gene returned his attention to Maggie. "So, you feel like your religion and your sexuality can't both be parts of your life? Am I close?"

Maggie shrugged. "I guess it's more that, y'know, religion was so important to my parents, and we don't talk anymore. I don't know how I'd worship without them."

"Mmmm." Darren leaned forward. "Maggie, I hope you know there's nothing that says Judaism and homosexuality are at odds with each other. You shouldn't feel like you have to choose one or another. I didn't. Look!"

He turned away from her to show her his kippah, and she burst into laughter. The base was the trans pride flag, with a rainbow Star of David embroidered in the center.

"Is that even allowed?" she asked as he turned back with a cheeky grin.

"I don't wear this in front of my grandmother," he said. "This is for special occasions like tonight."

"And it's not just us," Gene said reassuringly. "We play pickleball Thursdays at the SIJCC, and we've met so many LGBT people there."

"Sarah and Carol are nice, but they play mean," Darren complained.

"We're meeting them for brunch at Habayit next Sunday. Have you been?"

"No, I haven't heard of it," Maggie answered.

"We'll have to take you sometime," Darren declared. "Favorite kosher restaurant, hands down."

Gene grumbled, "They charge you almost fifteen dollars for middling shawarma though."

"Any shawarma that isn't your Bubbe's isn't good enough for you."

"Look, there's a right way and a wrong way to–"

"If you start talking about shawarma," Coral groaned, "we're going to be here all week." She placed a hand on Maggie's shoulder. "I'm almost sorry I'm saddling you with these two."

"Are you kidding?" Maggie clasped her hand over Coral's. "I haven't had a decent shawarma or falafel since I left home. I hadn't even looked for the local JCC."

"Oh, we have more than one, dear," Darren informed her. "This is a big city."

"And it's okay that it's taking you time," Gene emphasized. "My parents were more like yours when I was growing up. I mean, we were the kind of Orthodox where even my mom had to cover her hair. When I moved out here, the idea of trying to find another Jewish community and face that possible rejection again was intimidating."

"I…didn't realize it, but I think you hit the nail on the head," Maggie said softly. "I know there are more reformed Jewish sects out there, but I don't know how to find them without outing myself. How did you do it?"

"I found JQ International. They offer support groups for LGBT plus Jews," Gene said. "And I started attending events at the local JCCs."

"That's where we met," Darren said fondly.

"Oh my God, you should join us for Shabbat next week," Gene exclaimed "We're only, like, five blocks away from your apartment. Bring Coral."

"Really?" Maggie said, a rush of warmth filling her lungs. "You really mean it?"

"Of course." Gene placed a hand on her shoulder. "Everyone should feel spiritually well, whether that's not religious"—he nodded to Gwen—"or having your spiritual community supporting you. We'll be your community, honey."

As Maggie, Coral, Gwen, Gene, and Darren talked through the evening late into the night, Maggie found herself fighting tears. But they weren't the same tears she'd shed the first couple months in LA. She reached up to touch her new pride pin flag and gave herself permission to feel like she belonged.

Chapter Twelve

DESPITE NO LONGER frantically attending every audition she could find, Maggie had never been busier. Between play rehearsals, lessons with Gwen, Shabbat with Gene and Darren, and the occasional RiffTrax and popcorn night with Coral—each day passed Maggie by in a blink. She'd taken to carrying her pride flag pin in her pocket, a small reminder that she belonged to a community, and it gave her a smile whenever she ran her fingertips over it. Just when Maggie felt like she was starting to settle into a routine, Coral came along to throw things up in the air once again.

Maggie stepped into the back of the coffee shop Monday morning in mid-October and, checking her phone, found a text from Coral:

CALL ME WHEN YOU CAN

This was shortly followed by:

I'm not dying. I just need your help.

Maggie hastily dialed her phone and held it to her ear with one shoulder while she pulled a sandwich out of her bagged lunch. If she was going to have to run to Coral's location, there was no point in doing it on an empty stomach.

Coral picked up the phone after four rings. "Maggie, thank God. When are you off work today?"

"Um, four, why?"

"And you don't have rehearsal today?"

"No, that's Tuesday and Thursday."

"Can you pleeeeeeaaaaase come help me with this job after your shift? You'll get paid. I really need your help with this."

Maggie swallowed her mouthful and set her sandwich down, realizing she had more time. "What's going on?"

"I got a job. Hired on the spot. But it's more than I can do by myself."

"What are you doing, painting a fence?"

"C'mon, Maggie." Coral sounded hurt. "It's an acting gig. That's why I called you. It's a paid job, it's quick, and you could be seen by literally millions."

Maggie furrowed her brows. "And you can't do it by yourself?"

"I'll explain after your shift. Where's the coffee shop you work at again?"

"Griffith Park."

"Oh good! Text me the closest bus stop. I'll meet you at four and explain on the way."

*

MAGGIE FINISHED HER shift in a state of suppressed confusion. When she finally left for the day and found Coral waiting for her at the bus stop, she only became more confused. Coral was wearing an outfit she'd never seen her in before: a zipped hooded sweatshirt and joggers, white with black vertical stripes on the sides, and an embroidered… "Is that a donkey on your shirt?"

Coral glanced down at her clothes as she dug her phone out of her pocket and started clicking through apps. "Yes. Well, it's called an ass."

Maggie looked closer at Coral's face. "Your makeup is different. Did you use lip gloss?"

"Yeah, I call this the babydoll look."

Coral's dark brown hair was pulled into pigtails. She had bright pink eyeshadow on. The longer Maggie looked at her, the more details she found that made her question if this was really Coral standing in front of her.

"This is, um, part of the job?"

"Don't worry, you won't have to look like this," Coral reassured her. "I need your help with a different part."

"Coral, please tell me what's going on."

As they got on the bus, Coral finally found what she was looking for on her phone. She pulled out ear buds and handed one to Maggie. Once Maggie was set, she clicked Play on a video.

Maggie found herself staring at the face of a young man. Spiked bleached blond hair, tan skin, and bright white teeth practically leaped out of the screen.

"WHAT'S UP MY DUDES? IT'S ANOTHER VIDEEEEOOO!"

She tore the earbud out, shook her head, and put it back in.

"—that subscribe button, that like button, ring that bell, and SMASH THE—"

Coral reached over and double-tapped the screen a couple times, skipping the video ahead.

"—and that's why I'm announcing our NEW project. This is a BIG one. Are you ready for this?"

A voice behind the camera replied, "I don't think they're ready for this."

"You guys totally aren't ready for this. We're turning MY MANSION into a HAUNTED HOUSE! AND I need local actors to help really BRING IT TO LIFE! Here's what you do to apply—"

Maggie watched dumbfounded as the man walked backward through his house. He was supposedly giving instructions for the kinds of actors he wanted in his haunted house, but the video seemed to also serve as a tour of the mansion. As he walked through room after room, he outlined his many fantastical ideas. Throughout the video, he repeatedly said something along the lines of, "Hurry up and apply right now if you want to be a part of this!"

Coral took back her earbud and pocketed her phone. "I don't suppose you know who that was?"

"No clue."

"His name's Paul. He's a full-time YouTuber, claims he gets his money from being a social media influencer, but everyone knows he gets it from his rich father. He's obnoxious, but he has loads of loyal fans, and he keeps getting brand deals. He calls his followers 'asses.'" She plucked at the embroidered donkey on her shirt. "This is his merch. As you've probably guessed—"

"You applied for the job."

"Here's the problem… I'm the only one he's hired."

Maggie blinked in surprise. "How is that possible? If he has such a huge devoted fan base—"

"Well, most of his fans are children, so they can't work for him. And he has a bad reputation of being hard to work for. He's taken the video in question down since then, but three years ago, he ended up in a big controversy for not paying people who worked on it."

Maggie furrowed her brows in concern. "Why on earth would you try to work for this guy? Especially if he doesn't pay, and he's making you wear his merch, and do your makeup like that?"

"Oh, he pays now," Coral reassured her. "His dad got pissed at him for the controversy, so it's technically his dad who's hiring and paying me this time. He's overseeing the whole budget for this project to make sure he doesn't mess up again. And honestly, I don't mind looking like this. It's a character, you know?"

She twirled a finger in her pigtail, cocked her head to one side, and gave a gleaming smile. "I'm channeling my inner Elle Woods, or Heather Chandler. I'm a babydoll on the outside, but cunning on the inside." She stuck her lip out in a fake pout. "Don't you think I look pretty, Maggie? You don't hate me for being pretty, do you?"

Maggie's face flushed a violent red as Coral started laughing. Not waiting for an answer, Coral pressed on.

"So, I need your help. Paul only wants people with some kind of acting experience, and most actors don't want anything to do with him. My first suggestion was to film the haunted house in segments and edit it together so I can change costumes and be different monsters in between rooms, but he's not going for it. He wants to do a live walkthrough instead. It's not hard to move between rooms around him, but I can't possibly do everything he wants fast enough. I think if there's two of us, we can do it."

Shaking her head slowly, Maggie started to argue. "Unless you're try-ing to tell me we're going to film this whole thing tonight and get back home in time for me to sleep for work tomorrow—"

"Oh, no, we're not," Coral said, "but I was hoping if I take you now, get him to hire you on, and we talk through ideas with him, then we could film on one of your days off?"

"I mean…I study with Gwen on Wednesdays. I guess there's Satur-day, but that's Shabbat."

Coral sighed deeply. "Okay, we'll have to figure something out, but Maggie, I really need you on this. I posted in the Facebook group, and all the other actresses said no. I know Paul gives major creep vibes, but he's not that bad, just…entitled and stupid."

Maggie sighed even deeper than Coral. "I have so much going on right now. I don't know."

Coral took one of her hands and held it tightly. "I wouldn't ask if I didn't need the help. We can turn this around into a major promotional opportunity for us. Maybe even get him to promote the play you're in?"

"I thought you said most of his audience is kids."

"Yeah, but not all of it. Maybe you'll get his dad's attention, and he'll donate a ton of money to Peace Over Violence."

Maggie groaned. "Fine, fine, I'll talk to him. But if we can't come to a reasonable plan, I'm out."

Coral grinned and reached forward to give Maggie a tight hug. "You're the best roommate—no, the best friend I've ever had. Thank you so much. I owe you big time."

Maggie hugged her back. "Nah, consider this me repaying you for taking me into your apartment with such short notice." She pulled away.

"But I'm not wearing babydoll makeup—at least not without good reason."

Coral clicked her tongue, rolled her eyes, and twirled a pigtail. "Like, oh my God, you don't have to be a fashionista if you don't want to, you know?" She put on a more serious tone when Maggie groaned at her. "Maggie, it's a character. You gotta learn to be characters that aren't a hundred percent you sometimes. Have you ever done haunted houses or acted for creepy things before?"

"Kinda? When my community theater director found out they were making a *Beetlejuice* musical, he went kinda nuts and wrote his own version. I got to play a bunch of ghosts in that one. We weren't allowed to take any pictures so we wouldn't get sued, but I was told I did a great job."

"I can work with the *Beetlejuice* vibe." Coral pulled her phone back out and started flipping through photos. "I *love* haunted houses. I used to help out in our local haunted house every year when I was in high school. My favorite year was when I was the haunted nursemaid." She showed Maggie a picture of her in a bloodstained governess costume. "I got punched so many times by people who got too close and freaked out."

Maggie lifted an eyebrow. "Is that the real reason you're doing this job? You miss haunted houses?"

"What? Noooo, it's totally for the paycheck and the awesome work environment." Coral tapped the donkey on her shirt. "Plus, I get to wear high-end merch. What more could you ask for?"

A short ride later, they got off at the entrance to a neighborhood Maggie knew, deep down in her soul, she would never afford to live in. A stone wall with an iron fence encircled winding rows of giant mansions, each a different size and shape. Most had very small lawns, although some had huge driveways and rows of neatly mowed grass leading the way to elaborate front doors. It was the kind of opulence that made Maggie instinctively uncomfortable and afraid to touch anything.

Coral, on the other hand, waltzed up to the front gate and waved at a gentleman who appeared to be waiting for her. "Hey, I brought the actress I was talking about. We're good to go."

The young man, who appeared to be in his early twenties and had bleached hair similar to Paul's, punched in a code to open the gate for them. The three of them entered a black SUV. They drove through the decadent neighborhood, making their way to what Maggie realized was the humbler version of all of the homes. Although still larger than any home she could ever hope to have, it was dwarfed by some of the mansions with better views or larger lawns.

Still, she thought as they got out of the car, it was an influencer's dream. From what the video had shown, the mansion had six bedrooms, a living room, a parlor, an entertainment center, four bathrooms, a huge kitchen, an open dining room, and an indoor pool. Looking at it from the outside, with white pillars outlining each window and giant stairs leading to the front door, Maggie felt more than a little intimidated.

Once again, it was Coral who led the way up the stairs. "Get into character," she whispered as their escort reached to open the door. "We're acting both as monsters and as internet influencers. Choose a game face."

In the seconds between opening the door and entering, Maggie ran through a dozen different character choices. She could play the clever ditz, but Coral was already embracing that role. She could try to be the shy sweetheart with the bolder extravert friend, but somehow that didn't feel right. As her feet crossed the threshold, her character fell into place: A quiet but intense snob, someone who you felt was judging you with every glance. A cross between a librarian and a skater girl. Maggie threw back her shoulders, shoved her hands into her pockets, dropped her brows, and adopted the smallest of swaggers.

Coral seemed to have done a similar transformation. She moved with a bouncing gait and a bit more of a hip swivel than she usually had. Leading Maggie through the front entrance of the house, she gestured widely in front of her. "Welcome to the chaos!"

There were bits and pieces of haunted house everywhere. Under all the clutter, Maggie recognized the mansion from the video, but layers of dark cloths, cobwebs, and party streamers were in the process of transforming it. In a side room, a handful of men installed what appeared to be a fake candle chandelier from the ceiling and hung black fabric on the walls with staples.

A little farther in, and they were in the kitchen, away from the transformation.

Paul sat cross-legged on a kitchen counter, chewing his way through a greasy cheeseburger. He looked up when they entered and broke into a wide grin. "Hey, welcome back! Is this the chick you were talking about?"

"Best underground actress in all of LA," Coral crowed, shifting aside and drawing Maggie forward. "Maggie, say hi to Paul Jonas."

Maggie kept her hands in her pockets and gave her chin a small jerk up. "Sup."

"Yoooo, she's a keeper," Paul announced, standing up and walking over to them. "You're an actor?"

She grunted, and he got uncomfortably close. When he reached as if to hug her, she sidestepped. He recovered by gesturing at the kitchen.

"Welcome aboard! We're going to make the sickest haunted house

YouTube's ever seen! C'mon. Let me give you a tour, and you can tell the camera a little about yourself."

He reached for his phone, but Coral swiftly put her hand on his arm.

"Paul, you didn't even sign her on yet. Can't film her without a paycheck, y'know?"

"Oh, oh right," he said, looking sheepish. He went back to sit on the counter and resumed eating his cheeseburger. "Tom'll take care of ya."

Tom, apparently, was the young man who had driven them to the house. He'd disappeared to another room when they entered, but reappeared a moment later with a packet of papers. It was less comprehensive than the contract Maggie had signed with Gwen and Haleigh, but she read it thoroughly and couldn't find any problems with it. Then she got to the part about payment and choked slightly.

"If I wear your merch while working for you," she said, "you'll pay me a thousand dollars even. But if I wear my own clothes, you'll pay me minimum wage and clock my hours?"

"Gotta be part of the brand, hot stuff," Paul said through a mouthful of fries.

Maggie looked at Coral's outfit and gagged slightly. "I don't have to pay for the merch, do I?"

"Nah, I've got plenty."

Coral shrugged at Maggie's questioning glance. "They're actually pretty comfy. And he'll let you do your own makeup."

Groaning inwardly, Maggie circled the option to wear the merchandise, then signed her name. "There," she said, handing it over. "I'll help build some sets, act as a monster for your house, and talk on camera for your behind-the-scenes vid. And I'll do it in merch." She crossed her arms.

"You're a pretty generous guy paying me a thousand bucks for what might be less than twenty hours of work. I have another job, y'know. I can't be here every day."

Paul took a long sip of soda from a takeout cup and hopped off the counter. "Girl, chill, it's just cash. Get ready for some realness!"

He pulled out his phone, held it aloft, changed a few settings, and started speaking to the camera. "We got ourselves a new team member, check her out everybody!" He swiveled to put Maggie and Coral in the background, group-selfie-style. "What's your name, girl?"

"My friends call me Maggie."

"Maggie! And you're a friend of our friend Coral here?"

"Yeah, she's the best. Helped me out of a tough spot, so I'm here to help her in return." Maggie kept a blank face but gave Coral a nod of appreciation. "It's the least I can do."

Paul gave the camera a thumbs-up. "Isn't she a sweetheart? Coral, what do you like about Maggie?"

Coral threw her arms around Maggie and gave the camera a giant smile. "I know she's all tough on the outside, but inside she's a creative genius! You're going to love her as one of your monsters."

"All right all right all right!" Paul started walking them out of the kitchen. "Let's do the tour!"

Tom had quickly picked up a handheld camera with a visible microphone and expanding lenses. Paul put his phone away and talked through his vision as he guided Maggie and Coral through the different rooms.

"I want this to feel like the real thing, you know? So we're getting props, we're getting costumes, we're doing special effects makeup, the whole thing. You guys will get ready in here." He took them to a walk-in coat closet, which was mostly empty, except for hanging merchandise in multiple sizes. "Hey, Maggie, grab your size. What's your pleasure? Tank top? Bikini top?"

"In October? Sweatshirt, please." Maggie hastily grabbed a hoodie with a donkey silhouette on the back and pulled it on over her outfit.

"Great. So you're going to be inside as the monsters of the haunted house, right? And I'm going to come in from the front door and just walk through the whole house, bottom to top. I'm gonna wear a GoPro; it'll be sweet."

"The whole house?" Coral asked.

"Well, not the kitchen or my bedroom. I kinda need those this week. Gotta get my beauty rest and fitness fuel on, yo." Paul turned to the camera. "Don't forget; we're starting a brand of protein shakes. Hit us up on our Patreon if you want in on that action early."

Steering them out of the closet, he then went through the various props and craft supplies lying around the house. "It's gotta be dark. This ain't no little kid's haunted house. So we're covering every single window with the stuff they make blackout curtains out of, and we're lining all the walls in black fabric. Gonna drape the furniture in white. It's going to be so sweet."

Maggie continued to listen with growing concern as Paul described what sounded less and less like a video idea and more and more like his own personal haunted house. Rooms entirely in darkness, jump scares, liquid messes with no containment… Then Paul announced his plan to have them perform as ghouls in Ass Merch bikinis. At that point, Maggie looked over at Coral. With relief, she saw the same consternation in Coral's eyes.

As they reached the backyard, Paul turned and clapped his hands with excitement. "Yo, you guys so aren't ready for this; it's going to be so lit." He turned to the camera. "If you're watching this, it's because you already saw what happened, so you know how it's going to be. These girls got no idea!"

Tom lowered the camera. "Dude, where did you get that candle chandelier thing? It's so sick!"

As Paul and Tom excitedly discussed their plans, Maggie and Coral stepped aside.

"I thought this man made his living making videos," Maggie whispered. "How does he have no idea that everything he shoots is going to look like crap without any plan for lighting? Is he just going to shine a flashlight at everything?"

Coral rubbed her head. "I've tried showing him the kind of stuff we did at my old haunted houses, and he likes the ideas, but he doesn't seem to understand what actually goes into making it look good, and I don't know how to explain it to him so he will."

Maggie glanced over her shoulder. "Maybe you could just tell him what to do?"

Coral chewed on her bottom lip. "Some of it. But I don't know how to make all of it show up on camera or how to fit it into a house that isn't being renovated to be a haunted house, y'know?"

Maggie put her hands on her hips and stared up at the mansion, eyes flickering over the windows, half of which were blacked out. After a moment, a thought occurred to her. She glanced at Coral. "Do you think he'll mind if I add one more person to our crew?"

"We're not even halfway through his budget yet, from what I understand."

Maggie sighed, letting her shoulders droop slightly. She reached into her pocket for her phone. "I can't believe I'm doing this."

"Doing what?"

"I'm going to call Gwen."

Chapter Thirteen

"I DON'T UNDERSTAND why you called me. I'm not studying cinematography, and I don't vlog."

Gwen had been at a night class when Maggie called, so she discussed the details of the job at rehearsal the next day. As everyone packed up and put on their sweaters, Maggie hastily explained the situation to her, including showing her pictures of Coral in the merch.

Maggie, still in disbelief she was doing this, tried to sound encouraging. "But you know all about lighting and sound. You can direct and know how to engage the senses for storytelling. And Coral's really invested in this project; she keeps talking about what a promotional opportunity it is."

Gwen rubbed her temples as they left the rehearsal room and made their way outside. "This is crazy. Why do you care if it's a crappy video anyway? Just dress up, do the job, take the thousand bucks for the day, and get out. I'll even let you skip studying with me tomorrow so you can get it done. Easy money, and it's no skin off your nose."

Maggie nodded but pressed on. "Coral's been talking to Paul a lot about how to do the behind-the-scenes video he's shooting, to release right after the haunted house video. I think she has him convinced to use it, and us being in it, as a way to promote the play."

"The play?"

"This play. *Petty Oppression.* And maybe even gather donations for Peace Over Violence." Sensing Gwen wavering, Maggie kept building on the idea. "Paul's dad is rich, and although a lot of the audience is kids, there's also a lot of general publicity around his channel. Plus, Paul's trying to get back in the public's good graces after a controversy a couple years ago. Promoting a charity is exactly the kind of PR he's, well, his dad is looking for. If we reveal that the director and stage manager, Gwen Knowles, collaborated with Paul Jonas to make the haunted house as awesome as it was, plus, y'know, me as one of the actresses, we can make it a real, um, promotional opportunity or whatever you wanna call it."

Gwen started walking faster, a finger pressed to her lips. "I'd have to talk to Caleb. I'm not certain their organization wants to be associated with a bro-Tuber."

Maggie hadn't thought about that part. For a moment, she thought she'd lost Gwen's interest for good. Then she took another look at Gwen's face and was startled to see some determination in her eyes.

"I'll call him right now, try to get an answer from him before tomorrow," Gwen muttered, reaching for her phone with her other hand, one finger still tapping her lip intently. "It's not the kind of thing I'd usually do, but I've heard of Paul's dad—I think he runs a payroll company or huge temp agency. The 'invisible rich' type. Could be a solid partnership."

She paused in tapping through her phone, standing on the sidewalk with Maggie. "I'll ask Caleb. If he's on board, I'll skip class and come with you and Coral tomorrow. If we can get the right equipment, we'll set it up and shoot it all in one day, get it done and out of the way."

Maggie practically melted with relief. "Coral will be so happy. Thank you so much."

Gwen waved a hand dismissively. "I would hate to see Coral give a hundred percent to a project just for it to be crap anyway. Maybe this will help her get a lucky break; she's certainly earned it." Gwen held her hand out for a fist bump. "I'll text you when I know. Just text me with how to meet up with you—if Caleb says yes."

Maggie returned the fist bump. "See you tomorrow, I hope!"

*

CORAL WAS OVER the moon when Maggie's phone chirped the next morning, indicating Gwen's reply:

Caleb says do it, and he'll figure out the details with the dad later. How do I get there?

Coral snatched the phone from Maggie and typed instructions, then handed it back so Maggie could explain the best route to take. After Coral grabbed her own phone to email the news to Paul, she and Maggie began a flurry of activity, starting with putting their borrowed Ass merch back on.

Coral had decided the biggest problem with Paul's haunted house was it lacked a story. She'd spent the entire previous night throwing ideas around with Maggie until she'd created one of her own for them to implement. Maggie was relieved it barely involved any bikinis. During the bus ride there, they hunched over a notebook Coral had drawn ideas in, making plans for costumes they could assemble easily from the resources Paul had provided. When they got off the bus at the entrance to his neighborhood, they found Gwen waiting for them, looking tired and slightly annoyed but prepared. She leaned against a fairly old but sturdy-looking station wagon, which Maggie guessed must be her car. Despite the early October morning, she wore a black tank top with jeans.

Coral ran up to her and gave her a hug. "You are a lifesaver," she declared as they approached the gate. "This is going to be fun. I promise."

"Uh-huh," Gwen grunted, squinting up at the hill lined with mansions.

"No, really," Coral reassured her. "We get to basically design our very own quick little haunted house, to be seen by millions of people."

Gwen sighed. "Why do you have to go and make an inconvenience sound so inviting, Coral? How do you manage to do this to people?"

"I have no idea what you're talking about."

Maggie giggled as they climbed in Tom's SUV and started the drive. "Don't worry about it, Coral. You're just bringing us along for another adventure."

Gwen took less interest in the houses than Maggie had the night before and, instead, focused on drilling Coral and Tom about what equipment was available at the house. It appeared that Paul actually owned a variety of lighting options from several filming projects and gifts from sponsors. He just seemed to have no idea how to use them and usually chose to film in flattering natural lighting. When Gwen learned he owned a pack of lighting gels and a night vision camera, she actually smiled.

"Well, I can work with this. How many people are working on the project right now?"

"We've got a crew of guys waiting for us," Tom said. "They're mostly done with the decorating, hanging the fabric and stuff. Paul paid them an extra day to come help with all the stuff you girls are doing."

"Good. I shouldn't need them long."

They pulled into the driveway and got out of the car. Gwen turned to Maggie and Coral and said with a businesslike tone, "You two focus on rehearsing, costume, and makeup. Leave the rest to me."

Coral and Maggie both saluted.

"Aye aye, captain," Maggie said. "Just holler if you need us. It's a big place, but we'll still hear you."

Gwen murmured acknowledgement as Tom opened the door and entered ahead of them. She moved to follow and then immediately jumped back as a camera swung into her face.

"THE GIRLS ARE BAAAAAAAAAAAAAAACK," hollered Paul as he stepped out into the early light. "It's like, what, eight a.m.? GOOD MORNING, LADIES!"

Gwen sighed impatiently. "I suppose you're Paul Jonas."

"Girl, don't act like you don't know me. Starting today, you're one of the Asses!"

Gwen held up her hand. "I'm not working for you just yet. And I'm doing this as a representative of Peace Over Violence."

"Is that the charity your friend was talking about?" Paul lowered the camera. "Tom, get the paperwork, the one I printed out this morning?"

"The one I emailed you?" Coral piped up hopefully.

"Yeah, that one. It looked good."

Tom reemerged from the bowels of the house with a packet of paper and handed it to Gwen. Gwen took it hesitantly.

After a second, Maggie rushed forward and took the papers. "Oh, um, boss, why don't I look this over for you while you talk shop with the guys?"

"Yeah, let me know if it's good," Gwen said calmly. "Thank you."

"No problem, boss." Maggie started reading through the contract quickly while the group entered the foyer. Instantly, it became harder to read.

Paul's crew had successfully covered every window in the first several rooms with blackout curtains, and every light switch seemed to be hidden behind black drapes hung on the walls. She made her way to the untouched kitchen and flipped through pages while Gwen investigated rooms and gave Paul instructions on what lighting fixtures and equipment she wanted to work with.

After a moment, Maggie approached Gwen. "You'll be paid five thousand if you agree to wear merch, three thousand if you don't. Everything else looks fine. There's even a specific clause written in about promoting Peace Over Violence. They're going to use something called 'YouTube Giving,' and donate any ad revenue they get from the behind-the-scenes video for the first twenty-four hours. Plus, at the beginning and end of the video, there'll be clips where Paul and Coral talk about the play."

Gwen glanced at Coral, who was digging through a box of costume pieces.

Coral grinned. "Don't worry. Maggie's filled me in on the details. I'm gonna boost the Twilight too. In fact, if Maggie feels like she can get started with the costumes, I'm going to film that part with Paul right now."

Maggie handed Gwen the papers and a pen, pointing to where to sign.

Gwen scribbled her signature and handed the papers to Tom. "Fine, I'm in. The goal is to start your haunted house tour at sundown, right?"

"That's right. It's gonna be so dope."

"Then let's get cracking."

Paul whipped out his camera again. "Not so fast. First, it's time to meet the beautiful ladies who are working on this project. Say hi, ladies."

Coral, who had reimmersed herself in the role of the clever sorority girl, waved cheerily at the camera. "Hi everybody! We're so excited to be working on this. Maggie and I are making our costumes right now!"

Maggie flicked a finger from her forehead in a small, sullen salute. "Yo."

"And you guys won't believe this, but we got ourselves a real professional stage director for this video." Paul swung the camera into Gwen's face. "Talk about yourself, hot stuff. You've got a body that just won't quit; what do you do with it?"

Gwen crossed her arms. "Whoa, now, buddy. Let's get one thing straight. I'm a lesbian, and I don't need you getting all up in my space when I'm trying to work."

Paul instantly took a step backward. "Yo, yo, it's cool, man! Lesbian, huh? We're cool with gays here. Gays are cool. You like gay people, Tom?" He turned the camera to Tom.

"Yeah, gay people are cool. I'm not gay though."

"Oh, no, yeah, no. I'm not gay either, dude. But gay people are fine." Camera back to Gwen. "So, you've never had a boyfriend?"

"Nope. Not interested."

"Well, then, how about you ladies?"

Maggie spoke up quickly. "I'm also lesbian, actually."

Paul looked out from behind his camera viewfinder. "Wait, really? Did I manage to hire all lesbians?"

Coral opened her mouth, paused, then said, "Yep, I'm not straight either!"

Paul looked visibly disappointed but returned his focus to the camera. "Well…you know what they say about gay people; they have a great sense of fashion! So let's see those costumes you're making!"

Coral quickly went to Paul's side and looked into the camera. "Nuh-uh, you don't get to see. This house is going to be your surprise, right?"

"Uh—"

"Then it's not fair if you get to see before everyone else does. C'mon outside, and no peeking."

Coral guided Paul outside, presumably to film the video intro and outro. Tom went to retrieve some of the equipment Gwen had asked for. Gwen herself started tracing the edges of the walls along the floorboards, looking for an outlet through the black draping.

"I swear Coral sees the best in everybody," she muttered. "Never thought I'd be skipping class to work for a bro-Tuber."

Maggie chuckled as she picked up a bundle of white clothes to carry to the kitchen, where she could work in better light. "I guess where some people see a bro, she sees an opportunity?"

Gwen grunted. Just as Maggie was about to leave, Gwen called after her, "Well, at least I get to spend the day with you. Even if it's not in the way I usually look forward to."

"Ha ha, same," Maggie called back. She quickly walked to the kitchen, a goofy grin on her face.

Chapter Fourteen

THE SUN WAS struggling to maintain its reach on the Paul Jonas mansion at 6:30 p.m. when Gwen completed the last of her checklist. "All right, Tom, is the night vision camera on?"

"On and rolling."

"GoPro is on?"

Paul tapped his knuckles against the camera strapped to his head. "I'm always turned on, baby." Gwen lifted an eyebrow, and he chuckled sheepishly. "I mean, boss lady."

Gwen took a deep breath, then forced a smile. "You should be all set. Once you step in there, remember to follow the guide, or you'll walk into an unprepared room, and the whole thing will get thrown off."

Paul gave a thumbs-up, and Gwen reached for a camera set on a table beside her. Tom leaned over to show her how to turn it on, and then she hoisted it, aimed for Paul and Tom, and gave them the signal to start.

Paul started speaking in a raised whisper. "Guys, it's finally time, what you've all been waiting for. Through that door—*that door*—my house has been turned into a haunted mansion. I have no idea what's in there; I haven't been inside all day. We have no clue what's waiting for us. Tom, are you ready?"

"Oh, I'm ready."

"Tom here is going to record in case we catch any real haunted activity. Who knows what could happen? They say if you do those haunted games online, you invite ghosts into your house, right? And I've got this thing"—he gestured to the GoPro—"so you can see everything exactly as I'm seeing it. Now, I've got no flashlight, no weapon to protect myself, nothing. Tom, are you ready?"

"Man, I don't know if I am."

"C'mon. We've been through loads of haunted houses together. Best friends since fifth grade, man. We got this!"

"Yeah, yeah, let's do this!"

"It's gonna be dope!"

"This is so sick!"

"All right, everybody, my house–is a HAUNTED HOUSE! Let's go!"

Gwen turned her camera off and left the porch, allowing Tom and Paul to enter inside. Maggie, who had been watching and listening at one of the front windows behind Gwen, quickly dropped the blackout curtain, ran to her place, and texted a signal to Coral. Chattering with excitement, Paul led the way into a pitch-black entrance. Only a single, flickering red light in a wire bulb cage indicated where the doorway was.

"Oh God this is so scary; is this even my house?" Paul murmured as he went through to the next room.

White cloth layered in gray chalk covered whatever furniture had not been removed. Cobwebs hung from every corner and crevice. The fake candle chandelier was lit, as were a few more sputtering red lights at various doorways. The lights hummed, faint and low, every once in a while giving an unsettling pop whenever the light cut out.

As Paul and Tom slunk this way and that, recording the scene, Maggie silently edged into place behind them in the doorway. When they turned back to continue into the house, Paul and Tom jumped and shrieked.

"Oh my God, where did you come from?" Paul demanded. "That is so freaky, man!"

Maggie hid a grin. She'd matted down her curly hair with water and Vaseline so it hung heavy on her shoulders and in front of her face. She wore an Ass merch long-sleeved shirt and joggers, which she had embellished with rips, mud stains, and scraps of fabric from old white clothes. White paint covered her face, neck, arms, and hands, and black stockings practically hid her feet. Heavy eyeliner and cork ashes gave her a sunken appearance. It was the most typical ghost appearance she could think of, but that was the point—to make their audience think this was a typical haunted house.

She lifted a finger to her lips and warned them in a stage whisper, "If you keep making noise, Mama will hear you."

They both burst into half-hearted giggles.

"Who the hell is Mama?" Tom asked.

"This is so freaky, man," Paul repeated.

Maggie pointed further into the house. "We need to get out before Mama finds us. Follow me." She turned and went into the living room. Before the boys could exit the front parlor, she'd hidden herself behind one of the massive black wall hangings. They both walked straight past her, muttering to themselves and the camera.

She gave them some time to explore a few spooky surprises left in the giant living room: a hastily written note expressing fear of the monstrous Mama, a chained-up box with a motor in it that would randomly rattle as if trying to break free, and what looked like a half-eaten cat made from sadly demolished dollar store teddy bears. While they were preoccupied with the "cat," she reemerged, tiptoeing up behind them. Just as they were about to try to pick up the remains, she reached out to grab Tom's shoulder.

Tom screamed. Maggie had prepared for the worst and jumped backward after her grab so he didn't smack her in the face with his camera as he whirled around. Paul, on the other hand, nearly fell back into the wall. Both boys were still yelling as Maggie put her finger to her hand and again warned them.

"Mama can hear you. She knows you're here. Follow me."

This time, she didn't disappear as she wandered away, with the boys following close behind.

"Who are you?" Paul asked hesitantly.

"I'm Stacie," Maggie whispered. "I came here to live with Mama."

"But I thought you're afraid of Mama."

Maggie nodded. "Mama says she likes children. I think she likes them too much."

Paul and Tom tittered excitedly as Maggie led them through the dining room. The table was laid with the only plates and silverware the girls could find in the kitchen. In the serving bowls, they'd poured together whatever was expired in the pantry—cans of beans, soup, pasta, and fruit—

which they mashed with a blender and then decorated with olives. A frosted glass wall divided the table from where Paul kept his liquor cabinet, keeping it hidden from view during his videos. Maggie passed by the divider harmlessly but tapped her fingers against the cups and plates as she did so. As soon as Paul and Tom stepped up to the divider behind her, it was flooded with light, and Coral, covered in a white sheet, threw herself against the glass, wailing and crying. Paul and Tom nearly leapt out of their skin and hurried past Maggie into the hallway.

Maggie watched from the doorway to ensure they didn't backtrack and waved Coral on, who threw the sheet off, turned off the LED flashlight, and ran as quietly as she could toward the stairs. While Paul and Tom were distracted with the back game room, she would ready herself for the end of the story.

The game room had sheer white cloth strips hanging from thumbtacks in the ceiling. It was impossible to navigate the room without touching them. The boys shuddered as the cloth tickled their necks and arms. Toward the back, they found another rattling box. As they chuckled at it and prepared to leave the room, Maggie had been busy littering the hallway they'd just passed through with cheap baby doll pieces. She dumped the food from the dining table on fabric laid on the floor. The obstacles left them with one path—to the main stairway, leading to the bedrooms.

Paul and Tom were appropriately grossed out by the scene, but had clearly started to calm down from the dining room scare. Maggie decided to raise the tension again. As they approached the steps, she crept up behind them, reciting a rhyme she'd made up in a sing-song stage whisper.

"Two little boys climbing up the stairs. Mama will take them by the hair. Mama makes a crunch, Mama takes a munch, Mama loves to have company for lunch!"

"Yo, dude, knock that off." Paul laughed nervously. "Mama's gonna eat us?"

Maggie lifted her finger to her mouth again. "You have to get out, or Mama will catch you. She loves hide and seek."

Tom raised a fist to the camera. "I'm not scared of Mama. What is she, like, a vampire? Leather face?"

"Oh no," Maggie said. "Mama is sweet as can be. She doesn't look like she could hurt a fly."

"Oh, we can take care of her, definitely," Paul said.

"Yeah, we'll stop her from eating more kids," Tom said. Maggie bit back a laugh.

Up the stairs, there weren't any props, lights, rattles, or chains. It was pure black, with only the occasional faded light to illuminate the path. Maggie continued to follow behind them, encouraging them to find their way out. At the very end of the hallway, they finally found the largest guest bedroom, door ajar, strange scraping noises coming from deep inside.

The room had been turned into a maze. Maggie had found multiple sets of Ass merchandise hanging from portable clothing racks stored in guest bedrooms. She'd wheeled them in and set them up, obscuring the back of the room and creating a dizzying path with at least two dead ends. Paul and Tom wound their way through the clothing, with Maggie following close behind.

"We don't know why she eats so much," Maggie said sadly as they found themselves in a dead end of embroidered sweatpants. "But I think I know why she likes it."

"Why?" Tom asked, chuckling.

"She needs something meaty to chew on. And she says cats are just too small. You look pretty chewy."

Tom started to laugh, but was cut off as they rounded the last bend of clothes.

Maggie stepped to one side, leaving an exit, and whispered, "I think Mama found you."

In the very back of the room, hunched over a pot and scraping a metal spoon inside it, Coral sat with her back to the entrance. An LED light with a filter taped over the lens illuminated her harshly, in stark contrast to the rest of the house. She dropped the spoon and turned around, revealing what she'd spent the entire day doing while Maggie, Gwen, and the hired workers readied the house. Coral was dressed in a "bloodied" apron and dress, with rips and gashes everywhere. After almost nothing but black and white for fifteen minutes, the red was startling. But not as startling as her face. Dark holes in the place of her eyes and a huge, gaping mouth that overwhelmed her cheeks and chin completely transformed her. It was a face of primal hunger, and it made Maggie's stomach drop.

Paul and Tom screamed louder than they ever had. Coral lunged after them, and they went flying back into the maze, pushing clothing racks out of the way, hurtling toward the exit. Maggie hastily followed them, eager to see the finale.

Coral was in rare form. Without losing speed or agility, lurching in rigid, clockwork motions—the most unsettling movement Maggie had seen in her life—Coral chased the men down the stairs and out the hallway to the backyard, Paul and Tom tripping, swearing, and stumbling in their haste.

Outside in the cool air for the first time in hours, Maggie and Coral sat on the back porch, panting as Paul and Tom ran to the sign Gwen had painted: *Happy Halloween Asses!* Once they'd reached the sign and were certain they were in the clear, Paul and Tom ranted and raved into each other's cameras, listing what they'd thought were the scariest parts of the house.

Maggie looked over at Coral and chortled. "Simple, but effective."

Coral laughed. "If I've learned anything from my years at home, it's that a detailed story is nice, but the most important thing is to know your audience and make them feel unsteady."

"Do you think they'll get a good video out of it? It's not nearly as elaborate as the house he was imagining."

"But it's realistically what we could do." Coral patted the sweat off of her forehead with a bikini that had snagged on her costume. "Honestly, for his audience, I think it'll be…"

She trailed off as Paul and Tom approached the back porch. Paul ran up to Coral, a wide nervous smile on his face.

"Holy crap, that was amazing!"

"It was?" Coral asked, blinking.

Paul picked her up and spun her around in a tight hug. "That was so much more incredible than I had hoped. You were an absolute BEAST!" He let her down and reached to shake Maggie's hand. "Thank you both. Oh, and the blonde too. Gwen, was her name? You girls are mad awesome. We could not have done this without you."

Tom hoisted his camera. "C'mon, a good shot together? 'Happy Halloween' for the outro?"

"Totally," Paul replied.

Coral and Maggie stood shoulder to shoulder with Paul, Coral beaming through all the makeup.

Gwen was waiting on the front porch, chatting with the men who had arrived to help clean the house. As Tom waved the men in and started helping turn the lights back on, Gwen and Paul took a look at some of the camera footage. Coral and Maggie took the time to retrieve their clothes and wash the worst of the makeup off of their faces and hair. When they reemerged on the lawn, Gwen approached them, holding three checks.

"Payday, ladies. You did a fantastic job. We pulled an amateur haunted house together in a single day."

Maggie pocketed her check and wrapped an arm around Coral. "It's all thanks to one crazy girl who saw an opportunity where everyone else saw an idiot."

Coral grinned and returned the side hug. "This has been the best adventure I've been on in a year. Thank you both so, so much."

*

THE JOB HAD done more than fill their bank accounts. Coral walked around for weeks with refreshed confidence in her step. Apparently, Paul kept emailing her thanking her for her hard work and asking what kinds of jobs she was interested in for the future. There was a new sense of optimism throughout the whole apartment. That was why it hit Maggie so hard a short time later when Coral handed her a dinner plate with frozen chicken nuggets and asked, "So what are you doing for Thanksgiving?"

Maggie almost dropped the plate and had to flounder with both hands to steady it. "Oh crap. When's Thanksgiving?"

"Uh, next week." Coral squirted a generous serving of ketchup on her plate and passed the bottle. "I'm going to visit my folks in Wisconsin. So excited to see my niece for the first time. But I figured that's not really your plan, so, what is your plan?"

A lump formed in Maggie's throat. Memories from last year flooded her mind—Jess's parents opening the door, giving her bear hugs, introducing her to the aunts and uncles as part of the family. "I…I don't know. I haven't thought about it."

Coral paused, nugget halfway to her mouth. "Oh. Oh, Maggie, I wish I asked sooner. If I'd squeezed you in two weeks ago, you could have joined us. But Mom's filled all the extra space with work friends by now. My sister's family and the baby get a whole room to themselves, so I think I'm sleeping in a hammock in the attic."

"It's totally fine," Maggie reassured her, setting the ketchup down on the table. "I think I'm just going to take a couple days off and relax."

Coral didn't look convinced, chewing thoughtfully. "Maybe Gene and Darren will have room for you?"

"Maybe. I can ask."

"I'd feel better if you do. God, I feel awful. I'm a terrible roommate."

Maggie flicked a pea at her head. "Knock it off, you're fine. I'm going to be okay."

Maggie was about as convincing to herself as she was to Coral. She texted Gene after dinner but found out they were also traveling out of state for the holiday. Rather than try to invite herself into their family dinner, she wished them safe travels, put her phone down, and threw herself onto her bed. A sharp dig in her hip reminded her of the enamel pride flag pin in her pocket. She dug it out, gazed at it for a moment, and set it on her bedside table. She closed her eyes, buried her face in her pillow, and for just a few minutes, wallowed in memories of last Thanksgiving. Jess's mom handing her a piece of pie, explaining she tried to make everything kosher. Jess's dad bragging to everyone about their high school performances. Even Jess's grandma telling Jess she'd found a "nice gal." Maggie rolled onto her back. *Is it normal to miss your ex's family more than your ex?*

Her mind flashed to her own family. She wondered how her parents had explained her absence at last year's Thanksgiving to her aunts and uncles. She remembered baby cousins she used to bounce on her knee, older cousins who used to play football with her in the backyard. Did they remember her? Did they miss her? Composure she'd maintained for over a year crumbled. Sobs rose unbidden from her throat. She hurriedly grabbed a pillow to muffle her crying and curled into the fetal position, tears cascading down her flushed cheeks.

Chapter Fifteen

A GOOD CRY had helped, but Maggie walked through the next few days as though followed by a cloud. She reached out to her boss to see if she could work extra hours through the holiday but was reminded that Sofia was closing the coffee shop for the full week and cooking dinner for her extended family. Maggie tried to come up with projects or small jobs to give herself, to keep herself occupied for the week, but she hadn't had time for hobbies in so long she had no ideas. She tried to map out a route of LA to explore, but found most places were going to be closed at various inconvenient hours. By the end of the week, she'd sunk into a state of numb resignation. In the first improv group since *A Midsummer Night's Dream*, when they were playing "catch the sound," she failed numerous times to notice it was her turn to mimic the sound. Everyone was patient and understanding, but she grew frustrated with herself. No matter how hard she tried to focus, the only image her mind seemed to settle on was her alone in the apartment with a rotisserie chicken from the grocery store.

As she went to grab a bagel from the snack table, Gwen stepped alongside her.

"Hey, Maggie. How're you doing?"

"I'm good," Maggie said cheerily, spreading cream cheese with a plastic fork. "How are you?"

"I'm fine, but I'm serious. You seem not quite yourself today. Is everything okay?"

"Yeah, everything's fine," Maggie insisted, putting the bagel halves together for easier eating.

Gwen reached for her own bagel. "Valerie hasn't bothered you, has she?"

"Oh, no! No, I haven't heard or seen her at all."

"Good. But you still seem a little out of it."

"I guess I'm just tired." Maggie gave her a smile. "I'm good, I promise. How's school going?"

Gwen rolled her eyes. "I have a paper coming up. I get extra time to work on it, but we haven't finished covering the material in class, so I'm frustrated. I thought I'd reached a point where I was mostly done writing papers, then this one sneaks up on me."

"What's it about?"

Gwen and Maggie walked toward their things, which had somehow ended up next to each other. "Essentially, I have to explain why I would choose certain sound setups for different types of theaters. Like, traditional stage, versus black box, versus outside. And explain how different sound systems have historically been applied to different kinds of performances."

"That sounds…uh…"

"Boring?" She laughed. "It's fun to do in real life, but it's tedious to write about. Especially because I know from experience what works, but I have trouble explaining why it works."

"That sounds tough."

"Excuse me!"

Maggie and Gwen turned as Coral jogged up to them.

"Gwen, are you trying to steal my roommate? I thought we were going back together!"

Maggie hadn't realized she was halfway out of the auditorium, following Gwen to the doors. "Oh my gosh, Coral, I'm so sorry. I don't know where my head is at today."

Coral sniffed indignantly. "No, no, I understand. You're replacing me. I would too, if my roommate forgot to invite me to Thanksgiving. I still feel bad about that," she added earnestly.

"I told you, it's fine. Your family has enough people to worry about as it is."

"But I should have asked, you know?"

Gwen glanced between the two of them. "Wait. What about Thanksgiving?"

Coral pouted. "I didn't think to invite Maggie to Thanksgiving dinner with my family. Did Gene say they could take you?"

Maggie shrugged. "They're headed out of town. I don't want to be a bother. I'll be fine, I promise."

Gwen's brows furrowed. "Maggie, are you going to be alone for Thanksgiving?"

"I'll be fine!" Maggie's voice came out harsher than she intended, but her cheeks were tinting pink, and she was tired of trying to convince everyone.

Gwen shook her head. "Oh hell no. Give me a second." She dug her phone out of her pocket.

"What are you doing?" Coral asked excitedly.

"I'm taking Maggie with me to Thanksgiving." Gwen held a finger up as Maggie opened her mouth. "And before you try to argue with me, I'm calling my mother, and I dare you to argue with her."

"Gwen, this really isn't—"

"What did I just say?" Gwen grinned as she held her phone to her ear. "No one deserves to be alone for Thanksgiving, Maggie. Let us do this. It's our way of paying it forward from everyone who— Hi, Ma! Listen, I need you to meet someone. Can I put you on video chat?"

They were standing in the theater lobby at this point. Maggie considered taking Coral's hand and walking away. This was too much. But as she turned toward the door, Coral placed a hand on her shoulder.

"Maggie, listen. Gwen's had her Thanksgivings where she had to stay in the city. So have I. Someone was there for us and took us in. It's her turn. Okay?"

Maggie glanced at Gwen, who was trying to get her mom to pick up the video call successfully. She turned back to Coral and nodded. "If you'll stop beating yourself up, then, okay."

Coral grinned. "This is exciting. I think Gwen lives in Iowa or somewhere like that. Can you afford a plane ticket?"

"Probably not a whole one."

"I'll put in a little too, 'cause my parents are paying for mine. You can consider it your Christmas—sorry, I mean, Hanukkah present."

"There you are, Ma." Gwen bent her knees slightly to line up her face with Maggie and Coral. "I want you to meet a couple of my friends. This is Maggie and Coral."

The woman on the screen definitely bore a resemblance to Gwen, a shared jaw, nose, and complexion. But instead of Gwen's vivid blonde hair and green eyes, this woman had light-brown hair and eyes, and her frame was thinner than Gwen's. She gave a wide toothy grin. "Oh, Maggie! Hello! I've heard so much about you."

"Ma," Gwen chided her.

"All good things, all good things," the woman said calmly. "I'm Becky. It's nice to meet you both."

"Hi," Coral said, waving.

"Ma," Gwen cut in. "Maggie doesn't have anywhere to go for Thanksgiving. I'm gonna bring her over."

Maggie was taken aback by Gwen's blunt approach toward her mother, but Becky only grinned wider.

"That would be wonderful. Maggie, I can't wait to meet you in person."

"I, um—"

"What cute hair you have," Becky continued. "Gwen, lift the camera a little bit. Are those natural curls? You're gorgeous. No wonder she talks about—"

"Ma, you're embarrassing me."

"Oh, and we wouldn't want that, would we?" Becky's chuckle sounded a little like the evil laugh Maggie used when she dressed up as a witch for Halloween. "Have you ever been to Idaho before, Maggie?"

"Oh, no, I… Ma'am, I don't know if I'm coming yet. Gwen just brought this up."

Becky's smile immediately creased into a stern frown. "Well, is it true you don't have anywhere else to go? Or is Gwen trying to steal you from someone else?"

"Ma!"

Maggie half considered straight up lying. *It's okay, Ms. Becky. I'm going to my great-uncle's house; I just didn't tell Gwen because he's…part of the mafia?* "No, I don't have anywhere else to go. But I don't want to impose, really."

Becky clicked her tongue. "Now who said anything about imposing? You look like you don't take up much more room than a lap dog. I could fold you up in a full-sized suitcase and stick you in the corner." She waved her hand dismissively. "It's just going to be me and Gwen anyway, honey. We have plenty of room for you. Now I don't want to hear another word against it."

"Yes, ma'am." Usually, Maggie could continue to argue until she was blue in the face, but there was something in the finality of Becky's voice that reminded her of Jess's mom. Something she desperately wanted. She reached into her pocket and ran her fingertips over the enamel pin, a little warmth returning to her chest.

"Do you have any food allergies?" Becky was asking. "I'm not planning on making anything fancy, but I've got time to change things around if need be."

"I, um, I just need things to be kosher."

"Kosher?"

"Maggie's Jewish," Gwen said.

"Oh, that's right, I forgot you told me. Maggie, I don't know anything about Jewish cooking. Would you rather have Chinese food?"

Maggie smiled reassuringly at Gwen, who was looking unusually red in the cheeks. "No, normal Thanksgiving food is fine. I just can't eat meat and dairy at the same time. Like, they can't be in the same dish or the same oven. And the vegetables need to be really clean."

"Ma, we'll help you cook it when we get there," Gwen said. "You'd burn the turkey without me anyway."

That comment appeared to be one step too far. "I'll remind you, young lady," said a stern and tight-lipped Becky, "who exactly taught who how to cook a bird. Sure wasn't you who plucked those feathers off of the chicken when—"

"That was twelve years ago!"

"You hush, child. Don't make me yell at you in front of your friends."

With Becky's attention moved off of her, Maggie took a moment to get back in touch with her surroundings. She looked over at Coral, who seemed to be struggling to keep herself from laughing. But people from the improv group had been walking around them, trying to leave, with their loud conversation ringing off the theater walls. She tapped Gwen on the shoulder. "I think we should head out. They're going to need the theater empty in a bit."

Gwen nodded. "Ma, I'm going to call you back later."

"All right, sweetheart. Maggie, dear, it was nice to finally see you. I can't wait to meet you properly!"

"You too, ma'am."

"Stop ma'am-ing me. You can call me Becky." Her eyes wouldn't take "no" for an answer. "Oh, and it was nice meeting you, Carol, was it?"

"Coral. It was nice seeing you too. Have a good holiday."

"Have a good holiday. Gwen, call me later, okay?"

"Like always. Love you."

"Love you too. Bye, Maggie!"

"Bye!" Maggie waved as Gwen hung up the call. When the screen went black, Gwen's eyes were lined up with hers, practically cheek to cheek. Gwen was beaming. Blushing slightly, Maggie said, "Your mom seems really nice."

"She's my hero, but she's rough around the edges. I'm so sorry about the Chinese food comment. We don't have a lot of Jewish friends."

"I've heard way worse."

Coral cleared her throat. "Maggie, I'm gonna go on ahead if you're going to keep talking with Gwen."

"Oh, no, I'm coming."

"I'll follow you to your stop," Gwen said as she pocketed her phone, and the three walked out of the theater doors. "Maggie, I hope you don't mind, but I'm planning on driving."

"Driving?" Coral asked, aghast. "To Idaho?"

Gwen nodded. "It's a thirteen-hour drive. But I get horribly sick on airplanes, I can't do it."

Maggie furrowed her brows. "In that old station wagon?"

"It'll be fine for the trip. If you can help pay for gas money, that would be appreciated. I know it's not the easiest option, but there's no good train route, and—" Gwen shivered, a bitter look on her face. "My stomach cannot do planes."

Maggie shrugged. "If you were on a plane, I'd probably be hard-pressed to get a ticket on the same flight as you by this point. At least we can both fit in a car."

Coral threw an arm around Maggie's shoulders. "A road trip together? Just the two of you and the wide-open horizon?" She wiggled her eyebrows at Maggie, who raised one in response.

"I'm planning on heading out really early Wednesday morning," Gwen continued. "Would it be okay if I pick you up from your apartment around five a.m.?"

"Yeah, that's fine. Um, I don't mind helping drive, but I haven't driven in over a year."

"And I was planning on doing it alone anyway. This way, I'll have company, and you can take over if I get too tired." She grinned and winked. "Otherwise, you can help keep me awake."

"When will you be back?" Coral asked.

"Saturday night. When are you coming back? You're visiting family too, right?"

"Yeah, I'll be back Sunday. So Maggie, the apartment will be empty." Coral nudged Maggie hard in the ribs, making her stumble a bit, and she shot her a 'the-heck-was-that-for' look.

"It sounds like we have a plan," Gwen said. "Maggie, I know you don't want to be an imposition, but honestly, I'm looking forward to this. You're going to make a long, boring drive much better, and Ma's so excited to meet you. She loves having people over, and we don't get to host much."

"Thank you," Maggie said sincerely as they approached the bus stop. "Anything I can do to help, I will, especially gas money."

"I'd appreciate that." Gwen reached out for a fist-bump, which Maggie gave. "Have a good night, ladies. I'll see you on Wednesday, Maggie."

"Bye, Gwen," Coral called, waving cheerily as Gwen turned and walked away. Then she turned to Maggie, eyes gleaming. "Ooh, this is even better than I hoped."

"I don't know what you're on about," Maggie grumbled. "Why do you keep wiggling your eyebrows at me and stabbing me in the ribs?"

"You, Gwen, alone in the car for thirteen hours? And then she drops you off and you have the apartment all to yourself? And you're meeting her mom?" Coral was practically giggling through her words as the bus pulled up.

"You're crazy," Maggie said flatly as they walked up the steps and swiped their metro cards. "It's what you said earlier. Gwen's paying it forward for past Thanksgivings when she was alone. There's nothing else going on."

"Oh, yes, there is," Coral said confidently, sitting next to her and nudging her again in the ribs, more gently this time. "There most definitely is."

"You're crazy," Maggie repeated.

Coral smiled smugly to herself. Shaking her head at her, Maggie turned to watch the city lights going by. A small smile lingered behind her cheeks, not quite daring to appear.

Chapter Sixteen

MAGGIE WAS A bundle of nerves at five in the morning the day before Thanksgiving. She'd packed a small suitcase with her necessities and gone over her list several times but couldn't shake the feeling she'd forgotten something. Coral, who was leaving for the airport later in the morning, kept trying to calm her down with words of encouragement but couldn't seem to resist needling Maggie.

"You know if you forget something, you could always borrow from Gwen," she said as she chewed on her breakfast.

Maggie groaned and lifted her suitcase. "I'm enough of an intrusion as it is; I don't want to take her stuff on top of it all."

Coral shrugged. "Just have fun, worrywart. Drive safe and have a nice holiday. But when you get back, I want all the deets."

Maggie waved over her shoulder as she left. "Have a good flight. Try not to make friends with the entire plane."

"What else is there to do on a plane?"

Maggie took deep breaths as she walked down the stairs and stepped into the brisk morning air. She folded her arms for warmth and took in the relative quiet of the street. Usually, she only got to see LA in the early morning when she had the opening shift at the coffee shop. Knowing she wasn't going to work but would, instead, spend a personal holiday with her play director and acting tutor gave her the same strange feeling she'd felt the first couple days after moving to the new apartment.

Jess's face flashed to her mind. Maggie shook it away.

Gwen pulled into the parking lot moments later to where Maggie was standing. She got out to open the trunk and put Maggie's suitcase inside. "I am so, so glad you're coming," she said as they got in and buckled up. "I've been up since three, and I'm going to need the support."

Maggie frowned with concern. "Maybe we should plan to switch, like, halfway."

Gwen chuckled. "I mean, it's a thirteen-hour drive, no big deal." She glanced at Maggie and relented. "I promise I'll be honest about how I'm feeling, and we'll pull over if it gets bad. But I'm pretty used to operating on little sleep."

"Sure, but you don't usually have to drive for a whole day, and that gets tiring for people."

"Fair point. It's good I have you to look out for me."

Maggie was glad for the dark to hide another blush. "You're the one looking out for me. I wasn't looking forward to being alone this week."

Gwen nodded. "I can imagine. You ready? Let's hit the road!"

As she pulled out into traffic, a GPS chirped and gave her instructions, gradually leading them to US-101. The silence for the first fifteen minutes was the heaviest, most awkward silence Maggie had ever experienced, at least since leaving her parents' home. She stared out the window, desperate for some witty idea for a conversation starter. Eventually, as they idled in traffic, Gwen was the one who spoke.

"How do you feel about audio books?"

"Oh, um, yeah, I like them. I don't use them much. It's…um, it's faster if I just read them."

Gwen grinned. "I expected as much. But for me, it's way faster if I can listen. I try to get as many books as I can on audio. Doesn't always work for textbooks, but works great for fiction." She pointed to a backpack in the back seat. "Take a look and choose something you like? I checked a ton out of the library. Whatever looked interesting."

Maggie reached back and dragged the bag to the front seat. She unzipped it and was overwhelmed by the number inside. "Holy books, Batman. You got these all out of the library?"

"Well, no, some of those are mine. But I did get a bunch. Those tiny ones with the headphone jack? I have an aux cord in one of the smaller pockets that should work to play them through the car speakers. The rest should be on CD."

"Should be?"

Gwen paused, paying attention to traffic before making a left-hand turn. "Well, some of my audio books at home are on tape cassette."

"No way! You still have those?"

"They're great for books. I can just hit Stop and Play, and it resumes right where it was. Not every CD player does that."

"Where'd you even find something to play them on?"

"The internet, my friend, is a wonderful mistress," Gwen said loftily.

"Go on, pick something you like. I wasn't sure what genres you enjoy, so I tried to get a spread."

Maggie started digging through the books. A tiny bit of shame gnawed at her. Knowing what she did about Gwen's learning disorder, she'd assumed Gwen didn't like books the way she did. Looking at the sheer volume of audio books in the bag definitely disproved her assumption. "What are your favorites?" she asked eagerly.

"I'm a huge mystery fan. Agatha Christie, Sir Doyle, Lillian Jackson Braun…that stuff is my jam."

Maggie started sorting out mystery stories from the other genres in the bag. "Tell me more. Who's your favorite author? Favorite book?"

"Hmmm…that's hard. I think I'd have to go with Christie for my favorite consistently good author, but there isn't anything like a Sherlock Holmes mystery, is there?"

Maggie couldn't find a book for either category in the bag, so she kept looking. "I think my favorite Agatha Christie book is *Death on the Nile.*"

"Really? Not *Murder on the Orient Express?*"

Maggie looked up as they paused again, the GPS encouraging them to turn. "Well, I like that one too, but I think the people in *Death on the Nile* are more interesting. But for both of them, isn't it fascinating to imagine a time when travel could be such a luxury? Lovely teas and servants making your sleeping car beds for you, regardless of your station in life, so long as you could buy a ticket?"

Gwen chuckled. "Would you consider yourself a romantic for the old days, Maggie?"

Maggie laughed as well. "I think being a Jewish lesbian in the 'old days' would be rather difficult for me." She continued searching through the bag, then looked up again. "Well, what got you interested in mysteries in the first place? Were you assigned *Orient Express* in school?"

"Oh, no, that's all my Ma. We used to watch *Murder, She Wrote* reruns together all the time. I absolutely loved it and started looking for books like it. Didn't take me long to find the classics."

"Which do you prefer, famous well-known authors or authors fewer people know about?"

Gwen cocked her head to one side. "I don't worry about that kind of stuff, I guess. Most of what I read is what I can find in audio books. Thankfully, libraries are building their collections. You can even check them out online. But when I was a kid, it was mostly whatever was available. I guess that meant mostly famous authors. What about you?"

"I prefer small authors," Maggie said. "I like to support people who aren't getting as much attention. Those famous people get read and reread every generation."

"That's so thoughtful of you. What about your favorite genre, author, and book? I can ask interrogating questions, too, you know."

Maggie paused. "Honestly…I'm not sure what you call this genre. Slice of life, maybe? Did you ever read anything by Andrew Clements when you were a kid?"

"*Frindle*, right? I thought you weren't a fan of famous authors."

Maggie sniffed. "Just because I prefer smaller authors doesn't mean I ignore good books. Besides, *Frindle* isn't my favorite book by him. I liked *Lunch Money* and *No Talking* way more."

"So, you like books about everyday life?"

"Yeah, I guess. I like books that show everyone can have a story, even without special powers, or murders." She pulled a small audiobook device out of the bag. "This one looks interesting."

"Which one?"

"*On What Grounds* by Cleo Coyle." Maggie turned the device over and read the description on the back. "It's a mystery about a woman who works in a coffee shop. I guess it's the first in a series."

"Oh, that one! Yeah, I just checked that out. I haven't listened to it yet. It reminded me of somebody."

Maggie, who was looking for the aux cord, paused. "Oh? Who would that be?"

"Well, there's this awesome hardworking girl I know who has dreams of acting, but for now, she's a kickass coffee shop barista."

Maggie smiled to herself as she found the cord and plugged it in. "Well, let's take a listen. I bet this character is nothing like the girl you're thinking of."

"Mmmm, maybe not. But I hope that girl likes to talk about books with other people."

*

ON WHAT GROUNDS ended up being eight hours long. For the first chapter or so, Maggie and Gwen had sat back and listened in silence. Eventually, Gwen and Maggie started discussing the book as they listened, sometimes pausing the story for discussion, sometimes talking over yet another paragraph about proper coffee preparation and storage.

When the book was over, Gwen and Maggie finally went through a drive thru for lunch. Maggie was scarfing down her salad when Gwen gestured to the map.

"Hey, I think we're going to pass through a water reservation soon.

Do you mind if we stop to stretch our legs?"

"That's fine. Do you need a nap?"

"Nah, I feel great. Having you to talk to helped. Otherwise, I think that audio book might have lulled me to sleep."

"I didn't think it was that bad."

"Oh, I didn't think it was bad. I mean, it's another hetero romance disguised as a mystery book, but I'm used to those."

Maggie groaned. "No kidding. When I was a teen, I would have done anything to make half of the hetero romance subplots go away. I think I might need a break from audio books. Hearing the same voice in my head for such an extended period, talking about how I should be making coffee definitely messed with my head."

Gwen laughed. "That's fair. What should we do next?"

Maggie, who had spent half of her brain power preparing for this inevitable moment, screwed up her courage and said, "You could tell me about your hometown. I've never been to Idaho before."

"Sure thing. We might not get to see too much of it while we're there since I'm mostly going to be helping Ma around the house. But maybe we can stop by Stage Coach."

"Is that the theater your mom works at?"

"Yeah, I'm sure most people will be at home for the holiday, but we might catch Daryl or somebody working on fixing it up for the winter show season."

"I'd love to see it. Has your mom always worked there?"

"As long as I've been alive. Before that, I think she worked mostly retail jobs."

"She sounds like a hard worker. I can see where you got it from."

"I take that as a huge compliment, thank you," Gwen said. "Ma's my hero. It's never been easy, but she's always kept her head up and encouraged me to do the same. When I was starting to struggle in school, she's the one who pushed for me to get testing. I was in third grade when they figured out I had my learning disorder. But she never let that be an excuse, you know? It was like, now we knew what the problem was, we're going to move forward and keep working hard. She used to help read parts of my textbooks and homework problems to me, even though she was so busy."

Maggie gazed at the road in front of them, unfamiliar horizons stretching for miles. "She sounds amazing. I can't wait to meet her."

Gwen cleared her throat. "She's a good person, but she doesn't know a lot about the world. She grew up in Boise, and she doesn't plan on living anywhere else. She loves everybody but has some old-fashioned ideas."

Maggie chuckled grimly. "Oh, don't worry. I don't think she's going to be much compared to my folks."

"Mmm. I see your point." Gwen glanced over at Maggie, who pretended not to notice. Looking back at the road, she continued. "Well, to be more specific, we're actually from a little town called Eagle. It's close to Boise, where Ma works. When I was really little, we lived in an apartment close to the theater, but Ma eventually bought a trailer in Eagle when I was seven, and she's stayed there since. It's a pretty nice neighborhood, but with Ma's work schedule being the way it is, we never got close to any of the neighbors."

"So who was your friend group at school?"

"I had some friends I got along with in class, but I didn't get to hang out with people much," Gwen mused. "I'm still in touch with a couple on Facebook. I was closest with Jacob; we still talk sometimes. He has a single mom, too, but she worked in the childcare center in town."

She shrugged. "It's hard to hang out when you don't really have much free time. I'd go to school, then go with Ma to the Stage Coach to do my homework while she worked. When I was old enough, I got a weekend job at the bowling alley nearby, and we'd do double shifts together. Sometimes afterward, we'd get some fast food and go home to watch more *Murder, She Wrote* reruns."

"Wow…" Maggie propped her head on her knees, curled up to her chest and pulling against the seatbelt. "So you've always been this hard-working. It sounds like you really didn't have a lot of time to, well, do anything fun."

Gwen shook her head. "I don't want to make it sound like all I did was school and work. I wasn't in any clubs or anything just because I couldn't afford the extra time or fees. But I had a ton of free time at the theater. That's where I started learning what I know now. I was ten years old the first time Daryl let me up into the catwalk to see how the lights work. And Marcie used to pay me some pocket money for helping do things like put inserts into playbills, or stamp tickets, or help at the concession stand if they were really busy. I got to learn all the different ins and outs of running a theater from them. I couldn't have asked for better teachers."

Maggie grinned. "I get it. You grew up in the theater, and now you can't get yourself to leave it."

Gwen laughed out loud, eyes alight. "Who would want to leave it? You must feel the same way."

"You're right, I do." Maggie stretched her legs out again, curling her toes in her sneakers, before reaching down to rub her calves. "But I didn't have mentors the same way you did. I just did acting. I didn't learn all the stuff about how to make the theater run."

"Surely there must have been somebody who influenced you."

Maggie thought for a moment. "At the community theater, a lot of the people involved in the productions I was in were volunteers, and everyone was a volunteer for my school musicals. I didn't really get to know the theater employees themselves. But I did have a lot of friends at school who were in musicals with me, and some of them were in the community theater too. Oh, but there was Mrs. Whaite!"

"Who was Mrs. Whaite?"

"She was the conductor, anytime we had live music for a performance. The musicians tended to change over time, but I'm pretty sure Mrs. Whaite was immortal because she was there every single year and didn't age a day. She used to coach us in our vocal warm-ups, and if I got there early enough, she would let me practice my lines in front of her. She's the sweetest lady ever. She told me when I'm a movie star, I should send her my autograph so she can retire."

Gwen laughed. "She sounds like a very caring woman. More like a fan than an instructor though."

Maggie nodded. "Yeah…I guess I had a handful of instructors over the years but not a lot of consistent people. They were all talented though, and I learned a lot from them."

"Hmmm." Gwen was quiet for a moment. Maggie watched her fingers drumming on the steering wheel, quietly tapping the same rhythm Gwen tapped on her lips when deep in thought. After a moment, she spoke again. "It really seems like when you moved to LA, you moved there with almost nothing but the clothes on your back."

"Yeah. I mean, I had a small bank account my family started for me.

I'm pretty sure my grandparents bought some bonds for me when I was a baby, but my parents have those. I couldn't cash them before I left, so I'll probably never get them now. I basically closed my bank account, took about nine hundred bucks with me, and…" Maggie shrugged. "Never went back, I guess. Jess's parents helped set us up with the apartment, paid our security deposit for us."

"Your ex's parents?"

"Yeah."

Gwen went quiet again.

After a moment, Maggie spoke up, trying to sound chipper. "I think I did pretty well for myself. I got a job quickly, never went into the red. I'm actually at a point where I can buy food from a real grocery store now, not just whatever the dollar store has. And now, I'm in a real theater production about a year later!"

"Maggie," Gwen cut in gently, "you keep saying how hardworking I am, but you're just as hardworking yourself. It takes real guts to stick to your dreams after rejection the way you have. I hope you know I deeply respect you for that." She smiled. "I feel like we've said about everything nice there is to say about our hometowns."

Maggie chuckled nervously. "I guess just about."

"Tell you what. Let's pull over at the next truck stop, stretch our legs for a bit, and choose another audio book to get us the rest of the way. Maybe something having to do with moving out of a small hometown to make it in the big city?"

"Do you have a book in mind?"

"I can't remember what it's called, but I know it's in there some-where."

Maggie started looking through the audio books again. "What made you decide to move to LA? Why didn't you stay with the Stage Coach?"

"Honestly, I was tempted. I really love it there. When I was a kid, I told people that was where I was going to work. Ma's the one who made me go, really. She made me apply to every college she could find that did theater majors. Told me she didn't work her ass off for me to settle for small dreams." Gwen's expression became contemplative. "And then, once I was in LA, it was like I found home away from home. Everything I loved about Stage Coach and inner-city Boise, multiplied and glamorized. And, well, I met people I really grew to care about."

"Do you think you'll stay in LA when you graduate?"

"Definitely, if I can get a job. If not, I'll come back to Stage Coach. But I think I'm in LA to stay."

Maggie smiled to herself. She pulled out *Big Lies in a Small Town* by Diane Chamberlain. "This one looks interesting. It's about thirteen hours though."

"Let's finish it on the way back, then. Put it on."

Chapter Seventeen

BECKY KNOWLES'S HOUSE was a single trailer with sun-faded green siding, white window shutters, a tin roof, and a giant rustic star hanging on a shed at the head of the driveway. A sedan with a dent in one corner was parked near the front door. Gwen pulled her station wagon in behind it and honked the horn before she got out.

Becky opened the door, quickly descended the stairs, and wrapped Gwen in a hug. Gwen was a foot or more taller than her mother, but that didn't seem to stop Becky from enveloping her in her arms. "Oh, there's my girl," she said softly.

"Happy Thanksgiving, Ma," Gwen said, patting her on the shoulder. She pulled away and gestured to Maggie to come closer. "Ma, here's Maggie in the flesh, as promised. Maggie, my Ma. She doesn't bite."

Becky reached out to shake Maggie's hand. "Nice to meet you in person, dear. I hope the drive wasn't hard on you girls?"

Maggie shook her head. "We listened to books pretty much the whole time."

Becky smacked Gwen on the shoulder playfully. "You forced her into that, didn't you, bookworm?"

"Ma! She likes books too. I promise!"

Becky took Maggie's suitcase as Gwen opened the trunk of the car. "I apologize for Gwen. She's hopeless at keeping up conversation."

"Not at all," Maggie protested. "We talked about the books the whole time. It took us way longer to listen to them that way, but it was definitely more fun."

Becky ushered Maggie toward the door. "Well, I have a quick dinner waiting for you. I imagine you must be exhausted. I hope you like mac and cheese?"

"Yes, ma'am, I do," Maggie enthused, carrying in the backpack full of audio books. Gwen, who had another backpack filled with her clothes, led the way into the house.

They entered a combined kitchen, dining area, and living space. There appeared to be two bedrooms, one on each side of the house. The inside was decorated with a style Maggie was tempted to call "country meets city." Rustic and patriotic touches were scattered throughout—a stars-and-stripes banner here, a small cow figurine there. But everything inside was a little too streamlined to be completely rural in nature. Maggie recognized the dining set as something she'd seen in a catalog multiple years in a row when she was younger. Everything appeared to be well-loved, from the faded quilt on the back of the couch to the worn path in the carpet. What Maggie adored was the color. Each corner of the room, each surface, had some small pop of color in it. Nothing outlandish or neon, but enough to make it bright and cheerful. Maggie spied a tiny rainbow flag stuck next to a tiny American flag in a shot glass next to the TV.

"Set your things down in Gwen's room, then come wash your hands and eat," Becky was saying. She'd already taken Maggie's suitcase to the back room and returned to retrieve the mac and cheese from the oven. "Maggie, Gwen's already decided you can take the bed, and she's sleeping on the couch."

"Oh, Gwen, I couldn't possibly take your bed," Maggie protested as she set the audio books down. "This is your room."

"And the couch is super comfy," Gwen said. "Ask Mom. I used to sleep there all the time."

"She used to fall asleep watching TV," Becky confirmed.

"You look way too tall for it though," Maggie said, eyeing the furniture. It had three cushions, but was not nearly as long as Gwen was.

Gwen went to wash her hands in the kitchen. "I hang my feet off the edge. If it bothers you that much, we can swap tomorrow night. How's that?"

"I'll think about it," Maggie said, following Becky's gestures and washing her hands in the bathroom.

Before long, they were all seated, drinks poured, and food served. Just as she was about to take a bite, Becky cleared her throat.

"Maggie, um, do you want to say grace?"

Gwen looked bemused, but Maggie caught on.

"Oh, I'm used to eating without praying. Don't worry about me."

The stern look Maggie had seen on Becky's face the week before was back. "We might not be very religious here, but I won't be disrespectful to your practices while you're my guest. Please, feel free."

Maggie felt a blush spreading across her cheeks. The truth was, she hadn't recited a *brachah* since she'd left home over a year ago. Gene and Darren recited the prayers at Shabbat each week. Maggie gazed down at her food and concentrated as hard as she possibly could. After a few seconds, she felt words come back to her, like her feet finding their way on the pedals of a bike she'd left forgotten in the garage.

"*Barukh atah Adonai E…Eloheinu melech ha'olam*, um, *ha'olam… shehakol nihyah bed'varo.*" She searched her memory, realized she could not reliably remember any more *brachot*, and decided God would forgive her for half of a prayer. She looked up to see Becky and Gwen watching her expectantly. "Um, amen," she added.

"Well," Becky said as Gwen started shoveling mac and cheese in her mouth, "that was a beautiful prayer. What language was that?"

"Hebrew, Ma," Gwen said through her mouthful. "Jews speak Hebrew."

"Yeah," Maggie agreed. "Um, the prayer I said means 'Blessed are you, God, our Lord, Ruler of the world…' and, I think, 'Everything was created through His words.' Sometimes I forget the exact translation."

"Well, it's very lovely. I'm glad you shared it with us." Becky turned to Gwen. "And don't talk with your mouth full, young lady." Gwen rolled her eyes, then ducked as Becky swatted at her with a spoon. "Disrespect, young lady! I tell you, you send your kids out into the world and they come back all high and mighty with themselves." She clucked her tongue comically, as Gwen grinned mischievously. "Now, ladies, tell me all about this play you've been working on. Maggie, I'd love to hear about your part. Gwen tells me you're very talented."

The three ladies continued to sit and talk long after they had put their forks down and reclined in their chairs. It was almost nine o'clock when Becky finally stood up and reached to take the empty casserole dish from the table.

"Well, girls, it's about time to be getting myself ready for bed. I don't care how long you stay up so long as you respect my rest, please."

"Of course, Ma. What time do you want to start cooking tomorrow?"

"I'd like to have everyone seated at two o'clock for our big dinner. People can pick at the leftovers for supper. So, I'm getting up at eight. I have everything in the fridge."

"I'll get up with you, then." Gwen rose as well. "Let me help with the dishes, Ma."

"You wash, I'll dry."

Maggie stood up. "I'd like to help too."

Becky looked like she was going to protest but then thought differently about it. "Actually, if you dry the dishes, I'll get the sheets for the couch. Thank you, dear." Becky went to a small closet and retrieved a set of full-size sheets. "Gwen, do you want a blanket?"

"Two, please. It's a lot colder here than in LA."

"Fair point. Maggie, I'll make sure you have an extra blanket on Gwen's bed, okay?"

Maggie took the dishcloth hanging from the oven handle and stood by Gwen's side, watching her fill the sink with soapy water. "Thank you, ma'am."

"It's Becky, dear." Becky started covering the cushions of the couch with the fitted sheet, tucking it into the crevices. "Gwen, remember when I used to make the couch like this for you when you were sick?"

"Man, sick days were the best." Gwen handed Maggie a clean cup.

"Reading Rainbow, Cyberchase, napping whenever you felt like it…"

"Cleaning your vomit out of your hair."

Gwen pulled a face as Maggie giggled. "Sick days were the only days I was allowed to drink ginger ale," she said as she dried off a glass and set it on the table. "Supposedly, the carbonation is good for upset stomachs."

"So is ginger," Becky added.

"Remember the time I was sick with the stomach flu for a week, and Daryl drove all the way over to give me ginger tea?" Gwen asked.

"Do I ever! We were very lucky that Marcie and the rest of the crew were so understanding, I was allowed to stay home for every sick day."

Maggie continued to dry dishes until Becky had finished transforming the couch into a makeshift bed, complete with a pillow and extra blankets.

Becky then went to retrieve a blanket for Maggie. In the closet she exclaimed, "Oh, Gwen, look what I found." She pulled out a brightly colored fuzzy bundle. "It's your Care Bear blanket."

"Oh, God, Ma, put that back."

"Gwen used to *love* Care Bears," Becky said, a glint in her eye. She unfurled the blanket to show Maggie the larger-than-life pastel bears printed on the fleece. "At one time her whole room was decorated in these fuzzy butts."

"I love it," Maggie said immediately. "Is it warm?"

"It's super warm," Becky said, handing it to her. "You'll sleep like a baby."

"Ma, don't make her sleep in that."

"I want to," Maggie said firmly, hugging the blanket to her chest. "If that's okay with you, Gwen."

Gwen paused, then shrugged. She turned to the sink to drain the water. "It's fine by me if it's fine by you."

Each of the ladies said their good nights, took their turns in the bathroom, and separated for bed. Maggie closed the door to Gwen's bedroom behind her and took a deep breath, alone for the first time all day. She gazed around the room, drinking in every detail. It looked like teenage Gwen could walk through the door at any moment. Pictures of her and her mother lined the walls and shelves. There were sporadic spaces between the decorations, suggesting objects Gwen had taken with her when she moved out. A hand-colored pride flag hung over a tiny desk and chair. A bright red-and-blue plaid comforter covered the twin-sized bed, with a couple teddy bears settled on the pillow. The center focus of the room was a colorful bulletin board hanging over the headboard, covered in playbills for performances from the Stage Coach, the oldest from seventeen years ago.

Maggie gently moved the teddy bears to the top of the small corner dresser, pulled back the blankets, and slid under the sheets. She smiled at the Care Bears blanket at the foot of her bed, folded and ready to be pulled over her if needed. Lying down, she closed her eyes and pushed away memories of past years. She ran her fingers along the cloth of the comforter, made softer by years of use, and encouraged herself to bask in the warmth of the welcome she'd received that evening.

*

THE NEXT DAY passed surprisingly uneventfully. Gwen and Becky had both shooed Maggie away from the kitchen when she tried to help, insisting guests did not cook. They did ask her, however, to stay nearby and provide instructions on keeping the meal kosher. Maggie sat in one of the kitchen chairs and divided her attention between kosher food advice and keeping the cooks informed about the football game on TV. In the end, the food was delicious, the Chicago Bears won, and Becky had nearly depleted her store of embarrassing stories about Gwen's childhood to make Maggie laugh.

Maggie and Gwen agreed to take turns sleeping on the couch, so after eating some pie for supper and watching reruns of *Murder, She Wrote*, it was Maggie who situated herself to sleep on the couch.

"Look, it is a comfy couch," Gwen said. "But if you get cold, we can always switch. The front door has a bit of a draft sometimes."

"I'll be just fine with these." Maggie pointed to her pile of blankets—which included the Care Bear one. "Go on; you deserve to sleep in your own bed."

"All right, then." Gwen said, slowly closing her bedroom door. "Good night, Maggie. Sleep tight."

"Good night, Gwen," Maggie answered.

It was a comfortable couch, but Maggie didn't fall asleep quite as quickly as she had the night before. Perhaps it was the seconds of pie she'd eaten less than an hour earlier. Just as she was starting to drift off, she heard Becky's door creak open. To her surprise, Becky walked out, throwing a coat on over her pajamas. She cracked the front door open, then glanced over at Maggie.

"Hey, dear, want to join me?"

"Sure," Maggie whispered back. Burning with curiosity, she got up and slipped on a spare coat Becky handed to her. She slipped her feet into her sneakers by the front door and stepped out with Becky into the cold air.

Becky led her to the shed, where she quietly retrieved two folding lawn chairs. She set them up and pointed a finger in the air as if testing the wind. "You better sit by the shed." She took the other seat herself and pulled a pack of cigarettes and a lighter out of her coat pocket. "I told Gwen I quit a couple years ago, and I would hate for her to know I've backslid a bit."

"I won't tell her," Maggie said.

"Thank you." Becky inhaled deeply, then sat back and exhaled slowly. She dangled the cigarette from her fingers off the edge of the lawn chair arm. "Bet you can't see the stars like this out in LA, can you?"

Maggie looked up, letting her eyes adjust until hundreds of pinpoints of light popped into view. "You really can't. It's so beautiful out here."

"That it is." Becky took another drag of her cigarette and exhaled slowly again. "I like you a lot, dear. Definitely a lot more than the last girl she introduced me to. That bitch has a lot to answer for." She looked over at Maggie. "I don't suppose you know who I'm talking about?" Maggie shook her head. Becky looked back at the stars. "Well, I'm not gonna tell you if Gwen hasn't. It's her choice, telling people those kinds of things. And, well, you have the same choice too. But if you don't mind me saying, I get the feeling you and I could relate in a lot of ways."

"I hope so. I've really enjoyed my time here. You're a very kind hostess."

"Well thank you, dear, but that's not quite what I meant. Now, Maggie, I know you're Jewish and all. But it seems like something mighta happened with you and your church. You seemed a little hesitant about praying over the food yesterday and today."

"My parents are really conservative Jews," Maggie admitted. "And when I moved out, I kinda fell out of practice. I have some new friends I'm praying with though."

Becky nodded. "I'm right glad to hear that. It's a terrible thing to lose your church." She tapped the ash off of her cigarette. "I hope you don't mind me getting a bit personal, but I reckon Gwen hasn't told you a lot about us—except for anything having to do with the Stage Coach."

"She talks about the theater all the time."

"Well, that theater's about all the family we've got." Becky blew her smoke away from Maggie and cleared her throat. "I got pregnant at seventeen. I've got an idea who the father was, but I didn't want to be saddled with him, so I never really put in the effort to get him involved or confirm it was him. My parents were pretty strict Christians, so I got thrown out right on my ass."

She took another inhale before continuing. "Marcie took me in. Gave me a job, helped me get a place to stay. The first couple years, the theater practically raised Gwen. They'd take turns watching her so I could work. Only family we ever needed." She smiled grimly. "Gwen does look like her father though. All that height and those shoulders."

"I think she looks just like you. I can see it in the face and the way you hold yourself."

Becky chuckled. "She used to follow me around the theater and copy whatever I was doing. They called her my little twin." She tapped off more ashes. "I'm not telling you all this to look for pity. I just know Gwen can be a little secretive about herself, and I thought you deserve to know…Gwen's been through a lot more than she lets on. When she was twelve, I had to go to the hospital. Lung disease, thought it was cancer for a while. The doctor said my smoking caused it. I was in there for a couple months before

I could come home, then I couldn't work for a while."

"That must have been so scary for you."

"That girl," Becky continued, pointing to Gwen's bedroom window, "she didn't tell a single person at school what was going on. The administration knew because she was staying at Marcie's while all this was happening. But teachers and classmates had no idea. When I showed up at school a couple months later to pick her up, her English teacher asked me if I had changed job shifts again." She shook her head. "When I asked her about it, she just said she didn't want people to treat her any differently. Didn't want teachers to give her extended time for her assignments or anything; didn't want kids feeling sorry for her. She said she wanted to focus on her schoolwork and be on her best behavior until I came home. Her grades barely took a hit, thanks to Marcie and the crew's help."

"You raised an amazing young woman."

"Hmm, I did, didn't I?" Becky stretched in her chair, then relaxed again. "So, you're just friends with my girl, now?"

"Um, yes, ma'am, just friends," Maggie said, blushing furiously.

"Most of Gwen's friends aren't straight. Do you mind me asking…?"

"Um, no, I'm not straight. I'm a lesbian. Gwen's one of the first people I ever came out to."

"Well, let me say this," Becky said, giving Maggie a big smile. "She talks about you all the time."

"R-really?"

"We call nightly, and she mentions you a lot. You and all the actors in the play, but I know she spends extra time with you."

"She's helping me study acting."

"She says you're a lot of fun to work with. All I'm saying, Maggie, is thank you for being a good friend to my girl. She's made a lot more friends in LA than she did here. Just found the right crowd, I guess. But I'm glad you're one of them."

Maggie's blush calmed itself to a gentle heat in her cheeks. "Thank you. I'm so grateful to have a friend like her."

"Mmm." Becky exhaled again, long and slow, before reaching into her pocket and pulling out what appeared to be a tiny handmade Play-Doh ashtray. Becky put out her cigarette, stood up, entered the shed, and threw the butt out in the trash. She returned to Maggie and offered her a hand to stand. As they put their chairs away and headed back inside, Becky said quietly, "Take good care of my girl, Maggie."

"I promise, Becky."

Chapter Eighteen

THE FOLLOWING DAY, Gwen and Maggie hopped in the station wagon to go meet with members of the Stage Coach team in Boise. Gwen offered to take Becky, but she declined.

"I see those people every day. I don't want to have to see them on my day off too. Go have fun, and maybe I'll take a nap…or a bubble bath!"

Maggie loved the drive into Boise. While certainly smaller than LA, it was still exciting to see the skyline approaching, backed by a gorgeous mountain view. The city was replete with trees and open spaces, splattering it with autumn colors from the changing leaves. Even in places where the leaves had already fallen, the rivers of branches punctuating the streets gave a lovely feeling that nature and urban development had found a way to live together in peace.

"I wanted to meet up with everybody to do something fun," Gwen said as they drove through traffic. "But almost everything that isn't a retail store is closed today. So we're just meeting for pizza."

"I like pizza."

"Is pizza kosher?"

"Pretty much if I get it without meat toppings."

"What does 'pretty much' mean?"

Maggie quirked her mouth to one side. "Well, honestly, not a lot of restaurants or fast-food places have options that count as traditionally kosher. Kosher rules are really strict, and there's a whole system in place for getting your food and products certified as kosher."

"Wait, really?"

"Yeah, you can find kosher labels on products in grocery stores. But most places don't worry about following all of the rules, or even if they might qualify, they don't bother getting themselves kosher certified. So, like, cheese or veggie pizza is probably kosher, but it probably hasn't been certified as kosher. That stereotype your mom mentioned about Chinese food?"

"Ugh, that was so embarrassing. I'm so sorry."

"No, don't worry about it. I told you I've heard way worse. The reason why that stereotype is there is because a lot of Chinese food actually meets our kosher requirements. Not all of it, and it's certainly not traditional, but it works."

Gwen glanced at her as they paused at a red light. "So, should we try to find a kosher pizza place?"

"Don't worry about it. I, um, bend the rules a little sometimes. There's some stuff I stick to. But sometimes, I just tell myself it's close enough. Like frozen chicken nuggets—the ones we buy aren't kosher, but I justify it by not putting cheese on them or anything."

"If you don't mind me asking…I don't mean any judgment, I've just never thought about this. Why is kosher food important? At least, to you? It feels like that's the one thing you've stuck to all this time."

Maggie nodded. "Part of it might be habit. I'm a lot less strict about it than my parents were. But honestly, when you've grown up kosher, you don't even think about it. It's no different than a lifelong vegetarian not being interested in meat, I guess. And part of it is…I guess I broke a lot of God's rules. Most of them. But this was something I felt confident I could follow without screwing up."

Gwen looked at Maggie with concern. "Maggie, I hope you don't see yourself as a screw up. Those guys we met at the party, they don't seem to see you as a screw up at all."

"Gene and Darren? Yeah, they're nice. I'm starting to observe more, again. They make me feel like I can be a Jewish lesbian."

"Good," Gwen said firmly. "I can't think of anything worse than feeling like God made you the way you are just to punish you for being that way."

Maggie nodded. "I'm kind of jealous of you. Having such a supportive mom and everything."

"I'm lucky," Gwen acknowledged. "It wasn't just Ma. Wait until you meet everybody; you'll see what I mean."

They pulled into the parking lot for a family-owned pizzeria, a gathering of people just inside the door.

"They're already here!" Gwen said with excitement.

They had the attention of the room from the moment they opened the door. The group gathered around the entrance swept Gwen up into their arms, passing her around from hug to hug. Maggie was shocked to be swept up as well. Gwen spoke up over the chorus of greetings to be heard.

"Maggie, if these wild animals can calm down long enough, I'd like to introduce you. Daryl, don't hug her that tight. She doesn't even know you yet!"

The muscular, heavily tattooed arms wrapped around Maggie let her free. "Look at our Gwen, getting all bossy," said the red-bearded man.

"Sounds just like you, Henri," a lithe, gray-haired man joked while nudging a brunette in the ribs.

"Hush, Bart, or I'll have you repaint the old parlor set," the brunette replied, the crow's feet around her eyes crinkling.

As the group moved toward a table and loudly communicated with an amused but slightly overwhelmed young waiter, Gwen introduced them to Maggie one by one. Marcie, a woman with black hair cut into a shockingly angular bob, was the theater owner. Daryl, the bald man with a red beard and tattooed arms, was the lighting engineer. Henrietta, or Henri for short, was the stage manager, and wore a set of platform boots that almost brought her to the same height as Maggie. Bart, the gray-haired set designer and carpenter, wore a vest and pocket watch over a T-shirt and jeans. Also making up the group: a composer, conductor, and musical director named Garth; a stocky but soft-spoken audio engineer, Iggy; and a costume designer, Lilly, who was, aside from Gwen, the youngest of the group.

"Everyone wanted to come," Marcie said as they finally took their seats, "but a lot of them are out of town for the holiday or have their own families to host."

"I completely understand," Gwen stated, taking a seat next to Maggie. "I'm so happy I get to see you guys!"

"Not nearly as happy as we are to see you," Lilly said. "It's been, what, four years? Maybe more?"

"Four since she's seen you," Bart interjected. "I haven't seen her since she left for college six years ago."

"Oh God, has it been that long?" Garth murmured.

"Well, just look at how grown up she is now," Henri pointed out.

"I see my old car is still serving you well." Darcie nodded to the station wagon parked outside.

"I think it still has five years left in it," Gwen answered.

Daryl, sitting on Maggie's other side, said, "Tell us all about what you're doing now. You're still in school?"

"Your ma says you're directing a play?" Iggy added.

"I am," Gwen said, "to both of those."

"When are you finally going to graduate and come take Henri's job, then?" Bart chuckled.

"Henri's going to be stage manager forever." Gwen laughed. "When I retire, I'll move back up here to watch from the audience, and she'll still be yelling at actors to get their crap together."

"I can retire when actors learn to leave the goddamn prop table alone," Henri muttered.

"What's the play you're directing?" Iggy asked again.

"We can tell you about it together," Gwen said. "Maggie is one of the starring actresses."

Everyone at the table exclaimed interest.

"Maggie, is that how you met Gwen?" Marcie inquired.

"Actually, we met at improv group," Maggie said shyly. "I'm not really a professional like Gwen is."

"Maggie doesn't give herself enough credit," Gwen exclaimed. "She's been working as an actress for the past year or so. She just thinks being an extra and small parts don't count or something."

The group tittered. "Young lady," barked Garth, "we have all been in your position. Before I got this job, I did everything from bussing tables to repairing guitar strings."

"If you keep pushing to do what you love, you're no less a professional than the rest of us," Lilly added. "How old are you, anyway? You don't look a day over twenty."

"I'm nineteen."

"You see?" Lilly continued. "Nineteen and already has a starring role in a professional stage play. That's nothing to sneeze at."

"She's so good too," Gwen cut in. "You should see her sometime. I knew I wanted to work with her from the first day we met. We were doing this improv activity, something about bakeries…"

"You came up with the activity," Maggie added helpfully. "You had a problem with trying to buy donuts for group, so you told us to pretend we were customers and employees at a coffee shop where the customer asks for something the employee can't provide."

"Right! Right, and most of us all did what you would expect."

"Act like a Karen?" Lilly asked.

"Yeah, like an entitled customer," Gwen agreed. "But Maggie gets up, and the other person playing the cashier asks what she wants, and Maggie says she'll take a coffee, a muffin, and the guy's phone number." The group laughed in surprise. "And the poor guy tries to play it off as, oh, we're out of muffins, but Maggie didn't drop the phone number request. She proceeded to hit on this poor boy relentlessly for two straight minutes."

"Two minutes of improv?" Henri asked.

"Yes," Gwen affirmed, "and she was seamless. It was like she sexually harassed men with clever, creepy one-liners every day."

"Everyone else did two minutes too," Maggie interjected.

"I'm sure they're also talented people," Garth said reassuringly. "Other people's accomplishments don't minimize your own though."

"And it doesn't sound like they all stood out to Gwen the way you did," Marcie suggested.

"It was just such a unique take on the prompt," Gwen said. "And then at a later meeting, she and I did an activity together where we had to pretend we were on a Ferris wheel and make people guess where we were, based on our actions. How do you think she did it?"

People around the group shrugged.

"Talked about all the stuff you could see as you were going up?" Daryl asked.

"We did a little," Maggie said. "But we pretended Gwen was afraid of heights and described the motion a lot."

"Ooh, I like that," said Bart. "I hate heights, but I used to go up on Ferris wheels with my daughters all the time."

"She's a smart one you have here." Henri gestured at Maggie approvingly.

Maggie hid her blushing face in her hands. "Stop it, please. I surrender," she moaned as the group laughed.

"We'll take the focus off you for a little bit if you talk with us about this play you're in," Daryl promised her. "What's it like having Gwen as a director?"

Maggie opened her hands and took a deep breath to clear her blush. "She's great to work for. She's even giving me some extra time and attention to teach me acting theory since I haven't gone to college."

Marcie nodded with a smile. "That's our Gwen, all right. She could never just leave things 'just fine.' She's always polishing something or someone."

"A great eye for potential and the perseverance to develop it," Henri contemplated. "That's what directors do."

"Remember when she helped me rewire the whole lighting system in the catwalks so there were fewer tripping hazards?" Daryl asked.

"And she would let actors practice their lines with her all the time when it wasn't their turn to rehearse on stage," Garth added. "I remember when we were doing *A Christmas Carol*, and she challenged our Scrooge and his understudy to try to out-Scrooge each other."

"Oh, and the time she spent her free hours for two weeks helping us finish the costumes for *Henry VIII*," Lilly recalled.

"Guys, stop it," Gwen protested. "That's just what theater people do; you taught me that. Besides, Maggie could honestly do the studying without me. She's a natural. And she loves books. You should see how fast she can read."

"That's certainly useful," Marcie agreed. "But it sounds like she appreciates your help, Gwen."

"I really do," Maggie said. "Gwen's been more than just a good tutor and a director. She's one of my first true friends since I moved to LA." Maggie's mind flashed to their conversation at the LGBT Center fundraiser party. "I feel like I can be myself around her."

Daryl reached over and put his arm around Maggie's shoulders. "You can be yourself around us too. Any friend of Gwen's is a friend of ours."

"Well, any friend that treats her well," Garth cut in.

"Guys, Maggie's great," Gwen said. "She's one of the most hardworking people you'll ever meet."

"Gwen, I'm still waiting to hear about this play you're directing," Iggy interjected.

The group laughed. "We keep getting off topic!" Lilly said. "We're just so excited to share all of our Gwen stories with one of her new friends."

"Please, let's not do that," Gwen begged. "I'll tell you about the play. We have a local playwright named Haleigh Johnson. Marcie, you would love her; she's such a spitfire."

As Gwen explained the plot of the play to the group, with Maggie providing extra details and answering questions, Maggie felt herself relaxing more. She could see clearly how loving and accepting this theater family was of their adoptive daughter, but it was something more that was warming her heart.

She glanced over at Gwen, blonde hair brushed behind her ears, green eyes alight with excitement as she passionately discussed her directive decisions with these men and women she greatly respected. There was something about Gwen, something about the way she treated everyone in the room as though they were the most important person she could possibly spend her time with. Not just here, but everywhere—during tutoring, during the haunted house job, during play rehearsal, during improv group. It was as though Gwen were a bonfire, and everyone could light their torches in her flames without her burning out.

Suddenly, Gwen turned back to Maggie. "I've had more to be excited about this year than I've had in a long time. I hope we're going to keep working together after this play is over." In that moment, it hit Maggie. She, too, wanted to keep working with Gwen. Wanted to keep seeing Gwen.

Wanted to keep those Wednesdays in the library, just the two of them. Wanted to keep Gwen's viridescent eyes looking at her. Wanted to keep seeing her brilliant smile each day.

Maggie realized, heart dropping into her stomach so fast it made her lightheaded, that she could no longer ignore her massive crush on Gwen Knowles.

Chapter Nineteen

LOOKING BACK ON it, Maggie wasn't sure how she got through the rest of that Friday or the whole drive back to LA on Saturday. Somehow, she managed to keep her head on her shoulders and her blushing to a minimum. Becky was a huge help, and also audio books. They kept her mind focused on the positives and helped her push her confused feelings to the back of her mind until she exited the car at her apartment building.

"Hey," Gwen called through the car window as she prepared to drive away. "I'm really glad you came. This was so much more fun than it would have been by myself."

"Oh, no, thank you," Maggie replied. "I had a wonderful time meeting your family. It was way better than Thanksgiving solo."

Gwen grinned. "Well, I'll see you for rehearsal on Tuesday."

"See you then. Bye!"

They waved to each other as Maggie unlocked the door and went inside, telling herself it was the warmth in the apartment lobby flushing her cheeks.

As she unpacked her suitcase, Maggie tried to unpack her feelings. At the very least, she wanted to have more emotional control before Coral came home and teased her. Maggie tossed her dirty clothes into her hamper and told herself, *I just broke up with my girlfriend of about four years not that long ago. I'm not ready to date again, everything still hurts.*

She put her toiletries back in the bathroom and reasoned, *Gwen is kind of like my boss right now, as director of the play and my acting tutor. It's not professional to date your boss.*

Maggie put her suitcase away in the closet and decided firmly, *It's just a crush. I won't let it get in the way of my work. We can be very good friends. One day, I'll meet someone new who pushes her and Jess out of my mind.*

By the time Coral returned home, Maggie had settled her thoughts and, mostly, her feelings.

*

ON TUESDAY, MAGGIE spent the entire bus ride to rehearsal lecturing herself for being too excited to see Gwen. Part of her had spent the past two days wanting to text Gwen. She missed the conversations they'd had in the car. Three times, she'd picked up her phone, only to put it back down, telling herself if they hadn't texted frequently before Thanksgiving, there was no reason for her to start now. But Tuesday morning, she couldn't help herself anymore. In a rush of adrenaline, she had texted:

Finally rehearsal again today! Can't wait to get started again.

She then buried her phone under her pillow while she got ready for work. When she checked it again, to her shock there was a reply:

I'm so excited! See you there!

Once Maggie actually arrived, she was too busy to notice the way Gwen's eyes made her spine tingle—well, almost. At the door, Maggie was greeted by Georgia and Bel, who eagerly shared their stories about their Thanksgivings before diving into practicing their lines. Most of her lines were sharp in her memory, but Maggie appreciated the opportunity to refresh herself after a week off. Once Gwen and Haleigh arrived, Gwen spent the majority of her time with Skylar, Alyssa, and Donna, strengthening the parts of the play where the conservative women communicated with the mayor's wife. Maggie focused on her scenes with Georgia and Bel, with Haleigh helping with line memorization.

Rehearsal was over in the blink of an eye. As the ladies put on sweaters and coats, Georgia approached Maggie.

"I never asked, dear, how was your Thanksgiving?"

"Oh, it was really nice," Maggie said vaguely.

"Did you get to go see your family?" Georgia asked innocently.

Just as Maggie was working up her nerve to lie, Gwen dropped in.

"Actually, Maggie kept me company, and we drove up to see my mom."

"Oh, really," Georgia said, and Maggie could see Bel and Skylar look over, seemingly interested. "Where is your family, Gwen?"

"My ma lives in Idaho. Maggie even met part of the local theater crew I used to learn with." Gwen led the way out of the rehearsal room. "We drove, so Maggie kept me awake and entertained the whole ride."

"I, um, I wasn't able to go home this year," Maggie said, seeing Georgia was still following her. "So, Gwen's mom invited me to stay with them for the holiday."

"How kind of your mother," Georgia said sweetly.

"Yeah, she's the best," Gwen agreed. "Good night, Georgia." As the older woman waved and walked away, Gwen turned to Maggie and said softly, "I hope it's okay I cut in like that."

"That was a big help. Thank you."

"Can I walk you to your bus stop? I got so used to having conversations with you that it's been strange not talking to you the past couple days."

Maggie felt a jolt of warmth straight from her heart to her ears, a blush spreading everywhere in between. She mentally coached herself to breathe, relax, anything to make the blush calm down. "I don't want to take you out of your way getting home. But, yeah, it's been kind of weird not talking to you as much."

"Well, if I can't walk you to your bus, at least text me more often," Gwen said. "We're friends, remember? I want to know all about whatever books you're reading in your spare time."

"I actually don't read as much as I used to anymore. I'm really bad at making time for it."

"See, that's another reason to love audio books. You can put them on while you're doing stuff and listen. I have an audio book on every time I cook or I'm doing laundry."

"That's a great idea. I just tend to put music on or get caught up in my thoughts."

"Sometimes we just need to give our thoughts a break though. What kind of music do you listen to?"

"I know it's kind of cheesy, but I love musicals."

"As expected of a musical theater actress. Do you have a favorite right now?"

"Oh," said Maggie, getting excited, "I've been listening to *Hadestown* on repeat. It's so beautiful. I've never heard a musical that sounds like it."

"I don't think I've heard of that one."

"Do you know the myth of Eurydice and Orpheus?"

"That sounds Greek, but off the top of my head, I don't remember."

"The guy who goes into the Underworld to get his dead girlfriend, but Hades tells him he can't look behind him before he gets back to the surface world, and when he looks behind him, Eurydice gets sucked back into the Underworld."

"Oh! Yes. I do know that one. It's based on that story?"

"It is, but it combines it with folk and blues. It takes a melodrama and makes it the most heartbreaking story."

"That sounds gorgeous. I'd love to listen to it."

"What music do you like?"

"Hmm…I think the music I listen to the most is alternative rock. I guess there's a part of me that never grew out of being a teenager."

"Like…Coldplay?"

"Well, I listen to them too. But my ma and I love Blink-182."

"Well, of course, they're classic."

"Really, any music that makes me feel good, I throw on my playlist." Gwen smiled. "Well, it looks like I got to walk you to your stop anyway."

Maggie looked up with surprise, realizing she'd not only fallen into conversation with Gwen, but also into step with her, and they'd found their way to the bus stop. Maggie smiled sheepishly as the bus pulled up. "I'm sorry. I said I wasn't going to take you out of your way."

"You didn't. Talking with you is never out of my way." Gwen smiled and waved as Maggie boarded the bus. "Text me!"

"You got it!" Maggie hastily paid and sat in her seat, watching Gwen walk down the street and trying to hide the silly smile plastered on her cheeks.

*

MAGGIE AND GWEN did text, in part to discuss music, in part to confirm they were meeting for tutoring again the next morning. As Maggie woke and prepared for the day, she felt the same silly smile on her lips. As she was brushing her teeth, she received a text from Gwen:

I think 8am classes might be thdeath of me

Maggie chuckled and replied, *So don't sign up for one next semester.*

I have to its what lets me have a work schedule

Well, I can bring you a coffee when we meet?

Dont worry about it. Just getting to hand out will brighten my morning. Plus talking about acting there and thplay with you is way more interesting the this lecture. Ps sorry about mistakes. Cant use spechtotext in class

Maggie chose a warm pair of jeans but a cool, flowy purple top to balance the chill of the morning air against the warmth of the California sun in the afternoon. There was a part of her that couldn't help wondering what Gwen's favorite color was and if Maggie had any clothes in that color. Shaking the thought from her head, she packed her backpack with the borrowed textbooks and headed out into the morning.

She and Gwen exchanged a few more texts as she rode the bus to campus. Soon, Maggie stood in front of the beautiful fountain, scrolling through a playlist of Gwen's suggested songs. When she saw Gwen, she couldn't help but smile. The lime-green spaghetti strap top over jeans, in addition to her blonde hair and height, made her stand out a mile.

Gwen came straight toward her, rolling her eyes dramatically. "At last, freedom," she declared, setting down her bag and stretching. "I *hate* lectures."

"They definitely don't sound fun. But you made it."

"I did. And my reward is hanging out with you." Gwen put her bag back on her shoulders, then turned to the side and offered Maggie her elbow. "Shall we?"

Giggling, Maggie put her arm through Gwen's. She lifted her nose in the air. "Lead the way, m'lady." The two of them laughed and strode into the library together, arm in arm.

Today, Gwen was introducing Maggie to Michael Chekhov, the developer of an acting theory Gwen called the "psycho-physical approach."

"Chekhov went into acting in the decades after Freud had become popular and made psychology a household topic of discussion," Gwen explained, opening a book to Chekhov's grainy black-and-white photo. "And, amongst other things, Freud was famous for discussing the idea of the unconscious. Freud believed that many of our actions are heavily influenced by unconscious beliefs, desires, fears, and impulses. Chekhov wanted to connect that unconsciousness to our bodies by—"

"Hey, Gwen?"

Gwen looked up, surprised, as a young man approached their table. "Hey, James, what's up?"

He jerked his thumb toward the entrance to the study room. "Somebody outside said Dr. Lowell is looking for you. I told her I'd let you know if I saw you."

"Dr. Lowell is looking for me outside?"

"That's what it sounded like. Somewhere near the career center, I guess."

Gwen stood, looking perplexed. "I don't see why he wouldn't just email me. I'll be right back, Maggie. If I look around but don't see him, I'll just email him later."

"No worries," Maggie said, giving a small wave as Gwen walked away. She turned herself to the book and was immersed in studying Chekhov in moments.

She didn't hear or see anything behind her before she felt something poking at her back.

A familiar voice whispered before she could look up, "Don't move and don't react. We're going to talk, you and I."

Next to Maggie, the chair scraped against the floor, and a figure with long black hair sat down. She wore athleisure clothing, her chin came to a fine point, and she had piercing blue eyes. Her right arm stretched around Maggie, resting on the back of her chair, her hand clasping Maggie's shoulder. In her left hand, her fingers were curved around a pocket knife, pointing it straight at Maggie's side under the edge of the table.

Maggie sat very still.

"Now," said Valerie Harker in a low voice, "I don't know if you're reckless or stupid, but either way, you clearly don't know how to make a smart decision. I gave you multiple chances, kept an eye on you. And honestly, I was starting to think you were going to keep things professional with Gwen. But clearly, you just couldn't help yourself."

For a split second, Maggie had the horrified thought that Valerie could read her mind. She dismissed that thought and took a deep breath. "We are keeping it professional. Gwen's teaching me—"

"Do you think I'm as stupid as you are?" Valerie snapped. "You call

Thanksgiving dinner with her mom professional?"

Maggie's breath caught in her throat. Before she could think of a response, Valerie pressed on.

"Now, since you're clearly too infantile to think for yourself, I'm going to make this easy for you. I'm going to be right here in the library, watching you, to make sure you don't screw this up. When Gwen comes back, break up with her. Tell her things are over between you for good."

"We're not dating. I can't break up with her if we're not dating."

"You think you can lie to me?" Valerie sneered in contempt, the first emotion besides anger Maggie had ever seen on her face. "You think you can outsmart me, keep Gwen all to yourself. But which one of us arranged this little meeting? You, or me and my little reminder to keep your mouth shut?" She slid the knife across Maggie's shirt. "I have you all figured out, Maggie Fromm. You think that if you make yourself a pity case, play the shy little slut, Gwen will sweep you off your feet and rescue you. And Gwen, poor Gwen, she would fall for it too. She's not so good at making decisions either."

The knife went back to its place, firmly pointed at Maggie's waist. "You and I both know you don't deserve her. So just end this. Tell her it's over. Break her heart like you were going to later. Do it now, then leave the library and don't come back. Then I'll leave you be."

Maggie eyed the knife carefully. "If you hurt me with that, Gwen will come back and see it."

Valerie shrugged. "You attacked me. I had to defend myself."

Maggie's brows furrowed. There was no way Valerie could actually think that was a plausible excuse. She debated about calling her bluff, standing up and getting the attention of the room. She looked around to see who else was nearby.

Suddenly, there was a stinging pain in her side. Gasping, her hands flew to cover her waist. Valerie clucked her tongue, showing the pinprick of blood on the tip of her knife.

"I don't have to kill you to hurt you, you know," she said. "So don't go getting any clever ideas in that empty little head of yours. Break up with Gwen Knowles, and this will all be over."

"Fine, just go," Maggie hissed. She lifted her hands to see she had only received a small scratch and a slight rip in her shirt. She glared at Valerie. "Just leave me alone."

Valerie smiled, then pointed at the book on the table. "Be a good little girl and read. No peeking." When Maggie turned her eyes to the pages, Valerie stood and moved away, somewhere behind her.

In the next few moments, Maggie's mind raced. If she got up now and left, what could Valerie really do to stop her? She started to reach for her bag, determined to go find Gwen and tell her what was happening. Before she could, Gwen returned, striding past the study tables with a confused, slightly annoyed look on her face.

"Couldn't find him anywhere," she said as she approached. "I'll email him later. Where were we?"

Maggie stood, keeping her voice low. "We should leave. Try to look sad about it."

Gwen's brows only creased further. "Why should we leave? I'll talk with him later. If it was important, he'd have come and found me."

Maggie shook her head. "It's not your professor. It's Valerie Harker. She wants me to break things off with you and leave you alone."

Gwen's face went still and then white. She whispered, "Where is she?"

"Somewhere in here. Watching to make sure I do it."

Gwen reached into her pocket and pulled out her phone. "I'm contacting Public Safety. I can message them on the LiveSafe app."

Maggie hoisted her backpack onto her shoulders. "I really think we should leave the library."

Gwen nodded. "Yes…let's."

Maggie noticed how slowly Gwen's fingers were moving on her keyboard. "Here, I can type it out," she said, reaching for the phone. "Let's just start walking."

Gwen paused, then handed her the phone. "Tell them there's a person on campus threatening a student and her colleague at the Doheny Memorial Library."

Maggie nodded. As she and Gwen took their things and left the room, she quickly typed the message, adding that Valerie had a knife. She handed the phone back to Gwen, and they picked up their pace.

Gwen and Maggie stepped into the blaring sun but felt none of its warmth. As Maggie squinted into the sudden light, Gwen asked her, "Where do you want to go? Do you want to stay together, or do you want to head home?"

"I'm staying with you," Maggie said firmly.

"Then let's head to the Public Safety office. It's about ten minutes away."

Maggie opened her mouth, about to say some encouraging words, when she heard a cry behind her.

"Don't run away from me, Gwen Knowles."

Maggie was about to turn around, but Gwen gripped her arm tightly and lengthened her stride.

"Just keep walking," she said in a low voice. "As soon as you acknowledge her, you lose."

Maggie nodded, placed her hand over Gwen's, and hurried to keep up. She tried to think of something, anything she could say.

"Don't you fucking ignore me," Valerie yelled from behind. "You have no right to treat me like this, Gwen."

Maggie glanced at Gwen. Her face was white as a sheet, and her lips were drawn tight. They left the courtyard and the fountain behind them, weaving their way between brick buildings. With each corner, Maggie had the vain hope Valerie would choose to fall back and let them go. But as they stepped out into the main road, students and faculty occasionally driving and walking around them, she heard one voice raise itself again and again above the noise. The few people on the street were starting to look up in confusion and curiosity as they passed, eyes glued to a rapidly approaching figure behind them. Maggie heard Gwen curse under her breath.

"Let go of her, you slut!"

Maggie couldn't stop herself. She whipped around to look just as Valerie closed the distance between them. As they made eye contact, Valerie reached out and grabbed Maggie's wrist, yanking her out of Gwen's grip. Maggie cried out in pain as Valerie's fingernails dug into her skin.

Gwen immediately stopped and spun in her tracks, her hands raised in a protective stance. "Let her go, Val," she said, her voice still low and calm.

"Typical," Valerie spat. "You care more about a fling than you do about me."

In the blink of an eye, Gwen moved in. She grabbed Maggie's arm and hand, twisting Valerie's grip on her until her thumb was skyward, then yanked Maggie's arm down and out of the grip. As Maggie grunted from the sting, Gwen pushed her back, putting herself between Maggie and Valerie. "Keep going to the Public Safety office," she said. "It's at the intersection, next to—"

Valerie's hands snapped into place around Gwen's throat. Maggie screamed. Gwen, unnervingly calm, hunched up her shoulders and spun, breaking herself out of Valerie's grip. Gwen and Maggie leapt farther away and began moving backward down the street, trying to keep their distance from Valerie. At this point, the few passers-by on the street were watching closely.

"Hey, what are you trying to do?" someone called.

Valerie and Gwen didn't seem to hear them.

Maggie looked around desperately. "Call Public Safety, please," she begged.

"What's going on?" asked another voice.

"I don't know. We were just studying when—"

"Is that what you call it?" Valerie interrupted. "Studying? You two had no right to be so fucking indecent in the library."

"Don't listen to her, Maggie," Gwen said. "Keep getting to Public Safety."

"Should we call someone?" asked yet another voice. Some people were moving away. Some hadn't stopped to watch at all.

"Maggie, get out your phone," Gwen said calmly. "Dial two one three, sev—"

"You have no right to act like the victim, Gwen," Valerie snapped, speeding up to close the distance.

Gwen attempted to leap back, but Valerie gripped her by the shirt front. As she held on with one white-knuckled fist, she reached into her hoodie and pulled out the pocketknife. Gwen's eyes widened, and suddenly, she began to struggle. All her composure from a moment before was gone.

"You're the one who made it come to this," Valerie continued. She brought the knifepoint to Gwen's nose. "You ruined us, Gwen. You ruined me. Do you ever stop to think about the amount of pain you left me in?"

Maggie hastily pulled out her phone. She fumbled with the screen, trying to search for the phone number for Public Safety, praying it would be online.

"You made me feel like a monster," Valerie said. "All those horrible accusations. What were you trying to do? Slander me?"

Gwen strained to tear Valerie's hand off her shirt, but couldn't loosen her grip. She dropped her bag on the ground and bent her knees, seemingly to wiggle out of her shirt, but Valerie pulled her in closer and held the knife to her throat.

"If you want my forgiveness, you're going to have to beg me for it," Valerie hissed. "And I'm going to expect you to make some major changes. No more dating behind my back, no more prostituting yourself. I expect some dedication this time."

Maggie held her phone to her ear, hands shaking, breath shallow as it rang. She begged God, *Make me move. Make me do something. Something more than just dialing the phone like a helpless child…*

Valerie pulled Gwen so close that they stood nose to nose. She moved the knife edge carefully up and down Gwen's neck. Suddenly, Gwen's arms went limp and tears began to flood down her cheeks.

Valerie smiled. "Just say you're sorry, blondie."

Gwen sobbed.

Before anyone answered Maggie's phone, a white car peeled down the road. She had just enough time to recognize the university logo on the doors before two men in Public Safety uniforms jumped out of the car.

"Drop the knife!" one of them yelled, reaching for his belt.

Valerie released Gwen and ran. One of the men ran after her, yelling directions to stop and drop the weapon. Maggie rushed to Gwen and, holding her steady, lowered her to sit on the sidewalk. Gwen looked back and forth between Maggie and the remaining Public Safety officer, buried her face in her hands, and wept. She wept and wept until Maggie thought she would cough up her lungs.

Chapter Twenty

MAGGIE AND GWEN drove back to Public Safety in the car with the officer. After a brief discussion, the officer who had pursued Valerie Harker radioed in to inform them he'd lost her. At that time, they agreed to be driven to the police station to give statements. They spoke with separate officers in separate rooms. Maggie tried to give as much detail as she could possibly remember, and the officer helped her apply a bandage to the scratch on her waist.

When they were done and reunited in the lobby, Gwen urged her to go home. "I'm going to stay here for a while. Please, go and try to relax."

Maggie stood firm. "I'm not leaving until you do. Then I'm making sure you get home safely."

Gwen looked at her with weary eyes. "Maggie, I'm… I need try to file restraining order paperwork. I'll have to go to the courthouse to drop it off and everything. This will take a while."

"I won't let you be alone."

"I won't be. I'll call somebody. You should go home."

"Gwen." Maggie reached out, hesitantly at first, then took Gwen's hand in hers. "If you look me in the eyes and tell me you would rather do this alone and you genuinely want me to leave, I'll respect that. But if you're just worrying about me, forget about it. I'm happy to stay with you while you deal with this."

Gwen didn't look at her, but she put her other hand on top of Maggie's.

One of the officers nearby glanced up from her work. "Miss Fromm, we're going to call in an advocate and counselor to help support Miss Knowles. She won't be alone in this process. And they'd be happy to speak with you too. You've been through a traumatic moment."

Maggie peeked back at Gwen.

Gwen gave her a half-hearted smile. "They work with Caleb. You can trust them."

"Oh." Maggie chewed on her lip. "I don't think I need to speak to a counselor. I just…"

Gwen nodded understandingly. "You have a lot of questions. I owe you an explanation. But, Maggie, I don't think I can do it right now." She gripped Maggie's hand between both of hers. "Please, go home. And I promise, you and I will talk later. I'll call you."

"You promise?"

"Calling will be easier anyway. My text-to-speech function on my phone is great, but…"

Maggie nodded. "Okay. But you have to call."

"I promise." Gwen stood up, removing her hands, and excused

herself to the restroom.

Maggie checked that the officers were done with her, declined the invitation to speak with a counselor, and left the station with her hand wrapped around her phone in her pocket.

*

CORAL, ALMOST AS white in the face as Gwen had been, kept surprisingly quiet as Maggie explained to her where she'd been all day. When Maggie was done, Coral was momentarily silent, gripping one of the dining chairs tightly. "Well…" she finally said. "I'm glad we did call the police that one time."

Maggie nodded from her seat on the couch. "They pulled up my report and asked me about it while I was talking to them today."

Coral stood quietly for a few more minutes, then said, "Mom gave me a box of hot chocolate. I think I'm going to make some. Would you like a mug?"

"That'd be nice, thank you."

Coral set a kettle on the stove and opened the cardboard box of individual cocoa packets. "Maggie, is it safe for you to go to rehearsal tomorrow?"

"I'm going to talk to Gwen when she calls."

"What about work?"

Maggie thought for a moment. "I think it's safe if I'm not near Gwen."

"Mmm."

After a few minutes' pause, as Coral continued to prepare the chocolate, Maggie asked, "How well do you know Gwen?"

"Not very well. I think you two are closer, by this point. We met a couple years ago and move in the same circles, but we haven't spent a lot of time together. I'd like to," Coral added. "It just never really happened."

"Do you know if she ever dated anyone?"

Coral picked up the kettle. "Right around the time I met her, I think she was in a relationship. But her partner never came to anything I was involved in, not even the LGBT-plus meetups. Honestly, I never paid that close attention." She peeked at Maggie over her shoulder as she stirred the cocoa. "But someone's paying close attention to her. And you."

Maggie didn't reply. Coral brought her a mug of hot chocolate and sat next to her on the couch. They drank together for a moment. Maggie breathed deeply as the warmth spread from her mouth to her stomach, then slowly warmed her core. She cupped the mug as though it was a cold winter morning.

Both girls startled as Maggie's phone buzzed, indicating a text. She picked it up hastily. It was from Gwen.

They found her. Will call soon. Heading home now.

Maggie breathed a sigh of relief. She texted a reply quickly:

Stay safe.

Slumping back against the couch, she closed her eyes. "They found Valerie."

"Oh, good," Coral said bitterly. "I hope they lock her up."

Maggie shuddered. "Gwen said she would try to get a restraining order."

Coral laughed. "I don't think a crazy bitch is going to listen to a restraining order."

After a pause, she leaned back with Maggie, allowing Maggie to rest her head on her shoulder. "Tomorrow in the morning before you go to work, maybe we can call your boss, just so she's aware."

Maggie nodded. "The big guy, Tom, he should be working tomorrow on my shift."

"Good. And we should get you a self-defense weapon."

Maggie scoffed. "I don't think it'll do any good. I'll just freeze like I did this time." She groaned, lifting from Coral's shoulder and hiding her face behind the mug in her hands. "I was completely useless. I could have grabbed her, or kicked her, or—"

"Stop that kind of talk, Maggie," Coral said sharply. She reached over and lowered Maggie's mug. "You found the number for Public Safety and called them. Thankfully, they were on their way; someone else must have called too. But you didn't know that, so you were doing the only thing you could do."

Maggie's voice was hollow. "You didn't see her face, Coral. She looked...broken. Defenseless. And I did nothing."

"You did everything you could have. If you had tried to fight, you could have gotten hurt, and Gwen would never have forgiven herself for that." Coral rubbed Maggie's shoulder gently. "You didn't run away, you didn't freeze, you did what you could do that was safe. You're not expected to endanger yourself in those kinds of situations, Maggie. I know Gwen would tell you that too."

"She did it for me. She jumped in and saved me when Valerie grabbed me."

"Well, that was a grab, not a knife." Coral pulled over her laptop from where they had left it a few movie nights before. "Look, let's throw on something funny to watch while you wait for her to call, okay? I think you need to process with her. I can't make you feel better, but I can help pass the time."

"You do make me feel better." Maggie gave Coral a side hug and took another sip of hot chocolate. "I hope Gwen has someone with her."

*

GWEN CALLED ABOUT forty-five minutes later. Coral paused the *MST3K* episode on her laptop as Maggie excused herself to her bedroom. Closing the door behind her, she answered the phone and sat on her bed.

"Hey, Gwen. Are you okay?"

There was a pause. "No. No, I'm not okay. Are you?"

"Um…I mean, I'm safe. Coral's taking care of me."

"Good. That's all that matters." There was another pause. "I suppose I owe you an explanation."

"You don't owe me anything, Gwen," Maggie said firmly. "I can tell there's a complicated history between you and her. It's your decision what to tell me. You can tell me everything or nothing; it doesn't matter. I just want to know you're going to be safe."

Gwen paused again. When she spoke, her voice sounded heavier than it had before. "I think I want to tell you. But I don't want to burden you with it. It's not exactly a happy story."

"You listened to me talk about my parents, remember? And I'm sure if I'd told you more, if I'd wanted to keep talking about it, you would have let me and supported me." Maggie lay back on her bed. "I can listen as much as you want me to. We can talk about books if you want. We can stay on the phone and say nothing. But I'm here, Gwen."

"I…but…I mean, you lived through something really frightening today, Maggie. You need support too."

"I do," Maggie admitted. "I'm still not sure how to process it. But I don't think it's impacting me the same way it impacted you."

"I don't want you to pretend to be fine for my sake."

"I promise I'm not pretending anything. I was definitely scared. I'm pretty shook up. But I don't...I don't feel like I'm in danger. I feel like it might be hard to sleep tonight, but I'm going to be okay. Kind of like…like last year. There was a time I was on the Metro, and this car veered into our lane, and I thought there was going to be a terrible crash. The car ended up scraping another car's bumper, and it was a bad day, but no one got hurt. I was kinda freaked out when I got on the bus the next day, but over time, it got better. This feels like that, a little."

There was another pause. "You're a stronger person than I am, Maggie."

"I don't think I am," Maggie protested. "I think I'm responding differently because I don't have the same history as you do with her. It means different things to us."

"You might be feeling okay right now, but you might not feel okay tomorrow. And I don't want to unload all of my crap onto you to deal with on top of that."

"Like I said, it's your choice what you tell me. But I'm not going to be 'dealing with your crap.' I'm going to be supporting you. And if I need time or space to deal with my own stuff, I'll tell you."

"You promise?"

"Cross my heart."

For the next few moments, Maggie and Gwen just breathed. Maggie closed her eyes, focusing on Gwen's presence on the phone.

"Okay," said Gwen finally. "I guess…I guess it started when I moved to LA, when I was nineteen.

"I met Val at USC. She was a couple years ahead of me in the theater department. We started dating pretty quickly. I think I moved too fast, in the whole relationship, really. I hadn't ever really been paid attention to like that before. She used to do these spontaneous romantic gestures. Like, show up after class with flowers. She wrote me little love letters for a while. And, well, no one had ever made me feel like that. I was smitten. It wasn't hard to keep falling deeper into love with her. Over time, we were more and more entwined. When she graduated, I moved in with her to save money. We were together for over four years.

"I didn't see the red flags right away. They always start as small things. Excusable things, mistakes. She'd get frustrated, yell a couple words. She'd beg me for forgiveness, and I'd tell her not to worry about it; it's not a big deal. But when I moved in with her, it got weirder. Suddenly everything I did seemed suspicious to her. She had to know where I was and who I was with every minute of the day. When I'd tell her it wasn't necessary, she'd flare up at me. I've…I've learned a lot about domestic violence since then, and looking back now, I can see all the signs. But at the time…I just thought, this must be what love is like.

"And then when I realized it wasn't love, it was unhealthy…I remember begging her to go with me to counseling. USC has a counseling center. We could go there; it wouldn't cost us. Or she could choose a counselor of her own. And she'd keep saying she'd do it, but there were always these excuses to avoid it. We fell into this horrible pattern. Something would go wrong—I'd say something she didn't like, or she'd have a bad day at work and quit again, or something—and she'd yell and scream until she collapsed on the floor, crying, and I'd comfort her and put her to bed, and we'd wake up and pretend it never happened. And I just kept encouraging her. Let's go to counseling. We can fix this together. That's what adults in love do."

Maggie felt a lump in her throat. "I understand that feeling. I really do."

"Yeah… Well, we never did end up going to counseling. And looking back on it now, I know it's because she never was going to. All the yelling and crying, the flowers and the love notes, that was all to keep me where she wanted me. And…Maggie, it was like a drug. It would suck so, so bad when she was upset and screaming at me, telling me all these things about me. But when it was over, and we were sleeping next to each other? It was like a high. We were safe, we were still together, and I'd made her feel better in the end. If I hadn't been there to help her, I thought, she would have cried alone and hurt herself. I thought I was being such a good girlfriend. I was standing by her side through everything. It felt like I was proving I was the best partner in the world."

Gwen paused, seemingly lost in her thoughts.

After a moment, Maggie asked quietly, "Why aren't you dating anymore? Did you leave?"

"I'm not sure, sometimes, if I left or if we just combusted," Gwen answered. "I never really made the conscious choice to leave. But I knew something had to change. The last year we were together, I'd just turned twenty-four, and it didn't feel like we were in love anymore. I still loved her, very much, but it didn't feel like we were *in* love. In the years before, I told myself we were done with the honeymoon phase. But by the end, I knew things weren't okay. She wouldn't go to counseling, with or without me. She was monitoring where I was every minute of every day, and I had no close friends. She'd stopped pretending to try to keep down a job, and I was paying for everything. Anytime I tried to have a conversation with her about fixing things, that cycle would happen. I would try to tell her something she'd done had hurt my feelings, and by the end of the conversation, I was apologizing for making her feel bad. But the worst part was…she never showed me affection anymore. I had to earn touches, pats on the head. Sometimes, if I did something spectacular, she would hug me. But usually not."

"Oh, Gwen…that's so unfair to you."

"Well, no one said abuse was fair to anyone. I'm sure to anyone who could have looked into our apartment and seen what was going on, it would have been so obvious I needed to leave. But even when I knew it was bad, I didn't want to go. I still loved her. It's not like the abuse erased everything I'd liked about her to begin with. And besides, every time I tried to change the status quo, she'd get so nasty. It wasn't safe for me to leave, at least not on my own. I don't know if you're aware of this, but the most dangerous part of any domestic violent relationship is when the victim tries to leave."

"Really?"

"Because when the abuser loses the object of their control…well, they have nothing left to lose. 'If I can't have you, no one will.' That kind of thing."

"Oh my God."

"So I stayed, and I kept hoping if I was good enough, she'd see how devoted I was to her, and she'd get help, and it would be okay. Like…not that my love would fix her, but it would make her want to fix herself."

"That makes sense."

"Pff, no it doesn't. Why would my love make her want to fix

anything? She had everything exactly the way she wanted it. All that yelling and crying that was stressful to me was her normal. She was thriving."

Gwen took a deep breath and let it out in a slow exhale. "Eventually, she crossed the line though. One day, I told her I was going to go see a play at the university I'd helped build sets for. She had all these different reasons why I shouldn't go. I should be spending my time with her, I never make time for our relationship anymore, yadda yadda. I told her we could have a date night the next night, but I was going, no matter what. Didn't leave campus after class, just stayed until showtime. She showed up at the university and dragged me out of my seat in front of everybody."

"Holy crap."

"After she got me outside, she took out that damn pocket knife and cut off all my hair."

"Holy crap!"

"Told me she wasn't going to make it easy for me to go on dates without her. By the time Public Safety was there, most of it was gone. I had a couple scratches on my neck. They were bleeding pretty dramatically, but I wasn't actually hurt…it just looked a right mess."

Maggie's mind flashed to the look on Gwen's face when Valerie had shown her the knife on campus. "What happened then?"

"Oh, God, so much happened. One of my classmates let me stay in her dorm for a couple days. I called Ma, and she freaked out. Drove all the way to LA that night, brought Daryl with her. They were furious. Daryl went to the apartment with me and the cops and demanded all of my stuff. I got most of it back. Some of it was ripped and cut to shreds."

"And what happened to Val?"

"As far as I know? Nothing. I didn't press charges, didn't get a restraining order or anything. I just wanted out. I was tired. Val kept calling and texting and emailing me for a while, saying I had ruined her reputation, that everyone was treating her like a monster because I was going around lying about her. I spent the next couple weeks changing all of my contact information—number, email, everything. Eventually, I didn't hear anything until a classmate told me she'd left town."

"Why was she blaming you? You didn't do anything."

"I know. You have to understand. An abuser doesn't work on logic; they work on control and feelings. Like, on the one hand, she'd accuse me of sleeping around behind her back. On the other hand…" Gwen snickered. "She used to tell me I had fat arms, and my shoulders were manly. Said most lesbians wouldn't be interested in me because I looked too much like a dude. Too tall and muscular, I guess. I stopped working out for a while."

"She said you had fat arms? Was she blind?"

That made Gwen laugh. "I think she was picking up on a few insecurities I had from when I was younger. She encouraged me to wear long sleeves as often as possible; she said I looked better that way."

"I have never seen you wear long sleeves. Wait, no, once—the play audition."

"I will when winter hits. I'm not immune to the cold. But, yeah, it's kind of a stubborn point of pride for me now. I hope every time she stalked me and saw me showing off my arms it pissed her off."

After they both chuckled, Gwen continued, her voice sounding a little lighter than it had before. "See, I can laugh about that kind of stuff now. Because looking back on it, a lot of the things she used to nitpick or try to manipulate were really silly. They worked because I wanted to make her happy so badly."

"She didn't deserve your love." Maggie flushed, realizing the words had left her mouth.

"You're sweet, Maggie. I believe everyone deserves love… She wasn't ready for it. And I still think, if she decides to change her behavior, she could have a healthy relationship. But to do that, she has to let me go. Accept what she did was wrong, and accept that the consequence is we can't be together anymore because she hurt me too badly."

"It doesn't seem like she's accepted any of that, does it?"

"Not exactly. And, I mean, I knew it would take time. I did a lot to try to remove myself from her life. Ma and Marcie gave me the money for a security deposit on the safest apartment complex I could find in the city. It has number lock codes instead of keys; there's a guard in the lobby 24-7; there's an alarm system, everything."

"That sounds perfect."

"It's great, but it's pretty pricey. I can't live in it forever."

"Has she been stalking you since then?"

"I have no idea when she started actively stalking me. It couldn't have been too hard. I still have USC classes, so that was a good starting point. And she's always been pretty sneaky. Used to sneak up on me and scare me for laughs."

"Doesn't seem so funny now."

"Wasn't funny then either."

In the next pause, Maggie turned her thoughts over in her head, finally deciding on whether or not to ask about something she'd been wondering about for some time. "Gwen, I have a question. You don't have to answer if you don't want to."

"Fire away."

"Is all this how you got involved with Peace Over Violence?"

Gwen chuckled again. "You're clever, Miss Fromm. Yes, this is how I got involved with them. The counselor from USC recommended them. I've been engaged with them ever since. Well, as much as I can be as a broke, working student."

Maggie shook her head slightly. "You're amazing, Gwen. If I was in your place, I'd have gone back to Idaho. You chose to stay here, finish your education, and use your creativity to spread awareness about…about everything you survived."

"I'm not amazing," Gwen insisted. "I'm just stubborn. I'd been working on college classes full-time and part-time for over four years at that point. I wasn't going to give it up because my ex couldn't handle a breakup. And, I mean…I love Stage Coach. I always will. But LA is my home now. I'm building a group of friends again. I'm not about to let her run me out of this city."

"So what are you going to do now? With the play and everything?"

"Oh, I don't plan on stopping," Gwen declared. "The police filed an emergency protection order, and the judge is reviewing my request for a restraining order. I'm going to have to go to court in a couple weeks, but the EPO covers me for now. But, Maggie, I should be asking you the same question."

"I don't think I'm the one Valerie's actually after. I don't think I need a restraining order."

"Personally, I think it would be a good idea for you, but I won't press you on it. I meant, do you feel safe continuing in the play? And with tutoring?"

"You're willing to keep tutoring me?"

"Well, not in the library. I'm not going to feel safe there for a while," Gwen admitted. "I'm going to have to think of a new plan. But I don't want to give up on our work together, unless you feel it's best for your safety."

"No way. I'm seeing this through. Valerie Harker has no right to take any of this away from either of us. Besides, if I'm with you, then I get covered by your restraining order," Maggie added jokingly.

"Safer together than apart, eh?" Gwen laughed. "Listen, I really admire your dedication to the work. I really do. But promise me you're not going to neglect your emotional health or your safety over this."

"I feel like we've made a bunch of promises to each other tonight," Maggie said, grinning. "But I promise. I'll tell you if it's getting too much."

"Good." There was another pause. "I don't really know how to end this call."

They burst into nervous giggles. "Let's talk about something else, something random," Maggie suggested.

"Anytime we're in a conversation, we lose track of time," Gwen pointed out.

"Well, let's just talk until we're tired, then," Maggie said with forced confidence.

"That could be a long time, Miss Fromm."

Maggie reached over and turned off her bedside lamp. "I've got all night, Miss Knowles."

Chapter Twenty-One

THE NEXT DAY at rehearsal, Gwen arrived with Caleb Hughes. He was supposedly there to oversee the play's production, but Maggie had the sneaking suspicion Peace Over Violence representatives and other friends would be appearing regularly from now on for more than just production oversight. Her suspicions were strengthened when she noticed Caleb periodically but randomly getting up from his chair and walking around, peering into various crevices and empty spaces in the room, then leaving, seemingly to scope out the hallway.

Gwen and Haleigh also announced they would be moving rehearsals to a new location and would text or call the cast directly to inform them of where to go once a place had been chosen. When Bel asked why, Haleigh stated the university needed the room for other projects. The cast accepted this answer. Maggie was happy to learn, when Gwen texted her later, that rehearsals had been moved to a community center closer to her side of town.

Gwen and Maggie had an unspoken agreement to keep their distance more during rehearsals. Maggie didn't mind because when it was over, they resumed text conversations and sometimes calls to give Gwen a break from her speech-to-text function. At one point, when Maggie apologized for taking up Gwen's time, Gwen brushed it off saying, "These conversations are keeping me sane. They keep me grounded when I'm in my apartment, so I don't feel so alone."

"I thought that's what your audio books were for?"

"Those haven't been as helpful recently. I'm considering adopting a dog though."

Maggie, who was washing dishes with Gwen on speakerphone during this conversation, paused her scrubbing with a big smile on her face. "You are? That's so exciting."

"It is. I've never had a pet, but this complex allows dogs, and it would make Ma feel safer."

"Oh, I never asked. How did she take it when you told her about what happened at the library?"

"She wanted to drive down here again. I barely managed to convince her not to. When she found out Val wasn't incarcerated—"

"Wait, they didn't keep her?" Maggie asked, shocked.

"No. I am pursuing charges, but with the EPO and temporary restraining order granted, and because she wasn't determined a flight risk, she's still out." Gwen didn't sound bitter, just tired. "I have court for the restraining order in a couple weeks. My guess is you'll get a notice about the assault court appearance sometime around then, and they'll schedule it for a couple months after that."

"Why on earth is it taking so long?" Maggie asked, her face flushed with irritation.

"That's how courts work. They're slow to respond because they're already dealing with backlogs of cases all the time."

Maggie shook her head in frustration and continued scrubbing. "So your mom thinks a dog is a good idea? I agree with her."

"I mean, I've always wanted one," Gwen said, "I figured I was too busy. Plus, vet bills and stuff. But recent jobs have been paying well, and I think I figured out a good walk schedule so the dog isn't always stuck inside."

"Are you going to get a trained guard dog?"

"I've debated about it, but I don't think so. I don't have the money for training lessons on top of everything else. I think I'm going to adopt a big, scary-looking but sweet dog. Val isn't the biggest dog fan anyway, so I'm hoping that'll be enough to deter her."

"Well, most burglars won't mess with big dogs," Maggie said thoughtfully.

"Exactly. The thing is finding the time to actually go adopt one." Gwen laughed. "I have so little free time right now."

"Well, how about Wednesday? You let us take a break from tutoring to do that haunted house job, so we can use this week for you to go get your new furry friend."

"Well…that haunted house job is part of what's making it possible for me to afford the dog. That sounds fair. Want to come with me?"

Maggie smiled shyly. "That sounds like fun. But do you think it's safe?"

Gwen paused. "Honestly, I don't know. But I'd feel safer with you there than alone."

"Well, you do have the restraining order. Where were you thinking of go—" Maggie paused, glancing at her vibrating phone. "Hey, I'm getting a call from Darren."

"The guy you do Shabbat with?"

"Yeah. He never calls me. Can I call you back?"

"I'm going to go hop in the shower. We can text later."

"Sounds good. Talk to you later."

"Bye!"

Maggie dried her hands, took her phone off speaker, and accepted the call. "Hello?"

"Hey, Maggie. It's Darren."

"What's up?"

"Gene and I were talking. Hanukkah is coming pretty early this year."

Maggie blinked. "Oh, geez, you're right. It's in, like, two weeks."

"Little less than that, yeah. We like to throw parties, and we thought it would be nice to have a little Hanukkah party this year on the last day, to celebrate. If we do, would you come?"

"What day of the week is the last day?"

"Um…Sunday."

"What time?"

"We were thinking we'd invite people over as early as four, light the candles at sundown and everything with everybody around four forty-five."

"I can ask my manager to do the opening shift that day. I'd love to be there," Maggie said with excitement. "I haven't celebrated Hanukkah since I left home. I don't even have a menorah."

"Girl, not okay. Are you on Facebook?"

"Yeah."

"Do us a favor and friend request one of us. We tried looking you up and couldn't find you."

Maggie chuckled. "That's because I'm not using my real name on there."

"Oh, you're one of those people. Friend request me so we can invite you to the group for the party. After everyone RSVP's, we're going to decide whether or not to do a gift exchange."

"That sounds fun."

"Yeah, if enough people come, we're thinking of assigning everyone a secret Santa."

"Isn't that…um…"

"Ironic? Listen, it was that or a white elephant, and Gene gets way too competitive with those."

Maggie laughed. "Well, it still sounds fun. Who else might come?"

"Coral's already in the Facebook group."

"Of course."

"And there's a couple more people coming you might know. Remember Bobby from the party?"

"The one doing the fundraising?"

"Yes, exactly. Oh, and Maggie, you should invite Gwen."

For the third time that evening, Maggie felt her face flush. "Um, yeah, that'd be great. I don't know if she has a Facebook though, or if she's available."

Darren's voice got serious for a moment. "Coral let us know that something happened. Wanted to ask us to make sure you got here and back safely every Shabbat. She didn't tell us everything, but it sounds like Gwen could use a good group of friends right now, and a chance to relax."

"Yeah…I'll ask her about it."

"Great! Let us know. If she doesn't have a Facebook, we'll count her as your plus-one in the RSVP list."

"Sure thing."

"Okay, see you Friday."

After Darren ended the call, Maggie texted Gwen the details of the invite. She returned to washing her dishes, starting to feel excitement for the holiday season.

*

WEDNESDAY MORNING, MAGGIE found herself at a parking lot close to the spcaLA, waiting for Gwen to show up. When Gwen arrived, wearing a hooded zipped sweatshirt and jeans, Maggie gave her a smile. "Are you ready?"

"I'm excited," Gwen said. "I've never had a pet before. Have you?"

"My parents wouldn't let us get a dog. And my grandparents hated them. We had a pet bunny when I was younger. Do you have everything you need?"

As they walked toward the shelter, Gwen reached into her sweatshirt and pulled out a small packet of paper. "Proof of address, copy of my lease, ID, my checkbook… I think I'm all set."

"The website says you spend time with an adoption counselor. I wonder what that's like."

"I'm not sure but I'm excited." Gwen had a nervous grin she couldn't seem to get rid of.

"Did you take a look at the dogs online to see if there's one you want?"

"No, I want to see them in person. You don't really get to know someone through their picture, you know?"

Maggie nodded. She decided not to mention that she'd poured through the pictures and descriptions of the dogs, trying to figure out which one might be Gwen's best fit.

The shelter wasn't hard to find, with its large blue-and-white sign and an inviting doorway. They stepped into the bright lobby, and the receptionist, sitting behind a desk in a bright-blue Team spcaLA shirt, noticed them right away.

"Good morning," he said cheerily. "What can we help you with today?"

Gwen bounced a little on her toes, as if gearing herself up. "I'm looking to adopt a dog today."

"Fantastic," said the gentleman. "Come on up here, and I'll take care of you. My name's Walt. And you?"

"I'm Gwen Knowles," she said, reaching over the counter to shake his hand. "And this is Maggie."

"I'm here for support," Maggie said, shaking Walt's hand as well.

Walt's smile didn't fade but his eyes darted back and forth between Maggie and Gwen. "Will you also be living in the home with the pet?"

"Oh, no, I live in a different apartment."

"But she's going to be visiting me regularly," Gwen said. "So she might be the person the dog sees second-most." Catching Maggie's questioning look, Gwen added sheepishly, "I know I haven't mentioned this to you yet, but I was thinking of inviting you over to my apartment for studying instead of at the library."

"Oh." Maggie felt her cheeks warming. "Oh, yeah, that sounds nice.

If you're okay with it?"

Gwen nodded and returned her attention to Walt, who asked her questions regarding proof of address and ID. As she showed him her documents, Maggie took the time to get her blushing under control. Now was not the time to freak out over the idea of being alone with Gwen in her apartment!

Walt confirmed Gwen was approved for adoption, and she kept bouncing excitedly on the balls of her feet, looking around the room. The sound of dogs barking came from somewhere in the back. A large glass wall behind the receptionist's desk divided it from what appeared to be the break room. Maggie read the mission statement painted on the wall: "Dedicated to the prevention of cruelty to animals through education, law enforcement, intervention, and advocacy." To one side of Walt, a plastic stand with multiple sleeves held a combination of informational posters and fliers. Maggie noticed one for classes.

"Look, Gwen, they have obedience training," she said quietly, holding up the flier in her hand. "Five weeks for 150 dollars."

Gwen tapped her fingers against her lips. "That's…that's doable."

Walt looked up from typing on his computer. "If you're interested, our adoption counselor will be happy to talk with you about that after you make a choice. Some of our pets have already had some training to help them be more adoptable."

Gwen nodded, still tapping her fingers.

When everything was ready, Maggie and Gwen were finally led to the back. They had the dogs' immediate attention. Maggie was happy to see that instead of rows of cold, dark cages, the animals were kept in well-lit, clean kennels with comfy beds. Gwen let Walt know she was interested in adopting an older, larger dog.

Walt smiled with relief. "Puppies go so fast anyway. Go ahead and walk up and down the row, and let me know if someone stands out to you."

Maggie followed slightly behind Gwen as she passed the kennels slowly, stopping in front of each dog. Some bounced up and barked, some wagged their tails, and all of them were adorable. Maggie had no idea how Gwen could possibly make a decision.

Eventually, Gwen revisited a few of the dogs. Maggie glanced at her face as she did so. A tinge of pink colored her cheeks as if she was trying to restrain her elated anticipation.

"Which ones do you like?" Maggie asked.

"Right now, I think I'm between…the Labrador…or the pit bull." Gwen pointed to the two dogs.

Maggie read the slip of paper on the Labrador's kennel door. "His name's Harlem. He's a four-year-old, he's high energy, and loves to play. Says he would make a good cat companion."

She then examined the pit bull's door. "Her name's Bluebell. She's six years old, and it says she loves people, but she needs to be the only pet in the house." Maggie glanced over at Gwen. "She's a rescue from a home that didn't feed her enough, so she can get pretty territorial over food."

Gwen crouched in front of Bluebell's door. Bluebell was a gorgeous gray color, and her eyes looked just a little too big for her face. Instead of jumping up on the bars, she sat at attention. Her butt wiggled on the floor from her wagging tail, and she gazed up at them with a goofy smile. Maggie saw a light in Gwen's eyes. "How are ya, big girl?" Gwen asked the dog softly.

Bluebell answered with a gruff, "Harrumph," and licked her lips.

"I'm looking for a roommate," Gwen said. "It's a lot quieter than here. You would be spending a lot of time by yourself. Is that okay?"

Bluebell cocked her head to one side, as if thinking, then stood and wagged her tail even harder. She pawed the door and harrumphed again.

Gwen laughed and turned to Walt. "I'd like to spend some time with this one."

"If you come with me this way, I'll take you to the back yard, and Kelli our adoption counselor will bring Bluebell out to you." He opened the door for them.

Gwen tore herself away and hastened toward him. As Maggie followed, she glanced back at Bluebell, who seemed to be watching Gwen with those goofy eyes. In her heart, she knew they had just found Gwen's companion.

Chapter Twenty-Two

SATURDAY EVENING AT improv group, the first thing Coral did was to rush up to Gwen, gushing, "So how is the fur baby? Do you have pictures?"

Gwen, who hadn't even finished walking down the aisle to the stage, grinned and dug her phone out of her pocket. "Of course I have pictures! Everything she does is the cutest. Do you want to see?"

A small group crowded around Coral and Gwen as Gwen swiped through her phone. Everyone aaawwwwed.

"She's such a pretty lady," said one gentleman.

"When did you adopt her?"

"How old is she?"

The group continued to question Gwen until Professor Max took to the stage and cleared his throat loudly. "Unless today's improv group is about acting like pets," he said, a cheeky grin on his face, "I would like us to redirect our attention and get started, please."

The crowd laughed and split up, preparing to join Professor Max on-stage.

Maggie hung back with Gwen as she took off her jean jacket. "How's Bluebell doing?"

"She's adjusting well, I think, but Kelli was right, she's a little anxious. She's not destroying anything, but I think she tries to chew my welcome mat when I'm gone."

"Aw, poor thing," Maggie said as they approached the stage.

Gwen sighed. "I wish I could keep an eye on her during the day when I'm out, just to make sure she's okay. It would feel better to see her, you know?"

"Do you think you could get her approved as a service dog and take her with you?" Maggie felt a sudden rush of hope at the idea that Gwen could have a protective dog with her at all times.

Gwen shook her head. "Probably not. She's too old to be that well trained. I don't need her with me all the time, anyway. She just helps me feel safe when I'm home alone." Gwen turned her attention to the warm-ups that Professor Max was guiding them through, prompting Maggie to do the same.

The improv activity that evening was to make a continuous story, but every couple minutes, Professor Max would replace the actors, and the new actors would have to pick up the story where the old actors left off. Maggie and a sweet, slightly flustered lady went relatively early in the activity, where they added a twist to the story by "revealing" one of the characters was a spy.

As Maggie went to sit in the audience to laugh and clap with the other participants, she noticed a figure moving at the back of the theater. Her heart immediately jumped to her throat, and she froze, focusing her gaze, convinced for a split second that the figure had long black hair and athleisure clothing. Her vision sharpened, and she realized it was one of the theater cleaning staff, a gentleman with a newsboy cap and suspenders. Maggie took a deep breath, but found she was now too antsy to sit down. Maggie continued standing, stretching her legs, and kept gazing around the room, her attention wavering between the improv actors and the edges of the theater.

The kindly lady Maggie had acted with took notice. She and one of her friends, another lady in the group with red hair turning white, walked up to her when the activity was over. "Are you looking for something, sweetheart?" Maggie's activity partner asked.

"It's nothing, ma'am, I just thought I saw someone."

"Someone you're expecting to come?"

Maggie smiled ruefully. "Something like that, yeah."

The red-haired lady, who Maggie recognized from earlier improv sessions, spoke up. "I don't suppose you have a friend with beautiful black hair?"

Maggie's spine went cold. She felt the color drain from her face. Keeping her smile, she asked, "How did you know?"

"Oh, she and I chatted a couple times when group was done," the lady said sweetly. "Always said she was too shy to join in but enjoyed watching us. She used to sit so far in the back I almost didn't notice her most weeks."

"Well, someone should have told her to just jump in," said the kind lady. "I mean, you told me this would be fun, and you were absolutely right. And there's some strapping young men here too!"

The red-haired lady looked scandalized. "Now, Marge!" The two women wandered away, tittering, toward the snack table as Maggie stood still, gripping the back of a theater seat to hold herself steady, desperately trying to calm her beating heart.

Thankfully, Coral found her quickly. Before Maggie realized what was happening, Coral was pressing a bagel into her hand and whispering, "Is everything okay? You've seemed out of it all group."

"One of the ladies here," Maggie explained, fingers clutching the bagel, "she saw Valerie. She used to sit in the back to watch us."

Coral put a firm hand on Maggie's shoulder and squeezed. "Okay. Okay, yeah, that's pretty alarming. But, Maggie, we already knew she was stalking Gwen, right? She figured out where you went to work, she probably followed you guys to rehearsal. We knew about this, so it's being taken care of. There's the restraining order, right?"

Maggie shuddered. "It just… Before it was… She was like a ghost. And now I know she's real…"

Coral looked into Maggie's face with furrowed brows. "I think we should get you home. You're not making a lot of sense."

Maggie knew that she should, but her feet felt glued to the floor. She sat in the seat behind her, still gripping the bagel, and stared ahead, trying to make sense of her feelings.

Coral moved away quickly. When she came back, Gwen was with her.

"Maggie! Maggie, what happened?" Gwen asked, dropping to crouch so she was eye-to-eye with Maggie.

Maggie shook her head. "Nothing happened. I can't figure out why I'm so freaked out."

"She says one of the group ladies here noticed that crazy girl sometime in a past improv group," Coral explained. "Said she used to sit in the back."

Gwen immediately straightened her spine and looked around the auditorium, scanning the seats. Returning her attention to Maggie, she softened her voice. "Hey, Maggie, let's do a quick exercise, okay?"

"Sure."

"What are five things you can see around you?"

Maggie looked up and turned her gaze around the room slowly. "Um…I see you, and Coral, the theater seats, the stage, and the orchestra pit."

"Great job. What are four things you can hear?"

Maggie closed her eyes and focused. "I can hear…your voice, people talking, people walking…and the buzz of the lights."

"You're doing great. What are three things you can feel?"

"The seat I'm sitting on. Um… This bagel. And my heartbeat."

"Is it slowing down?"

"Yeah…yeah, it is."

"Fantastic. What are two things you can smell?"

Maggie breathed in through her nose slowly. "Musky velvet theater seats and the hot air from the theater lights."

"One more, Maggie. What's something you can taste?"

Maggie opened her eyes and took a bite of the bagel. She lifted the bitten bagel in answer and smiled through her chewing.

Gwen chuckled. "That's a great answer. How are you feeling now?"

Maggie stood up and stretched. "I feel a lot better. What did you do?"

"I didn't do it," Gwen said, "you did it. You grounded yourself. Maggie, I told you what happened at the library was going to impact you eventually." Gwen reached over to hand Maggie her sweater. "You just survived an attack. You're on the alert. My old counselor called that hypervigilance and hyperarousal. A small thing makes your body think you have to protect yourself again, but you can't actually find the threat. It's really disorienting."

Coral, Gwen, and Maggie started walking toward the back of the theater.

Maggie's face was slowly flushing scarlet. "I don't want you to think I can't go anywhere without freaking out," she muttered.

"This is all new to you," Gwen reassured her, "so it's completely normal to have moments like that. But if you use strategies to help ground yourself, like the one we just practiced together, you'll help your brain and body recover from what happened."

As she held the door open for them to leave, Coral asked, "Does it go away?"

Gwen paused. When she answered, her gaze was focused far away. "For some people, yes. Especially if you take care of it really early on, use the right strategies right away, and have a lot of love and safety and support. And I think it matters what you experienced. Like, was it a one-time event or was it a chronic problem."

Gwen tapped her fingers against her lips, eyes coming back into focus. "Maggie, I know you're always asking if I'm okay and safe, but make sure you're taking care of yourself too."

"I don't want you to worry about me."

"Too late," Coral said. "I've been worried about you since that chick singled you out at work." She wrapped an arm around Maggie's shoulders. "That's what friends do, they make sure you're okay and take care of you when you're not."

Gwen, from Maggie's other side, reached out and overlapped her arm with Coral's. "You got this, Maggie."

Maggie hesitated, then pulled both of them closer. "Nah, we got this." She hoped the confidence in her voice would dispel her blush. "Gwen, which way is your car parked? It's my turn to walk you this time."

Before Gwen could protest, Coral cut in. "We insist on it!"

Smiling, Gwen conceded. "It's just around the block. But we have to turn back the way we came."

The three girls laughed and separated so they could walk more steadily. In a matter of minutes, with some chatter and chuckles, Coral and Maggie were waving good-bye as Gwen closed the car door and pulled away.

Coral and Maggie turned back in the direction of their bus stop.

"We're going to have to wait a little bit longer for a bus now," Maggie commented.

Coral shrugged. "I don't mind; it's worth it to make sure she's safe."

Maggie nodded in agreement. She was about to reply but was interrupted by her phone buzzing. She pulled it out of her pocket, opened the text message, and felt the blush she had fought so hard to eliminate return to her face.

Glancing over, Coral asked, "What's wrong? She didn't find your number, did she?"

"No, nothing like that. It's just…Gene and Darren did the Secret Santa assignments for the party."

"Oh?" Coral pulled out her phone to check for a message. "Ooh, I got Bobby. That's perfect; she adores chocolate. Easy gift. Who did you get?"

Maggie covered her face with her hands. "I got Gwen."

*

SUNDAY EVENING FOUND Maggie standing at the entrance to a super-center store, trying to decide what section to go to. She texted Coral.

I don't even know where to start.

Wait for me to get off work, and i'll come with you.

Maggie could practically hear the squealing, pleading voice through the screen.

It'll be late by the time you're out. I just want to get this over with so I can go home and wrap it and not have to worry about it anymore.

You're no fun. If you don't want my help, why do you keep texting me about it?

Maggie groaned as she typed back.

Procrastinating?

Come on, Maggie. Just think about something Gwen likes. You have to know something she likes.

That was the problem. It wasn't that Maggie had no ideas about what to buy Gwen; it was that she had too many. Should she buy Gwen an audiobook? But what if she picked a book she hated or already owned? Should she buy Gwen a set of highlighters, tabs, and other organizational tools? But what if she got things Gwen already had, or didn't like, or didn't use? Should she buy Gwen self-defense tools? Maggie threw that idea out with a shake of her head. This was meant to be festive.

For a brief moment, Maggie thought back to past holidays when she and Jess exchanged presents. They hadn't observed Hanukkah, but had celebrated a small Christmas. Jess had given her a copper beaded bracelet, and Maggie had given her a pair of leather boots. They ate dinner with candles, giggling over a small bouquet of poinsettias they'd found in the grocery store. Maggie's imagination ran wild. What if she gave Gwen a beautiful armband to ornament her arms? What if she gave her a dozen roses? What would make Gwen feel swept off her feet?

Maggie groaned again and tapped her forehead firmly, shaking the ideas free. *You're buying a gift for a friend. Just a friend. Knock it off,* she told herself. Deciding that perusing the aisles would help, she marched off, face set in concentration.

The store itself was not very helpful. Above almost every aisle, giant advertisements hung portraying smiling families, couples, and friends. It seemed like the store had gone all-in on a romantic Christmas marketing strategy because everywhere she turned, Maggie saw pictures of guys giving girls jewelry, flowers, mixers… Did Gwen like baking? She lived alone; she probably cooked alone. Would she like a mixer? What if Gwen was actually hopeless in the kitchen? Maggie shuddered and swiftly left the kitchen aisle.

Maggie looked for audiobooks, but the selection was small, and nothing stood out to her. The organizational tools seemed lifeless and flat. Maggie even wandered up and down the gardening section, searching for inspiration.

Eventually, an employee in a blue polo, who she had crossed paths with multiple times, asked her, "Can I help you?"

Maggie smiled apologetically. "I'm looking for a present for a friend."

"Uh-huh." The employee nodded, possibly looking her up and down to check if she'd been pocketing anything. "Well, maybe I can help. You've been wandering for a while."

Maggie covered her eyes with her hands and groaned. "I know. It's so bad. I want it to be really meaningful, you know? Something she'll genuinely use and feel happy about. I hate giving people crap that collects dust."

"I understand. I'm the same way. What I usually do is try to remember something they talked about recently. If it's important enough for them to have a conversation about, it's probably good enough to be a gift. Maybe something they started doing recently and are still getting into, so they don't have a lot of stuff for it." He gave her a hopeful smile. "Does that help?"

Maggie stared blankly at him for a moment, then smiled back. "Do you have a pet section?"

He moved back into the open aisle and pointed to his left. "Right over that way, section fourteen."

Maggie started to power walk away. "That's perfect, thank you so much." As she swiftly approached the pet aisle, she took out her phone to text Coral.

I think I figured it out!

Chapter Twenty-Three

ON WEDNESDAY MIDMORNING, Maggie found herself taking a bus route she had never taken before, all the way to Gwen's apartment complex in Glassell Park. Maggie was a bit in awe of the building when she found it. The outside was a glimmering white box. Some of the higher apartments had balconies. A quick scan of the property showed a fenced-in pool in the back. Maggie was willing to bet this place had a gym, and maybe the laundry was in unit, not three floors down in the basement with the smelly cobweb-draped rafters.

Maggie and Gwen had agreed it would be best if Maggie approached the building alone once certain no one had followed her. There was a chance Valerie didn't actually know where Gwen lived, they reasoned, because she hadn't tried to approach Gwen there at any point. It was still risky, but even if Valerie figured out what Maggie was doing and did try to follow her into the building, the lobby security guard had been informed Valerie was not allowed inside due to Gwen's restraining order.

Maggie inspected the panel of buttons next to the main door and pressed the one labeled with Gwen's apartment number.

After a quick pause Gwen's scratchy voice over the speaker asked, "Who is it?"

"It's Maggie Fromm, ready to learn!"

"Great. Come on in and take the elevator straight ahead." Gwen buzzed her in.

Maggie entered a chic lobby with minimalist furniture and wavy patterns in the carpet. She stopped by the security guard's desk to sign in, then headed to the elevator.

Gwen was waiting for her when the elevator doors opened on the fifth floor. She gave Maggie a quick side hug and a bright smile. "Mine's over here," she said, leading the way. "You kinda have to go around this corner toward the back of the building."

"This is an amazing complex," Maggie said, staring around her. "Everything's so bright and clean."

Gwen grimaced. "It's a bit expensive. I'm stretching to make it work, but so far it works."

Maggie glanced at the doors as they passed. "Are those…keypad locks?"

"Isn't it cool? I'll show you how it works when we get to mine. You can customize the combination for your door. I change mine every so often."

As they rounded the bend, Gwen came to a halt in front of a large gray door. "No peeking," she said jokingly.

As Gwen typed in her combination, the door to their left creaked open, and a red-headed girl poked her head out.

"Hey, Gwen, I thought I heard you."

"Hi, Bea," Gwen said, stopping. "Maggie, this is Bea, my favorite neighbor."

Bea reached a freckled hand out to shake Maggie's. "My name's Beatrice. Nice to meet you."

"Nice to meet you too."

Bea returned her attention to Gwen. "I wanted to let you know I think I saw a package get delivered for you in the mailroom."

"That's probably Ma's holiday care package," Gwen said brightly. "Thanks."

"No problem. Tell Bluebell hi for me," Bea said as she closed her door.

"I'm glad you have a friend right here," Maggie said as Gwen pushed her door open.

"Yeah, Bea's sweet. She's a little naive, but she's good-hearted. And she's offered to have Bluebell over if— There you are, girl!" Gwen dropped to a crouch and put her arms out. "See, I wasn't gone long!"

Bluebell trotted toward Gwen, her wagging behind putting a wiggle into her step. She bundled herself in Gwen's arms, covering her in slobbering kisses.

Gwen petted her firmly on her back and sides with both hands. "You went to look for me under the bed, didn't you? Didn't you, Blue?" She turned and looked up at Maggie. "Do you remember Maggie, girl? She was there the day we met."

Maggie crouched and held out a hand calmly. "Hi, Bluebell. You're looking really good in your new home."

Bluebell humphed, sniffed Maggie's hand, and wiggled over to her, pushing her body against Maggie's knees.

Maggie fell back into a sitting position, laughing, and rubbed Bluebell's sides and back like Gwen had. "Aren't you a strong girl?"

Gwen stood and reached to help Maggie to her feet. "I hope you don't mind our new study buddy. She's a bit of a cuddler. I won't let her on the bed, but I can't resist snuggling with her on the couch."

"I don't mind at all." Maggie laughed, accepting Gwen's hand. As she rose, she took a good look at her surroundings for the first time.

Gwen's apartment was small, but a striking lack of furniture made it seem stark and cavernous. An eat-in kitchen area lay to her immediate right, much bigger than hers and Coral's, with actual cupboards and a dishwasher. Gwen had a folding table and two folding chairs set up on the tile floor. Forward was a living space with three square windows. A small gray loveseat sat next to a tiny coffee table with a laptop set up on it. A door to the right led to what Maggie assumed was the bathroom. The surprisingly high ceiling and the unexpected reason for it made her eyes light up.

"Is that a loft?" Maggie asked, eyes gliding over the spiral staircase rising from the living space to Gwen's bedroom fifteen feet in the air. Gwen's bed was situated with the headboard against the left wall, leaving three more square windows clear. In the back corner, piles of textbooks, audio books, and other supplies filled milk crates.

"That's my favorite part about this apartment," Gwen said. "Bluebell doesn't like the stairs very much though. She's a little clumsy on the turns." Gwen held her arms up and gestured around her. "It's not much, but it's cozy."

"I love it," Maggie enthused, following Bluebell to the loveseat.

Bluebell jumped up, waited for Maggie to sit, then lay down with her front legs on Maggie's lap. Maggie chuckled and petted Bluebell with long, soft strokes. "What do you think of your new home, Blue?" Blue wagged her tail and laid her head down on her paws.

"You can push her off if she's too heavy," Gwen said.

"I wouldn't dream of it."

"I'm just saying, don't make yourself uncomfortable for her sake. She has a dog bed she can use for once. Oh, and before I forget, I have a message from Alyssa for you."

"A message?"

Gwen pulled her phone out of her pocket and opened her texts. "Alyssa didn't have your phone number, so she asked me to tell you. She's having a birthday party for the cast in February." She showed Maggie the screen so she could read the information for herself.

Maggie looked at Gwen quizzically. "This says it's just a couple nights before opening."

"I gave Alyssa my blessing for this," Gwen reassured her. "This is going to be our celebration night as a cast too."

"In that case, I'd be happy to go."

"Great!" Gwen started climbing the stairs. "I'm grabbing a couple books; remind me where we were?"

"We were about to talk about Chekhov."

"Oh, good. I think you're going to like him a lot." Gwen returned, carrying a few books in hand. "Chekhov's techniques are focused on expressing the psychology of the character through the body. The idea that you should fully understand your character not just intellectually but in your whole body, and not through script study but through experience. The best way to be the character is to feel the character."

"I love that." Maggie reached to accept the textbook Gwen handed to her.

"Before we dive further in, a good way to start is by asking yourself a simple question. Right now, before you develop your skills in this theory, what is the part of your body that doesn't get into character? Some part you don't have a lot of control over, that is distinctly you, no matter what character you're trying to play?"

Maggie blinked at her. "Can you phrase that a different way?"

"Well…" Gwen scooched Bluebell over an inch as she sat down next to Maggie. "Let's say the script says you have to open a door. You could either open the door exactly the same way the character would in that moment, or you might just open the door the way you, Maggie, open all doors. Maybe you can't help walking like yourself. Maybe you tend to brush your hair away. Maybe your eyes always look like your eyes no matter what your character is feeling in that scene."

Maggie sat back and thought. "I feel like I'd have to watch a video of myself acting to notice it. It's hard to name something specific. I'm so focused on remembering blocking that I don't think I'd notice something I'm doing that's just…me."

"Let's look at it a different way, then. Let's start with something about your body or the way you move that you can't control or seem to change."

"Oh, that's easy," Maggie said. "My blushing."

"That was a quick answer!"

"It's the truth," Maggie groaned. "I think it's not bad on stage because everything's scripted, so I know what will happen, or I can just keep myself in character until I get off stage. But in real life, oh my God, my blushing is the worst." Maggie covered her face with one hand. "I can feel one coming on now. The smallest thing will happen, and *bam*. Tomato face."

"I don't think you look like a tomato when you blush. It's honestly kind of cute."

Maggie groaned louder and put both hands over her cheeks. "You're making it worse."

Gwen smiled and reached to rub Bluebell's ears. "Sorry, sorry. But I see what you mean. Do you know why it happens?"

"My parents actually asked a doctor about it when I was a kid. I flush when I eat certain foods, when I have the slightest emotional response. I blush at everything. The doctor said it's fine; I just have active blood vessels, I guess." She exhaled with exasperation. "Believe it or not, it's better now than it used to be. I mostly use deep breaths to make it calm down, but it takes concentration."

Gwen nodded. "That sounds frustrating for acting."

"Oh, it is." Maggie sat upright and turned to Gwen. "I used to turn scarlet at every audition. Anytime I made a mistake during rehearsal. When someone else made a mistake. It was awful." She resumed petting Blue. "I think I have it mostly under control, but it's annoyingly involuntary."

Gwen tapped her lips thoughtfully. "How do you get it so under control for acting? Something that involuntary is incredibly hard to turn off."

Maggie paused again for thought. "Well, the predictability of a scene is probably the biggest thing, to be honest."

"I've seen you in improv though," Gwen pointed out. "You don't blush in improv."

Maggie cocked her head to the side. "I guess that's true… I think it's because I'm so focused on trying to be someone else. I know that doesn't make sense, but I'm not sure how else to word it."

"Hmm. Perhaps what you're saying is—Maggie gets flustered and blushes easily, but your characters do not?"

Maggie shrugged. "Something like that?"

"That actually fits with Chekhov perfectly," Gwen said, opening one of her other books. "Chekhov teaches us when we act, we're not trying to insert our own emotions and experiences into the scripted situation. We ask the character how they would feel, what they would do, how they would do it. Unlike method actors, who ask themselves, 'How would I respond in this situation,' a Chekhov-trained actor asks the character what to do." Gwen glanced at Maggie. "Go ahead and open that book to the page with the blue tab on it. Let's talk about the energy center."

*

GWEN SUDDENLY TORE her attention away from the notes Maggie was scribbling. "You must be starving; we haven't stopped for lunch!"

Maggie glanced up, pencil poised on paper. "Why? What time is it?"

Gwen checked her phone. "It's almost five. Aw, geez. Maggie, I'm so sorry. With this new schedule, I completely forgot."

"It's fine. I ate before I came. I'm not starving; I promise."

Before Gwen could reply, Maggie's stomach grumbled. Bluebell, who had moved to the floor, looked up with curiosity.

"I swear that wasn't me," Maggie said, a blush already creeping through her cheeks.

"I have to make it up to you. By the time you get back home, you'll be dead on your feet. Can I make you a quick dinner here?"

"I don't want to eat up all your food," Maggie protested as she and

Gwen stood up.

"I know I'm stretching it for rent, but I have enough food for two. I really don't have to pay a lot for groceries." She walked into her kitchen. "First thing's first though. Blue, dinner!"

Bluebell trotted over as Gwen opened a container of dog food and put two scoops into one of two metal bowls next to the fridge.

"Try to get it all in your stomach and not on the floor this time, silly goose," she said as Bluebell chowed down. She went to the sink and washed her hands. "I can make you something in a jiffy. Help me look through and see what's kosher. Check the fridge for me? I'll check the cupboards."

Maggie opened the fridge, expecting to see the stereotypical college student diet. She took a step back in surprise when she was instead greeted by fresh produce. "You have the good stuff," she said in admiration.

Gwen looked at her with a raised eyebrow. "What do you mean?"

"Like, real vegetables and fruit and stuff. I don't know if I can eat your food, Gwen. It looks expensive."

Gwen stopped looking through cupboards, turned to Maggie, and put her hands on her hips. "Maggie, what have you been eating?"

"Um…" The blush she was fighting from earlier was back. "You know, the usual…chicken nuggets…ramen…frozen vegetables."

Gwen's brows furrowed. "Oh, God, Maggie, why?"

Maggie shrugged. "Mostly because it's cheap? I eat healthier now that I live with Coral, but with Jess, it was kinda just food we could eat on the go. Something quick, no dishes to wash, that kind of thing."

"Is that kind of stuff kosher?"

"Like I said about pizza," Maggie muttered, "I bend the rules."

Gwen took Maggie by the shoulders and directed her back to the loveseat. "Sit on the couch and relax. I'm going to cook you stir fry. Real vegetables. It'll take me twenty, thirty minutes tops. And you're going to ask yourself why you've been eating straight crap for over a year."

"In my defense," Maggie protested as Gwen pushed her to sit, "it's hard to find cheap and fresh groceries."

"I know there's food deserts in LA," Gwen acknowledged as she walked away. "That's as much your problem as cost, finding where it's provided."

"I mean, I found grocery stores when I first moved here. But—"

"Let me guess. The first time you and Jess went grocery shopping, you bought a huge list of food you didn't end up eating and weren't sure how to cook?"

"How'd you know?" Maggie said grumpily.

"I made similar mistakes," Gwen said as she pulled vegetables from the fridge. "Thankfully, Ma gave me lessons before I moved out on my own completely. First thing you need to do is identify what kind of food you actually like to eat. Second thing you do is find the affordable ingredients. Buy only what you need, only as much as you need. And learn a bunch of recipes that are quick, or freeze easy so you can prep them in advance and then microwave them when you need them."

She opened the freezer and pulled out a container. "See? I have meals set aside for days when I know I won't be able to cook."

"Meal prep sounds tiring."

"Oh, it is. I kinda hate it," Gwen admitted, pulling a cutting board and knife out of a drawer. "So, on the days I can set aside the time, I just cook fresh. Look, nothing I'm cooking in this is expensive." She lifted an onion she was about to slice. "This onion is less than a dollar, and I don't need the whole thing for a recipe, so I'll cut up what I need now and stick the rest in a container to use in another recipe later. And some foods are super filling and cheap in bulk, like beans and rice."

Maggie watched with curiosity, scooching over so Bluebell could join her on the couch. "Fine, I will learn your ways, oh wise guru of food."

"I promise you. You don't have to buy fancy, and honestly, keep buying the frozen vegetables if that works for you. But if you eat real food more often, you're going to feel so much more prepared for the day."

Watching Gwen cook was an experience. While she wouldn't be mistaken for a five-star chef, Maggie was still mesmerized by the way she carried herself as she completed her tasks. There was an air of confidence, almost assertiveness, in the way she handled her knife, the way she whirled around gathering her ingredients. Maggie noticed she didn't use measuring cups or spoons, despite a set of them hanging on a hook on the wall.

While they talked about books, improv group, and *Petty Oppression*, Gwen finished her stir fry with a final flourish and invited Maggie to come sit at the table.

"Sorry it's not a real table or anything," she said as Maggie sat. "I didn't have any furniture when I moved in."

"I don't mind. It smells amazing. Can I help with anything?"

"You just sit there and get ready to eat," Gwen ordered. She started scooping rice into bowls. "I don't want you doing anything but enjoying the taste. What would you like to drink?"

"Water's fine."

Gwen set the bowls on the table and handed Maggie a fork. "I'll grab you a glass. Dig in."

Maggie bowed her head and quietly recited a *brachah*, then took her first bite. "Oh my God," she said through a mouthful of rice and snap peas. "How did you do this?"

Gwen set the glasses of water down and sat across from Maggie. "I'm not exactly a prodigy, Maggie. I just dedicate resources to taking care of myself. Do you? I know you're a busy worker, but your health is what lets you do all that."

Maggie took another bite quickly, chewing this one more slowly, and swallowed. "I promise. I'm not bad about sleeping, and I keep active. I'll try to buy fresh food more when I can." She took another bite hurriedly.

Gwen's green eyes watched Maggie for a moment more before she picked up her own fork. "I'm really flattered you like it."

"It's so good." Maggie put her fork down, pressed her hands together, and closed her eyes. "Thank you so, so much."

"You're very welcome to eat with me anytime," Gwen said. "Tell me what else you like besides mac and cheese, pizza, and stir fry. I'd love to cook for you more."

An image of Gwen cooking daily meals for her, sitting and talking with her as they ate, flashed quickly across Maggie's mind. She hastily took another bite to distract herself.

Gwen watched her eating. "I'm serious. I don't get to cook for other people very often. And being able to make you this happy more often would be an absolute treat."

Maggie's face flared up instantly. She tried to keep her cool. "I, um, I'd enjoy that."

"I've been researching kosher foods," Gwen said between bites. "I hope you'll teach me more about it. I want to make food you know is made with you in mind."

Deep breaths, Maggie told herself, *deep breaths.* "Sure. Maybe you could teach me a little too. About cooking."

"I'd love that. I think there's a lot I could teach you." Gwen wiggled her eyebrows.

"That's it," Maggie said, putting her fork down and pointing accusingly at Gwen. "You're making me blush on purpose. I can tell."

Gwen hid her mouth behind a loose fist, but Maggie could see the sheepish grin. "I can't help it. I'm sorry. It's just... It's really cute."

"You're doing it again!"

Gwen burst into laughter and lifted her hands in surrender. "I'm sorry, I'm sorry. I promise I'll stop." A mischievous smile lingered as she resumed eating.

Maggie gave a humph of approval and picked her fork back up. "You will be sorry when I figure out what your weakness is and exploit it against you."

Gwen's smile remained, but her eyes, twinkling with mischief a moment before, were suddenly deep and serious. "I better be careful, then. I suspect it won't take you long to learn my weakness, Miss Fromm."

Chapter Twenty-Four

THE TWILIGHT HAD another performance coming for the holiday season, so improv classes were put on hold until January. Maggie didn't mind. Rehearsals for *Petty Oppression* and regular phone conversations with Gwen filled her need for creative expression and connection to theater. And, of course, there were always evenings spent watching Coral practice a new skill for her upcoming audition. Saturday night it was moonwalking.

As Coral went through the motions slowly, trying to get her toe to slide properly, she asked, "Are you all set for tomorrow's party?"

"Yep. Present's wrapped. We're bringing a platter of *sufganiyot*. I even picked an outfit."

"You picked an outfit?"

Maggie chuckled wryly. "I didn't want a repeat of the fundraiser party where I was stressed the whole evening before. I chose my favorite blue sweater and white dress pants. I think that'll be festive."

"Geez, talk about prepared." Coral turned on her heel and attempted the motions in the reverse direction. "I still have to wrap Bobby's chocolate. You never told me what you got Gwen."

"I'm keeping it a surprise. I'm super nervous about it, and I'm afraid if I tell other people what it is and find out it's a dumb gift, I'll freak out."

"I'm positive you didn't buy Gwen anything dumb."

"Well…not dumb, I guess. But what if it's, like, too much? Or too little?"

"Gwen's not the kind of shallow person to care about present cost."

Maggie shook her head. "I don't mean like that. I mean, what if I come on too strong? Or what if I make it too casual?" Maggie brushed her curls out of her face with exasperation. "I just don't want her to get the wrong idea from it."

"Oh?" Coral paused, toe poised on the floor, and glanced at Maggie expectantly. "And what is the 'right' idea?"

Maggie flushed. "I don't know. That we can be good friends?"

"Ha! God, you're so deep in denial." Coral returned her attention to her feet. "I always mess up right here where the toe goes—"

"Wait, what do you mean 'in denial'? I'm not in denial," Maggie protested.

"You're up to your nose in denial. 'Good friends,' my foot. Why don't you just ask Gwen out?"

"Coral!"

"What? You don't have to act like that's a scandal or something." Coral stood firmly, hands akimbo. "Look, you've been single for, like, four months now almost."

"That's not a lot of time."

"It's not a short time either. And, honestly, how happy were things in your relationship before it ended? You're past the point of having to maintain, I don't know…an image of modesty?" Coral's brows scrunched together in confusion. "Why do people make a fuss about how soon you get a new girlfriend, anyway?"

Maggie ignored the question. "Aren't you being a bit of a hypocrite, Miss I'm-not-looking-for-a-relationship-right-now?"

Coral waved a dismissive hand. "See, there's a difference between looking for someone and having someone standing smack dab in front of you. I'm just not going out of my way to find somebody. But you?" Coral rapidly waved her hand in front of her eyes. "You've got a blonde Amazonian lesbian giving you all kinds of signals, and you're just choosing to ignore it."

"She's not giving me signals—"

"Denial!"

"—and what if I don't like her that way anyway?"

"Ha!" Coral said again. "You're an amazing actress, Maggie, but you're a terrible liar. Of course you like Gwen. And you should! She's great!" Coral shrugged dramatically. "Look, you do things at your pace, I guess. I just don't want you to miss out on an opportunity to be happy with someone amazing."

Maggie hid her blushing face in her hands, fingertips massaging her forehead. "Coral, even if I like Gwen—and I'm not saying I do—she's practically my boss. It'd be so inappropriate."

Coral clucked her tongue. "I've seen way weirder in this field. But fine, I can respect your career." Coral turned to the side again. "I'm just saying. You both deserve to be happy."

"I am," Maggie insisted. "Come on, show me the moonwalk. You've been practicing in slow motion for, like, half an hour."

"All right, all right. Here we go!" With a deep breath, Coral poised a toe on the floor in front of her, paused, then started gliding backward across the floor. She looked up at Maggie, beaming. "I got it!"

"You got it!"

Coral turned around and did it again, only stumbling a little at the end. "Ooh, I got this audition in the bag. Can't wait to show everyone at the party tomorrow."

"What's the audition for again?"

"Used car sales commercial. This is going to be sweet."

*

THE FOLLOWING EVENING, Coral and Maggie grabbed their presents and the *sufganiyot* and walked the couple blocks to Darren and Gene's apartment. Their building was definitely nicer than Coral and Maggie's tiny brick building, although not the lockdown fortress Gwen's was. It was spacious, had a balcony, and was filled with goofy pictures and figurines of giraffes for no other reason than to make their guests laugh. Maggie and Coral had been over several times for Shabbat but were pleasantly surprised to find the apartment decorated for the event when they arrived. Streamers hung from the ceiling, and the dining table was beautifully laid with candles, dreidels, and food arranged buffet-style. The whole apartment smelled like baking sugar.

Gene took their sweaters as Darren took their platter. "You can put the presents over on the coffee table," Gene told them. "You're just in time; we're about to light the menorah."

"And don't you even think of lifting a finger to help," Darren warned Maggie. "Remember, this is your time to celebrate."

Maggie held a hand up in surrender, still balancing a wrapped box in the other hand. "Hey now, I didn't even say anything."

"You didn't have to."

The gentlemen moved farther into the apartment, with the ladies following behind. Maggie's eyes sorted through the room, taking stock of who was there. Gwen had told her Bobby was going to escort her to the party, so she figured the two of them would arrive together soon. She recognized a number of other faces from the LGBT gathering but was surprised when a head of familiar silver hair turned around and revealed Skylar.

"Maggie," Skylar said, raising a glass of soda in greeting. "Fancy seeing you here."

"Hey." Maggie gave Sky a fist bump. "I didn't know you knew Gene and Darren."

"Believe it or not, Gene is my cousin," Sky said in a conspiratorial whisper.

"Wait, really?"

"I mean, kinda. His cousin married my cousin. We mostly know each other because our friend groups overlap a bit, and we play a lot of World of Warcraft."

Coral, who had branched off to say hello to familiar faces, found her way back to Maggie at that moment. "Sky," she said cheerfully. "How's it going? I haven't seen you in ages."

Maggie was shocked to see a tint of color rise to Sky's cheeks. The usually amicable but hard-lined face softened, and Sky smiled almost shyly.

"Hey, Coral. Happy Hanukkah."

"Happy Hanukkah. What have you been up to? You're in the play Maggie's in, right?"

"Yeah, I am. Are you going to come see it?"

"I wouldn't dream of missing it."

"What have you been up to?"

"You know me, searching for opportunity. I learned how to moonwalk, want to see it?"

"Absolutely," Sky said with the dead-set conviction of a person who wanted nothing more in their life than to watch their friend do an amateur moonwalk. As they walked away to where Coral would have more space, Maggie couldn't shake a feeling something ironic was happening.

Gwen and Bobby arrived not long after. Gwen carried a giant plate of latkes, and Bobby had her hands busy with both their gifts. Maggie couldn't help admiring Gwen in her emerald blouse and jeans. "I hope I made them right," Gwen told Gene as he took the plate from her. "I followed all the instructions I found online."

"It's hard to mess up latkes. I'm sure they're delicious," Gene reassured her.

"My mother would take issue with that statement," Darren called from the kitchen.

"Well, she's not making latkes tonight, is she?"

Gwen's eyes fell on Maggie, and she smiled. "Happy Hanukkah," she cried, giving Maggie a quick side hug.

"Same to you," Maggie said. "Hi, Bobby, nice to see you again."

"Nice to see you too, dear. Where do the presents go again?"

Maggie pointed to the coffee table, which was partially hidden by the crowd inside. "You'll recognize it. There's all sorts of presents on it already."

Maggie and Gwen followed as Bobby made her way to the presents table.

Bobby gave a small squeal. "Gwen, come look at this one that has your name on it. The wrapping paper is covered in puppies."

Gwen rushed over to examine the box. "Oh my gosh, that's so cute. I wonder who it's from?"

"Well, I think everyone knows you got a new dog you love," Maggie said casually. "Seems like the wrapping paper was a winning pick?"

"I love it," Gwen said with a huge grin. She looked around the table. "Oh, Maggie, I found yours. It's wrapped in purple." She pointed to a thin, tall square. "I wonder what it could be?"

"Are we going to investigate everyone's presents?" Maggie asked chidingly.

"I can't help it. This time of year is exciting." Gwen looked up as people started moving toward the balcony. "But I think we're being summoned."

"Oh, it's time to light the menorah," Maggie explained, seeing Gene and Darren make their way to the front of the group.

"Well let's go. I've been so excited for this all week," Gwen said, grabbing Maggie's hand and moving to join the rest. Maggie, surprised, hurriedly matched her stride to Gwen's. Her hands were strong and dotted with calluses. Maggie fought the urge to interlace her fingers with Gwen's and hold tighter.

Gene and Darren encouraged Maggie and a few other Jewish guests to join them in the front. Thankfully, the space was large enough that everyone was able to see, especially people as tall as Gwen, who stayed to the back. The menorah, made in beautiful silver with a shining gold star on the center, was set lovingly on a small end table Gene and Darren had positioned directly in front of the balcony sliding doors.

"We tried doing this outside on the porch last year," Gene said, gesturing to the beautiful sunset view, "but the wind kept blowing out the candles." Darren shushed him as he picked up the matchbox.

As the sun's last rays slipped over the balcony railing and away over the horizon, Darren lit the match and held it to the center *shamash* candle. When it took the flame, he blew out the match and handed it to Gene. Then he carefully took the *shamash* and proceeded to light each of the candles. When all eight were lit, he replaced the *shamash* in the center and stepped back.

Maggie became mesmerized by the nine bright flames and stared deeply at them as they flickered. Warmth filled her chest, spreading through each rib and her spine, settling inside her heart. Memories of stories her grandparents had shared with her over the years came flooding back to her—stories of ancestors who had survived incredible hardship only to lead their family to the peace and prosperity they enjoyed now. She thought about her own year, how, in a few short months, she had overcome a broken heart, become a professional stage actress, and found a place to worship again. Tears stung at the corners of her eyes, but she smiled with pride.

With a nod from Darren, the Jewish members of the group began the first *brachah*. "*Barukh atah Adonai Eloheinu, melekh ha'olam, asher kid'shanu b'mitzvotav v'tzivanu l'hadlik ner shel Hanukkah.*"

Maggie stumbled over a few of the first words, but found they came back to her quickly. She recited the second *brachah* with more confidence. "*Barukh atah Adonai Eloheinu, melekh ha'olam, she'asa nisim la'avoteinu ba'yamim ha'heim ba'z'man ha'ze.*"

Gene and Darren then began to recite a *Hanerot Halalu*. Maggie did not recognize this version, so she focused on the candles and listened reverently.

When the *brachot* were completed, Gene and Darren turned to the group with welcoming arms. "*G'mar chatimah tovah!*"

"*G'mar chatimah tovah!*" Maggie and a few others said back.

"The candles will remain lit for at least another half hour," Gene said, "but we went all out with candles this year so they might last longer than that, and we're not planning on blowing them out unless we have to. Thank you, everyone, for joining us to celebrate today. Let's eat!"

As the group turned to the table, Gwen hung back and caught Maggie's attention.

"I was hoping you could explain what happened," Gwen said a bit shyly. "I know what a menorah is, but…"

"You don't speak Hebrew," Maggie said.

"Nope."

"Neither do I, really," Maggie said. "I know a little bit but not enough to be fluent. I just know what our *brachot* mean. Do you know why we celebrate Hanukkah?"

Gwen shook her head. "I know Christians celebrate Christmas because it's the birth of Jesus. Is it connected?"

"Uh, no. No connection at all." As they selected food, Maggie explained the story of the rededication of the temple of Jerusalem. "Technically," Maggie continued as they found seats in a couple chairs, "Hanukkah isn't a recognized holiday in our most important scripture, the Tanakh."

"I thought it was called the Torah."

"The Torah is part of the Tanakh. We have a lot of scripture. The point is, there are a lot of Jewish holidays that are technically considered more important. None of which I've been great about acknowledging for the past year," Maggie admitted regrettably.

"How come Hanukkah is the only holiday I know about, then?" Gwen asked.

A gentleman with buzzed, white-colored hair and a shiny blue bow tie, who had been lingering on the edge of their conversation for a few minutes spoke up. "I think it's mostly for two reasons. Firstly, in the 1970s, there was a push to increase the visibility of Hanukkah in America. America loves its Christmas; there's a huge culture around treating the winter as the time to renew your soul and bond with your family. Hanukkah became largely accepted in that light, which helped increase some public acceptance of Judaism."

Maggie resisted rolling her eyes. "Growing up I used to hear people call Hanukkah 'Jewish Christmas' all the time, and it's annoying. Hanukkah is way older."

The gentleman laughed. "Sometimes, I think Christians have a bad attitude because God gave them a whole new section of the Bible and told them they had to memorize the whole thing. But then I remember it's not just Christians, it's Americans and their love of turning holidays into spending extravaganzas."

Gwen eyed the presents table. "I am easily distracted by shiny things," she acknowledged.

"The other reason I believe Hanukkah is well-known and loved," the gentleman continued, "is because it's such a joyful message that anyone can celebrate. God shows His love for us and continues to watch over us through little miracles. No matter what we have survived as a people, He has been with us. And," he said, gesturing to the mound of cheese on Maggie's plate, "everyone has an important role to play, regardless of identity or social role."

Gwen glanced at the cheese and then back at the gentleman.

Maggie explained. "There was a Jewish woman named Judith who beheaded a Babylonian official after getting him intoxicated with wine and cheese. So, once a year, I get to eat a ton of cheese in the name of feminism."

"Metal."

The gentleman reached to shake Maggie's hand. "I'm Nathaniel, by the way."

"Maggie. Nice to meet you."

"Are you, like so many I know here, returning to the faith after some time away?"

Maggie nodded. "Once I wasn't with my parents anymore, I guess I just couldn't find a reason to keep practicing. I didn't have anyone to worship with."

"What about Jess?" Gwen asked.

This time, Maggie did roll her eyes. "Jess wasn't exactly torn up when I stopped practicing. In fact, at one point, she mentioned it was good I was 'letting myself loose.'" Maggie shrugged. "I think Jess just didn't like rules, to be honest. She kept trying to put bacon in mac and cheese."

Nathaniel tutted.

Gwen frowned. "Well, that's rude. You deserve to be with somebody who respects your religion, even if it's not theirs."

"Oh, are you two not together?" Nathaniel asked with a tone of surprise.

Maggie choked on her cheese.

"No," Gwen replied as Maggie took a sip of water. "Why?"

"You seemed to be interested in learning from Maggie," Nathaniel replied.

"I am. I definitely am."

"Ahh, I see," Nathaniel said, sitting back and winking.

Thankfully for Maggie, Darren chose that moment to stand up and announce, "Let's get the Secret Santa gift exchange started, shall we?"

"Boooooo," called a brunette across the room. "Do we have to call it that?"

"Fine, fine, Hanukkah Harry," Darren replied, causing laughter in the group. "I'll be Harry."

"So I shouldn't get out the red-and-white hat we have shoved in the closet?" Gene asked from the kitchen doorway.

"C'mon, Gene, let me have my one celebration where I don't have to hear 'ho ho ho' or feckin' *Jingle Bells* one more time," the brunette demanded, with a chorus of agreement from the group.

"I'm just kidding, Janice!"

Darren clapped his hands. "All right, let's get started. Now, there's no prize for guessing who gave you your present, but it is fun to do. Who should we start with first?" He scanned the presents, then picked up a tiny ruby gift bag with its string handles tied together. "Coral, since you're always bursting with energy, how about you?"

Coral took the bag and, in a gesture that made Maggie cringe, ripped it open from top to bottom.

"What did you do that for?" she asked as Coral started unwrapping tissue paper. "It's a perfectly reusable bag."

"It's fine," Coral shushed her as she revealed her present: a shimmering four-leaf clover pendant hanging from a fine gold chain. "Oooh," Coral breathed, holding it lovingly in her hands. "Oh, I love it."

"Well, who do you think gave it to you?" Darren urged her.

Coral examined the faces of everyone in the room intently, squinting at certain suspicious gigglers. Initially, she pointed at Nathaniel, but he shook his head.

"I'm afraid I don't have that good of taste," he said.

"Hmmm, who here has good taste…" Coral murmured.

"That narrows it down a little," Bobby joked.

Eventually, Coral's eyes landed on Sky, and she pointed at them. Sky, grinning, nodded their head.

"A while ago when we were talking, you said you needed a lucky charm to help you get your big break," Sky explained. "So…I hope this can be your lucky charm."

Coral immediately put the necklace on, brushing her dark brown locks out of the way. "I'll wear it to every audition," she promised. "It's beautiful. Thank you so much!"

As Darren moved on to the next gifts, Maggie noticed Gwen chuckling next to her.

"What's up?" she asked.

Gwen moved close to Maggie and whispered in her ear, "It's perfect Sky got to be Coral's Secret Santa."

"Why's that?"

"Because Sky's had a massive crush on Coral for years. Anyone who knows them knows it. It's so obvious."

Maggie glared across the room at Coral, who was intently watching another partygoer opening their present. "You don't say."

After Nathaniel opened his present—a set of fun bow ties from Bobby—Darren handed Maggie her large, slim purple box. The sides were taped together, so with a few slices with her fingernails Maggie was able to lift the lid of the box and see inside.

She gasped. "I…I don't know what to say. This is amazing."

"Hold it up," Bobby called.

Maggie obliged, carefully lifting up a glass menorah. Each curve was a different color, creating a beautiful ombre rainbow. Maggie gazed at it with awe before looking back to Darren. "You did this, didn't you?"

Darren nodded, and Gene, who had stepped out of the kitchen to join them, said, "When you said you didn't even have your own menorah, it just broke our hearts. We wanted you to have a reminder that your faith and your sexuality need never be separated again." The others in the room, including Nathaniel, nodded approvingly.

Maggie fought tears as she carefully laid the menorah back in its box. "I'll treasure it forever," she said, her voice choked up.

"We want to see it lit up next year," Darren said as he turned back to the present table.

A few gifts and many laughs later, it was Gwen's turn to open her present.

"I don't want to rip the wrapping paper," she said, examining the box. "The puppies are so cute."

"Rip tear rip!" Coral cheered.

"It's okay," Maggie reassured Gwen. "You have a cuter, real dog at home you can see all the time."

Gwen nodded, but still did her best to open the paper without tearing it, much to Coral's disappointment. When Gwen revealed the box, her eyebrows furrowed in confusion at first and then suddenly lifted in excitement.

"It's a puppy cam!" she said, turning the box to show the rest of the room. "So I can keep an eye on Bluebell even when I'm not at home." The group exclaimed excitedly as Gwen started reading the features on the box. "It uses an app on my phone, it has a battery reserve in case the power goes out, it can record, and it even does sound. I can actually talk to my dog over the phone with this thing!"

"Who do you think gave it to you?" Bobby called. "Guess!"

Gwen scanned the room. "Running out of options here. Let's see, process of elimination…" She paused, then turned her head quickly to the side. "Maggie?"

Maggie blushed but spoke with false confidence. "You got it in one try."

Gwen beamed. She threw her arms around Maggie, wrapping her in a tight hug. "Thank you so, so much. I'm going to set it up as soon as I get home. This is perfect. How can I ever thank you?"

Maggie, feeling a little lightheaded, hugged Gwen back as tightly as she dared. "Just show me how Blue is doing whenever I ask, and we're even," she joked.

When Gwen ended the hug to show Bobby and Sky more about the puppy cam, Maggie reclined and breathed deeply, pointedly ignoring Coral's cheeky grin.

Chapter Twenty-Five

IN JANUARY, HALEIGH and Gwen announced rehearsals were moving to the Twilight. For three more weeks, they would meet on Tuesdays and Thursdays before increasing to daily rehearsals until opening night. Maggie couldn't help the shimmers of excitement as she thought about finally getting into costume and running through the play beginning to end, set pieces and props complete.

The first time she walked into Twilight for rehearsal, she barely recognized the stage. The set designers had outdone themselves with painted fabric backdrops. Backstage, a small crew worked on refinishing a dining table and set of chairs. While a couple women brushed the table with varnish, a gentleman used a wood stapler to reupholster the chair seats with dark-gray fabric. Behind them, Roy, the stage manager, talked with Gwen and Haleigh.

"I don't know how you want to handle the town hall scene," he said.

"Are we thinking loose chairs, or benches? Do you want a podium, or a long table?"

"A podium should be fine," Haleigh replied. "If you can manage benches, I'd love to see benches."

"I don't like the blocking with benches though," Gwen said. "We'd have to arrange everyone so that they don't block each other when they get up and move around…"

"Tell you what," Roy said. "I'll ask one of the crew, Xinyan, to get those short benches we used for the court scene in *Christmas Carol*, and we can try those out. If you like them, they just need to be repainted. They're a ghastly eggshell."

"Thanks, Roy," Gwen said. "Anything we can do to be most helpful?"

Roy shook his head. "Let's just jump into this. I've memorized the script, but I still need to get the feel of how the show runs."

"You got it."

Maggie placed her things in an audience seat and eagerly climbed onto the stage as Gwen summoned the group. She joined Alyssa, Bel, Georgia, Donna, and Sky in a semicircle around Gwen, Haleigh, and Roy.

"Thank you, everyone, for arriving promptly," Gwen began, "because it's going to be a big day. I'd like to officially introduce Roy Sharpe, the stage manager."

Roy nodded. "I've been a stage manager with Twilight for about five years, graduated from USC. Gwen and I have worked on a lot of projects together."

"Roy's job is to make my creative ramblings function like a well-oiled machine," Gwen said. "So today, we're going to do a run-through, no stops."

"You say that," Donna piped up, "but I've literally never done a run-through without stops."

The group laughed, including Roy.

"Well, we're going to do our best," Gwen emphasized. "Roy is mostly going to watch from the audience. He'll be joined by our lighting and sound engineers. We're going to establish all the cues and start practicing them properly from now on as a team."

"Definitely stops, then," Bel muttered.

"I heard that," Gwen responded. She clapped her hands. "Everyone backstage. I'll be over here in the corner, but try your best to act like it's a performance. Here we go."

Maggie rushed backstage with the rest, her heart fluttering. From the moment Gwen called, "Act one, scene one, go!" Maggie practically melted into her comfort zone. Finally, at long last, she was performing, truly performing again.

Well, almost. True to Donna's prediction, the run-through had many, many stops. Sometimes, the actors stood for up to five minutes at a time while Roy and his engineers discussed cues with Gwen. At one point, Maggie and Georgia sat on the stage floor, waiting for a particularly heated discussion about lighting to finish. Roy and Gwen had similar communication styles, throwing ideas at each other until they passed the same idea back and forth, at which point they polished the details, then moved on to the next question.

Even with all the stops, the hours flew by. Maggie was pleasantly tired when Gwen clapped her hands and announced, "That's all the time we have for today. Please see Haleigh to pick up your rehearsal notes. If you have any questions about them, feel free to contact me and we can discuss them."

Maggie stretched her arms, letting Georgia and Donna go first to collect their notes so they could head home to their families. Roy had already moved back to his crew, who had finished the dining room set and moved on to cleaning up an old bicycle and podium. When Maggie went to pick up her notes, she noticed Alyssa hadn't left after getting hers. In fact, she handed out something of her own to everyone as they left.

"Maggie," she said upon her approach. "Here, have an invite."

Maggie took a little pink envelope in hand. "Can I open it now?"

"Of course. It's just a reminder for my birthday party, especially for people who didn't get a text from me the first time."

Maggie looked the invite over. "Why is it called 'Party Three'?"

Gwen chuckled as Maggie took out the invite. "Alyssa's a bit of a party animal. She's having one party with family, one party with work friends, one party with us…"

"Hush, I didn't hear you complaining last time when I brought a cake to rehearsal." Alyssa sniffed. "I'm turning twenty-five. I want to really celebrate."

"No kidding," Maggie murmured. "Isn't Coastal Harbor a bar? I don't know if I can go."

"It's a bar and restaurant," Alyssa reassured her. "You'll be allowed in; I promise. I'm looking forward to it. They have live music that night. I reserved us a couple tables so we get a good view. And no presents," Alyssa told her. "Just your company."

"Really?" Maggie asked, surprised. "Are you sure?"

Gwen rolled her eyes. "I told you, she's a party animal. The last time she invited me to something, I gave her a gift card. That should be fine."

"You're actually coming to the party this time, aren't you?" Alyssa asked.

"I promise," Gwen said. "I wouldn't miss it."

*

MAGGIE DIDN'T HAVE a lot of free time to think about the party in the weeks that followed. She worked with Sofia to set her work schedule at the coffee shop for the next couple months, making sure her time for upcoming play rehearsals and performances would be secure. More and more nights and afternoons found her at the Twilight, with rehearsals becoming increasingly frantic with activity. Costumes were created, altered, worn, and fixed again. Props were chosen, used, then discarded in exchange for better fits. Set pieces were repainted, and the stage marked with various colors of tape. Roy and Gwen were a power team, guiding the actors as though they had always shared the same creative vision. And through it all, Maggie and Gwen still found the time each Wednesday to meet and study acting—now with the addition of freshly cooked dinners, at Gwen's insistence.

Maggie had started wondering what she was going to do with her time when the play was over. She was already scanning audition postings, looking for a potential next job, but she couldn't bring herself to go to them yet, not if it meant sacrificing her last afternoons with Gwen.

As one of these study sessions wrapped up, Gwen threw together a Mexican casserole to bake in the oven while Maggie wrote notes about Practical Aesthetics. As Maggie reviewed her notes, checking she had included all four steps of the theory's particular analysis, Bluebell trotted clumsily down the spiral staircase. Blue plopped herself on the couch next to Maggie and, before she could properly react, started ripping a packet of paper with her teeth.

"Blue, no! Give me that!" Maggie took the packet from between Blue's paws and spoke to her sternly. "Bad. Chewing paper will give you papercuts."

Gwen hurried over. "Ugh, I must have left something on the floor. I don't know what her fascination is with paper. What'd she get?"

Maggie handed it over, but noticed what it was from the straggling pieces—a court summons.

Gwen looked it over, then sighed deeply. "Well, that's fine. This was for last week. I already went." She set the paper on the kitchen counter, safely out of Blue's reach.

"How did it go?" Maggie asked cautiously, closing the textbook she had been writing notes from.

"Court was adjourned."

"What does that mean?"

Gwen slid the casserole into the oven, closed the door, and set the timer as she answered. "Val never showed up. Her lawyer said they hadn't had a chance to talk yet. So the judge had to adjourn. We rescheduled for next month, and the judge extended my restraining order until then."

"Ugh," Maggie groaned. "I'm sorry; that's so irritating."

Gwen nodded, cleaning up ingredients on the counter. "I'm not surprised. Wouldn't put it past Val to have one more opportunity to inconvenience me."

Maggie joined Gwen in the kitchen. Gwen's shoulders were slumped, though her movements stayed quick and precise. "Can I help?" Maggie asked, trying to distract her.

"I'm almost done. The casserole will be done in about half an hour, so we have time to finish."

"How's the puppy cam working?"

Gwen's face lit up. "I love it so much. I don't know if you noticed I check it during rehearsals, but it's perfect. It pretty much shows the whole apartment."

"Really?" Maggie looked around. "I don't see it."

"It's really discreet." Gwen pointed next to her door. "I put it right above the intercom, and it just looks like a doorbell or something."

"Oh yeah. It blends right in." Maggie took a closer look. "I didn't even notice it when I came in."

Gwen took her phone out and tapped open the app before showing Maggie the screen. "Look how clear the picture is."

Maggie was impressed. "This is incredible. And everything works?"

"Look at this, it's so cool." Gwen tapped a speaker button on the app. "And now I can hear anything in the apartment." Her voice reverberated from the phone. She quickly clicked the speaker back off, then clicked on a microphone. "And you can hear me, can't you Blue?" This time, the voice echoed from the camera unit above the door.

"I'm so glad that works," Maggie said. "There were more expensive, fancier ones, but…"

"This is perfect the way it is. You outdid yourself."

"Really, after all the time you've spent tutoring me for free, and now you're even feeding me." Maggie fought an incoming blush. "It's honestly the least I could do in return."

"Stop it," Gwen said casually, heading back over to the couch. "This has been so enjoyable for me; you have no idea. But I did want to talk to you about the tutoring."

"Sure…what can I do?"

Gwen looked at Maggie with a serious expression, one that reminded Maggie of their first sessions in the library. "You've been a fast learner, but you're not getting a complete education with me. I really think you should consider applying to college."

Maggie flushed. "I don't think that's realistic for me right now."

"I'm not saying do it right away," Gwen replied. "But seriously. With the grades you had in high school, and the work I've seen you do since we met, you're a perfect candidate for an academic scholarship. I think you should apply sooner rather than later."

Maggie sat next to her on the couch. She could feel herself getting defensive, and encouraged herself to keep her voice calm. "I don't see how I'm supposed to make that work. Once *Petty Oppression* is over, I'm back to just making ends meet."

"Maybe you don't do it full-time. Maybe you do it full-time, but you find a different mix of jobs. Look, I have some experience in this; I'm willing to sit down with you to try to help you figure out how to make it work. But Maggie, it could be a huge benefit to your career." Gwen gestured to the pile of notes from *Petty Oppression* collected on her kitchen table. "Look at how many of our cast come from local schools. With your talent, and your student skills, a little bit of networking…I think it's the path that could work best for you."

Maggie sat and thought in silence for a few moments. Gwen gave her time, petting Bluebell's ears.

"I'll take a look at some things," Maggie said. "Look around for good tuition rates. Maybe an acting academy."

"Keep your options open," Gwen said. "And I'm here to help. I just ask one thing."

Maggie looked at Gwen, whose face had softened into a smile. "What's that?"

"Promise me we'll still hang out when the play is over."

"Oh! Oh, Gwen, of course." Maggie gripped her fingers together nervously. "However we can make it work. I still want to hang out. You're…you're my best friend."

"What about Coral?"

"Coral's…a different kind of best friend." Maggie scrunched her eyebrows together. "A silly kind."

"But earnest," Gwen said, leaning back as Bluebell climbed up onto her lap. "I hope she gets a good, steady job soon. She's worked so hard for it, and when she puts down the silly hijinks and tricks, she does have the talent. I'm glad you have her for a roommate."

"Why don't you have a roommate? I know this apartment is small, but you said it's expensive. You could, I don't know, hang a curtain from the loft and make this a second bedroom."

Gwen shrugged. "I've made it work so far. After what happened, y'know, with my ex…I just didn't feel comfortable asking anyone else to risk living with me."

Maggie furrowed her brows. "I'd think it would be safer if you lived with someone."

"Maybe. But honestly, I think living alone is safer. If I lived with someone else, Val would just assume we're dating, and that could provoke her."

"That's ridiculous."

Gwen ran a hand through her hair. "I know it is, but…that's what it's like, dealing with that kind of controlling person. You learn to start reading their signals, to understand their emotions better than they do. With Val, it was kind of my job to help her regulate her emotions. I used to do it because I wanted her to be happy. Now I do it just to keep her off my back."

Gwen sighed, holding her chin in one hand. "Those emails and stuff she started sending me after the breakup…I read a couple before I wised up and changed my contact info. She seemed to think I was having some kind of extended temper tantrum, and eventually, I'd get over it and ask for her back. The more I keep my distance from people, the more she leaves everyone involved alone."

"But that's not fair," Maggie protested. "You can't expect to live your whole life with no friends or roommates to appease one person."

"I'm not. Honestly, when the emails stopped, I thought she was finally letting go. Now that I know she's still around, and still, well, angry…I have the restraining order. And before you worry about my safety, I'm friendly with my neighbors, so if I ever need someone, they'll come help." Gwen smiled. "Bea actually came over for coffee and to hang out with Blue the other day. She has a new girlfriend but says she hates dogs, so Blue is her puppy fix."

Maggie watched Gwen carefully, looking for signs that she was faking being fine, but Gwen seemed to have shifted her focus back to Bluebell with little struggle. "I don't know how you do all this," Maggie said. "I respect you so much."

"I respect you too. Thanks for letting me talk about this kind of stuff with you. I know it's not the happiest stuff to listen to."

Maggie shook her head firmly. "Don't ever apologize. I'll always listen. And, when you need a positive distraction, I'm filled with ideas."

"Oh, really? Well, lay it on me." Gwen sat back. "What's a positive distraction?"

Maggie grinned. "Have you ever watched *Mystery Science Theater 3000*?"

Chapter Twenty-Six

COASTAL HARBOR WAS located in the Ocean Avenue neighborhood, so the bus ride to it was a lengthy one. Maggie leaned her head against the window, watching the February sun gleam against skyscraper windows, and wondered if she should just give in and buy a clunker car. So far, she had avoided it, but if she was going to attend school again, she might find herself in situations where being dependent on the Metro's reliability wasn't an option.

Somehow, she made it, only a little later than the rest. Alyssa's attire, a gold, glimmering dress with a cutoff shoulder, at first had her wondering if she was underdressed. Taking a look around at the rest of the cast, dressed in jeans and nice shirts, Maggie decided her jean jacket with black leggings and a purple dress was suitable, and Alyssa was just being a birthday queen. When Bel helped Alyssa put on a shiny plastic tiara, this confirmed her suspicions.

Gwen noticed Maggie's arrival immediately and waved her over. "You look really nice," she said, speaking over the chatter of the bar patrons.

"Thank you." Maggie hoped the warm lights of the bar hid her blush. "You look really nice too."

Gwen laughed and gestured to her blouse and jeans. "This is literally what I wore to the Hanukkah party."

"I know. I really like it. It matches your eyes." The words slipped out before she could stop them.

Gwen smiled and was about to reply, but Bel cut in.

"Maggie! You're just in time. We're about to play a trivia game up at the bar. You do musical theater, right?"

"Yeah, all the time in high school."

"Great. I want you on my team. Let's go."

Bel dragged Maggie up near the bar, where she was given a glass of water and carefully watched by a bartender whose bushy eyebrows indicated a no-nonsense attitude. She sipped her water demurely as they played the game, competing against one another to answer questions about musical theater, classic rock, hair metal, and country music. After Donna won the winning point for Alyssa's team (answering, "Who wrote the song 'Roses on My Grave,'" with the band Alleycat Scratch), the group made their way to the next room.

The room was relatively large but somehow still gave the appearance of an intimate gathering place. Warm burgundy walls decorated with vinyl records directed attention toward a dance floor and a stage at the back wall. A set of drums and a keyboard, already set up, waited on the stage next to an empty guitar stand, a microphone, and a couple amplifiers. Circular tables and chairs for dining took up the rest of the room. The cast sat at two tables, four each, with Haleigh, Alyssa, Bel, and Donna at one and Skylar, Georgia, Gwen, and Maggie at the other. There were almost no empty tables to be seen. The rest of the crowd had less of a "party" aesthetic than Alyssa, mostly wearing jeans and graphic band tees, but the room was abuzz with excitement.

"So how is this working?" Gwen asked Alyssa. "I don't see menus."

"Oh, it's performance night," Alyssa explained. "We're getting some munchies family-style to share. Sit-down restaurant-style isn't exactly made for getting up and dancing. Pick what you want from that appetizer list over there"—she pointed to a chalkboard against the wall—"and we can order at the bar."

"Ah." Gwen sat back and leaned over to Maggie next to her. "This is a bit more club-scene than I was anticipating," she said just loudly enough to be heard.

"I think it's fun," Maggie said. "I've been to a couple things like this. Not in a while though."

"Are there kosher options here for you to eat from that list?"

Maggie smiled at Gwen. "I can bend the rules a little. Thanks for asking though."

Maggie, Gwen, Georgia, and Skylar decided to chip in to buy a couple appetizer platters to share. As Georgia took the order up to the bar, the lights in the room adjusted, illuminating the stage and dimming the dining area.

"I forgot to ask," Georgia said, "What band is playing?"

"Some up-and-commers called Chimera," Skylar said. "Alyssa says she's heard them around."

It was as if someone had just dumped ice water on Maggie's heart.

She gripped the table edge. "Chimera?"

"Yeah, have you heard of them?"

"You could say that." Maggie stared at the stage as familiar figures emerged. Steve and Jay took their place at the keyboard and drums to do their sound checks. Ethan walked out with his electric guitar, hooked it up, and played a few test chords to cheers from the crowd.

Then, out came Jess, wearing her favorite leather jacket, half her hair buzzed and the other half purple, but otherwise looking every bit the same as she had the last time Maggie saw her five months prior.

Jess took the microphone and called out, "I don't know what you're all sitting down for. Our music is meant for you to rock!"

Many people, including Alyssa, leapt to their feet and rushed to the dance floor. Maggie was grateful the people at her table chose to stay behind because she couldn't have moved if she tried. She sat, frozen, eyes glued to the suddenly fascinating dessert menu on the table.

"Ladies and gentlemen, welcome to the Coastal Harbor, and we're Chimera!"

Jay ticked the beat on his drumsticks, and with no further ado, the band launched into their first song of the night.

They performed for almost an hour. Maggie operated on autopilot, mindlessly eating mozzarella sticks and french fries, prompting another order of appetizers from the bar. It was a strange feeling, almost out-of-body, while also firmly anchored to one spot with no idea how to escape. As Jess sang, in her mind, Maggie involuntarily sang along to every word, each lyric leaping forward as if they had been branded into her brain. Maggie tried everything she could think of to keep herself sane, staring at the dancing audience, inspecting the dessert menu, even trying to have a conversation with Sky, Georgia, and Gwen over the music when possible.

Just when she thought maybe she could get through this, just push through until the performance was over, it happened. Maggie was watching Ethan intently, silently urging him to do his last-song ritual of resting his guitar on the stand for a moment and stretching, when Jess looked across the audience, and their eyes met. Perhaps it was a coincidence. But when Maggie immediately looked away—maybe it was her imagination—she heard a change in Jess's voice.

And when that song was over, Jess called out, "Hey, pretty girls, who came here alone?" eliciting some cries from the dancers and making Maggie's face flush scarlet.

When the final song was over, Maggie practically slumped in her seat as the band exited the stage, ushered off by enthusiastic cheers.

Alyssa, who had spent a large part of the hour dancing, made her way over to the table. "You guys, you barely got up at all," she said, tapping Skylar on the shoulder. "Are you at least going to dance now that you've eaten?"

Georgia and Skylar stepped away with Alyssa over to her birthday table, talking about the performance as the restaurant's sound system started playing recorded music again.

Gwen glanced over at Maggie, who hadn't moved or replied at all. "Are you feeling okay? You don't look great."

Maggie groaned, rubbing her face with her hands. "I'm good. I just need a moment."

"Not a fan of the music?"

"Oh, no, the music was fine," Maggie said almost bitterly. She straightened up in her seat and reached for another mozzarella stick. "In fact, at one time I was their biggest fan."

Before Gwen could ask any more questions, there was a slight commotion from the dance floor. Maggie watched, horrified, as the dancers parted to reveal Jess walking toward their table.

"Heeeeey, Mags," Jess called out as she approached. It took all of Maggie's strength to stay upright in her chair and not slouch out of sight. Jess leaned an elbow on the table, flipped her hair out of her eyes, and grinned. "God, I haven't seen you since… Well. You look good."

"Thanks, Jess." Maggie formed the words as if she were pushing them through steel punch cards. "Cool hair."

"Aw, you like it? I'm thinking of trying green next." Jess combed her fingers through her hair. She leaned closer to Maggie. "It's awesome to see you. What are you doing here?"

"I'm at a friend's birthday party." Maggie pointed to Alyssa, who was up and dancing again, surrounded by the cast.

Gwen scooched her chair slightly closer to Maggie and reached across the table to shake Jess's hand. "Hey, it seems you're a friend of Maggie's. I'm Gwen. It's nice to meet you."

Jess looked surprised, then shook Gwen's hand. Maggie noticed Gwen seemed to shake it pretty firmly. "Oh, yeah, hi. Yeah, we're kinda friends. Maggie's actually my ex."

"Oh," Gwen said as she sat back. "You must be the one she moved here with. It sounds like it was quite the adventure."

"Oh, yeah," Jess said casually. "Yeah, Maggie and I came here with the guys. She held down the fort while we got business up and running. I mean, she's no housewife"—she laughed—"but she was sweet to me. Mags, listen, I know I was a bit of a jerk. I hope all is forgiven. You know me, I just like to go with the flow."

Maggie grunted.

Gwen said, "I never asked— How did things end between you?"

"Oh, that was all my fault," Jess said, shifting on her feet. Her smile was starting to look forced. "I was running around at night, you know. Had a thing going where I spent time with some girls after performances. You know how it is; you get up on stage, you play your heart out, and then your adrenaline is just racing… And, um, I wasn't really honest about it."

Gwen's face went from cordial to cool faster than Maggie could blink.

"Hey, are you Mag's new girl?" Jess asked, flicking a finger back and forth between the two of them.

Gwen's arm instantly wrapped around Maggie's shoulders. "Yeah, I am," she said firmly. "We're trying not to make tonight all about us though; we're here to celebrate."

"Oh, yeah, your friend." Jess turned around, balancing both elbows on the table. "The one in the gold dress, right? She looks fun. Do you know which team she bats for?" She winked at Maggie. "To be honest, I was kinda hoping you were free, but it seems like you're not. You got hot friends though."

Maggie was about to scream. Gwen's hand tightened on her shoulder. Thankfully, at that moment, the crowd parted again as Ethan and Jay pushed their way through, Steve fending off enthusiastic and observant fans behind them.

"Jess," Jay snapped, marching toward her. "The fuck are you doing?"

"Heeeey, man, be chill," Jess said, raising her hands in protest. "I'm just saying hi."

"You get the fuck back to the truck and help me pack up the

equipment," Jay ordered her, gripping her by the elbow. "You're in no shape to be out here right now. I saw the cans you snuck in right before the show."

"God, you're such a narc," Jess said, rolling her eyes as Jay dragged her away.

Ethan stayed behind, with Steve joining him quickly. "Hey, are you okay?" Ethan asked Maggie, brow creased in concern.

Maggie rubbed her forehead. "Yeah, I'm fine. Hi, guys. Long time no talk."

"We're so sorry about her," Steve said. "We told her over and over to just leave you alone."

"Maggie, are these friends of yours?" Gwen asked cautiously.

"Yeah, no, they're cool. This is Steve and Ethan. The third guy was Jay. We all went to high school together."

Steve reached across the table to shake Gwen's hand, who took it apprehensively. "Glad to see Maggie has a friend looking out for her," he said. "She's been through some shit."

"You're friends with her ex?" Gwen asked.

"They're cool," Maggie repeated. "Ethan's actually the one who told me Jess was cheating."

Gwen's lips pulled taut, and Maggie thought there was a red tint to her ears. "You guys know what she did and you keep her around?" Her voice sounded labored, as though she was fighting to keep calm.

Ethan bowed his head. "She fucked up bad, but she's our mate. We've been best friends since grade school."

"And she needs us," Steve said. "Maggie, I don't know how much you saw of this at the end, but Jess… Well, we're working on some new expectations for her. Less drinking, less partying."

"As talented as she is," Ethan continued, "we've made it clear if she doesn't clean up her act, we'll drive her back to Ashland."

Gwen's face relaxed slightly. "Well. Thanks for intervening. There was about to be a fight."

"Hell, wouldn't be the first time," Ethan said. "Maggie, it was really nice seeing you again. I hope things are working out for you."

"Yeah, I've got a job as an actress for a stage play."

"Word! That's all you ever wanted." Steve reached across the table to give her a fist bump, then turned to Gwen. "If you're a friend of Maggie, take good care of her. She's a gem."

"I know," Gwen said, pulling Maggie slightly closer.

As Steve and Ethan walked off, Maggie finally let herself slump in her chair. She sullenly took another fry.

"Are you okay?" Gwen asked, taking her arm back but turning to face her.

"I'm going to eat my feelings, then I'll be fine." Maggie chewed on the fry and fought tears. "I just wasn't expecting that."

"No kidding. I hope you don't mind me saying this, but…oh my God, what a bitch."

Maggie laughed wryly. "I mean, she's nowhere near as bad as your ex."

"Hey, don't go trying to dismiss your pain by comparing it to mine," Gwen said, a little sternly. "That chick had the nerve to come over here and try to—ugh." Gwen's hands balled up into fists. "I was this close to socking her in the nose. Was she always so vain?"

Maggie waggled her hand in the so-so motion. "Eh. She's always known she's talented and desirable. When we were in high school, she was a lot more attentive. Things just got weird after we moved here." She reached for another fry. "I dunno. I've tried to not think about it much. I think once we were here and she had the freedom, had girls flocking to meet her, she just wanted different things. I'm not mad about it. I accept that we drifted apart." She sighed deeply. "I don't know why I'm feeling so drained, really."

"I don't have a lot of normal experiences with dating, but it's my understanding that meeting an ex in public is never the nicest thing, especially when it ends on a sour note. Is that why you broke up?" she asked gently.

"Because she cheated on me? I guess so. That, and she didn't even have the guts to tell me until Ethan texted me pictures, and the band forced her to apologize." Maggie swallowed her fry and reached for a mozzarella stick. "And, I mean, she was never home anymore. I know you have to work hard to make a band successful, but the conversation we had that day was the longest one we'd had in months, and it only lasted about fifteen minutes."

"Wait, what?" Gwen looked like she was trying to solve an equation in her head. "You didn't spend any time together?"

Maggie shrugged. "Unless I went to her gigs. I used to whenever I didn't have work or an audition."

Gwen placed her hands together and rested them against the tip of her nose. "So…you didn't, like, go on dates or anything? Spend time together at home to unwind?"

Maggie shook her head, taking the last cheesy bite. She gazed sadly at the empty appetizer platter.

Gwen stood up. "Hey, how are you feeling?"

"I still want to eat my feelings."

"Perfect. Go out with me."

Maggie nearly fell out of her chair. She gripped the table and pulled herself upright. "Wh-what?"

"Let's go on a date. Right now."

"Right now?" Maggie felt dizzy.

"You deserve to have a good time with someone who's just paying attention to you—and not for the sake of your career." Gwen jerked her thumb toward the restaurant entrance. "I have my car outside; let's go. Anywhere you want."

"Ah—but— We're here to celebrate with Alyssa and the cast." Maggie knew there was no fighting the blush spreading from ear to ear. "Won't leaving be rude?"

"I don't think they'll care if we tell them we're bowing out a little early." Gwen looked over at Alyssa, who was whooping and whirling her tiara in the air. "Besides, from what I remember last time, Alyssa gets obnoxious after five drinks. I'll give Georgia the money to cover our part of the bill. Hang on." Gwen slipped onto the dance floor, weaving her way toward Georgia and digging into her pocket for her wallet.

Maggie stumbled to her feet, her mind somehow going a million miles a minute and standing completely still. Part of her desperately, frantically searched for an excuse, telling herself, *Don't do this. This isn't a good idea.* But another part of her, an increasingly loud part, asked, *Why?*

By the time Gwen returned to the table, Maggie had decided. Gwen held out her elbow. "So, is it a date?"

Maggie slipped her arm through Gwen's and smiled, embracing the flush in her face. "It's a date. You deserve some attention, too, Gwen."

Gwen smiled softly. "A first date for both of us, then." She gestured to the door. "Onward, Miss Fromm. Adventure awaits!"

Chapter Twenty-Seven

MAGGIE FELT NOSTALGIC sitting in the front seat of Gwen's station wagon.

Gwen pulled out her phone. "So, what shall it be? Late night bowling? Romantic date to the observatory? Shopping at Universal Studios citywalk?"

Maggie giggled. "I don't know. This is all a little sudden."

To Maggie's surprise, Gwen giggled too. "It is! What time is it?"

"About eight," Maggie read, checking the car clock.

"Well, that limits a few options, but there's plenty of time. What would you like to do? Is there some part of LA you haven't seen?"

Maggie chewed on her bottom lip, a sudden dark thought rising unbidden to her mind. "There's a lot of LA I haven't really explored. But…" She tried to find the kindest way to ask her question. "Will you be okay going out in public with just me?"

"What do you mean?"

"I mean…" She didn't want to ruin the mood. If asking this question canceled the date right then and there, she would regret it. *Gwen's safety comes first,* Maggie told herself, and she asked, "What if we run into Val on accident or something? Will you be okay?"

Gwen smiled sadly. "Oh, Maggie. I promise I'll be okay. We'll be careful."

Maggie couldn't help creasing her eyebrows. "I worry about it all the time," she admitted. "Most of the time, I just keep too busy to let myself think about it. But sometimes when I'm getting ready for work, I'm like, what if she shows up? And I run through all these scenarios in my head about what I'd do."

Gwen nodded. "I do that every day."

"How do you handle it?"

Gwen took a deep breath and let it out slowly, leaning back in her driver's seat. "Honestly? I'm not sure. It's hard. Out of everything that happened in our relationship, in some ways, us breaking up is the scariest thing because I don't know where she is. She could be out looking for me, or she could be minding her damn business, and I have no clue." Gwen rubbed the heels of her hands against her forehead. "I guess I just tell myself that I didn't work this hard to let her box me out of my own life. But honestly, I've thought about moving back to Idaho."

She leaned her head back and closed her eyes for a moment. When she opened them, she turned to Maggie, smiling. "But it's a good thing I didn't because if I had, I wouldn't be on a date with a cute girl right now."

Maggie, who was pretty sure her face was permanently stained pink at this point, started to protest, but Gwen cut her off.

"Maggie, I know you're worried about me, but I promise it's okay. I worked with a counselor for a long time. I have a safety plan of strategies to handle if something goes wrong. I brushed up on the safety plan after the library incident, and I've been using my coping skills. I'm okay." Her eyes suddenly became serious. "Are you?"

Maggie nodded. "When I think about what if she shows up, what do I do, I just start doing the five-senses exercise you taught me."

"That's perfect. So, feel safe enough to go on a date? If you still want to?"

"Yes! Yes, I still want to."

Gwen's shoulders relaxed, and she picked her phone back up. "Fantastic. Choose an adventure."

Maggie thought hard. Suddenly, she was thinking of the hours she had spent in her high school computer lab googling attractions in Los Angeles. She'd spent most of the time looking for theaters and band gigs, but a few ideas sprang to mind. "I've never been to Santa Monica pier."

Gwen's face split into a huge grin. "You haven't? Oh, we have to go check that out now. We're so close too." She typed the address into her phone, handed it to Maggie, and started the car. "Hold on to that so I can hear the GPS? We'll be there in a jiffy. You can control the radio."

Maggie turned the radio on and searched through channels until she found a catchy song. As Gwen drove through the streets, slowly bringing them closer and closer to an unobstructed ocean view, Maggie watched excitedly through the windows. When the entrance to the parking lot suddenly loomed ahead, she couldn't help but cry out, "There it is!"

Gwen chuckled as she turned in. "God, you're so cute. If I'd known you wanted to see the pier this badly, we'd have gone ages ago."

"You didn't ask me out before now," Maggie sniffed jokingly.

Gwen laughed again. "You got me there. But you never asked me out either," she needled. "Who wears the pants in this relationship?"

"You can wear the pants. I'm more comfortable in leggings."

"Good, because I love when you wear leggings with dresses," Gwen said, scanning the lot for an available spot. "You do this thing where the skirt twirls no matter how you move. It's almost magical."

Maggie buried her face in her hands. "Gwen, stop it. If you keep saying those kinds of things, I'll blow up."

Gwen didn't reply at first. She'd found someone pulling out of a spot and maneuvered to pull in after them. When they were safely parked, she turned the car off and turned to Maggie. "Now, Miss Fromm. I believe I said I was taking you on a date and showing you that you deserve some undivided attention."

"And you," Maggie shot back.

"Fine, both of us. Well, that includes the whole package. You're going to get every compliment I can think of, and you're going to feel good about it because I have no ulterior motives for this. I just want to make you blush and see you smile."

"Well, what am I supposed to do while you're flooding me with blush-inducing comments, then?"

"Accept them," Gwen urged her, opening her car door. "Come on, the pier awaits!"

Maggie hastily opened her door and climbed out. For once when she and Gwen started walking, she set the pace, eagerly making her way to the pier bridge. Maggie reached the railing first and gripped it in her excitement, gazing out over the expanse of rippling water, glimmering with moonlight and the illumination of LA's skyline. She closed her eyes and took a deep breath of brisk salty air before opening them again and turning back to Gwen. "I could stare at this all night."

"The ocean?"

"It's magnificent." Maggie turned back to the view. "I've only ever seen it a few times."

"Wait, you've lived in LA for over a year, and you've only seen the ocean *a few times*?" Gwen shook her head in disbelief and wrapped an arm around Maggie's shoulder. "Maggie, we are definitely spending more time together when this play is over. What kinds of things do you enjoy? Hiking? Biking? Bowling?" She hugged Maggie closer. "Or we could sit on the shore together and listen to the ocean."

Maggie closed her eyes again. "That sounds wonderful. I wish this humidity wasn't so bad for my hair." She tangled her fingers in her curls. "Look at me, I'm like an overgrown bush."

"I think your hair is gorgeous. It has so much life to it."

"It has a mind of its own," Maggie complained, tugging at it. "I've broken so many brushes, trying to make it decently presentable."

"It's not just presentable," Gwen said. "It's beautiful. It has character. Your hair can do things my hair could never do." She took her arm from Maggie's shoulder and instead reached for her hand. "Come on, let's check out the pier. We can stay by the railing for the view, but I believe you mentioned something about eating your feelings, and there's a guy with a churro stand I think should be here by now. And if you like this view of the ocean, wait until we actually reach the edge of the pier and it's not blocked by a giant parking lot."

Maggie accepted Gwen's hand and almost skipped forward. "Thank you for bringing me here. It's as pretty as I hoped it would be. Look at how they light up the Ferris wheel!"

"Should we go up? Or are you scared of heights?" Gwen teased. "I'll hold your hand the whole time."

Maggie laughed. "Maybe. I don't know. There's so much to see."

"I'm not sure if it's still open this late. But we can see. Let's walk the whole pier."

It was crowded, but not so much that they couldn't easily navigate. Maggie and Gwen kept tight hold of each other so as not to get separated. Gwen showed her where the carousel was housed (closed for the night but still whimsical through the windows). She pointed out the aquarium and Bubba Gump Shrimp, promising to set those aside for another trip. Soon, they found the arcade and, across from it, Gwen's prized churro cart. Gwen insisted on paying for a churro for each of them.

As Maggie took her first bite, she couldn't help but smile. "It's so good. I could eat ten of these."

Gwen laughed. "You really have a weakness for unhealthy food, don't you? Chicken nuggets, pizza, churros…"

"I can't help it that God gave me a sweet tooth. And unhealthy food is everywhere."

"I know, but I really want to help you learn to appreciate the finer things in life. Like nutrients. And vitamins."

Maggie stuck her tongue out at Gwen, then took another big bite of churro.

"Shall we take a look in the arcade?" Gwen offered as they licked sugar from their fingers.

Maggie pointed farther down the pier. "What's going on over there?"

The faintest sound of music rose slightly above all the other noise of the crowd and attractions.

"Let's go check it out." Gwen took her hand again, and together, they wove their way through the foot traffic until they had reached their destination.

Three musicians—gentlemen in jeans, collared shirts, ties, and suspenders—stood surrounded by a growing crowd. They played a tambourine, a harmonica, and a guitar hooked up to a portable amp. A small light set up at their feet illuminated them; to its side Maggie spied the guitar case, with coins and bills thrown inside. The people who had stopped to listen clapped their hands along to an upbeat, cheerful melody. Maggie soon found her toes tapping as she and Gwen listened.

When the song ended, the gentlemen each took a quick drink from thermoses by their sides. As some of the crowd wandered off and others joined for the first time, the one who had been playing the harmonica spoke to the crowd.

"Thank you everyone who's here with us on a beautiful night like tonight. We'd like to do something a little different. We'd like to play a song by the Beatles."

The people listening murmured with approval.

"But here's the problem," he continued. "There were four Beatles, were there not? And only three of us. Do we have any musicians or singers in the crowd tonight? Anyone who would care to join?" At that question, more people left the crowd, seemingly anxious that if no one volunteered, the musician would drag an unwilling participant to the front.

Gwen nudged Maggie. "You sing, right? Why don't you give it a try?"

Maggie blushed, but only a little. "You won't mind?"

"Not at all. I'll be right here."

Maggie nodded, then shyly lifted her hand. The gentleman with the harmonica smiled brightly.

"Fantastic! Come on right up here, young lady. But you seem a bit young to know the Beatles," he joked as he guided her next to him.

"Everyone knows the Beatles." Maggie laughed. "They're classics."

"Then do you know the words to 'Love Me Do?'"

Maggie thought for a minute. "Is that the one that goes...'" She hummed a few bars of melody.

"That's the one." The gentleman nodded to his peers, who started to play. Maggie and the man with the harmonica tapped their feet to the rhythm, finding the beat. The man played the opening riff on his harmonica, then nodded to Maggie. With a deep breath, she sang for an audience for the first time since high school.

Maggie's voice resonated sweetly as she sang the first verse. The words were simple, allowing her freedom to play with the melody. Her performance danced on the line between flirty and earnest.

The gentleman stopped his harmonica and joined her to repeat the verse, singing the harmony to her melody, then returning to the harmonica as Maggie continued. Maggie quite admired his tone, not as rock-star quality as John Lennon, but filled with spirit, making the lyrics shine brighter than they would on their own.

As she continued singing, Maggie gazed out to the audience and caught Gwen's eyes, shining emerald in the dark. Gwen clapped to the music, along with an increasingly large group of listeners. Maggie noticed that Gwen was singing along. As their gaze stayed connected, Maggie found herself singing clearer, louder, directing her words straight to Gwen's ears.

With a final riff on the harmonica, a final chorus, and enthusiastic applause from the listeners, the song came to an end.

"Very nice, very nice! Another hand for the lovely young lady." The man with the harmonica clapped his hands loudly. He leaned closer to Maggie and said privately, "You have a very nice voice. Thank you so much for sharing with us."

"It was my pleasure. I haven't sung in a long time." Maggie shook his hand.

"We hope to see you again. Maybe join us for another song," the gentleman said, waving as Maggie retreated back to Gwen.

Gwen took Maggie's hand as soon as they were in reach of each other. "You were amazing," she crowed as they resumed strolling, leaving a couple bills in the guitar case.

Maggie blushed again and ducked her head to one side. "Aw, it's nothing. That's one of the easiest songs to sing in the world."

"Well, your style made it more interesting. I can see why so many of your starring roles were in musical theater. Is that what you want to return to eventually?"

Maggie shrugged. "Maybe, if Lady Luck strikes me."

"I'm sure she will, with pipes like that and acting talent like yours. Maybe we should do karaoke together sometime. When you're old enough, there's a bar I know we could go to."

"Gwen." Maggie laughed. "You make it sound like I'm a child. 'When I'm old enough,' good grief."

"I'm six years your senior, young lady," Gwen scolded her jokingly. "You be respectful."

There were several places Maggie was tempted to stop along the pier, but they decided to press on. Maggie wanted to get as close to the ocean as she could. As they continued, the crowd thinned slightly, and it became easier to hear each other.

"How often have you been here?" Maggie asked.

Gwen thought for a moment. "I came here once or twice the past couple years, just to spend some time at the beach. But, honestly, most of my time here was with Val."

"I'm sorry, I shouldn't have—"

"Nope, hey, stop that," Gwen said quickly. "Whatever you think you need to apologize for, you don't. A lot of my time in this city was with Val, so of course there's a lot of places here tied to memories with her. I don't want to focus on that. I want to make new memories at these places." Gwen grinned. "I'm making an amazing one right now."

"Well, then, which do you prefer? The ocean or the mountains?"

"That's a hard choice." Gwen pressed a finger to her lips and eyed Maggie up and down.

"What are you doing?"

"Trying to figure out which I want to see you in more, a swimsuit or a cute hiking outfit."

"Gwen!" Maggie swatted Gwen on the arm.

Gwen just laughed. "I like both. Both are fun. I'm more used to mountains, but there's nothing like the ocean on a hot day, is there?"

"I don't know," Maggie admitted. "I think I went to the beach once when I was, like, five? My parents had pictures, but I barely remember it. Most of our vacations were to theme parks and stuff. Mom didn't like outdoors much."

"Oh, we're definitely coming back for the beach, then."

"Even though I don't know how to surf or anything?"

"We can get lessons, if you want."

"No thanks. I'd be too embarrassed. I'll keep my feet on firm ground, thanks."

"Then let's sit out under an umbrella and read like two old secretly married lesbians."

Eventually, they walked out past the Ferris wheel to the part of the pier that fishermen favored.

Maggie found a clear stretch of railing and leaned against it, admiring the skyline across the bay. She sighed deeply, mesmerized by the glitter of lights on the water. "It's really pretty, isn't it?" she said dreamily.

"Yes, really pretty."

Maggie turned to talk to her but lost her words when she realized Gwen was staring at her, smiling. After tripping on her tongue for a few moments, she said, "H-how about we try the arcade before it closes? I can try to win you something."

"Sure," Gwen said, not moving. "But let's enjoy the view here for a moment longer. It's peaceful, isn't it?"

Maggie listened to the lapping waves against the pier boards, beating in time with her heart. "Yes…yes, it is."

*

MAGGIE AND GWEN finally called it a night around ten, reasoning that they had one more day before opening night and needed to get their rest. On the car ride back to Maggie's apartment, they sat in content silence, with Maggie switching the radio to skip commercial breaks, stretching her legs to recover from the walking, and watching the moon outside the car window.

Maggie's heart sank a sliver as the car pulled into her apartment's small lot. For a moment, her brain frantically searched for ways to keep the night going. *Invite her in for a movie night. Ask her to sleep over and cook breakfast for her and Coral in the morning. Ask if she needs to use the bathroom before she goes home?* Maggie shook off these ideas and stepped out of the car. It was time for the date to end, as all good things do.

"I had a wonderful time tonight," she said as Gwen walked her to the door.

"Me too. And I mean it, let's go again soon. Maybe when it's a little warmer though."

"Yeah." Maggie stood on the doorstep awkwardly. "What are you planning on doing tomorrow before rehearsal?"

"I have a thing at USC I need to do, a couple classes, and I'm helping with some lighting for a student production. Then, all my attention is with you guys and with Roy, doing, I'm sure, just one more fix of all the cues."

"You're so busy. You should have been home sleeping by now."

"This was worth it. Thank you for going out with me, Miss Fromm."

Maggie blushed. "I enjoyed it. Thank you for taking me." She paused. "Well…see you tomorrow."

She turned to reach for the doorknob, but Gwen's voice stopped her.

"Maggie, wait."

Maggie turned back to her, and found Gwen fidgeting with the fingers on one hand. She looked as though she was making up her mind.

"I have…I have something I want to tell you," Gwen said. "And if I don't tell you tonight, I know I'm going to regret it."

Maggie took a deep breath. "What is it?"

Gwen closed her eyes, taking a deep breath of her own. When she opened them, her brilliant green eyes shone in a whole new way, captivating Maggie as if Gwen didn't already have her undivided attention. "I want you to know that what I'm about to say…whatever you say back, if you say anything at all…it doesn't change anything about how much I respect you. As a hard worker, as an actress, as a colleague, none of it changes. I will always be one of your biggest fans, and I'm cheering you on, no matter what."

Maggie felt a rush of anxiety. What was going on? "Is something wrong with my role in the play?"

Gwen gave a burst of laughter and clapped a hand over her mouth. "Ah—no, oh God no, Maggie, you're perfect. That's what I mean, you're an amazing actress, and I enjoy working with you, no matter what. Okay?"

Maggie nodded, only feeling more confused. "Is it because I haven't gone to college? I'm, um, I am thinking about it—"

"Maggie, it's that I really want to kiss you!" As soon as the words left Gwen's lips, her cheeks turned bright pink, but her eyes stayed locked on Maggie's.

Maggie's heart dropped, then instantly rose straight back up into her throat. Her ears burned red hot.

"I want to kiss you," Gwen repeated more calmly. "I've wanted to kiss you this whole night. You look amazing in that dress… I've been trying to keep things professional and friendly between us. But I can't hide from what I'm feeling for you anymore. Since you came into my life, I can't stop thinking about you. And, if you'll have me, I'd be honored to be your girlfriend."

Maggie felt herself burning up all over. She took a moment to find her voice. "Is this real?" she breathed. "You're not messing with me?"

"Maggie, I would never." Gwen gently reached for Maggie's hand, only taking it into her grasp when Maggie's fingers curled around hers. "Do you know how much joy you've given me? Those nights you're in my apartment, and I cook for us, and you're petting Blue, and it feels like a little family? Those nights keep me going. Talking about books and music with you, it seems like such a little thing, but I can't stop smiling when I'm listening to your voice."

She held Maggie's other hand and pulled them both close. "I used to think I was never going to love again, that I could never trust anyone. And, well, I don't think I'm going to love the same way again. But I want something different with you. I want to love you in a way I've never loved anyone else." Gwen bit her lip. "If you'll have me."

Maggie interlaced her fingers with Gwen's, and she held on tightly. "I've been going crazy for months," she whispered, still searching for her full voice, her head spinning. "Telling myself there's no way we could ever get together. All these different excuses—"

"Don't listen to them," Gwen urged her. "Just be honest about how you feel. I promise I'll listen."

Maggie fought tears, but her smile shone as bright as Gwen's eyes. "I want to be your girlfriend," she said, finally speaking with her full voice. In that moment, she didn't care who heard. "And if you still want to kiss me, I want that too."

Maggie saw Gwen's chest rise, as did her cheeks as her smile grew bigger. Gwen pressed a hand to Maggie's cheek, brushing her hair aside. She leaned down until they were nose to nose, eyes searching Maggie's. Maggie closed her eyes as Gwen pressed her lips to hers.

Her heart sang as though she'd been looking for this moment her whole life. Maggie melted into the kiss, letting go of Gwen's other hand so she could wrap both her arms around her. Gwen kept her hand on Maggie's cheek but slid her other arm around Maggie's waist and pulled her close. When their lips separated, it was only for a moment, a quick look into their eyes to reassure each other that this moment was real, and it was theirs alone. Then Maggie pulled Gwen to her again, joining with her again, lost in her soft lips, warm touch, and tight embrace.

Chapter Twenty-Eight

OPENING NIGHT BEGAN with an all-too-familiar feeling of butterflies in the stomach and worms in the head. Even though tech week had been positive and productive, Maggie had a gnawing feeling in the back of her mind that nothing she did would be good enough. As she showered, brushed her hair, and threw on a comfy set of clothes, she lectured herself over and over. She knew her lines, she knew her blocking, and after the months of tutoring from Gwen, she knew Ruth better than any character she'd ever played. In only a handful of hours, there would be a whole crowd of people who knew her face as the face of Ruth.

Coral came with her as she headed for the Twilight, her ticket tucked into her purse. She'd dressed up for the occasion in ironed dress pants and a glittering cream sweater. "I can't wait to finally see this with my own eyes," she said on the bus. "After all your practicing and rehearsing and ranting about it, I'll finally get to see everything you've been talking about. Do you think you can sneak me backstage?"

"Not during the performance," Maggie said, nudging Coral in the ribs. "Plus, you got one of the best seats in the house. But I'll sneak you into the dressing rooms to say hi to everybody for a little if you want."

"Yes, please. I want a sneak peek." Coral's eyes lit up.

Maggie chuckled at Coral's enthusiasm, but it was lifting her spirits too. When they entered the theater, she kept her word and led the way to the dressing rooms: in a door to the side of the stage, through backstage, down a flight of stairs, and under the stage itself. Before Maggie could get very far though, Coral got distracted by a basket of playbills left on the concession stand. She quickly grabbed one and flipped through it.

"Maggie, look," Coral said gleefully. "Paul is listed as a producer."

"Who?"

"Paul Jonas. You know, the guy we did the Halloween video with." Coral pointed to his name on the second page. "He donated money to the production. This dude mentioned above him is probably his dad." Coral flipped through the rest of the program, then laughed triumphantly. "There's an advertisement for his YouTube channel in here. And he mentions you by name."

"No way." Maggie grabbed the pamphlet and stared at the full-page ad. A giant movie poster–style image featured several key moments from the Haunted House video with the caption, *Like Margaret Fromm? You'll love to see her scare your pants off!*

Maggie handed the pamphlet back to Coral and laughed. "I cannot believe your one weird job has had this much of an impact."

"Right? I've actually had a few people recognize me at auditions from the behind-the-scenes video," Coral said as they continued. "Just shows, opportunity comes in weird ways!"

As they made their way backstage, they passed Roy, Gwen, and other theater technical crew doing a final check to make sure every single item was in place. Gwen paused when she saw Coral and Maggie passing by.

"Hey, you two, no getting into trouble down there," she said.

"I'm not keeping her down there long, but I promised to show her a sneak peak," Maggie said. "Roy, do you mind?"

"Who is she?"

"This is my roommate. She's an actress too."

Gwen spoke up. "I know her; she's in my improv group. She's friends with the theater."

Roy snorted. "'Friends with the theater.' Good one. Listen, I don't want a bunch of foot traffic in here…but since Gwen knows you, I'll allow it this once." He lifted a finger in warning. "Just once."

Coral saluted. "You got it, sir. Thank you so much, Gwen."

"Anything for you, Coral. If you hadn't brought Maggie to improv, she wouldn't even be in this play."

Coral laughed. "How's the puppy? Can I see her?"

"Sorry, 'fraid you can't. My phone's up in the office, and I left Blue with my neighbor until I get home since it's such a long day."

"Beatrice?" Maggie asked.

"Yeah, she's been a real blessing." Gwen made a shooing motion with her hands. "Well, Coral, don't distract my stars, please. It's time for Maggie to get ready."

Coral saluted one more time, then turned excitedly toward the stairs to the dressing rooms. Behind Roy and Coral's backs, Gwen and Maggie shared a special smile. Fingertips to lips, they blew each other a tiny, secret kiss.

Roy and Gwen had their own troubles to resolve; the world of technical theater was never calm. Happy to leave them to it, Maggie attended to her own responsibilities. Thankfully, prepping for this play was a relatively easy feat, with no special effects makeup needed and easy, comfortable costumes. Maggie tucked her backpack under a vanity in the dressing room she shared with Bel and Georgia.

"If you don't mind sitting out in the hallway, I have to change into my costume," she told Coral.

Coral, inspecting the costume pieces hung along one wall, said, "Sure thing. Which one's yours?"

"My first costume is the yellow and brown one."

Coral pulled out a pair of brown capris and a yellow blouse with little fluttering caps at the end of the sleeves. "Grooooovy," she said, holding out the sleeves to admire them. "What else do you wear?"

Maggie giggled and ushered Coral out of the room. "You'll see when you watch the play. Go say hi to people; I'll be right back."

Maggie closed the door behind Coral and changed quickly. A couple minutes later, she opened the door again to invite Coral back in while she did her hair and makeup. She smirked, seeing Skylar had found Coral, who was chatting them up excitedly.

"Hey, Sky," Maggie said innocently. "Hope you don't mind I brought Coral down for a little before we get started."

"No, not at all," Skylar replied, turning to Maggie with a slightly goofy grin. Seeing that usually cool and collected face tinged pink would never stop being entertaining.

"I never did ask," Maggie said as she sat at her vanity and pulled her hair back. "How did you two meet?"

"We were in a production of *Guys and Dolls* a couple years ago," Coral replied, speaking from where she sat on a bench in the hallway. "Skylar played Society Max. I was one of the Salvation Army band members."

"You got the biggest laugh out of everybody," Skylar cut in from where they were brushing their wig. "That night you pretended to trip and almost fell into your own tuba—"

"That wasn't pretend. I really tripped." Coral laughed. "I just had to go with it. The show must go on."

"You fell into a tuba? The prop master must have wanted to kill you," said Maggie.

"Oh, she did," Coral said. "I had to avoid her for the rest of that production. Skylar, guess what I have?" Coral reached into the neck of her sweater and pulled out the chain of her clover pendant necklace. "I'm wearing the good luck charm you gave me. I hope it helps you guys tonight too."

In her mirror, Maggie saw Skylar poke their head out of their dressing room, adjusting their wig on their head. That goofy smile had returned.

"Oh, wow, thank you, Coral. I'm glad you like it enough to wear it."

"Are you kidding?" Coral said. "I've worn it to three auditions now. And, honestly, I have a really good feeling about the second one."

"What's that audition for?" Bel had arrived and inserted herself into the conversation as easily as if she and Coral had known each other as long as she and Skylar had.

Coral answered with zero hesitation. "It's for a character on a new sci-fi TV show. I really like the idea for it, and the audition was one of the better ones I've been to. They even asked me to a callback."

"Coral, that's great," Maggie said, pausing from applying her lipstick.

"Why didn't you tell me about this?"

"Things got busy." Coral shrugged. "I'm keeping my fingers crossed though. They're holding a last round of auditions in New York next week. Then they're going to announce their casting choices."

"I'll keep my fingers crossed for you," Skylar said.

"No need. I have your lucky charm, remember?" Coral pinched the clover pendant, laughing.

Maggie giggled mischievously as Coral and Bel started chatting together, completely oblivious to Skylar burying their head in a throw pillow to hide their blushing. Maggie decided she would have to make sure Skylar and Coral stayed in closer touch from now on and not just at mutual friends' parties. After all that needling Coral had done about her and Gwen, it was only fair!

The time passed in a blur, and soon, Coral headed to the lobby, where she would wait until the house doors opened. Maggie accompanied her out to make sure Roy didn't think the house doors had opened on accident, then hurried backstage. She and Georgia had a ritual of doing vocal warm-ups together. Even though there was no singing in this performance, there was quite a deal of emotional screaming, and the last thing Maggie needed was to strain her vocal cords. They did a bit of line reading and then a group meeting on the stage with Roy and Gwen.

The stage manager and director were dressed in black jeans and a black button-up. All the crew—stagehands, directors, engineers—were dressed in stage blacks instead of their paint-stained work clothes. They had the same excitement alight in their eyes as Maggie felt.

Roy, however, was apparently the kind of stage manager who presented as angry when he was excited, with his flushed face and stern voice.

"Ladies, during tech week we had a major problem with delays before walking out onto stage," he lectured them. "I need you following the prompts as they're given. No adjusting your costume first, no hair primping, no wig fixing, just go out there. If there is a major problem, the stagehands will stop you. If Emmie or Xinyan are telling you to go, then you go."

"Yes, Roy," the cast echoed back.

"Don't 'yes Roy' me. I'm talking about it because it keeps happening," Roy huffed, crossing his arms. "And, Donna, stop trying to turn your mic off. I'll cut your mic remotely."

"Sorry, old habits," Donna apologized. "I'll keep my hands off the box."

"Good." Roy uncrossed his arms and put his hands on his hips. "Otherwise, I don't have anything to add. You've all been a pleasure to work with. I especially appreciate that you've been polite and respectful to my crew. We're excited that we get to do this show for almost a whole month with this team. Just remember. You killed it in rehearsal; you're going to do fantastic here." He turned to Gwen. "Any last words?"

Gwen, beaming and tapping her toes with excitement, stepped forward, and warmth surged in Maggie's chest as their eyes briefly met. "I want to say I've been so proud to work with all of you. This is a wonderful adventure. We're going to bring a powerful story to the city of Los Angeles tonight. Who knows where it will go from here? But no matter how it ends, it all starts tonight. So let's do what we do best and bring this fantastic piece of art to the world. Bring it in everybody!"

Gwen held out one hand palm facing down and gestured for everyone to do the same. Soon her hand was joined by the cast, the stagehands, Roy, and the entire crew. "On three, what do we say?" Gwen asked.

"How about liberation?" Bel suggested. "For the liberation movement."

"Perfect," Gwen agreed. "On three, we shout liberation. One, two, three."

"Liberation!" the crew cheered, lifting their hands in the air.

Roy clapped his hands. "Okay, everyone, to your stations! Xinyan, you're stage left. Emmie you're stage right. I'm up in the box above house. Actors, below stage, waiting for your cues. Gwen?"

"I'm starting down here. I have my spiel at the beginning with Caleb to introduce Peace Over Violence."

"Right. As soon as that's done, grab your headset from Xinyan." Roy clapped his hands again. "What are you all hanging around for? Let's go!"

*

UNFORTUNATELY, THE NATURE of stage theater was that actors had to be ready and waiting long before the theater itself was ready for them. And with the dressing rooms situated directly below the stage, the actors had to be nearly silent in order to avoid being heard. Maggie spent a good twenty minutes sitting with her own anxious energy, trying to have a quiet conversation with the cast. When they finally received their cues to go backstage in preparation for the first scene, she almost rushed up the stairs before reminding herself it was time to be in character.

From the other side of the curtain, Gwen's voice echoed throughout the house. "…the profit we make as a production goes straight to Peace Over Violence. We're honored to be associated with such a meaningful organization, and hope our story can help spread the message of the work they do for women and survivors across Los Angeles."

The spotlight illuminating Gwen went dark, and the curtain barely fluttered as Gwen made her way backstage.

"And now, presenting," Haleigh's recorded voice said over loudspeaker, "*Petty Oppression.*"

The curtain opened, and Maggie walked out, pushing a small shopping cart in front of her. In one step, she dropped her preconceptions, beliefs, biases, perspectives, and quirks that made her Maggie. In the next, she stepped into Ruth's shoes: reckless, passionate, determined, goal-driven, an inspiration to young women who had nothing to lose. With the third step she asked Ruth, *What are we doing? What do we feel? What needs to be done about it?*

And in the fourth step, Ruth answered from deep inside her heart, *Tell my story as honestly as we can, and damn the consequences.*

By the time the stage was lit, Maggie was gone, and Ruth was grocery shopping with her sister, Mary. They discussed an upcoming rally, unaware that just a few aisles over, two church wives were criticizing the liberation movement.

Maggie swept through the play with no stumbles, no hesitation. In the scene where she and Georgia were supposed to drink coffee and the coffee cups were missing, Ruth put the coffeepot on the windowsill to cool. When Bel couldn't find her shoes, Maggie found them where they had been thrown in the back of the dressing room, then ran onstage so Ruth could hand out pamphlets to the public. She wavered in a strange state of mind that was both her and Ruth, both creating art and reliving life in 1960.

In the final fight with Mary, Ruth took full force on stage. Maggie embraced her rage, her pain, as she never had before. "You know the truth," she said coolly, dangerously calm. "But you never stood up for me. Not once. Not a single word in my defense."

"That's not true." Mary/Georgia looked close to tears.

"Don't lie to me!" Ruth stood, her chair clattering to the floor behind her, her voice echoing off the walls and tainted with sorrow. "You could have stopped all of this if you had just been honest. Why do you lie to everyone?"

"It's not my business."

"I'm not your business? I'm your sister!"

"But it's your personal—"

"I don't have personal business anymore." Ruth turned her back to Mary, fingers digging into her crossed arms. "Not since the doctor told the church board about my baby. But didn't tell the whole story. No, no one cares about the whole story. I'm just Ruth, the slut who got herself knocked up, then killed her baby—"

"Don't say those things—"

"But you could have told them." Ruth whirled back around, her hands clasped, almost pleading. "You could have told the church board. Told them it was Jared—what his treatment did to our baby."

"You shouldn't care what they think. Let people think what they want—"

"Do you realize you're the only reason I'm still in this godforsaken town?" Ruth sobbed, stopped, and took a deep breath. "You're the only family I have, Mary."

"I know that…and I love you, Ruth."

"Then why…why won't you say anything?"

"When Mom died—"

"No, don't say it like that." Ruth reached out and took Mary's hands.

"Say the truth. Say what happened."

"When Dad killed Mom—"

In the back of her consciousness, Maggie heard the audience gasp. At the forefront of her mind, Ruth heard nothing but the pain in Mary's voice.

"—you and I told the police what he was like," Mary continued. "How he used to treat her. And what did they do?"

"They arrested him."

"But Ruth…I told them about him the first time he threw a plate at her. I went to the police all by myself to tell them. At first, I thought they did nothing. But years later, I found out that's why Mom lost her job at the library."

Ruth walked away, then gripped the table edge for support. "I…I never knew. I thought—"

"I tried." Mary rushed over to Ruth and took her in her arms, the embrace of a big sister who must, in this moment, be mother as well. "I tried to save Mom, and I couldn't. So, I…I thought I would try to play by their rules. I told people you had been misled, but I was taking care of you, and you wouldn't make any more mistakes. They talk about you, but they left you alone."

Ruth looked out into the distance. Somewhere in the future, the audience was wiping tears from their eyes. In the decade 1960, Ruth saw a home tainted by painful memories. "I don't want to be left alone," she said, her strength returning. "Not anymore. I'm not content to survive, not under these conditions."

She stepped away from Mary's hug and strode toward her coat on the hat rack. "We're going to change this town," she swore to Mary, pulling her arms through the sleeves. "We're going to make them see the ugliness they're protecting. And we'll either heal together or burn it to the ground." She tore open the kitchen door, prepared to leave. "And I don't really care which way it happens," she spat before walking out and slamming the door behind her to cheers from a far-away audience.

In the final scene, that burning energy had spread to Mary's heart as well. Susan approached them, gloved fingers clutching her purse, voice at a conspiratorial whisper.

"It's a terrible thing," she said, "a terrible thing when a community is divided. I believe it is most important that we stick together, as women, during such times as this. Would you ladies agree?"

Mary and Ruth looked at each other. "Women must stand for women," Mary said, gripping Ruth's hand.

Susan nodded. "I'd like to invite you to come speak to a circle of women in the library next week. A nice, calm gathering. No more of these…violent words, these frightful exchanges. You can hand out your pamphlets there. A nice, friendly conversation, for the good of our community."

Ruth sneered at her. "You say that you're listening, but you hear nothing. We're not going to just talk to each other anymore. We need to speak in a public forum, where all the town can hear us. Everyone needs to be a part of the change."

Susan looked pained. "Really, Ruth, must you be so rash in this? These new beliefs, they could be just as well for your younger generation, but…can't we agree to disagree? You can come speak to us in the library. That way no one will be offended—"

"Let them be offended," Mary said, cutting her off. "If they're offended, it means they need to hear it most."

"This fight continues whether you support us or not, Mrs. Mayor," Ruth said dismissively. "We won't play by the same rules that have kept us held down any longer."

Mary handed Susan a flier. "We're going to march to the town park tomorrow for a public discussion. Perhaps you would like to join us." The sisters marched off, arm in arm, as the lights fell.

When the lights rose again, Ruth quickly slipped away from Maggie as though shedding a robe. Maggie stepped into the lights with Georgia, Donna, Bel, Alyssa, and Skylar to give their bows, holding hands and grinning from ear to ear. They gestured to the lights and the backstage crew, then looked to the balcony seats, where a spotlight focused on Haleigh Johnson. Haleigh was radiant in an embroidered purple gown, decked with strings of golden beads that shone as brightly as her eyes in the spotlight. Maggie thought she could see tear tracks on her cheeks, but her smile had never been more joyful. The audience practically roared with applause, and Maggie spied at least a third of them rising to their feet. Haleigh blew kisses to the crowd. Beaming, Maggie and the cast backed up and gave their final bow.

Once the curtain fell, all structure fell with it. The cast and several stagehands clumped together in a circle, whooping and cheering from post-production adrenaline.

"Did you see how many people were standing?" Bel squealed, hopping up and down. "For an independent play?"

"That was flawless acting," Donna cried, gathering as many girls as she could reach into a group hug. "I felt like I was living every moment of it."

Maggie was a little jittery, a little tired, mostly wired. She clasped hands with Georgia. "Oh my God, I almost cried on stage," she gasped. "You were so convincing. That hug…"

The actors gradually shepherded themselves down the stairs to their dressing rooms, weaving between a still-active set of stagehands. They continued reliving the play as costumes came off and leisure clothing was donned, makeup was wiped, hair was let down, and belongings were packed into bags.

Maggie had decided to leave her makeup for when she got home to wash. She expected Gwen would call them back on stage any minute to deliver notes and looked around for ways to be helpful in the meantime. She was helping Skylar remove all the pins holding their wig in place when she realized the clatter and commotion from upstairs on the stage didn't sound quite right. Somewhere, Roy's voice was raised, and he sounded furious.

"Guys, can you hear that?" Maggie said, lifting a finger to shush the chatter. The group around her paused, listening closely.

Roy was definitely shouting, with words like "—broken headset, but no one bothered to—" and "—car is still parked out back, why—" ringing down the stairs. Exchanging cautious looks with the cast members, Maggie headed upstairs and poked her head into a scene of chaos.

Stage hands were running in various directions but not attending to scenery or props. Someone was climbing the catwalk, even though the lights weren't lowered. In the middle of it all stood Roy, his hair falling free of its ponytail.

He caught sight of Maggie and pointed to her, barking, "Do you know where Gwen is?"

Chapter Twenty-Nine

MAGGIE SHOOK HER head. "What's going on?"

"Gwen never put on her headset," Emma explained, pausing as she raced by. "Roy thought her headset was broken, so he just operated through Xinyan and me the whole night. We got so busy running things that we didn't stop to think about where she was—"

"What do you mean?" Maggie interrupted, her voice rising. "No one knows where she is?"

"No. She's not answering her phone. We've looked all over backstage. We're searching through the house now."

Maggie's blood ran cold. She hurtled toward the door at the rear of backstage, ignoring Emma's questions. Throwing open the door let in a burst of February air. She scanned the alley for Gwen's car. It was still there. She ran to it but found it empty. Sprinting inside to the dressing room, Maggie almost fell down the stairs as her feet fumbled to keep up with her mad dash.

Upstairs, Xinyan's voice called over the theater speakers: "Gwen Knowles, if you're in the building, please come to the ticket office."

Maggie practically skidded to the floor in front of the dressing room vanity, dragged out her backpack, and dug wildly for her phone. She unlocked it—no messages or calls. She quickly dialed Gwen's number and clutched the phone to her ear, waiting. No answer.

"What's going on?" Georgia asked, with the other cast members poking their heads in the dressing room door.

Maggie swallowed hard, finding her voice. "We're looking for Gwen. She never put on her headset." She hit Redial and held the phone to her ear, eyes closed, waiting. Nothing.

She ignored the others' questions and concerns. A thought was burrowing into her brain. Grabbing her bag, she ran upstairs, searching for Roy. With the help of the stage crew, she found him as he made his way up to the theater office.

"Roy," Maggie said, panting, "how much do you know about Gwen's past?"

Roy paused. He studied Maggie critically. "How much do you know?"

"I know about her ex."

Roy's gaze sharpened, and he descended the steps to square up to Maggie. "Gwen hasn't talked about Val to me recently. Is there something going on?"

"Val attacked Gwen and me a couple months ago. Gwen has a restraining order against her, but—"

"Whoa, whoa, slow down," Roy interjected, holding up a hand. "What do you mean 'attacked'?"

"I mean she came up to us with a knife and threatened Gwen." Maggie had trouble keeping her voice calm.

"Aw, hell." Roy ran his fingers through his hair, pulling more strands loose from his ponytail. "I kinda knew she was a crazy bitch but… You think she has something to do with this?"

"She has to," Maggie said, trying to hold back tears. "Gwen would never abandon us on opening night. She's put her heart and soul into this."

"Roy!"

They both turned around as one of the stagehands approached Roy with a bundle of items.

"We checked the theater offices. Gwen's stuff was still up where she left it. Everything's here." The stagehand showed them her sweatshirt, phone, keys, and wallet.

Roy picked up the phone. The screen lit at his touch, showing missed calls from Maggie and a "MOTION DETECTED" notification from the Puppy Cam app, but nothing else. He gave the phone back. "Her headset is still on the table where we left it. How the fuck can a woman disappear right after making an announcement in the spotlight, in front of an almost full house?"

He shook his head, then took out his hair tie to regather his hair into a new ponytail, a determined look in his eyes. "I'm calling the owner. Maggie, can you come wait with me in the tech booth? If something happened with Val…"

"Can…can I hold on to Gwen's stuff for you?"

Roy nodded, and the stagehand passed Gwen's things to her. Maggie took Gwen's bundle and, clutching it to her chest, walked numbly after Roy. On her way, she pulled out her phone and texted Coral:

Hey, you're going to need to head home without me. It might be a Valerie thing. I promise to keep in touch and explain when I get home.

A handful of seconds later, Coral sent back:

If u promise me u won't head back by yourself if it's not safe, then okay.

Maggie texted a reassuring reply, then pocketed her phone.

Most theaters Maggie had been in had a prompting corner, usually stage left, where the stage manager stood to oversee the production and cues. The Twilight, instead, had a system that involved two deputy stage managers backstage and Roy up in the tech booth, a dark room set up behind the balcony seats, where Roy could observe the entire play alongside the electrical and sound engineers. Gwen was supposed to be a secondary stage manager backstage that night.

Roy was already on the phone with someone, presumably the owner, when Maggie entered. "No, she didn't just leave; her car is still here," Roy was saying, clearly irritated. "Look, sir, I wouldn't call if I didn't think it was an emergency. At the very least, what am I supposed to do with all her stuff? We found her fucking wallet!"

As they continued arguing, Maggie found a chair and sat. She held Gwen's sweatshirt tightly in one fist, resisting the urge to bury her face in it and cry.

She felt the hard surface of Gwen's phone and retrieved it. A second, new "MOTION DETECTED" notification came up from the puppy cam, over a blurry picture of Blue's face for the lock screen. Maggie stared at the phone, unfocused, for a few moments. Then something in her brain clicked. Bluebell was supposed to be at Beatrice's apartment until Gwen got home. Why would the puppy cam detect any motion if neither Bluebell nor Gwen were home?

Maggie pressed the button to unlock the phone, which brought up six little dots for a passcode. Maggie recalled Gwen saying that she changed her passcode for her apartment frequently. Maybe she'd do the same with her phone. If she did, it couldn't be something too difficult to remember. Maggie stared at the number pad. What should she try?

She tried the date Gwen had adopted Bluebell. No luck.

She tried the opening night for the play. No luck.

She tried Gwen's phone number, first with no last digit, then with no first digit. No luck.

Maggie sat back and thought, eyes closed, as Roy's discussion continued in the distance. A sudden thought came to her. She ignored it for a moment, considering other possibilities, but it tugged again at her. What if…?

Biting the inside of her cheek, embarrassed that the idea had even crossed her mind, she typed in 624443. MAGGIE.

The passcode was accepted.

Maggie straightened suddenly in her chair, thumb hovering over Gwen's phone. The home screen was a picture of Maggie on stage, reading over lines with Georgia. Maggie felt tears stinging at her eyes, but she pulled up the notifications and tapped on the most recent one for the puppy cam. With Maggie's tap, the app opened, and she clapped a hand over her mouth to stifle a scream.

Roy glanced at her questioningly.

Maggie turned the phone to him, trembling. "Valerie has her. They're in her apartment."

"Oh fuck." Roy jumped to his feet and rushed over, looking at the phone over Maggie's shoulder as she turned the screen back to herself.

Gwen sat on the floor, back to one wall, arms wrapped around her knees. Black-clad Valerie paced back and forth, seemingly agitated. Bluebell was nowhere to be seen.

Hesitantly, Maggie tapped the sound icon. Valerie Harker's voice, slightly scratchy but distinct, rang out.

"—made this happen. If you had just done as you were told, I wouldn't've had to go this far to get things straightened out. We could have just talked about it. You know, like mature adults do? But you decided to make a big drama out of it, so here I am." Valerie crouched on her heels, facing Gwen. She pointed something—her pocket knife?—at Gwen's face. "Stop pouting like a child. Nothing's going to be fixed until you grow up and face this with me."

Gwen shrugged. "There's nothing to face."

"Oh, blondie." Valerie chuckled. "Now you're just making me mad."

Maggie started searching the folds of the sweatshirt.

"What are you doing?" Roy asked.

Maggie didn't answer. She snatched Gwen's car keys. She threw Gwen's things in her bag, zipped it, and ran out of the tech booth, down the hallway, and to the stairs.

Roy followed only a moment behind, leaving his phone on the table. "Maggie, stop!"

Maggie didn't listen. She was halfway through the auditorium and still running, blood pounding in her ears, blind to everything but the alley door.

"Maggie, for fuck's sake, wait for the goddamn police." Roy caught up to her, grabbed her by the arm, and held her. "You can't go rushing into this. What are you going to do about it?"

"I can't just leave her alone," Maggie screamed at him, trying to tear her arm free.

"She's not going to be alone," Roy snapped, tightening his grip. "We can call the cops. They'll take care of it. Snap out of it."

Maggie kept struggling. "Roy, let me go!"

"You think I don't know how you feel?" Roy grasped Maggie by the shoulders and forced her to face him. "Gwen and I have been friends and colleagues for years. I saw what being with Val did to her. I know what that woman's capable of. But we aren't the professionals, Maggie. If we go running mad-dash in, we're putting everyone in danger, including Gwen." He shook her slightly. "Do you understand?"

Maggie looked into his eyes, tears brimming. She nodded hesitantly.

Roy let go of her. "Good. Come back to the booth with me. We'll let the owner know what's going on and call the cops."

Maggie took a shaky breath in. "I'm going to use the ladies' room real quick. I need a minute."

Roy eyed her suspiciously as they walked to the lobby. "Do I need to watch outside the door to make sure you don't bolt again?"

Maggie shook her head. "No, you don't need to. But, after calling the police…is there any water I could drink?"

Roy softened. "I'll grab something from the concession stand for you. Come up to the booth when you're done."

After Roy dropped her off in the ladies' room, Maggie stood and waited, listening until she heard him walking toward the concession stand. She cautiously, silently opened the door and poked her head out. Roy was nowhere to be seen. As carefully as she dared, as quietly as she could muster on the aged squeaky floors, Maggie crept back to the house, down the aisle, to backstage, out the door…

Amazed she had escaped detection, she bolted to Gwen's car. Her fingers fumbled as she unlocked it, but in a moment, she had thrown her bag in the passenger seat. She whipped out her phone, opened up the map function, and typed in Gwen's address. As the satellites searched for a route, she got herself adjusted in the car. She hadn't driven in almost two years and questioned if she knew what she was doing. Was she just going to crash Gwen's car, adding another emergency? Was this worth the risk?

She thought of Gwen, curled up and alone on the floor. Alone in the apartment that was supposed to be her fortress. Alone, with a knife pointed at her by the person she used to love.

Gwen was not going to face this alone anymore.

By the time Roy ran out of the door and started sprinting toward the car, Maggie was peeling out of the parking spot, fingers white-knuckled on the steering wheel.

Chapter Thirty

MAGGIE HAD NO idea how she got to Gwen's apartment in one piece. Although LA traffic was less strenuous at ten at night, it certainly wasn't anything like the streets she had driven as a teenager in Oregon. But somehow, in what felt like entirely too much time, she found herself pulling into the apartment parking lot.

She was shocked to find it completely devoid of cop cars. Gripping the steering wheel and breathing hard, she told herself that Roy had definitely called the cops. There was no way he hadn't.

Then a nagging voice suggested, *What if he doesn't know where to send them?*

She froze. *Addresses are part of employment records; he could look it up.*

Gwen's an employee of the university, said the nagging voice, *not the theater.*

Maggie groaned. How could she be so stupid? Hastily, she reached for her phone, and in moments, 911 was ringing in her ear.

"Nine one one, what's your emergency?" It was a deep, low voice, the kind that reminded her of her father whenever he wore his badge and uniform.

Maggie's knuckles went white. She fought to speak, urging her voice to overwhelm the panic that clouded her throat and lungs. "Gwen Knowles is being kept captive in her own apartment by Valerie Harker. She— Gwen—has a restraining order against Valerie. I think Valerie has a knife."

"Who are you?"

"Margaret Fromm."

"And where are you?"

"I'm in the parking lot. I unlocked her phone and can see into her apartment through her Puppy Cam app." Maggie pushed the words out of her mouth as if she were testifying before God. Her heart pounded from the effort of keeping herself focused and calm. "You need to send police to her apartment building."

"Do you know the address?"

Maggie gave it to him, speaking slowly, desperately trying not to trip over her words. She closed her eyes to block out the image of Valerie pacing in front of Gwen like a hungry wild cat and forced herself to focus on answering the operator's questions.

Finally, he said, "Officers are on their way. Please wait where you are until they arrive."

"Wait?" She imagined Gwen's huddled form, small and alone on the floor of her apartment. "I can't wait here. I have to go to Gwen." The blood that had been frozen cold in her chest thawed and spread to her limbs. She felt lightheaded. "I can't just wait here and do nothing."

"Miss Fromm, you're describing a dangerous situation, one with a weapon and a hostage," the operator said in a kind but firm voice. "You need to stay where you are safe and trust the police to help your friend. They—"

Maggie hung up. She stared up at the apartment windows, trying to think of what to do. She needed to get inside, but she didn't know the code. The guard wouldn't recognize her as a resident. There was only one solution.

Maggie hurried to the door and searched for the buzzer for Gwen's apartment, then pressed its neighbor. She rang twice before the intercom clicked in and Beatrice's confused voice asked, "Hello?"

"Bea, hi. It's Maggie Fromm. Gwen Knowles's friend," Maggie said, almost tripping over her words. "Gwen's having an emergency. Can you let me in?"

There was a pause. "What kind of emergency? Is she okay?"

Maggie searched for an answer. Bea sounded like she didn't know what was going on next door, and Maggie didn't want to alarm her. But she needed to be sincere.

"No, she's in danger. I need to get Bluebell for her. You can come with me. I know you're responsible for her right now. But Gwen really needs her."

There was another pause. Then Bea said, "You better come up and explain what's going on." The door lock buzzed, allowing Maggie in.

Maggie had planned to ask the security guard for help but found the desk surprisingly empty. A quickly scribbled sign on a sheet of notebook paper indicated the guard was taking a bathroom break. She bounced on her heels, wondering if she should wait, but the ding of the elevator as a couple exited into the lobby prompted her onward. She ran to the elevator and hurriedly pressed the fifth floor and door close buttons.

An eerie rush of dread enveloped Maggie as she sprinted down the hallway to Gwen's room. She halted at the door and listened closely to the murmur of Valerie's voice but couldn't make out what she was saying. She pulled out Gwen's phone, unlocked it, and pulled up the Puppy Cam app. Valerie sat on a folding chair she'd set in front of Gwen, toying with her knife in her hands.

Maggie stepped back into the hallway and cautiously turned on the sound for the app. Valerie's voice drifted quietly through the speakers.

"—don't understand how you've managed to convince yourself of this narrative where you're always the victim. You're not doing anyone any good by doing that, you know. It just makes people start resenting you. People are much more accepting of you if you acknowledge your faults and apologize, than if you act like you never do anything wrong."

Gwen remained curled in the same position as before. She didn't look up at Valerie when she spoke, only stared at the floor by her feet. "Just tell me where my dog is, Val."

"I told you," Valerie responded, sighing impatiently. She stood up and resumed pacing. "You'll get your dog back when you start acting maturely. You aren't ready for the responsibility of a pet until you can…"

As Valerie spoke, Gwen's shoulders sank even lower, her hands adjusting their grip around her knees. Maggie had never seen her look so small.

Maggie went back to the door. She lifted her free hand, paused for the barest second, then curled it into a fist and pounded. "Gwen!" she called. "Gwen, it's Maggie."

On the phone screen, she saw Gwen jolt. Valerie stopped dead in her tracks, seemingly frozen.

"Oh, no, Gwen," she snarled. "Your precious little side chick is here. Whatever shall you do?"

"Leave her alone," Gwen said in a low voice. "She doesn't have anything to do with this."

"Oh, she doesn't, does she? Then what is she doing here?" Valerie turned on her heel and marched over to Gwen. Grabbing her by the hair, she pulled her up until she was kneeling, then slammed her head against the wall, making a horrible thud. Maggie screamed, causing Valerie to whirl around. "So, you're there, you slut," she said through the door. "I told you once; you had the chance to walk away."

Beatrice's door opened suddenly, and she looked out into the hallway, wide-eyed, pajama-clad, and bed-headed. "Maggie, it is you. What are you doing?"

Maggie was about to answer when Bluebell came padding out of Bea's apartment. She trotted over to Maggie, tail wagging in excitement and a goofy grin on her muzzle. Maggie pounded on the door again. "Gwen, Beatrice and I have Bluebell. She's safe here with us."

This time she could hear Gwen's voice through the door as well as the phone. "Bea? You have Bluebell?"

"Of course, I do," Beatrice yelled through the door. "Gwen, what's going on? Why didn't you come get Bluebell when you came home? Why's Maggie here?"

Maggie showed Beatrice Gwen's phone. "Gwen's trapped. The person in there is someone she has a restraining order ag—"

"Wait, no," Bea interrupted, grabbing Gwen's phone. She stared at the screen. "That's…that's Val."

"You know Valerie Harker?" Maggie's head spun.

"Know her? She's my girlfriend." Bea knocked on the door. "Valerie, is that you? What's going on? Why are you here?"

Maggie heard Valerie groaning and glanced at the phone again, still in Bea's hand, which showed Valerie pacing the floor with her hand against her forehead. Valerie turned back to the door.

"Bea, listen," she called out. "Everything's fine. If you take Blue back to your apartment and lie back down, I can come over soon, and we can talk about what's going on."

Bea shook her head and clutched Gwen's phone. "Val, I don't understand. Why are you even in there?"

"Just—" Valerie placed her fists against her temples, eyes squeezed shut for a moment. "Just take the dog, Bea. And call security. Tell them to kick Maggie out. She's trespassing. Just close the door and lie down, and I'll be right over."

"Come over now," Bea said. "I'll give Gwen Blue back, and we can talk. Babe, you're scaring me."

Gwen glanced at the door and then at Val. "'Babe?'" she echoed. Maggie wasn't sure, but it looked like an incredulous smile was on her face. "Are you kidding me?" Gwen stumbled up onto her knees, leaning on the wall for support. "You spent years accusing me of cheating on you, and now…" She burst into laughter, a pain-laced hilarity.

Valerie marched toward her and swung to slap her, but Gwen dodged.

"You have the audacity," Gwen said with a chuckle, "to make demands of me while dating my neighbor?"

"You made me do what I had to do," Valerie snarled, grabbing

Gwen's forearm.

Bea abandoned watching the phone and pounded on the door. "Valerie, open the door! What the hell are you doing?"

"She doesn't have an answer that will make this okay, Bea," Maggie told her. She gripped Blue's collar as the dog strained, trying to paw at the door.

Gwen kept laughing. She was unsteady on her feet, but she started moving, circling around Valerie to reach the door. "You sly, two-faced bitch. That's how you had a photo of Bluebell. Bea shared it with you. You never even had to get near the dog."

"Gwen, shut up and listen for once," Valerie snapped. "I didn't want to trick you into having this discussion. You didn't give me any choice."

Neighbors now poked their heads out of their doors, muttering about security but not daring to come closer with Bluebell pulling at her collar. Maggie took Gwen's phone back from Beatrice, who leaned against the door with both fists, her eyes wide with shock.

"Valerie, what is she talking about?" Bea pleaded.

"I'll tell you what I'm talking about," Gwen yelled back. "Valerie showed up at the theater dressed like a stagehand with a picture of Blue and told me to do as she said if I wanted to see her alive again. And you had her this whole time. Let me guess, was that Bea's car you made me drive here in, Val? Did you snag her spare set of keys?"

"I have Bluebell right here, Gwen," Maggie said. "We're here for you. And the police are on their way."

"Police?" Bea gasped.

"Beatrice, go back inside," Valerie ordered. "It's all going to be okay."

"Why are you still leading her on?" Gwen asked. "Does it make you feel good every time a starry-eyed young lady falls for your flowery words and sweet gestures?" Gwen started to approach Valerie with her hands raised. "Does it make you feel powerful?"

Valerie moved so fast Maggie thought the app camera had malfunctioned. Valerie stepped forward and kicked her foot against the inside of Gwen's, sweeping her leg out to the side and unbalancing her. Gwen raised her arms to defend herself, but Valerie pushed down on Gwen's shoulders and lifted her knee to Gwen's face, knocking her to the floor. Maggie watched in horror as Gwen's face twisted in pain, blood trickling from her nose.

Valerie crouched in front of Gwen and cocked her head to one side. "You threatened me," she said, eerily calm. "I won't accept a relationship where I'm afraid for my safety, Gwen."

Beatrice knocked on the door, tears leaking from her eyes. "Valerie, this isn't like you! Something's wrong. Maybe you need a doctor. Please, come out. We can get through this."

Valerie put her fists at her temples again. After a small pause she yelled out, "Beatrice, I need closure with Gwen. I'm sorry I never told you about her. I didn't want things to be awkward. We have…have unfinished business to—"

Gwen started chuckling again. "Closure? This is your idea of closure?"

Valerie's posture relaxed. She reached out and attempted to pet Gwen's head. When Gwen flinched away, she gripped her hair in her fist instead. "We can't leave things uncertain like this, blondie," she said matter-of-factly. "It's time for you to stop playing games. Just apologize, and we can be together again."

Beatrice clapped her hands to her mouth and backed against the opposite wall, tears running down her face.

Every inch of Maggie's skin burned like fire, blood pumping so hard she could hear it in her ears. She dropped the phone, turned to the door, and screamed, gripping Blue's collar, "Gwen! Tell me the passcode!"

A rustling and mutter of voices came through the phone on the floor, but no response.

"Gwen, listen to me." Maggie screamed, ignoring the neighbors' stares and Bea's sobs. "You've been facing this alone for so long because you were trying to keep us safe. But that doesn't matter anymore, can't you see? She isn't going to play nice just because you do. I'm here, and Blue's here. Tell me the passcode, and let's face her together."

For a heartbeat, she wondered if she had made the right choice, if her words would put Gwen in more danger.

Then Gwen yelled, "Ten-twelve-sixteen!"

Valerie screamed something in a rage, but Maggie wasn't listening. In seconds, she typed in the code. She shoved the door open and let go of Blue, who bolted inside with Maggie racing after her.

Valerie had pulled Gwen off the floor and now held her pocket knife to her throat, facing the door, struggling to keep Gwen's hands pinned behind her back. Gwen's face was horribly swollen and bruised, and blood dripped from her nose to her chest. Blue ran to Gwen, attempting to force herself between their bodies, but Valerie had planted one leg between Gwen's, keeping herself anchored firmly. Valerie looked up at Maggie, sneered, and kicked Bluebell firmly in the side. Bluebell yelped in pain, tail between her legs.

"Get the fuck out!" Valerie screeched.

Gwen broke her arms free and grabbed Valerie's knife hand, pushing it away while twisting herself out of Valerie's grip. She shoved Valerie backward and jumped away to give herself space. Bluebell instantly moved in front of her, trembling but snarling.

Maggie darted to Gwen's side and curled her hands into fists. "The police are coming," she warned Valerie. "And this time, you're not running away."

The sound of movement came from the doorway behind her.

"How could you?" Bea sobbed. "You promised me…you said…"

"Beatrice," Gwen yelled at her. "When did you and Valerie start dating? Was it just before Christmas?" Bea went quiet. "She swept you off your feet, didn't she?" Gwen continued. "I bet she's been real charming and sensitive. Big romantic gestures, like cute creative dates in the park, right?"

Maggie glanced at Gwen, whose face was set in a look of quiet, festering rage.

"Well, it doesn't stay that way," Gwen continued. "You're lucky, Bea. You get to see the real her now and not a year later when she has you wrapped around her finger, so in love with her—so afraid of her—that you can't bear to leave."

Valerie's eyes looked icier than Maggie had ever seen them. She seemed poised to attack; her knife dangled from her fingers, but Bluebell was in the way. "You have no right to talk of being in love," she said coldly, "after the way you've been treating me for years."

"Shut up," Gwen said. "We're done talking. We're waiting for the police, and then you are leaving us alone. Me, Beatrice, Maggie, everyone."

"Ah, yes, Maggie." Valerie's eyes cut into her, and for a split second, Maggie felt the sting of the knife's blade in her side. "I knew there was something different about her. The first person you ever touched, after all this time. It was like you couldn't help yourself."

Maggie fought to keep her face neutral. "That's why you found me at work? Because Gwen shook my hand or something?"

"She touched your shoulder," Valerie snarled. "Suddenly feeling so free to be touchy-feely, weren't we, blondie? And then the next week, you were just bouncing into her lap!"

Gwen stiffened but kept her fists raised. "You don't get to decide where I go or who I touch," she said quietly. "You're not entitled to me—or Beatrice."

"Again," Valerie spat back. "Labeling yourself the victim. It's no wonder no one else ever wanted to date you. I spent years dealing with your crap, trying to show you how to be a true partner, a strong and loving girlfriend. You never talk about *my* feelings. You never stop to think about how *I* feel! How do you think I felt watching you fondle her—" She pointed to Maggie with the knife. "—when you've been ignoring me, starving me for affection all this time?"

Maggie started to speak, but Gwen cut her off.

"Those kinds of words don't work on me anymore. Save your breath."

Suddenly, Beatrice's broken voice cut through the air. "She has a knife! Please hurry!"

The pounding of feet sounded, and it seemed multiple people approached. Beatrice's sobs became fainter. In her periphery, Maggie saw a cop with his hands up, walking through the kitchen.

"Valerie Harker," he said in a low, calm voice. "You're in a bad spot right now. Set down the knife and come talk with me."

From the way Valerie's face darted about the room, Maggie guessed there were two officers. Maggie focused her eyes on the knife. Valerie had tightened her grip, but she seemed unfocused.

"Come on, Valerie," the cop said again. "Nothing good is going to happen by staying around here. Drop the knife, and let's figure things out."

Valerie looked down at the floor. Her grip on the knife relaxed. Maggie's heartbeat started to slow, the flush in her cheeks calming. Then Valerie looked up and locked eyes with Gwen.

"Gwen, please," she whispered, her voice softer than Maggie had ever heard it. "I may have been harsh. Rash. But it's because I care so much for you. I always have. I can't bear to be without you."

Gwen didn't answer.

"Please!" Valerie looked pitiful. Tears welled in her eyes, and her voice was wretched with sorrow. "No one knows me like you do. You know I have anger issues. We can work on these things together. I need you. I love you, blondie. I just want things to be like they were before."

Gwen reached down and patted Bluebell calmly.

After a pause, Valerie straightened up, eyes hard. When she spoke, all traces of tears were gone from her voice and eyes. "So be it. This was your choice, Gwen Knowles." And she plunged the knife into her stomach.

It was so sudden that Maggie didn't know what she was seeing until Valerie fell to her knees. Her black shirt made it almost impossible to see the growing bloodstain under her hands, still clutching the knife handle. As one cop approached Valerie, the other pulled Maggie back. The cop's voice rang hollow in the back of her mind, sounding miles away.

Gwen was frozen in place, eyes glued to Valerie's until the officer's body obstructed her view. Maggie saw her knees shaking. Before the cop could turn to her too, Maggie reached for Gwen, clasping one hand over Gwen's, still holding Blue's collar. She put her other hand on Gwen's arm and pulled, guiding a quivering Gwen and snarling Bluebell out the door, into the hallway, and away from the apartment.

Beatrice huddled with someone Maggie assumed to be another neighbor, who provided cautious comfort in the form of shoulder pats and uneasy glances. When Bea saw them coming down the hallway, she said something Maggie's ears couldn't process. It wasn't until Bea broke away from the neighbor and started to rush down the hallway that Maggie's brain started to click back into place.

Maggie let go of Gwen's arm and grabbed Bea's hand. "Don't go down there. You don't want to see it."

Beatrice looked between Maggie and Gwen's faces. "What happened? Is she okay?"

Gwen still stared into the distance, shivering. Maggie swallowed hard and tried to sound calm and reassuring.

"They're going to… They're going to put Valerie in an ambulance. They'll take care of her. But you shouldn't—"

"An ambulance!" Beatrice looked like she had no more tears left to cry. She wailed, clasping her face, "Is she going to be okay? What do I do?"

Before Maggie could respond, Gwen suddenly spun on her heel and wrapped both her arms around Bea, leaving Maggie holding Blue by the collar. Gwen pulled Beatrice tight against her chest, facing her away from the apartment. She petted Bea's hair and spoke in a firm tone.

"I'll tell you exactly what to do. She's done this before. She gave herself an injury, a bad one, one that's supposed to make me feel guilty and go running to her side to take care of her. She'll live, and she'll wait for me.

And when I don't arrive, she'll turn to you."

Gwen held Bea even tighter. "Block her number. Block her on social media. If she makes more accounts, block those too, and report her for harassment. Cry to heal your broken heart. Be mad, hurt, lonely, and scared. Spend time with your friends and family. Start a new hobby. See a counselor. Go on vacation. But do not. Go. Back."

Beatrice wept, dry sobs, fists clinging to Gwen's shirt. Maggie and Gwen watched as a stretcher was brought around the corner and hurried into the apartment. Gwen seemed too tired for tears, but her arms were no longer shaking as she held Beatrice tight. Maggie gazed into Gwen's eyes and, after a moment, Gwen looked back at her. Maggie gave her a small nod, then stood slightly in front of her, holding Bluebell alert and at the ready. In a few moments, the stretcher exited, rolling away with a flash of long black hair.

Epilogue

"…HAPPY BIRTHDAY, DEAR Maggie, Happy Birthday to you!"

Maggie laughed and blew out the 2-0 candles on the miniature cake. Gwen clapped, and Blue barked with excitement.

Gwen pulled out the candles and sliced the cake. "So what did you wish for?"

"Why are you asking? You know if I tell you, it won't come true."

Gwen took the knife and candles over to the sink. She grabbed a couple small plates and added the slices. "Eh, it was worth a try."

Maggie took an eager bite, then said, "I can't believe you found a kosher bakery just for this."

Gwen reached across the folding table and booped Maggie's nose with frosting. "You deserve it. You've been working so hard lately."

Maggie wiped the tip of her nose, sighed, and reclined in her chair, thinking about the half-finished college applications on Coral's borrowed laptop back in her apartment. "I'm never going to get them all turned in on time."

"Maggie, it's August. You have until February." Gwen took a quick drink of milk. "Remember, you're applying for next fall semester, not this fall."

"I know," Maggie groaned. "I've rewritten my personal essay almost ten times. There isn't anything about me that would make me stand out."

Gwen almost choked on her cake. "Oh, absolutely," she said after she recovered. "You've had no interesting life experiences that you've pushed through, whatsoever." Maggie threw her napkin at her. She ducked, then bent to pick up the napkin before Blue could chew on it. "Seriously, Maggie. You have so much you could write about. Moving out on your own, being in *Petty Oppression*? Colleges love those kinds of stories."

"I don't know how to make it sound interesting."

Gwen snorted and put her face in her hands. "Honey, seriously, just write about it honestly. I promise it'll be amazing."

Maggie pouted for a moment but decided to turn her attention back to the delicious marble cake. She let her gaze roam about Gwen's apartment. After everything that had happened in February, Gwen couldn't justify the cost of rent for a building she no longer felt safe in. She'd moved into an apartment on the ground floor of Coral and Maggie's building—a one-bedroom, shoved into the corner at the back of the building. The landlord had been very understanding about accepting Bluebell. They'd added a little more furniture—some garage sale items she and Maggie had found over the past couple months—to make it feel more like home. And when the sun started to set, as it was doing now, it gave the tiny kitchen a warm glow that made Maggie feel completely at peace.

Maggie pulled herself out of her thoughts to find Gwen staring at her, smiling. "What?" she asked, chuckling self-consciously.

"Just admiring," Gwen said cheekily, scraping the last bit of cake off her plate. Maggie hid her blushing, finished her last bite, and then Gwen collected their plates and carried them to the sink for a quick wash. "Did Coral have her first day on set?"

"Yeah, she's had a couple," Maggie said, petting Blue.

"We should celebrate with her sometime soon. Find out her favorite thing to eat, and I'll make it for her."

"We should invite Skylar," Maggie suggested mischievously.

Gwen laughed. "Oh, absolutely. So how's our new star holding up?"

"She seemed exhausted this morning but happy."

"I'm sure," Gwen said, smiling. "She just got booked as the protagonist of a twenty-episode sci-fi series. I think she's going to be tired for a while."

"Mmm." Maggie scratched behind Blue's ears. "She has a long commute. She mentioned that a handful of the cast were considering getting an apartment closer to the set."

"Is she considering joining them?"

Maggie shrugged. "I didn't ask yet. It seemed like she was still thinking about it."

Gwen rinsed off the plates and forks for a few minutes before asking, "What will you do if she moves out?"

"I'm not sure. I think I could afford to keep paying the rent myself for a little while." Maggie got up and moved next to Gwen at the sink as she dried her hands.

Gwen pulled Maggie into a soft hug, resting her hands on her hips.

"Hmmm. I'd hate for you to cut into your savings just before going to college," she said quietly. "Maybe you should get a roommate."

"Maybe." Maggie rested her head on Gwen's shoulder. "Maybe I should ask someone I already know well. Someone whose apartment I already lurk in during most of my waking hours anyway?"

Gwen chortled. "Maybe you should try a few sleeping hours with that person, first, to see if it's something manageable for you."

"Are you inviting me to a sleepover?" Maggie said with a grin, glancing up at Gwen.

"Did you bring a toothbrush?"

"I can run and grab mine. I'm only two floors up."

Gwen laughed out loud, leaned down, and kissed Maggie softly on the forehead. Then she straightened, looking as though a thought had jumped to mind. "Oh. I wanted to ask before I forgot. Did you talk with Carrie about the headaches?"

Carrie was a Peace Over Violence therapist who led Maggie's healing arts group.

Maggie nodded. "She thinks it might be a good idea if I switch over to their trauma informed yoga group. She said it'll help me address the physiological stuff."

Gwen nodded, then pulled Maggie back in for a closer hug. "Good. I worry, you know?"

Maggie's heart grew heavy, and she tightened her hold around Gwen's waist. "You're the one I'm worried about. I didn't get involved with anything until right at the end. You had to live with her for years." Neither of them ever said Valerie Harker's name. Maggie usually tried not to even remember her face, although it kept poking up during group therapy sessions.

Gwen nuzzled Maggie's curly hair. "I'm fine, love. I'm back with my old counselor. I've been through this before. I'm going to be okay."

Maggie took a deep breath and let it out slowly. She let go of bad memories and focused on the present—the feel of her head against Gwen's strong shoulder, the warmth of Gwen's hands, Bluebell poking their knees with her nose, asking for attention. She reached down and patted her ears a little absentmindedly.

Gwen kissed Maggie's forehead again. "So, how does my love want to finish her birthday celebration? We can do anything you want—within reason since we both have work tomorrow."

Maggie grinned. "I brought just the thing." She reached into her pocket and took out a USB drive. "Bad movie riff night, with popcorn."

Gwen groaned slightly, eyes closing in mental anguish. "Oh no… What trash heap did you find this time?"

Maggie giggled madly as she went to Gwen's laptop on the loveseat. "It's one of my favorites. *Ninja III: The Domination.*"

"This one doesn't have a ton of gore like the last one, does it?"

"No, I'm sorry about that. This one's just good old-fashioned camp. Trust me."

Gwen sighed with a smirk on her face and threw a bag of popcorn in the microwave while Maggie set up the movie. When the popcorn was done, she scooched Blue off the couch so she could settle next to Maggie, bag between them and the movie loaded.

"You know," Gwen said, opening the bag, "there's only one type of girl I'd be willing to watch these awful movies with."

"Oh, yeah?" Maggie asked brazenly. "What type of girl is that?"

"The type I'll probably ask to marry me some day."

A flood of emotions rushed through Maggie simultaneously, conflicting and powerful ones. She fixed her eyes on Gwen's, ignoring her pounding heartbeat. "Marriage is…a big commitment."

"And it's not one I suggest lightly," Gwen replied, serious eyes shining behind her smile.

"What…what if I decide to go to school in New York, to work on Broadway?" Maggie's mind started to run wild. "Or if you decide to work at Stage Coach, and I get hired here? And what about—"

Gwen gently put a finger to Maggie's lips. "We can make all those kinds of decisions when we get there, together. Whatever happens, we'll make the decision that's best for us."

Maggie took Gwen's hand in her own, stroking the knuckles. She pressed their palms together, lacing their fingers. "I feel like I just found you. I don't want to lose you."

"Then don't think about that," Gwen said, gripping her hand tighter. "Whether we're together for a month, a year, or a lifetime, I'm going to treasure every moment I have with you."

Maggie's heart nearly burst. She stammered for a moment, then buried her blushing face against Gwen's shoulder. Gwen, smiling, placed a finger under Maggie's chin, lifting her lips to her own. Maggie melted into the kiss, breathless, warmth spreading through every inch. Nothing mattered but holding Gwen and being held, home together in the space they made their own.

Gwen broke the kiss briefly, lips still brushing, and whispered, "I love you, Miss Fromm."

"I love you too." Maggie pulled her back, fingers weaving in Gwen's hair, lips pressed tenderly together, and everything perfect.

About the Author

Jennifer earned her minor in creative writing from Alfred University in 2016. As a pansexual genderflux individual and a trauma-informed mental health counselor, they're passionate about representation in fiction. Each story she tells is an opportunity to explore the beauty in nonconformity, healing, and diversity. After a lifetime of putting imagination to paper, Jennifer's debut novel, Getting to Know You, came into being as a promise kept to a friend. Jennifer lives in the Finger Lakes with her family, where they enjoy tabletop roleplaying games, sewing, and cuddling their cat.

Email

cox.augrad.2018@gmail.com

Facebook

www.facebook.com/profile.php?id=100071897927037

Website

www.jennifermdcox.wordpress.com

Instagram

www.instagram.com/jenivere_the_wit

YouTube

www.youtube.com/@jenivere-the-wit

Threads

www.threads.net/@jenivere_the_wit

TikTok

www.tiktok.com/@jenivere_the_wit